Rumer Godden was born in Sussex in 1907, but she spent much of her life in India. Her prolific writing covers plays, poetry and novels, though it is probably for the latter that she is most well known.

Also by Rumer Godden in Futura:

The Battle of the Villa Fiorita
In This House of Brede
Five for Sorrow, Ten for Joy
A Candle for St Jude

RUMER GODDEN

Breakfast with the Nikolides

Futura

A Futura BOOK

Copyright © Rumer Godden 1942

First published by Peter Davies 1942
Reissued by Macmillan London Limited 1965

First Futura edition 1983

This edition published in 1985
by Futura Publications, a Division of
Macdonald & Co (Publishers) Ltd
London & Sydney

ISBN 7088 2781 0

Printed in Great Britain by
The Guernsey Press Co Ltd, Guernsey, Channel Islands.

Futura Publications
A Division of
Macdonald & Co (Publishers) Ltd
Maxwell House
74 Worship Street
London EC2A 2EN

A BPCC plc Company

To the families of Mangos and Elethriades — now in
Athens — who were once, for me, the Nikolides.

I should like to thank Kumar Krishna Das for his courtesy and help.

BREAKFAST WITH THE NIKOLIDES

Chapter I

IT WAS in the little agricultural town of Amorra, East Bengal, India.

In the night Emily Pool's small black spaniel, Don, slipped down the stairs. He ran into the garden and out through the gate into the College grounds where the lawns lay smoothly between the buildings and the trees and ended in grass beside the tank. He ran with curious intentness, his head down, his wide ears brushing either side of his hot serious face, and very soon his ears were soaked with dew and stuck with twigs and ends of grass. The featherings of his legs were filthy too.

He was hot. He lay down and panted; but in a moment, pricked with some intense discomfort, he was up to run again, round and round without any point or reason. There was nothing he wanted, but he could not be still, he could not feel or behave like himself at all. He had been a serene and normal dog, quietly engaged in completing himself

[3]

from a puppy to an adult, but now, and all day, he was like the mirage of a spaniel, lifted out of himself and thrown distorted and heightened on the air. He was forced to run, and run, and run — foolishly to run.

At times he was invisible, quite lost in the shadows and the leaves, and presently he was invisible altogether because he had lain down behind a small balustraded platform that led down to the water tank; it was here the old professors of the staff liked to bring their chairs and their shawls and sit out in the evening. Now it was deserted. Don lay on the grass and pressed his side against the stone. He needed to press himself down where it was cool. The stone was warm from the day's sun but underneath that veneer of warmth there was a real old coldness, damp and chill, and it eased him to feel it beyond the warmth. He needed to be cool, to be still, to be dark, but he was mysteriously compelled to stand up and run in circles round and back to his place below the platform; he did it again and again and each time he circled back to lie invisibly there.

Chapter II

IN THE night the Government Farm at Amorra seemed to grow smaller. By day it was impressive with its colonnaded buildings, its straight well-sanded roads with railings that led through model fields; through the seasons the fields had model crops of jute and paddy-rice, grasses and pulses and fruits, sugar-cane and cotton and wheat; they stretched field by field towards the horizon sweeping in a wide half-wheel with the bank of the river, acre after acre. Only Charles Pool knew how big it really was; he knew exactly, because he had made it. He had pushed it out and across the plain, patch after patch, crop after crop; and it had not been easy, for with every field he pushed out into the waste, he was pushing the whole of India before him.

The Indian cultivator is rooted in deep slow prejudice and he is convinced that he is without hope. He knows too well that he is born to live and die in monotony and poverty with nothing but toil, and debts and perhaps hunger and still more toil. Charles's talk of manures and water-conservation and crop-rotation only made the villagers lift their eyes for a moment and sink back into the ways of their great-grandfathers' great-grandfathers' grandfathers again.

Charles talked of peculiar things — of pits for instance; and at first thought, what had pits to do with farming? Charles still talked of pits, pits for rubbish, compost pits, pit-latrines. He talked of dreams, of –85 per cent germinating seed, of bigger crops and better crops and different crops and crop-rotation. "It does not matter how we farm," they said. "If we farm well in a bad year, still we get bad crops; if we farm badly in a good year, still we get good crops. What is to be will be. What does it matter how we farm?" "There shall be no bad years," said Charles and talked of wells, and Persian wheels, and levelling and terracing the rain-fed land to hold the water and conserve the top-soil.

"Do it now. Combine," said Charles.

"We'll do it to-morrow."

"No, now. Now. To-day." He was like a gnat in their ears. Grudgingly, in one or two villages, they began to follow him.

Charles's young men went with white banners like preachers or warriors into the villages. They took with them a bull, and an English cock and hen, and the people's eyes stayed open with astonishment when they saw the size of these creatures. The young men showed them eggs from the hen, they talked of stall-fed milkers for the bull. They had a model village, a model house, a haybox, mosquito nets and quinine, and they had a magic lantern with slides: *Cowdung for Manure, Not for Fuel. Use the Haybox. Light and Air. The Poor Man's Pestilence — Litigation. Good Seed Costs Four Annas More, Bad Seed Loses Twenty Rupees.* They had posters to match the slides — *Fever is Cheap, Quinine is Cheaper; Motherly Love* (the mother who drives away the vaccinator — "Go away, you cruel man!" — while her baby's ears and nose are pierced for ornaments); *Send Your Girls to School, the Mother Makes the Home; Who Profits?* (when the crocodile of litigation holds its clients in its jaws) — all with lurid highly coloured pictures. They had gramophones and records. Later they had wireless.

There were not enough young men, not one for a hundred villages. The Indian lives to and for himself and his family, his sense of social service and citizenship is small, and voluntary workers were almost nil. The Legislative Government was slow and very cautious in providing paid ones. Already Charles was the fellow who always wanted money and when money was given to him it went like drops of water on dry sand. "But you only give me drops," said Charles. "I want bucketfuls and gallons."

"That is impossible," they said.

"It may be impossible but it must be possible," said Charles. "It may be useless but it shall be of use. I don't know how you can do it, but you must do it, all the same."

Charles won. Results are quick in India, once work is started and sustained, and in eight years the Farm had become an Industrial and Research Centre, with an annual exhibition; it had a Stud Farm and a Veterinary Research Annex, and recently the College had been added to it with a roll of nearly three hundred students who came from all parts of the Province to study livestock, crop-husbandry, bacteriology, agricultural botany, mycology and entomology.

Now, the mail steamers came up to Amorra; it had a light railway; it was visited and conferred upon; its grant had been raised and doubled, and raised and doubled again. It had equally outstripped its boundaries in land, the gates led one into the other along its roads and new houses were springing up for its staff all along the river in surprising shapes and colours, "Primrose Villa," "Lucknow," "Jolly Garden," "Riviera View." One was pink concrete with wrought-iron balconies in silver, one had strips of looking-glass let into its walls, one was completely in the shape of a ship with a railed bridge, a ventilator and a concrete life-belt on the roof. Charles looked at it through his monocle. "It seems I started more than I knew," said Charles.

He was held to be a connoisseur of houses though no one quite knew why; rumour also said that his own house was very beautiful and very peculiar, but not many people had been in it to see.

Everyone knew Charles but no one knew him very well, except perhaps the Principal of the College, Sir Monmatha Ghose. Charles was the old as well as the new Amorra, and he never left it. He lived alone in a fixed ray of limelight as the only European in Amorra except for an Anglo-Grecian combine managed by a Greek, Yorgo Nikolides, on the river two miles away. The whole town knew everything Charles did, but that told them very little about him. Naturally a network of rumour and gossip and small coloured lies had woven themselves round his name; his appearance encouraged them.

He looked a little like a pirate; he was burnt so brown that he hardly looked European — though he was too big, his bones too heavy, for an Indian; his walk was commanding; though it was commanding it had a slight roll. He was tattooed on the inside of his arms, and his eyes were a peculiarly brilliant blue, and he had a small cast in one of them that gave him a blind, wilfully obstinate look, a suggestion of a patch, particularly as in it he wore a monocle without a string. His hair was as black as his eyes were blue, and he had hair on his chest and arms and legs. The students to whom he lectured occasionally called him "One-eyed Carlos" or "Charlie Chang" — but unlike a pirate he had sober tastes, and unlike a monkey he would never chatter and never hurry. Sometimes he was terse and explosive and the students were in awe of him, but usually he was genial, venial and serene; and on the whole he was popular.

Among the rumours there was one that persisted; it said he had been degraded to Amorra from a very senior post. The curious tried delicately, or bluntly, to find out from Sir Monmatha Ghose if it were true. Sir Monmatha Ghose did not know, but he had been in Charles's house and knew that many of the rumours told of it were not far wrong.

The house was old and deep-walled and cool and spacious, but Charles had insisted on having the whole of it altered. That was odd in Charles, who liked and valued true old Indian things. It was washed yellow, and turreted at one side, with long verandahs and a columned porch, where creepers grew. It stood like a fort with a moat of old bazaar on three sides of it, trenched in upon by the new houses and new streets that were spreading out across the plain. On its fourth side it was joined to the College, and its garden led into the College grounds.

Inside the rooms were still immense, the doors and windows nearly as high as the rooms, the verandahs nearly as deep; it was floored with Mexican red stone except the drawing-rooms, which now had marble in faint grey and white squares; the floors were carefully kept and oiled so that they shone like mirrors, the walls were leeped in delicate lime washes, the panelling and the furniture polished and waxed, and the gardener spent an hour every morning arranging bowls and vases of flowers that were beautiful in the empty rooms.

"Where did you get your *mali?*" said Sir Monmatha Ghose. "He has one heavenly arrangement of flowers after another." There was a square glass jar that held marguerites and lupins in blue and pink and orchid colours, with forget-me-nots and deep red carnations, and a vase flat against the wall, with roses, and the small cream double jasmine that has flat, pale green glossy leaves; and a ring on the table in the next room, where they were to dine, that picked up every colour on the tablecloth: nasturtiums and white candytuft, marigolds, and tips of stock. "But I suppose," said Sir Monmatha, "you imported him with the others."

Charles's servants were hill-men, of high order and meticulous, who did not gossip in the bazaar.

Sir Monmatha noticed them, and he noticed the flowers, the faint exquisite colourings of the rooms and furniture; and he noticed — what many people would not have seen — that, under the polish and orderliness, nearly all of it had been broken or defaced and put together again.

"This poor table," said Sir Monmatha Ghose, running his finger down an ugly joining, "why do you live with it like this? It is so badly broken that it is a pity it has ever been mended. Why do you keep it like that?" As Charles did not answer he took it that he might go on. "This house," he said, "is like a shrine that has been defaced," and he turned his small deep-seeing eyes on Charles and said, "It isn't good for you, Pool."

"On the contrary," said Charles, "it's very good for me."

"You should try to forget."

"No, I should try to remember," answered Charles, and after a moment he added, defensively, "I'm perfectly happy."

He was perfectly happy. He lived chiefly in two small rooms beside the office; he woke up at dawn and worked into the night — and that was what he liked to do, get up at dawn and work all day into the night. That was how he had made Amorra; but in spite of all his years of work, in the night it looked curiously small in the plain. Its edges seemed to shrink back on themselves as if the plain might swallow them, and the night picked out the great belt of the river that changed its course and its bed through the years, that could perhaps defy the engineers and change its course again and sweep the farm and Amorra out of sight with one twist of its flank. The farm in the night was small between two enemies, the snake river and the tiger plain, but Charles did not see them in the night; in the night he went to sleep.

"You are not afraid of the river?" asked Louise, his wife. "It might turn again."

"It might. If the dams won't prevent it, I can't."

"Why didn't you build more inland?"

"We are growing inland, but we have to irri-gate."

"But there are the rains . . ."

"The rains might fail and the crops would dry."

"So — famine and flood — even here!" Her eyes were dark with melodramatic lashes. "Even here."

"Everywhere," said Charles.

Suddenly after eight years Charles had produced a wife. That had disconcerted, most horribly, his Indian friends. Granted that it was quite possible and usual for anyone in a foreign country to have a hidden past, in spite of the rumours they had not really believed it of Charles. Europeans in India are like cut flowers; that is why most of them wither and grow sterile: they cannot live without their roots, and so few of them take root; but Charles had taken root. They had almost forgotten that India was not his native soil, and they were deeply hurt. They were deeply curious too.

One morning Charles went down to the jetty to meet the steamer; and on the steamer was his wife, and not only his wife — there were two children of perhaps eleven and eight. What were they like? The wife was elegant, handsome but fragile, with a very white skin that made her more than ever noticeable in an Indian community. Her hair was a deep dark gold; "The colour," said the sentimental students, "of the wheat of the fields when it is ripe"; "The colour of curry powder," said the not-so-sentimental, "very hot indeed."

Her dark eyes under the small veil tied over her hat looked this way and that, quickly as if she were afraid or searching for something, and she lifted her hand to shield her face to ward off the stares, or the sun, as she walked down the jetty to the car. Her hand was small and gloved; gloves had not been seen in Amorra before, nor had the Pekingese, the two dogs feathered like birds that walked down after her. The little girls came behind, one larger, one smaller, like the pictures of the British Princesses; they were dressed alike, one had long hair and one had not, one was pretty and one was not, and they carried attaché cases with foreign hotel labels. Except for the beauty of the mother, they looked very neat and urban, not at all the sort of family anyone would have imagined for Charles. His friends were disconcerted and an immediate unbridgeable gulf opened between them.

Where had this family come from? It appeared that they had been driven out of Paris by the war, and escaped by Lisbon to the Canaries, where they had taken a ship round the Cape to Colombo, and another from Colombo to Calcutta.

Why had they come? Why had they not come before? Why had no one ever heard of them? On all these questions Charles shut his door and gave no word of explanation. Soon, Louise and the little girls might have been living in the house in the bazaar always.

* * * They came in on the paddle-wheeled mail steamer, Louise and Emily and Binnie, on the last stage of the journey from Paris, by Spain and Portugal, by the Canaries and the Cape, by hot little ports on the Eastern edge of Africa, by Madagascar and Ceylon to Calcutta; from Calcutta they caught the steamer that took them down the mighty tributaries of the Brahmaputra through East Bengal; and, as they went, a line like a taut string unwound from a tightness under the child Emily's heart, between her heart and her stomach;

it slackened as if the thread were casting her off. As the water of the river closed over the track of the steamer, smoothing it back again into calm, these hours began to close over the track in Emily's mind, smoothing it away.

The steamer rode high above the plain, and the hot empty landscape suited Emily. It was the end of the rains; though it was hot there was a promise of freshness; there was a small wind and the river was full to the brim, and on the plain were flat expanses of water, like shallow lakes, rippled by the wind and touched with brilliant green of floating water weeds. There was nothing else but the steamer going slowly and quietly along, coming in now and then to touch the bank near a village of huts in the trees; a plank was put out from the lower deck, a few people with bundles or a wicker crate of hens walked off, a few more people walked on, and the plank was drawn in, the steamer backed off and turned upstream again. It was gentle, unhurried and completely quiet.

Emily rested her arms on the wooden rail that was hot from the sun; she rested her chin on her arms and shut her eyes and the sun began to warm her eyelids and her face. She sighed, and the sigh ran through her like a ripple from the same warm wind that blew across the lakes, and she settled down more comfortably to lean on the rail. Then she opened her eyes and saw her mother's face.

Louise was standing at the rail too, looking down into the water, but what did she see in it to make her look like that?

Louise did not see the water; she was looking at a ghost and the ghost was herself. She was on another steamer, like this with the flat land falling away on either side; and Emily, standing beside her, was not Emily but Charles. Then they had been going back to the town, not away from it — and somewhere ahead, beyond the horizon that met the sky like the edge of a bowl, there waited, too, another unknown house that she would live in, and a life that she must live. . . .

"What are you thinking about?" said Binnie, thrusting her head up beside Louise.

"Of a house I used to live in — once."

"What — here?" asked Binnie.

"Yes," said Louise.

"What was it like?"

"It was particularly beautiful — to me, because I made it," Louise answered slowly.

"Where is it now?"

"Broken to pieces long ago," said Louise. "Don't talk to me now." Binnie stared.

Nothing had changed on the river; it might have shifted a little, eaten away a foot or two of earth from the bank, uncovered a new shoal of sand, swept away another, but it was the same; the banks were the same with the same nude brown children running to play in the wash that spread in the same way up the banks as the steamer went along, and the fishing boats moved with the same lilting crescent movement as they passed. . . . It was the end of our honeymoon, the beginning of my married life with Charles — thought Louise; and suddenly the vibrating of the deck under her feet, the slowly passing scenery, sharpened with a nightmare quality. It was happening over again. ("No!" cried Louise. "No!")

She was wearing a narrow veil tied over her hat and the two ends blown back resolved into the two long ribbons of the steamer wash, and for her, unlike Emily, they broke the quiet of the river with a sustained inexorable break.

("Stop!" she cried. "Stop. Please stop. I must go back!" But this was a nightmare and her cry had not made a sound.) The steamer went on. It had started, it would arrive at the terminus. It might stick on a sandbank, but that would only be a delay. It would arrive.

Louise had lately been having a dream. It was a dream in which a man rode on a horse, and the man was Pestilence or Famine or Death or simply a rider, an ordinary man, but Louise did not know what he was because she would not look at him. That was the dream; she knew that if she looked at him she might be saved, but she refused to look till he was close, riding her down, and then it was too late. The dream was a symbol for what was happening now, in this terrifying repetition that washed away the years and made her catch her breath with panic. It was too late.

Someone else, not Emily, was standing beside her at the rail. She barely came to his shoulder, she could see the outline of his shoulder behind her cheek, his arm by hers on the rail, the wind ruffling the dark hairiness of it. . . . She gave a little gasp and put out her hand and touched — Emily.

"Oh, Emily!" she said, "oh, Emily! ' and Emily stiffened as if she had winced. A sulky, almost resentful look came into the child's face.

"What's the matter, Emily?" Her voice was sharp.

"Nothing."

"Then why do you wince away like that?"

"I was thinking."

After a contact with Emily, Louise often grew angry like this. . . . Charles ought to have told me, she cried angrily. He should have warned me. Why didn't he warn me? . . . And like a cold thought, the answer slid into her mind: "Why should he warn you? He didn't ask you to come."

* * * Just before they reached Amorra the steamer passed a line of buildings along the farther bank: a factory chimney, great sheds of cor-

rugated iron, trucks on rails that ran down to a jetty, and a flotilla of grey launches with a blue-and-white key design round their funnels. Attached to the buildings was a strange yellow house, with gables and turrets and a dark red roof; it had a garden with a row of trees and a jetty of its own. It looked curiously complete: small, foreign and fascinating, like the picture in a French reading book. . . . I should like to visit it one day, thought Emily.

Then on the jetty she saw two children, waving to the steamer; she could see them quite clearly, they appeared to be wearing dark clothes and dark socks and one had a white pinafore. They did not move but stood and stolidly waved. In the middle, holding a hand of each, was an Indian nurse, an ayah. "They are too big to have an ayah, holding on to them," said Binnie scornfully. "Imagine if we were afraid of tumbling in the water!"

"They are not like us," said Emily. "I wonder who they are."

* * * When Louise's first cable was brought in and he read it, the whole of Charles had been flooded with such a surge of relief that he felt sick. Louise had left Paris at the beginning of the war, he knew that, and he knew she had gone confidently back soon afterwards, but he had not known whether she had been too late to get away again.

During all the weeks of desperate anxiety and burning heat, the wirelesses of Amorra had poured out the news; they could be heard blaring in Hindustani and Bengali in the bazaar, in Bengali and English in the College, in Hindustani, Bengali and English in the houses.

Charles went to the Principal's big tall house. It was a blisteringly hot evening. In the College, as he passed, the professors were sitting out on the platform above the tank with small palm-leaf fans in their hands, and the students were walking listlessly in twos or threes or sitting on their beds on the verandahs. The dry nervous heat accelerated the tension, and the loud-speakers still blared.

Sir Monmatha Ghose was in, and he too was listening to the wireless, dressed in a thin muslin vest and beautifully looped *dhoti,* the graceful Hindu nether garment, and toeless slippers, though in College he usually wore European clothes.

"Can I listen to the news with you?" asked Charles.

"Assuredly. Bring a chair for the sahib and bring a whisky peg."

They listened in silence, smoking. Charles smoked cigarettes, which he stubbed out before they were finished; Sir Monmatha Ghose smoked a hookah with silver chasings and a gay green-and-pink piping to the mouthpiece, and the hookah punctuated the news with a soft hubble-bubble of sound that was echoed by the regular puffing of smoke from Sir Monmatha Ghose's lips.

"May I come again?" said Charles when it was over and he rose to go.

"Come every night."

Charles hesitated on the step and said suddenly, as if it were torn from him, "I cannot sit and listen to it alone."

Sir Monmatha Ghose took out his mouthpiece. "You need not, I am here." And he asked, "Then you think she is in Paris?"

"I don't know!" cried Charles. "I don't know."

Louise's cable came a few days later. It had taken nine days on the way. He stared at it and then he realized that he was filled only with triumph that in her desperate moment Louise had wanted him; immediately he crushed that down; it made him faintly pitiful and he had every objection to being pitied. He read the cable again and said definitely and finally "No," and crumpled it up and dropped it on the table. "No, thank you," said Charles, and then he picked it up and smoothed it out, and said "Why not?" He answered: "MAKES NO DIFFERENCE TO ME IF YOU COME."

After his cable had gone he would have given anything to get it back. "She won't come," said Charles, "it was only panic."

(Louise's panic came up like wings out of the grass before the footstep was anywhere near. He had cause to remember that, and he cried, "I can't start that again!")

("I shall not start it again, whatever happens," said Charles; "I could not. It is over and it is dead. It can't begin again.")

The last words Louise had written came back to him now. "*Understand; nothing — nothing — will make me alter my mind. You have finished this for us, for ever.*" He wrote them now, in a letter to meet her in Calcutta. "*This is what you said when you went away. This is what I say now. Nothing shall make me alter my mind or anything else about me. You can go or you can stay. It makes no difference to me. Nothing can alter me now.*" As he wrote it he had altered already.

He had grown a certain laziness in these years; perhaps, like most Indians, he wished more than he did — hoping, almost believing, that wishing is the same as thinking, and thinking is tantamount to doing. He had been contented and that had made him lazier still; laziness, dilatoriness, is natural to India; the sun steals the marrow from the bones, and Charles had worked for eight years out under the sun in the fields, in the lazy certain rhythm of the land, and he had not finished yet. . . . Because I believe in it, said Charles. Why? Because this is my work that I have found for myself, and I shall not finish it till I die; because I believe that India is one of the new countries; like

China and like Russia it is so old that it is beginning to be new. I am of the country now, I am not an exile, I am not even an alien. When I pick up a handful of earth to feel its quality, I know it as I crumble it. I know it better than the Indians themselves. I have studied it, tested it, doctored it, made it better than itself. My results are creeping like a tide across the land — no, they are coming out of the land, because they come from the soil — and when I die, said Charles, don't let anyone have me cremated. Put me into the soil where I belong, where I may do some final good to a patch of wheat or a mango-tree. Louise called me a clod. Well, so I am; and I shall stay a clod, come or stay as you like. There's nothing you can do to me now. . . .

In all his calculations he had forgotten the children. For the children, their father was a little far-away man on the part of the map that was shaped like a deep pink tear-drop. Emily, it was true, had invested him with a personality from a picture she had seen in the *Illustré*, a picture of the Patagonian Consul in a white pressed suit, white sun-hat, dark face and beard. No one knew how Binnie had imagined him, but she was certainly as surprised as Emily when Louise pointed down from the deck of the steamer and said, "That's Charles," and added as if it were an unfamiliar word, "that's your father."

"*Father?*" said Binnie, and she and Emily looked

down at the man standing on the wharf among the coolies. Emily knew that the same dreadful thought had struck them both. "Is he — black?" Binnie was just going to ask it when he looked up at them and they saw the blueness of his eyes. He stood on the wharf in the midday sun without a hat, in shorts and a khaki shirt, no coat and no collar or tie or socks. He looked to them wild, not at all their idea of a father, and Emily felt a little stir of excitement and anticipation as she watched him; he was totally unexpected and new. He did not wave or smile. "Isn't he expecting us?" said Binnie.

He came up on the deck of the steamer that made a stage high up above the town, and Louise stood up like a child to meet him. In her white cheeks there was a hot flood of colour. Emily watched them from the rail; Louise, who had always seemed tall to her, looked quite small, and the sun striking across the deck made her skirts transparent, showing her legs, and thighs, making her look flimsy. They did not kiss. They stood with those few yards of deck between them and looked at one another and there was a pricking silence as they looked. Charles spoke first. "How do you do, Louise?"

Emily savoured the oddness of that. She looked at Louise, but Louise said nothing and the moment seemed to be given to Charles. He said, "You look very well — after all these years."

"So do you."

"You are prettier than ever, but you know that of course."

Why did he speak to her in that curious taunting way? Emily and Binnie were staring in surprise. He did not look at them. It seemed to Emily he would not look at them.

"You haven't seen the children," said Louise.

"You can hardly expect me to recognize them, can you?" He spoke roughly and, as he said it, Emily with a peculiar little shock recognized herself: that was just how she herself spoke when she had something unbearable she wanted to hide.

Then Binnie walked straight across the deck and shook hands. She looked up at him and he, very slowly, looked down at her. "How do you do, Father?" said Binnie.

He stood, swinging her hand a little in his, and his face had altered. . . . He was — frightened — before, thought Emily. Why should he be frightened of Binnie? . . .

"I don't remember hearing an English child's voice before," said Charles. "Funny." And he looked over Binnie's head to Emily. "Can't Emily say something too?" Emily was hotly embarrassed, but under the mockery in his voice she thought he sounded eager. "Emily — " he said again as if he liked to say it, then his eyes came back to Binnie. "What's your name?" he asked.

"You don't know my *name?*" Binnie was shocked.

"I haven't seen you before," said Charles, and he said to Louise a little triumphantly, "She gets her eyes from me," and immediately he dropped back into his bantering. "But of course, hers are steadier than mine."

Emily had a sudden unaccountable pang of pity.

They drove through the bazaar to the house, and as they turned in at the gate, a young Indian, dressed like a soldier in khaki with a puggaree and a polished belt and a cane, clicked his heels and saluted. "That's Mahomed Shah," said Charles to the children. "He used to be a sepoy, now he's our porter. You'll like him."

Louise spoke for the first time. "Are there any other Europeans here?" she asked, and her voice was tense.

"None," said Charles, "except the Nikolides."

"What a funny name," said Binnie.

"There are Mr. and Mrs. Nikolides," said Charles, "and they have two funny children, funnier than you. Their names are Alexandra and Jason."

"They sound funny," said Binnie, "but I like the sound of them."

"Those must be the children we saw on the jetty as we came," said Emily.

The car drove under the porch where the servants were standing in clean white clothes. As they came into the hall, Louise stopped with a sharp catch of her breath and put out her hand as if she were giddy; her hand found Emily's shoulder and tightened on it so that it hurt, but Emily, with her new awareness, said nothing. She looked round the hall; it was exceptionally pretty and she could see nothing in it to startle Louise. It was panelled in white, and the stairs leading up were stone with a solid side instead of a banister rail and a shelf where a row of Canton enamels, like the ones Louise collected, shone with coloured flowers and birds. "Remember those?" asked Charles pleasantly.

The dining-room had white furniture, with a deep red floor and curtains of patterned red and gold leaves on white silk. "That material has worn wonderfully well, hasn't it?" said Charles. Over the fireplace was a curious huge axe, with a handle of wood carved with a crest and a blade-edge that looked sharp and clean.

"Does it really cut?" asked Binnie.

"Does it, Louise?" asked Charles; and then he said, "Of course it does. It's Dutch; did you know you had a Dutch great-grandfather? He built his house with that."

"And what do you use it for?"

"Now I have decided to keep it up here," said Charles.

Upstairs was the drawing-room stretching away to the windows in a high curved bay. "Some of the pictures are new, of course. I couldn't save those, but this is your piano — " he ran his fingers down the notes — "you see it's managed to keep its tune without you."

Louise said nothing at all; she still held Emily's shoulder and she looked suddenly exhausted. "You want to go to your room," said Charles; "I've put the children in the spare room. This is yours — " and they followed him across the passage. Emily thought Louise did not want to come, but Charles led the way in through double white doors.

"What a lovely room!" said Binnie.

"Like it, Louise?" asked Charles.

"Why did you keep it — exactly the same?" Louise cried, and her voice was breaking. "How could you? It was broken for ever."

"It's still broken," said Charles.

"It isn't, it's lovely," said Binnie. "Look at the lovely table and the brushes. Whose are they? These are not your brushes, are they, Mother? Three mirrors and lights! Look at the light in the bed. Mother, is that your bed? Are you going to sleep in it?"

"She has made it, so she's going to lie in it, isn't that it, Louise?" said Charles, and, as if he could no longer bear the sight of them, he shook his shoulders and went out and downstairs. Louise went slowly across the room as if a weight were dragging at her knees and sat down. Emily watched, standing still and clumsy and cold in the middle of the floor. She was beginning to feel sick.

"What nonsense," said Binnie cheerfully, bouncing up and down on the bed. "You didn't make it, did you, Mother? You needn't ever make your beds in India, need you?"

* * * In the night Louise lay and listened to the drums. The bazaar lay close beside the garden walls and the drums and cymbals in the temple by the banyan tree were very constantly beaten. It was a harmless cheerful little temple; it was lined inside with bathroom tiles, and the roots of the grey old tree appeared surprisingly among them. It was used chiefly as a meeting place, for argument or gossip, but in the night its drums had a baleful throbbing sound. Louise had never noticed the life of the temple and the tomtoms started in her the beating of panic in her heart. She lay and listened, her heart beating, beating, and painfully awake. . . . If I go to sleep I shall dream. I shall have my dream again and I shall dream we are not safe. But are we safe? Is anything safe? Why did I come? Oh why, why did I come? What have I done? But what else could I do? I didn't know what to do. And, what else was there to do? It was mad, an impulse; a silly impulse, but anything then had to be an im-

pulse. There was no time for anything else. No time to think. Every night I see again that road we drove along. The car went slowly, so slowly; I was faster than the wheels all the way, trying to urge them on. Why was it so dreadful? Dreadful — so that it will be with me to the end of my days. There was nothing spectacular. The only fear all the way was the petrol. I had forgotten the petrol. We nearly ran out of petrol and I saw those two British officers in the square — where? I don't know where — and they gave me a five-gallon tin. Later on we found one petrol pump that was working, but they would only part with ten litres. No one stopped us or questioned us. We were not alone. Cars passed us, or we passed them all the way, and pony-carts and bicycles and horses, and people walking and people with wheelbarrows and perambulators. The children seemed sunk away to nothing, with small tired faces, and Emily was abominably cross. Then she was car sick and I had to keep stopping the car for her. Binnie said nothing but Emily kept asking why we didn't stay where we were. . . .

("Because the Germans are coming.")

("Oh. Have they come? Will they kill us?")

("Of course not" — hastily.)

("Then why didn't we stay where we were?")

Emily's face was green-white, and she had on her new winter coat, black-and-white check; its smartness was all crumpled by her sleepy sitting. So was Binnie's. . . . Now in the night it seemed to Louise that she had dragged them in those coats across the world, by sea and by land and by road, by Europe and Africa and Asia — to safety. Safety. Was it safety? . . . It must be, cried Louise. I am so tired, she said. If only the drums would stop beating I would go to sleep. But — if I go to sleep I shall dream. . . . She lay on her side and listened to the drums and presently she went to sleep and presently she did begin to dream.

* * * All over the Farm the lights were going out. In the coolie lines fires were still burning, with the men squatting round them to smoke and talk and play cards on a mat spread out on the ground. They would burn till long past midnight. In the Hostels the Superintendent had made a perfunctory round and the lights in the windows went out one by one. The staff quarters were silent long ago. On verandahs were the shapes of beds under mosquito-nets, and in handy places, on porch steps, beside the kitchens, the servants carried out their beds or their bedding to sleep in the cool. Some lay simply on the ground with quilts wrapped round their heads and looked like bodies wrapped in shrouds, and others lay on the steps or the shelves of the verandah rails; the watchman stood his lantern in the middle of the drive to keep watch by itself and fell into profound slumber standing up against a wall.

Mahomed Shah put his hurricane lantern inside his door, where it turned his room into a cave of deep soft yellow light. The room was a hut beside the gate, so small that he could not stand up in it, and he could touch from wall to wall without stretching his arms. It had a floor of beaten dried mud, a few pots and *lotas*, and an earthenware pitcher of water in the corner and a shelf with a broken mirror and a comb. He kept his clothes in a tin trunk painted with roses that usually stood under the bed, but to-night he had carried the bed outside. The walls were plastered with pictures from the European papers, *Post* and *Bystander* and *Illustrated London News;* in the night it was singularly inviting.

He sat down on his bed and took off his twisted soldier's turban with its falling end and pointed centre cap and placed it whole on the end; he leant his *lathee* against the head and drew up his legs, dropping off his wooden pattens that stayed on because they had a peg to hold between the toes. He sat for a few moments staring into the garden where the moon was advancing up the sky, and then he lay down and went to sleep.

* * * The last house on the New Road along the river belonged to Narayan Das, the new young veterinary surgeon. It lay outside the limits of the Amorra Electric Company, and in the night it was lit by oil lamps; each room was filled with a soft bubble of light, the same refulgence that Shah's hut walls had. The garden of the house was only half made, but it had been the garden of an old pavilion on the river, and the light fell from the windows across a square of grass where a pillar had fallen down and was slowly crumbling away. Now it made a seat with a flowering creeper growing over it. Narayan's young wife, Shila, stood beside it and listened to his footsteps going away from her down the road with his friend Anil.

She had waited up for him; he had sent her to bed but she waited up, listening to the voices talking and rising, talking and falling in the next room.

Tarala, the maidservant, had come in and sat on her heels on the ground beside her. Tarala was an old widow crone; her face was dark and wrinkled out of all coherence, she had a rag of grey hair on the top of her head and was dressed in a meagre dun-white piece of cotton. She appeared quite garrulous and senseless, but she had two senses left, a sense of scandal and a sense of enjoyment, and occasionally she would delve down into some other former mind and produce a gentle brand of wisdom. She began to press Shila's feet, squeezing them in her hands, pulling out the toes.

"The dinner was beautiful, Ma," said Tarala.

"Yes," said Shila.

"Anil Babu said it was beautiful." She lifted an eyelid to see Shila's answer to this but Shila kept even her foot still in the old woman's hands.

"It was a pity Narayan Babu did not eat the *jilipis* — they are his favourite sweets."

"He never knows what he eats when he is talking," said Shila bitterly.

Tarala squeezed and pressed in silence for a minute, a cord with keys on it sliding up and down her forearms that were black and skinny as shinbones. Then she said, "It's natural, Ma, for a young man to see his friends."

"But not only *one* friend; and he is only a boy."

"Narayan Babu has many friends," said Tarala, pressing steadily. "Even the One-Eyed Sahib, Pool Sahib, is his friend. Naturally. He is a very clever man, though some of his ways I *don't* understand," said Tarala. She, like Shila, had come from an orthodox home, but Shila had been to school and she was young; Tarala clung with obstinate ferocity to all the old customs and beliefs that Narayan condemned as superstition, and she continually combatted his ungodliness with private rituals of her own. He would find a pole with a flag tied to it, outside the kitchen door, a marigold and a sprinkling of rice below it, or he would come back to see the courtyard washed over with the cowdung he had forbidden her to use and, on the ground in front of the door, a fresh line of patterns that she had made with rice flour and the Ganges water; the mixture dried to a creamy white, and the patterns were pleasing, but it infuriated Narayan, and Tarala would silently rub it all out and do it again as soon as he had gone. "He is a clever young man," sighed Tarala. "With a man as clever as that you must expect foolishness, Ma." She stood, getting straight up from her heels in one movement in spite of her age. "Well, let God take care of the father," she said. "We must take care of the child. Come, let me put you to bed."

There was the sound of chairs pushed back and Narayan came through the door; his brows came together in quick annoyance when he saw them. "Shila, I told you to go to bed." Tarala could not get used to his calling his wife directly by her name. Shila, herself, could hardly force her tongue to use his, but she tried it now, hoping to please him.

"It isn't late. I waited for you — Indro."

She looked at him pleadingly. She had on a sari of fine blue gauze that almost hid, in its draperies, the present vase shape of her body; the light lay deeply in its folds, turning them deeper blue, her arms and neck were bare in a cut-away bodice edged with silver; the tinsel threads in the silver shone, her skin shone and her hair shone too, glossy blue-black in its coil, and on her forehead, between eyebrows shaped like crescent moons, she had painted a tiny scarlet mark, her *tika* mark that Narayan did not like her to wear.

Narayan did not look at her. He said hastily, "Go to bed. I am walking home with Anil."

"But it's late."

"It's late. It isn't late." He mocked her. "You are asleep. You don't know what you say."

"I'm not asleep." Her voice burned with feeling, and then she dropped into a pleading whisper. "Don't go. Stay with me. Just one night."

"Am I never to be free?" Now he was angry. "Can I not have one friend or one thought to myself? Leave me alone."

It was she who was left alone. Neither of them counted Tarala. Shila followed him to the garden door and heard him and Anil go out by the gate in the wall; she heard the pedals of his bicycle ticking as he wheeled it beside Anil; they stopped outside in the road to light the lamp and she heard the match on the box, and then she heard them going away laughing, quiet intimate laughter. The child inside her gave a convulsive leap. Did she move or did the child?

The little garden was full of dim moonlight, it brimmed over the walls and above the trees; everything was clear in it, every blade and leaf and stem, dark on pale and pale on dark. She walked out in it, though the grass was wet and chill on her bare feet and Tarala would scold. The river was shining like an unearthly lake, its edges disappearing into mist, and it seemed to Shila to be running extra quietly. She listened to the footsteps going away along the road.

In the distance Anil began to sing; his voice came back to her on the wind.

"I hate him," whispered Shila.

Anil was a student at the College. Its grounds were lit, too, by the moon as Anil and Narayan walked past the sleeping watchman and in at the gate. It was a Romeo and Juliet moon, and along the path, as separated as those lovers, moonflowers and sunflowers grew together, and though it was late in the year, there were still some flowers on the trees. The lawns unrolled to the verges of the tank, where the steps led down to the water; the water was still and pale and held a long reflection of the moon, and between the darkness of the leaves the sky showed in little brilliant spaces. Near the Hindu Students' Hostel another tree was shaped like a weeping willow and had small scented flowers on its stems.

The College perfectly matched the night — it might have been a palace in Verona; whitened by the moon, its whiteness had a milky lustre as if it had changed to marble, and in its arches and its pinnacles, its balconied verandahs and under its cupolas, were shadows of dim convolvulus blue.

Narayan and Anil walked hand in hand along the path, not to the Hostel but along the lawns. Anil pulled Narayan forward; their figures moved in and out of the shadows that bordered the path, in under the trees, out into the moon again. Narayan had European clothes, but Anil's loose white draperies moulded his thighs and flowed around him. He was still singing, not listening to the words, not even pronouncing them, singing and wandering with Narayan's hand in his, feeling the moonlight, letting it eat into his skin.

Narayan followed, willingly and unwillingly. Anil shared for him the overstudied graces of the night; Anil troubled him as the moon and the scent of the moonflowers troubled him, and the scent of the flowers on the weeping tree that blew into his nostrils with every stir of wind. He enjoyed them but they troubled him and he thought it would be better to be working or to be in bed. He was hot and he had a slight pain of indigestion that came from eating while he talked too much, and his feet in the wet grass were chill. He gave a sad little belch but Anil, singing louder, led him on.

They stopped at the platform by the tank; it was empty, lit softly by the moonlight, so that its edges were indistinct and the canna flowers by it had no colours. It was forbidden to the students, but Anil stepped up on it now. "Teacher, teacher, do you see me?" he sang.

"Be quiet. We shall be heard. You should have been in an hour ago."

"Not I," said Anil. "I settled that long before. I go and come as I please."

"Not if you are reported to the Principal."

"I shall not be reported to the Principal."

"You have too much money," said Narayan, suddenly disagreeable. "You will get into trouble all the same, one of these days." He sounded as if he wanted it, and in that moment he did.

He loved Anil, he was in love with Anil, but in some way he resented him. . . .

I can never see you quite properly, Anil, because you dazzle me. This is ridiculous when I am much older than you, but you dazzle me, Anil. You are something in yourself that has not touched my life before. How did we come to be friends? Really, I do not know. I remember the facts: I came to your rescue when the Police interrupted a meeting — a meeting of the Onward Movement, the Students' League, the Social Reform; you were in all of them, it was any of them — and I interceded for you and undertook to see you to your room. I do not remember what made me do it and it does not explain how the friendship began, but as we walked to the Hostel, both of us silent, you a little sulky, we looked at one another; I talked to you, you answered me, and I think we have been talking ever since. We have not been friends for long, but everything that came before I knew you seems unsatisfactory to me now.

I cannot forget you for a moment, when I am with you I cannot forget myself. I have crossed blood in me that makes me dark and thick and slightly squat; your stride is longer than mine, and your body is built so that you go forward strongly and gracefully; my hair grows close to my head like a Negro's, but yours grows loose and most poetically. When you take my hand I see our wrists together and mine is heavy and dark-looking beside yours. Most of all I am conscious of your family. You are a Bengali Brahmin, the child of tradition that you trace back for twenty-seven generations; the son of a landowner, you will inherit land and wealth. You came to College because you inherit, too, your father's idealistic notions; you came to feed an ideal, not because one day you must feed your mouth or starve. Now you are bored, probably you have forgotten what that particular ideal was; you forget so quickly. You would not stay here except that your father says you must get your B. Ag. degree. The class of student is not high, that is natural in an Agricultural College; young men prefer the Universities, they don't like to dirty themselves with peasants' work. You are bored, and that is why you talk to me.

I started in a street in the back streets of Calcutta. The street was like any other street in a big commercial city, it had houses far too tall and far too close together, it had noise and smells and its gutters were full of litter and garbage and stray dogs and cats and it was interesting because it was so diverse. A rich street is much the same all down its length, it betrays nothing, but a poor street betrays everything; you cannot be private in hot, small, bug-and-cockroach–infested rooms, so everyone is everyone else's business and there is a kinship that is almost friendliness. I missed it when I was picked out of the garbage and taken to school — and that was done by the detestable British, my dear Anil; the Imperialistic British, who bothered to take up a gutter-boy and give him life.

Am I grateful? I need not be so very; the British have a passion for alteration. I was educated at the Slane Memorial Scottish School for Orphan Boys; they had my mind and my body for seven years, and for seven years I learnt to keep my heart shut away in darkness and starvation. Perhaps that is why it grows such extravagant one-sided branches now I have let it out; I am shamed by it and think I shall put it away again.

Till now I have avoided any kind of friendliness and kept to acquaintance; only this last year since I came here, married to Shila, I seem to be learning friendship — I have even a beginning of friendship with Mr. Pool — and through friendship I have learnt to love you, Anil; but you make me feel the marks of that street more than ever; they are on me, I shall never lose them, they are the only caste-marks I shall ever know. . . . And he thought again of Anil's father. . . .

What would your father think if he saw us together? I know quite well. I make you describe your father to me over and over again, his stateliness, his rigid orthodoxy; and we laugh at him, but for me it is like pricking at a wound. I have no father. I see your father, as you have told me, on the terrace of your house above the fields; he sits on his bed, his feet drawn up, his shawl hanging in fresh cream folds, his hands and his feet still. He would look at me and his eyes would see at once what kind of a fellow I am and then he would turn his eyes away and not be interested to look at me again, in spite of anything you could tell him. He has retired from the city never to go there again; he hopes, when you have grown wiser and older, to leave his possessions and his family in your hands and retire completely from the world. He holds minutely to the ideal of non-contamination, even a shadow in the street would defile him. Well, it is easy for him; the fields and the land all about him are his, he is the lord of the land and the house where his family and his son's family live, where his son's sons' families shall live. His is the tradition and the heritage of Brahma. It is in him and in you; even if you laugh and are lazy, you cannot deny it.

And I? I am of the city garbage, raised on its litter; my emancipation and position make me accepted here, they allowed me to marry Shila; but if you took me to your home I should contaminate your house. Your young wife and your cousins' wives might peep and stare, but your old aunts, the uncles' wives, would take one look through the curtain and say to your sisters, "Wherever has Dada picked up such a person?" And they would have my shadow cleaned from the house wherever it had fallen. . . .

Narayan sighed and sat down on the balustrade behind Anil. Too many shadows had fallen on him; he was soiled, impure for life; and now everything he had most desired and striven for seemed to him far removed from truth. . . .

I have been wrong all this time, I have been going in the wrong direction; all this force and striving, this breaking away and smashing down of obstacles, has been wrong — is still wrong. I should have left it alone. I wish I had left it alone; but what else could I do? I had to make myself, and make myself strong. Now I want to go back, behind that street, behind my birth, accepting them, go back to the only mother I have, to India herself. . . . He could not say more than that; an inarticulate longing filled him with humbleness and passion, so that he trembled, and in that moment he was happy, with a happiness that came from a sudden rightness of the balance in himself, as if he had touched truth. . . . I am, he said, this is myself — and immediately from habit he began to think of himself and his grievances and difficulties, and his ambitious discontent swamped and put out that glimmer of light that was anyhow small as one of the wicks burning in a little saucer of butter that they sold in the temples. . . . What was I thinking of? What do I want? And his mind cried angrily, but still silently: Really, it is impossible for me to be friends with you, Anil.

And yet — and yet . . . To move about the garden as we do to-night, to talk a little madly and to laugh, to wander in the light and the darkness with the scents and the still shadows, to laugh and to talk a little nonsense, to hold your hand, Anil, and swing it lightly — why should I not do this? It is nothing if not a waste of time, I am getting nothing for it — and yet . . . You sit turned away, Anil, looking into the water; I see your shoulder, thin in its fine white muslin shirt; I see the line of your cheek, thin too, but softly young and dark, and I see the darkness of your hair. I see you but I don't know what thoughts you are thinking, I only know that I could never think them and if you told them to me they would cause surprise and perhaps excitement in my mind. The things you think of and say are often quite absurd and childish, but they are pristine and curiously complete and they make my profoundest efforts clumsy and like a boy's. I don't know what you are thinking. . . . And aloud he said, "What are you thinking, Anil?"

"I was looking into the water and I thought about the river," said Anil dreamily. "Did you see the colour of the river this evening, Narayan? It was like the inside of a shell. All the colours are deeper when they lie on that mother-of-pearl, the water-lilies are milk-white and crimson instead of pink and cream, and the hyacinth clumps are purple. Didn't you see them like that, Indro?"

"No," said Narayan sourly. Anil knew very well he did not.

A speck of light sailed across the sky towards them; but it was not a shooting star, it was a firefly.

"I sometimes think my thoughts will end like that," said Anil: "Not a star. A very common insect."

"You only say that to hear me contradict you."

"Really. Really. You are very cross to-night. What is it? Something, or somebody, has disagreed with you, I think." He stood up on the edge of the platform and stretched himself, leaning backwards a little so that the line of his body made a taut, clean curve; he looked as if he might fly with the strong springing lines that he made, and his loose clothes fell in long folds, gracefully, as he stood.

Without thinking Narayan followed him and

stretched himself as he stood up; but cheap European clothes are not made for stretching — there was the sharp sound of a tear and the back of his coat split and at the same time his collar stud gave way and one side of his collar sprang up against his cheek.

"That comes of wearing what does not suit you," said Anil, laughing at him. "You don't look half as much grand as you did."

An extraordinary wave of temper came over Narayan. Everything was horrible — Anil's bantering, half-sneering laughter, the hot sticky night, his own heat and his wet feet, the fantastic shadow-strewn College, and the long road he must travel home to his house where Shila, if he knew her, would still be waiting up to greet him with reproachful eyes. He hated Anil. "You damned impertinent boy!" he cried and inexpertly, with a clumsy gesture, he knocked Anil backwards across the chest. Anil was laughing, and he purposely let himself be knocked, still laughing, off the platform, landing lightly on his feet in the grass below it. Immediately there was a howl, and he screamed, a real shrill scream of fear with pain in it, and something ran away in the grass. Anil staggered and fell theatrically against the balustrade, hiding his face.

Narayan did not move; he could not move, he could only stand, watching Anil stagger and fall against the stone. The moment drew out in fantastic coldness and still he could not move and chill drops ran down his neck. When he did speak his voice sounded rusty. "Anil, Anil," he rasped, "Anil, for God's sake what has happened? What is it? Oh, what did you do?" His voice was shriller than Anil's, but Anil still leant on the balustrade, his face hidden and his shoulders shaking. In agony he pulled the hands away from Anil's face and Anil was laughing, and now he laughed aloud. Narayan flung away from him in disgust.

"Another silly trick."

Anil's face went stiff and furious too. "Not at all. I thought I had been bitten by a snake. It was not a snake, that is all."

"You *were* bitten. Show me. Where are you hurt?" There was concern and authority in Narayan's voice. "You were not play-acting me. Show me where it is."

Anil stepped back coldly. "Don't concern yourself. It was not a snake."

"I know it was not a snake," said Narayan irritably in his anxiety. "Other things are dangerous as well. Tell me. I must know."

"You won't know if I do not choose to tell you."

"Anil, I am sorry. I was not myself just now."

"You were very much yourself. Don't mind about it. It does not interest me."

"Anil, please. Did it touch you?"

"It did or it did not. That is my affair."

"Please don't take this attitude. Tell me what has happened."

"Nothing has happened," said Anil impatiently. "I thought I had trodden on a snake. It was not a snake. That is all."

"What was it, then?"

"I don't know. It has gone."

"Didn't you see it? You must have seen it."

Anil shrugged. "It was invisible. Let it remain so. In any case I am a damned impertinent boy. What does it matter what happens to me?" And he turned on his heel, but Narayan saw the flash of tears in his eyes before he had time to turn.

"Anil." He caught him by the hand, there was a moment's childish struggle and Anil suddenly gave way.

Presently, as they were walking back together, Anil said: "I am overwrought, I think. I have been working so much, too late for the Examination."

"You have to work," said Narayan callously. "You have to pass first, with first-class honours; and you will get the Kailash Chandra Prize for Bacteriology, and the MacEwen Purse — "

"So you say."

"Anil, this is something I want worst in the world."

"But why? For me? I am not your brother."

"You are more than my brother. You are myself. You are all that I want to be." And that was true, and though he spoke lightly, Anil's results were desperately important to Narayan. Anil was unreliable. Narayan sighed. "You must not be too late. You have much to do to-morrow. Professor Dutt is giving you some private coaching, I think." But still they did not go to bed.

They walked lightly on, while it grew very late. Anil was half touched, half bored; Narayan was blurred with remorse and tenderness. They had both forgotten what had happened, but on Anil's *dhoti* was a trail of small dark spots, bloodstains from a gash across his shin, a small deep gash where the blood had dried already. Anil did not notice it again.

They paused at the door of the Hostel and looked across the College to the outer walls. The moon was sinking in the sky, it was growing darker. In the Pools' house was a light.

"Charlie Chang is working late to-night. He shouldn't be. His wife is here. Why does he need a light?" said Anil; and laughing, sniggering a little, they said good night themselves.

* * * It was not Charles, it was his daughter Emily. Anil's scream had woken her and she put out her hand in the darkness to find her spaniel and he was not there.

The scream woke Emily out of a dream and the

voice that had been screaming went on to laugh. It was entirely natural to Emily that screams and laughing should be mingled and entirely natural that on hearing them she should be nipped cold and still with fear. (Louise would not let them scream, nor would Madame Chastel at school in Paris. "We shall not scream or cry, we shall laugh instead," and so they did, a high snapping sort of laughing, while fear was naked in Louise's eyes.) Now Emily woke confused. What was that scream and that laughing, high with fright? What was it? . . . ("What was it, Mother?" "Nothing." "What was that?" "Nothing." That was a lie, it was almost next door, but Louise told lies. At least she never exactly told the truth.) . . . Will there be a crash? Will there?

Remember, Emily, remember. This is not France, this is India. Remember! India. . . . Slowly she began to relax.

She had been born in India; she, Emily — not Binnie. . . . If you are born in a place does a little of it get into your bones? Yes. I think it does. . . .

("What do you call people who live in a country always, Charles?")

("Natives, I suppose.")

("No, not natives. People who come to it and want to belong to it and never go away.")

("Domiciled citizens.")

("Then Binnie and I should like to be domiciled citizens of India, please Charles.")

Why did Emily like it so much? The only way in and out of it was by the river. It had taken ten hours of winding through the plain to reach Amorra from the depot, and all that way they had seen only the fields and the villages and the empty sky; and Amorra was much the same, only a town along the riverbank; the high College buildings that seemed like skyscrapers against the huts looked pygmy against the sky, and all the fields and paddocks were only a little patch upon the plain.

The strange wide land with its heavy weight of sky and water that oppressed Louise was beautiful to Emily; there was more sky here than anywhere she had seen, and the river was a mile wide from bank to bank, swirled with rapids that churned the sand up into yellow-green water, and beyond the river on each side stretched the plain. . . . We are divided from everything else. We are in another world. Nothing can get at us here. . . .

And Charles was here. Why had they been without him so long? There had been no one like Charles in the house at Bellevue; none of the men they saw — Félix, dear Félix the cook whom they had laughed at her for loving, or the postman or Madame's nephew Jean André or Louise's friends — were in the least like Charles. Charles was strong and bold and different. Even the smell of him was different; Charles smelled of man; he smelled, too, of tobacco and the grass and herbs he touched all day long, and of soap and Eau-de-Cologne, and when he came in from riding he smelled strongly of leather and horse, a good live smell though Louise wrinkled up her nose in disgust. . . . I would rather smell of doing things than being clean, said Emily . . . and the smell of Charles seemed to chase the last sickly shadows from her mind.

Now, except when she woke in the night, the life in Paris was like a shadow or a dream; the house with the balconies and paved garden had been the centre of the world, now it was like a dream — all of it; Madame Chastel, the despot whom they thought would go on and on for ever, was gone, left without them; the voices of Félix and the cross old Albertine were speaking where she could not hear them; other people were walking up the road, picking their steps between the *pavé*, walking in and out of the pattern that the chestnut trees threw down on the stones. . . . For ten years I lived in that house and walked up and down that road, said Emily, ten times I have seen the leaves change, opening in the spring, spreading a still canopy in summer, drifting in the autumn, rustling along the gutters in the frost of winter — ten times, and all the while Amorra and Charles were here alone.

("Why didn't you bring us out here before, Mother? Why did you keep us at home?")

("I shouldn't have brought you now if it were not for the war. India isn't good for little girls.")

Phaugh! Rubbish!

("Charles, why didn't Mother let us come here before?")

("Because she wanted to keep you at home," said Charles.)

That was the natural explanation. It did not seem in the least odd to Emily. It had not occurred to her that a father had any rights over his children or could make decisions for them. In Emily's experience Louise was omnipotent. Then, she had listened with close attention to a conversation she overheard between Charles and Louise. . . .

"I suppose you will want someone to teach the children," Charles began it. "Perhaps one of the professors at the College could do it in his spare time. I'll speak to Ghose."

"Is it worth it?" answered Louise. "They won't be staying here for long."

"Won't they?" asked Charles, and Louise looked at him quickly.

"They can't stay here, Charles."

"Why not?"

"How can they? It's not — fit for them."

"I'm afraid it must be," said Charles crisply. Louise did not answer; she was facing Emily, and Emily saw her hysterical look come into her face; it made her cheeks very white, her eyes very black.

"You came. I didn't ask you to. You came," said Charles. "Why did you come?"

"I don't know," said Louise in a whisper, "I don't know," and she cried, "Can't you understand? It was like being hunted. There was no time to think — "

(Oh, there *was*, Mother, Emily contradicted silently, we were in that nice hotel for days.)

"There seemed nowhere on earth that was safe or quiet — "

(Lisbon was perfectly quiet.)

"I had no one to turn to, no one to help me — "

(Oh, *Mother!*)

"Now — now I know that I was mad."

"I don't think you were mad at all," said Charles pleasantly, and all Emily's nerves approved of his light, almost conversational voice, after Louise's overwrought cry. "I think it was very sensible. My house was half yours even if you didn't care to use it. It's comfortable and it's as safe as any place can be — though naturally you don't like living quite alone, as you have to here. I understand that. I didn't like it either — to begin with — "

"Charles — "

"And we don't need reminding, do we," asked Charles with a peculiar edge to the words, "that Emily — and Binnie — are my children?" Louise's answer was silent on her lips. "I'll ask Ghose to recommend a tutor for them," said Charles, suddenly, tersely, bringing the subject to an end. "They have been so well stuffed that it won't hurt them to forget a little."

Louise still did not answer, and a fear was born in Emily's mind; and now, in the night, it recurred to her. . . .

Louise had brought them to Amorra, Louise could take them away. They could not prevent her, children could not be real citizens of any country; they could not choose where they would live. Louise had many weapons and she would use them. Could Charles defend himself against them all? Could Charles? Emily herself constituted one. Emily was delicate and she had an unlucky stomach; often, herself, she had been undone by it. If she should get ill . . . The heat had already made her most unbecomingly pale. She was a pretext Louise had often used before; often she and Binnie had been forced away from a party, an occupation, a holiday or a dream. ("Why?" "Because I say so." "Explain!" And Louise could always explain.) . . . That was it, thought Emily, she had all the reasons, the arguments, all the words and all the power. The only thing Emily had learnt was to make herself expressionless, to give nothing away, above all never to show she liked or loved. Now she set her teeth in her despair. . . . But one day, Mother, it will be my turn to win. Charles will help me, and

I shall win. I shall win over this. I shall stay here — always — with Charles. . . .

She had grown a violent hero-love for Charles, but Charles, it seemed, was curiously abstracted and had no time to return it. She, the undemonstrative Emily, would push her face against his hot shoulder, tighter and tighter: "Let me stay with you, always — always." He said: "Yes, but not now, that's a good girl" — but sometimes he stroked her hair and turned up her chin and looked into her face, and he had given her a puppy for herself. He had given her Don. . . .

She put out her hand in the darkness to feel him. Her finger touched the edge of his drinking-bowl, not the top but the side, and her hand found his bed, but it was empty. Shaken out of herself she was able to sit up and switch on the light. The bed was empty and the bowl was turned over, with the water running away across the verandah, and the side of the bed, a wooden frame plaited with webbing, was bitten into splinters all along it and the lead bitten in half. "Oh, Don!" cried Emily. "Don!"

Immediately Don appeared like a sprite from under her bed. "What have you done? Where have you been?" asked Emily sternly, but he showed none of the guilt that customarily filled him at the least tinge of scolding in her voice. He wiped his paws down the side of her net, fawning and leaping and trying to lick her hand with overwhelming love. "Don't be sloppy," said Emily sternly again, and at last she coaxed him onto his bed and, leaning on the edge of hers rather than getting out on the floor, though the bed's edge cut across her chest, she managed to tie him up with the end of his bitten lead. She turned out the light and lay down and her hand stroked his warm, sleek-feeling body. Now her hand felt sparser hair and a patch of hot bare skin; he had turned on his back and she was stroking his stomach. "You're very hot, my love," she crooned.

If she put her two hands round Don from behind she could feel his heart beating like a little engine; but in some way when he was still and asleep it seemed to be beating all over his body, everywhere except in the rough pads of his feet and in his ears; that was natural, the pads were like shoes and a spaniel's ears were largely ornamental, like long hair. You could not feel much of Emily, could you, in the ends of her hair?

She kept her hand on Don's stomach and the pulse of it seemed to be beating up her arm, very quickly as if it were part of her. But he is quicker than I am. He goes quicker than I do, thought Emily drowsily, but he seems to be going very quickly now. . . . She was not concerned; with her hand on him all her troubles had gone.

They had never had a dog before. . . . Of

course, Mother has the Pekingese, but they are no more dogs, said Emily, than goldfish are fish; though they are charming, of course. Besides, they are Mother's, and she adores them and they are far removed from us.

On Don's collar she had tied a label —

> Don
> Pool
> *Government Farm*
> *Amorra*
> *Bengal*
> *India*
> *Asia*
> *The World*
> *The Universe*

— because that seemed to be a satisfactory explanation of her feeling for him. Suddenly, she had entered into richness; she had Don, and, nearly, she had Charles. She was drowsy, she was not afraid any more. . . . This is India, this is not France. Nothing can happen here. Don is under my hand. He is beating, beating under my hand. Don . . . Don . . .

Don settled more deeply on his back and sighed. Emily's hand, limp and heavy with sleep, slipped off him to the rug. He started up and began to bite the bed, straining and worrying at his lead.

Chapter III

THE MORNING came early to Amorra. First the river began to pale and to look solid against its farther bank where the mist hung down. Soon, beyond the town, the fields seemed to draw themselves out away from the banks on either side; and this drawing away, this look of stretching, was because the horizon now showed. The sky grew pale too, separated from the earth, divided pale from dark. Soon the fields began to show their shapes — in chequers of pale and dark, in a glimmer of water from the rice-fields, in running criss-crossed paths of white. Now it was possible to pick out the road banked high in case of flood; it looked pale, bleached and colourless; but presently, as the trees changed from dark to green, it changed from a pale thread to a line of pinkish dry brick-dust, with the humped shapes of bridges and the white pepper-pot turrets of a country temple beside the road; the railway lines behind it ran on, on and away.

Now there were no more stars in the sky, and the sky was growing green and faintly luminous above the plain. Green was the first colour to come, faint green in the sky after the stars, a dark blackish green on the trees and pure bright green, limpid, on the rice-fields. Then appeared the clay colours of the earth, the dry fields and the mud walls and village huts and after them, clear as the rice, the mauve spikes of water hyacinth in the pools. There was a little of that colour in the sky, as in one village and then in another a fire was lit and smoke went up dark into the sky. The sky was soon colourless again with daylight, and white mist chill with dew began to creep across the fields and round the town.

The shaggy old town of Amorra woke before the new.

The first to wake in the bazaar were the cats; they ran along the drains under the steps and leaped over refuse and old tins and heaps of leaves without a sound, skirting the sleeping bodies on beds and mats or on the ground; and as they ran the light ran after them, drawing streaks across the houses. The sun came up and filled the light with warm yellow, and struck across the bathing tanks, where presently the people would go for their ablutions and to clean their cooking-pots.

A dog sitting on a dung-heap stood up and stretched his hind legs; as the sun began to warm the street, a thousand indelicate smells rose to his nostrils. In every tree the crows began their cawing. Someone took the cloth off the cockatoo's cage and it walked backwards and forwards along its perch examining its feathers that were green with purple points.

A thin little boy was the first human to come out; he wore nothing but a coat that came to the top of his stomach and his stomach was blown out into the shape of a melon and his head was newly shaven except for one lock in the middle. He shivered, his eyes were dull with sleep and he went to the tap that stood in the street and began to splash his face. Two other boys ran out from a hut and hailed him; they left the door of the hut open and new smoke and scoldings came out after them and an old woman, bent so that her face was near her knees, brought out a basket. She stepped aside to blow her nose with her fingers, then went to the end wall of the hut and in the sun began to plaster dung cakes on the wall to dry; each cake was patterned with the print of all her fingers and she slapped them on one after the other with a heavy regular rhythm that was soothing in the early morning. The little boys began to play.

Soon after the huts were awake the houses woke too. Soon the families came out on the verandahs.

In a small house a thin old man came out to sit in the sun and near him he had a table of books. He shivered gently and wiped his nose and gathered his grey shawl round him and put on his spectacles and picked up a book. He was Professor Dutt from the College, and he had two extra classes to prepare; after his morning lecture he was to coach that brilliant, uncertain and rather tiresome student, Anil Krishna Banerjee, in his room; and at three o'clock he was to go to Mr. Pool's house, where, every afternoon, he taught certain subjects to the Misses Emily and Barbara Pool. That gave him a little welcome extra money every month, but it worried him; he could not decide if it were an honour or an ignominy that Sir Monmatha Ghose had recommended, and Charles had chosen, him; and he could not make up his mind what, and how much, the children ought to know or what, and how much, he ought to teach them, and he varied startlingly between the kindergarten and the academic; also he was terrified by Mrs. Pool. She said "my children" as if they were some rare sort of animal, she attended the lessons and interrupted them and had the effect, he noticed, of nonplussing Miss Emily as well as himself. He sighed as he turned over the pages in search of some small problems that would not harass the brains of the children too much and yet would please and impress Mrs. Pool.

A goat and two kids pattered down the road to the bazaar, past houses where oleanders showed in knots between the dusty little gardens, and cows were being milked in front of their suspicious owners. The goat had discharged her milk and now, with her udders done up in a neat white bag, she walked along in front of her disappointed kids. They walked in and out of the legs of fathers coming back from the family shopping, of cake-sellers and bread-sellers and the betel-leaf man. Water dropped on their heads and along their backs as the water-skins and pots were carried in for the day, and from the tanks the sound of splashings and scourings came to their ears.

For the goat the bazaar was a pleasant place to wander, full of pickings and leavings, though her kids became entangled with legs and wheels and the butchers' shops had heads and entrails and whole corpses of little kids hung up on hooks. The live kids filled the air with their hungry bleatings but no one heard them, they were only one more noise in the hubbub of noises; the kids danced on their miniature hooves over leaves and litter and betel stains and droppings and the goat stayed by the side of the road munching a succulent paper. The bull took no notice of any of them, nor of his patient relations the buffaloes, as they walked leadenly along with their carts, overloaded, hot and dusty. The bull swung his dewlap and went off to lick a pile of soft sugar in the sweet-shop; his horns were tipped with brass and he wore a necklace and

a hump cap made of blue-and-white beads; and —
another side of veneration — a little sick cow stood
on three legs and shivered before it limped off
starving down the road. Eventually it wandered
into the College grounds while the porter was
round at the kitchens gleaning his morning meal.

Anil saw it as he was getting up. He stood in his
room with nothing on his body but a cotton cloth
around his thighs. He had just come up from the
privy and his Thread, the sacred Thread that hung
from his left shoulder to his right thigh, was twisted
round his ear. Slowly humming a song, he un-
twisted it and began to put on his clothes. At home
he could not have dressed like this. There he went
to wash himself in the tank beside the house; praying, then facing the sun, soaking himself with pour-
ings from his *lota,* saying again the prayers pre-
scribed as he poured, pouring water after he had
prayed, thinking of the seven sacred rivers; and as
he plunged finally into the water of the tank, as it
closed around his shoulders, it was the water of the
Mother of All Rivers, the river Ganges; he was
bathing by intention in its waters, his spirit floated
away to join it in its course.

When he had finished, he turned towards the
sun, taking the water in his hands, letting it run off
his fingers. He came out of the water putting a
pure cloth round his waist and on his shoulders

and waited with his face turned to the East for the house priest, the Purohit, to touch his forehead with a paste of sandalwood making the red mark of his caste, and hang round his neck a string of flowers. After saying his last prayers he put on his clean clothes and carrying his *lota* and his flowers went towards the house. That was his morning ritual and now, getting up as he had done this morning, washing himself quickly and putting on his clothes as he looked out of the window, Anil felt slothful and impure. : . . Why do I not keep to the rites in College? My father thinks I do, I vowed to him I would, then why don't I? I do not know. Why do I think of this now? What suddenly has made me think of this? Narayan is always talking of it. Is it Narayan or is it that little cow tearing up the College grass as if she were in heaven? . . .

"*It is acknowledged that the poverty of the Indian breed of cattle is due to the fact that their slaughter is forbidden by ancient Hindu religion; old and useless herds are thus maintained that take from the healthy young animals their share of food.*" That is what Anil himself had written in his essays, but would he have killed the little cow outside? No, he would not. . . . Would I prevent Narayan from killing it? I do not know. I do not know. . . . And suddenly he found it was nearly eight o'clock and bent down to pick up his shoes. On his leg the red mark had nearly healed.

* * * Narayan sat in his office and made up his book. It was his case book and though he would not have shown it to Anil or anyone else, or mentioned its existence even, it was precious to him. It was a collection of notes on his cases, not for showing to officials but written for himself; they might even have been called notes on himself. Each one was a record of more than a case, each one was a battle; they were a series of small tough battles in which he had won through from the new deeply inhibited student to Dr. Das, the young research man at the Government Farm, the marked-out Government servant. . . .

And it is quite right, said Narayan, I am good. At present I have to do routine jobs, I have to practise, but I shall get a better post and a better. And I shall deserve it. Each page I turn brings me nearer to that. The pages of the book were deeply serious to him — "*A bullock . . . An imported goat . . . A cow in calf . . . An infected herd of buffalo.*"

When he was young Narayan had had the thoughtless terrible cruelty of most Indians to animals, a cruelty that reaches from high to low, that runs through high days and ordinary days; it stains the land with the blood of annual sacrifice in temples and holy places; it tortures the cows for their milk and starves their calves to death; it lets sores gather and stream under the yokes of bullocks and buffaloes and on the thin hard-driven tikka gharry ponies; it lets dogs lie out in the road when they have been run over till they die by slow hours, and throws kittens and blind puppies on the rubbish heaps to starve — native, thoughtless cruelty. Now he was not cruel and he was not kind. He was intensely practical and he was a good and skilful doctor; and besides his passionate ambition, and the research that lifted him towards it, lately he had liked his work. Every time he was called to the ordinary and routine work he was conscious of a new deep satisfaction. Even while he grumbled and pulled up his sleeves, the whole of him was filled with a good accustomed feeling of skill and ease.

That was how he had first met Charles; it was soon after he came on the farm, one evening when he had managed to save a calf that might — so easily — have died. It was a hot evening and the shed stank after the calf birth, of blood and urine and soaked stale straw, but as he knelt on one knee over the calf Narayan had been full of ease and quiet peaceful emotion — emotion is too strong a word, happiness too light, but he was filled with serene and utter peace. He, who was usually obsessed with futility, in the shed that evening had a quiet responsible power, reasonable and just, capable of joy and strength and a wisdom of its own. In saving the calf he had in some part saved the world, and his, that evening, were the quiet and the strength of a saviour. At least till Charles came in. When Charles came in Narayan did not move but every hair of him altered and stiffened into defence. He waited for whatever it might be, a question or a criticism or an order, perhaps praise, because no one could deny that he had done good work with the calf — but it was nothing.

Charles, who was smoking a pipe, leaned against the door of the shed and was completely silent, watching Narayan — watching his hands and watching the calf laid down on the straw and the cow turning her head on the rope to look, watching the sunset through the half-door; and the sun going down seemed to look back at him, winking on his eyeglass; imperceptibly, Narayan relaxed.

The cow sheds were on the edge of the farm buildings; and over the half-door of the shed he could see outside, to the fields where the sun was going down behind the flat plain; the people were going home to their villages along the narrow raised partitions of the fields; they moved to the dim distance — a man driving two bullocks, his plough left standing till to-morrow in the earth; a child, a woman with a bundle on her head, a woman carrying a child; a man, a boy, a child. He could see the village in the distance raised in its clump of trees and the land stretching from it like a sea from an island. The flat land with its bare earth fields, for it was summer then, took for a moment the reflection of the sky; the last light lay on them turning them a deep Indian yellow; it was an unmistakably evening light, and somewhere near the shed, but out of sight, a cowherd began to play a tune upon a flute.

The calf moved, jerking its legs, and Narayan forgot Charles; presently he lifted it and put it by the mother; it was dark cocoa colour streaked with white, it had white on its legs and a white star on its forehead. "Star of good luck," said Charles; "I didn't think it would live."

"It will do now I think," said Narayan.

"It's a good thing we have you and not old Babu Bhobatosh Babbletalk. That is one of our imported Frisians."

Narayan was so surprised at his knowing and using the students' nickname for old Dr. Bhobatosh that he forgot to answer. Charles was looking at him as Narayan wiped his hands on a towel.

"You should have been a doctor."

"I should have — did funds permit." After a moment he added, "They did not permit."

"Perhaps that was lucky," said Charles, and gravely he looked at Narayan. "You couldn't do any more important work than this." And he asked, "You go to the Onward Movement meetings, don't you?"

Narayan flushed. "I — have gone. But they are silly boys, I think."

"I wish you would go more often," said Charles and Narayan stared. "Tell them — tell them — " said Charles, and his pipe smoked alone in his hand — "tell them that the future of India may lie in this — in this calf, or a pod, or a bud, or a healthy blade of rice. Tell them not to talk so much. Politicians talk, and they start at the top and they never reach bottom, or earth — or truth. Young men are talkative and they like to be politicians — tell them to forbear," said Charles; "tell them to start at the bottom with the soil. They have inherited it. It is theirs. They are always telling us that. Tell them they should learn how to use it."

That was what Charles had said — and each word struck a note from another word like it in Narayan. It was as if he had been tuned; and he flushed and cried, "I will tell them to hold their tongues and use their hands!" As soon as he had said it, he saw the absurdity of what he had said and he burned with the ridicule of it so painfully that his eyes and his throat hurt him almost to tears; but Charles did not appear to have heard and presently Narayan was able to stammer: "That is — I — I think you should tell them yourself, Sir."

"I?" said Charles and laughed. "They are frightened of me."

That was true. They found Charles disconcerting. He had a way, not of tripping them up, but of making them give an exact attention to everything they said; the mind of Narayan appreciated that, while his own cheeks burned, but the students were not robust enough for it, and those who loved hyperbole and smartness disliked Charles. Narayan had heard him in conference and debate and, from curiosity, had gone to hear him lecture; the lecture was vigorous and engrossing, Charles was magnetic and he had fired some of the students into action.

They came to Charles after the lecture. "You need voluntary workers," they said grandly. "We shall go."

"Very well, go," said Charles.

That left them in the air. They felt snubbed and they resented it. They felt entitled to his consideration; they had offered their services, free. "We said *voluntary* workers," they reminded him.

"I said voluntary workers, too," said Charles. "You know where the organization is. If you want to work, go there."

"Sir, if you do not want us — "

Charles's answer came swiftly and hard. "*I* don't want you. *It* wants you. Don't make it anything to do with me." But they did not understand and they were offended.

Narayan wondered over this: Charles knew the young Bengalis; under their buoyancy they were

deeply sensitive, and if he had been more gentle
with them his words would have gone twice as far.
Narayan was certain he knew this, himself; then
why was he not more gentle? He deliberately discouraged affection and Narayan, who had just begun to cultivate it, found this hard to accept.
Charles was friendly to him, Charles was interested
in his work, but Narayan felt that they were still
waiting for their intimacy. He knew it was most
unlikely that Charles should be his friend, but he
felt, quite certainly, that presently this would be.

He tried to interest him in Anil. "No, thanks,
Das," said Charles, "I haven't time for protégés,"
and Anil refused most firmly to further it either.

"Let me show your poems to Pool, Anil?"

"To *Pool*? To Charlie Chang? What a foolman
you are, Indro. He only deals in seeds and cattle
breeds" — but under his lofty derision was the
same note of fear.

He had once encountered Charles; Narayan did
not know that. It was at another lecture that
Charles had given in the College. "And we must
take a wider, broader view of what agriculture
means to India," said Charles, concluding. And he
asked, "Has anybody anything to say?"

Anil always had something to say. "Sir," said
Anil, standing up, "I see the whole pattern of agriculture as a circle . . ."

Charles had never thought of it, but now he was

suddenly and most definitely against that; if he saw a pattern at all, he saw it as a long, long line, like a road beginning far back out of vision, continuing broader and broader out of sight.

Anil was still speaking: ". . . Everything is a circle," said Anil. "The rhythm of the year, the seasons, make a rhythm of the land — the preparing of the land, the seeding, germination, ripening, harvest, the return to earth as seed again — full circle is come; and is it not strange," said Anil, waxing louder, "is it not strange that everything that is symbolic of the life of the people is also the shape of a circle? The grindstone, the feeding bowl, the basket, the wheel — "

"What about a plough?" asked Charles.

No. Anil would not come and speak to Charles. But one day, thought Narayan that morning in his study, I shall ask him to dinner, and Anil too, and they shall learn to know one another under my roof. We shall have a charming dinner, we shall talk. And he shut his book and called, "Shila!"

Shila came to the door.

"One day I shall ask Charles Pool to dinner," said Narayan.

"Mr. Pool — to *dinner*? But — but — what does he eat? What could we do? How shall we do it?" Her eyes widened and then she said, "He will never come."

"Certainly he will come and we shall give him dinner." They would sit in the study, though they must borrow another chair, for the study only had two chairs, and Shila should send in a tray of sweets and they would sit talking while the light died on the river and Shila came softly in and trimmed the lamps; talking in friendly understanding talk. "Certainly he will come." And at Shila's dismayed face he laughed in good spirits and said, "Tell Tarala."

"Tarala has gone to the bazaar."

"And you? What do you do?" he teased.

"There is plenty to do in the house." She was delighted that he was in this mood and talking to her. "What do you think I should do?"

"Sit by the river and dream," said Narayan.

Much of that was true. On the tumbledown pillar in the garden Shila would sit while minutes and whole half-hours slid away. "Where is the knitting they taught you at school? Where are the books I like you to read?" They lay forgotten, and the small red ants that inhabited the pillar came out and ran across them. The sun lay hot there, and in the evening there was a breeze warm from the river, and Shila like one of the ants or a little lizard could never have enough of warmth and sun. The creeper by the pillar was an allamanda with big trumpet-shaped flowers of bright yellow and a heavy scent of honey — and all the time the river ran below and she watched the water running, running past.

"You sit there and dream of all the things you wish for," teased Narayan.

"No, I dream of all the things I have," said Shila softly, and she shut her eyes to see them. . . .

When I am too happy and when I am too miserable I come and sit beside the river and a little of the sorrow or the joy is drained off by the flowing water and runs away with it; then I can go into the house again and no one will see anything unusual in me. No one knows I have to do this but the river. I should not do it, I am a wife and a wife should spend her days evenly; if she has moods they should reflect her husband's; when he is glad, she is glad and when he is unhappy, she is unhappy too. My mother taught me this, but she was not married to Narayan.

Narayan has so many moods and he does not like me to watch him, it irritates him, and still I cannot help watching him. He does not want a wife like the wife I have been taught to be; he calls her a slave and a shadow, and he says he wants me to be myself. He makes me call him Narayan or Indro, as if he were not my husband at all; he makes me sit down in the room with his friend and he has asked me to eat with him, but this I cannot learn to do.

I am not clever enough for him; I was sent to school but I did not pay much attention; the bus used to call for me with the other girls and we sat in it, in two rows, facing each other behind drawn curtains and from that moment we began to giggle and we giggled till we came home. There were serious girls, and girls who used really to study; I laughed at them but now I wish I had been with them. Narayan likes mixed schools for girls and boys; what would my mother say to that? He says that girls can learn as well as men, but I have not found that yet; I find the books so very hard to learn, I cannot talk about them — like Anil Banerjee.

Don't think I am unhappy. I am the luckiest girl in the world. I only wish I were clever and not shy and then I could amuse Narayan — like Anil.

I have so much. I never thought, for instance, that when I was married Narayan would have a home of his own. The house is small, the little rooms lead out of one another, but it is all ours; the study is larger and has a window facing the court, and a door facing the steps; it has a desk and two chairs and a bookcase with all Narayan's books and a cabinet for his instruments. I should like our friends to see it, but would they come to see us now? I dare not ask them; they might say "No." Narayan is not orthodox; he is not even Hindu nor is he Christian; he is against religion.

He says it is superstition, he says it is nothing and he will talk against it for hours. He forbade me to go to the temple or to keep the Holy Days or to fast — and yet I think he wanted me to go. At first — I obeyed him and said nothing.

("Why don't you answer?" he asked. "Don't you want to go to the temple?")

("Yes.")

("Why don't you go?")

("Because you tell me not to go.")

("Oh. Go! Go! Go! Go! How many times have I told you not to do everything I say?")

Now I don't know whether to go or not to go; neither will please him; but there is one day that I must go. I must make my *puja* to Shasti . . . Her lips curved of themselves into a smile. . . . I shall pray to the Goddess of all children and she will keep my child.

It is not long to wait now. I sit out in the sun and the sun shines on me warming me all through and the river runs very softly and the sound of it goes in at my ear through all my body. My baby stirs and moves gently at the warmth and sound. He will be plump like a little pigeon and his skin will be soft like the petal of a champac flower to touch. Narayan says it will be a girl. He will be delighted with the baby. Will he? Will he? I am not sure. I am never quite sure of Narayan. . . .

She opened her eyes and asked Narayan timidly, "Has Anil Banerjee's wife a son?"

"I do not think so."

"Ah!" said Shila softly, and she asked, "He has been married — how long?"

"He has been married for nearly two years," said Narayan crossly. "The marriage was consummated ten months ago. I have told him it is absurd. The girl is not fully developed. She is only fourteen."

"Fourteen is developed," said Shila suddenly and boldly; there was a distinct gleam in her eyes. "And he — what does he say?"

"He does not say anything at all. It is not his fault. He married her to please his father; if his father tells him, he will send her away. Meanwhile she is his wife, a little girl. It is a good thing he has to leave her and come to College."

"All the same," said Shila softly, "he must want a son."

Narayan was tired of it. He said, "Here is Tarala, come back from the bazaar. Shouldn't you go and see what she has brought?" But Shila had already gone.

Shila saw the bazaar through Tarala's basket; everything that was important to her in the bazaar was in it. At the beginning of the month the stores were brought; sugar, rice, oil, spices and grain to last the month; but every day Tarala went down and came back with a triumphant expression on her face and a coolie boy carrying her basket. "What have you brought, Tarala?"

Vegetables — young sweet carrots, and glossy purple knobs of brinjals, and a pomeloe that opened like a big pink-fleshed orange; sour-milk curd in an earthenware pot, some fresh firm hilsa fish.

"Is that all?"

"Yes, Ma."

Neither Shila nor Tarala would look at one another. At last Shila spoke. "Was there — no mutton?"

"No, Ma, none."

"Tarala — did you look?"

(Looked, and turned my head away quickly!) And aloud Tarala cried: "None, Ma, anywhere. Narayan Babu must have fish for his dinner." ("And that is bad enough, God knows!" she said under her breath.) "But we shall make it so good," she reassured Shila, "you will see he is pleased. Narayan Babu likes hilsa fish, Ma."

"He likes mutton," said Shila, and as firmly as she could make herself say the horrible word, she said: "There must be mutton to-morrow."

* * * Before she woke, Louise saw the horse and the rider going along behind the hedge, a tall white horse with a dreadful boniness that she most strangely knew; the rider's face was turned away from her, hidden by a hat with a long plume that trailed into lines of mist and lay on hedges and trees; a dim half-white, half-hidden landscape, where any noise was muffled in the mist. She stood in long grass wet above her knees and as she stepped back, the grass drew after her drawing all the landscape with it, the hedge and the horse and the rider. To stop it she must stand still and look at the rider and then he would turn his head and she would see — she would see . . . But she would not look; she stepped back and back, though the grass grew heavier and wetter and the mist was lapping round her in tenuous spirals and folds. . . . *Look at the rider! Look him in the face. Look. Look. Look!* . . . And she screamed dreadfully and silently, and the trees were immediately distorted and the mist changed to smoke that was coming to scorch and burn her. It was in her tongue and her throat, burning, tasteless, burning, and her throat began to swell. The swelling rose in her mouth and the landscape began to swell as well, swollen trees and leaves and hedge, and the malformed horse came backwards towards her, bearing its rider backwards while it went stepping on in a terrible duplication of itself. There was a bony grating — Ah! *crepitus!* She recognized it from the First Aid Lectures — but that meant the rider was turning his head. . . . I must look. I must look. *Look. Look. Look!* And the swelling choked her and before she died, she woke.

The room was full of pale light and the grating, the *crepitus,* was the noise of the bee-catcher birds waking in the garden. It was hardly morning, but to Louise the room was full of heat; it ached with heat like her head, and her eyelids felt like egg-shells, brittle and dry. Through the windows she could see the sky turning from grey to white with a line of hyacinth above the dark dusty tops of trees. Everything was dry, hot, dusty; and the dream filled her mind with a sharp horror of fear. She picked up a glass of water that was on the table by her bed and drank, but the water had been standing and was warm with a horrible body warmth, and she retched and in spite of the heat her skin was suddenly goose-fleshed and cold. She trembled so that the whole bed trembled too — and snatched up her dressing-gown and went out on the verandah.

After her padded the Pekingese, Sun and Picotee, that she had snatched with the children from France. She had refused to leave them behind — she bullied and cajoled to get them on the steamer; her love for them, for all animals, was touched with fanaticism, and now she lived in continual fear that they would pick up something from the bazaar.

Louise saw the bazaar as a patch like plague against the walls of the house. . . . I see the bazaar, she said — at least I am prevented for ever from seeing it by smelling it first. I smell the street and the nest of lanes behind it as one foul latrine. I swear the Indians can have no sense of smell. If I walk through it I am contaminated even through my shoes, even through the high heels of them — soiled and contaminated. It is filthy, unhealthy, dangerous; there is cess in the gutters where the men squat down even while I am passing, there are stains and patches where betel-nut and cough-phlegm are spat out on the stones, there are flies that rise up from litter heaps and settle on the sweets and foodstuff in the shops. I smell the rancid ghee in these shops and the smell of mustard oil and garlic and rotting fruit and meat that has hung too long, and in the road all round me is the smell of refuse and the smell of unwashed sweat and oil from the coolies, the smell of musk and sandalwood from the cleanest white-clad clerk; and on some days I smell the burning of a body from the burning *ghat* and that I cannot bear. Charles, I cannot bear to go into the bazaar. I cannot bear to stay here where I must see it and hear it all day long.

It is hideous and cruel. I see the woman with elephantiasis, and the beggars withered, distorted, deformed, and among them the leper who is allowed to wander here for begging. The children's stomachs are swollen with fever and spleen, and the babies have flyblown ophthalmic eyes. The dogs have mangy backs and bruised outstanding ribs, the buffaloes pull the carts in the sun all day long — buffaloes, that are water beasts and meant for water and for coolness; the iron bullock-wheels turn and creak along the road, so that I cannot forget them. I see a kitten lying where a crow has pecked its eyes, and the men are as cruel as the crows, they have birds hung in tiny cruel cages and sometimes they have put out their eyes to make them sing. I can forgive them their babies but I cannot forgive them the birds.

There is nothing picturesque or attractive in the bazaar, it is sordid and poor, it has no products of its own; it has no muslins or silk or pottery or weaving or rugs or ivory. Even the temple is hideous and cheap, even the sacred bull has a sore on its rump and filth on its tail. There is nothing but filth and squalor and misery in the bazaar. I hate to go there, I hate the children to go there and I am terrified the dogs will stray and catch some disease in the bazaar.

I asked Charles not to give the children a dog. I asked him not to give them Don. He gave them Don. . . .

He gave him to Emily.
"Why Emily? Why not Binnie? Why Emily?"

"I think," he said, "that that little girl needs love."

In her surprise Louise had stared. "*Emily!* Why, Emily won't have love. That shows how little you know of her. She is hard. She is completely oblivious of everyone but herself. She doesn't care an atom for anyone. She is almost unnatural."

"You don't like her, do you?"

She answered icily, "I love Emily more than you could begin to understand."

"You may love her. You don't like her."

"I love her and I know her better than she knows herself." And she said, "I must ask you not to interfere with the children."

Charles's eyes went dark and the cast in them showed plainly. "If you didn't want me to interfere, why did you bring them here?" he asked. "Did it never occur to you that I might get interested — in the children?"

"You are — insufferable," said Louise, and she cried: "You know nothing about children. You don't like children. You don't know them. Why should you interfere?"

He said nothing to that. He gave Don to Emily . . .

Now, as the Pekingese poured in a wave of tails and feathers down the stairs, Don whined from between the children's beds. Louise went quickly up the verandah where the two white-netted beds stood. Under Emily's on the floor lay a watch face downwards.

("Emily, don't take your watch to bed.")

("I will put it under my pillow.")

("If you do, you will break it. If it falls on the stone floor it will break. You know how you toss and turn. Don't take your watch to bed.")

Louise set her lips and picked up the watch. It was not broken.

Don was tearing at his rug and whining. She went round Emily's bed to set him free and she stopped. She bent down to look at him, and looked again. For a long while she stood there looking down at him. Then she ran down the verandah calling for Charles and Kokil, the sweeper.

* * * The world is square, said Charles in his sleep, and I shall have it square. . . . That was the last moment he slept. He was awake; he still lay with his eyes shut, but he was awake, aware of the light on the outer side of his lids, and the hardness of the bed under him where before he had been floating — floating — floating. . . . He was nearly asleep again and again he was awake. He stretched a little and yawned.

He began to consider the day. Before he went to sleep Charles added up his day, as soon as he woke up he forecast it, and tried to read it out. It was one of his fixed, lonely habits; he knew exactly what he would do in the day and he liked to know; but now, since Louise had come, it was not as clear and not as easy to read. Anything might happen in the day. . . . And I can't predict, said Charles, how well I can behave. He felt tired. . . . Lying in bed is easy; to get up and face the day is not. I shall not get up — just yet. . . . And he turned resolutely on his face, but a little pulse beating against his pillow, somewhere in his head, seemed to beat *Louise . . . Louise . . . Louise* — and impatiently he sat up.

The morning had a milky coolness under its promise of heat, the wind blew across the garden that still had dew in all its shady places. There still was freshness in the wind, there still was dew and freshness in the garden, on the lawns under the trees, on the undersides of leaves, between the shafts of the bamboo, inside the striped cyclamen trumpets of the blue convolvulus, in the lemon-yellow allamandas. His skin felt cool and dewy, he was strong and he moved in bed stretching, sending the sleep from his bones as he stretched and stretched, stretching his annoyance away. There was the sound of someone running and Louise herself came in without knocking, swinging the door back. "Charles! Charles! Charles!"

"I'm here," said Charles quietly.

She stopped abruptly and the urgency faded on

her face. She looked at the room: his clothes put out on a chair, the bath running in the bathroom, his dressing-table and shoe-stands, his crop and hat on the table, a row of photographs on the wall, cups on a shelf, a pile of papers; Charles's room that she had not seen for years. It arranged itself in front of her eyes with a series of pricking shocks — and Charles was lying on the bed and watching her, raised on one elbow, wearing nothing but a *lungi* wound round his waist. His chest and legs and arms seemed brilliantly brown and strong on the white sheet, and the sun shone on his head and made hundreds of dark bright points on the hair on his legs and arms and chest. "Haven't you a dressing-gown?" cried Louise.

"You didn't knock," said Charles, and she blushed. He made no attempt to get up; he lay there looking at her and his gaze went slowly down from her face over her body to the hem of her skirt. She wore a wrapper of thin white silk, tied at the wrists and neck and waist with rose-coloured woollen cords; it swung open at the hem to show the chiffon nightgown and her bare feet in mules. Her hair was down, loose on her shoulders; she tried to stem the hot colour that flooded her cheeks and neck but it grew hotter. "This is quite like old times, isn't it?" he said pleasantly.

For a moment he thought she would go, but she controlled herself. "You know I shouldn't have come if . . ." Her voice broke into genuine panic. "Charles. Please come quickly. It's Don. Oh, Charles. Please come."

They took Don downstairs while the children were still asleep.

* * * For Emily the morning broke in streaks of green and white: white on sunlight, and flying bands of green; and she woke in her bed under the white net high above the garden. In the garden on the trees every tip and frond was waving in the morning light; there were the tall exciting shapes of palms, petrified, in colours of greys and greens like palm-trees in old prints; there were the emerald diaphanous sprays of the cassias, and another tree whose leaves were like countless little coins or seals moving in the sun. The sun spread like a fan over the garden, the same shape but upside down as the tails of the cook's pigeons that sat on the roof and round the stables; one fan-stick of sunlight lay across Emily's bed and touched her cheek, it had not touched Binnie or anyone else, it touched only Emily. It altered as the sun came up, now it was long and thin like a spear. A golden spear.

"Bring me my spear. O clouds unfold . . ."

Charles sang that. Charles's voice was big and rather rough and it had notes that were so deep and vibrant that they woke a literal echo in Emily, as if she had harpstrings inside her.

"He makes an awful noise," said Binnie, her head cocked to listen. "It's like listening to a whole band."

"I like it," said Emily.

In the early morning, waiting for his horse, he always stood on the steps above the garden and sang "Jerusalem."

> "Bring me my bow of burning gold,
> Bring me my arrows of desire,
> Bring me my spear. O clouds unfold,
> Bring me my chariot of fire . . ."

"Oh, hush!" said Binnie, scandalized. "They'll hear you the other side of the river."

"It will do them good," said Charles. "It's the most beautiful song in the world."

"Mother doesn't think so," said Binnie.

What possessed her to say that? Charles sang no more and called for his pony and Emily beat at the plumbago bushes with the switch that she was carrying. They went a little way with Charles and then suddenly, over some stupidity like this, they lost him; always Emily was turning up, from him or from Louise, continual proof of what she did not want to know.

"*There are circumstances over which we have no control.*" Louise said that often, but Emily had never quite believed her. . . . I shall *not* let them spoil it. I shall stay here, said Emily. Nothing, nothing must happen here to spoil it.

"Jerusalem," Binnie was saying, "is a place in Palestine. How could it be in England too?"

She spoke to Charles, and Charles, who had one foot in the stirrup of his nervous and very lively little country-bred, before he mounted paused to answer her; at however inconvenient a time, Charles always answered. "*That* Jerusalem wasn't a place," said Charles, and swung himself up.

Delilah, the pony, went dancing away, sending up the gravel in a cloud of red dust. Presently she came fidgeting back again.

"What was it then?" asked Binnie.

Emily waited for his answer. He hesitated, looking down at Binnie who stood by his foot; from Emily's view she looked foreshortened, all gathered frock and round pink face and a neat little pate of curls, and her heart gave a jealous pang at the tenderness on Charles's face. They did — they did like Binnie best.

"What was it then?" asked Binnie.

"Your heart's desire," said Charles, and Emily forgot her jealousy in her interest. That was the first question he had not answered properly, he seemed to feel that; he was looking not at Binnie but over Emily's head. "Your heart's desire," he repeated, and he said it with a mocking bitterness that appalled her. "And if you can't get it," said Charles, "don't lose your temper. Be reasonable. Take something else instead."

Emily knew, without turning, that Louise was standing behind her.

Lying in bed, thinking of that, she shut it quickly out of her mind. . . .

This is how I used to wake when I was a baby, thought Emily hastily, in another house that seems in some way joined to this. Now I am back again as if I had never been away. I am back again exactly where I started from. I am back. I am back. . . . But was she? Could she be? Was she? . . . Yes I *am,* insisted Emily, I have forgotten I have ever been away. . . . But she said it as Charles said the world was square — for Emily had been away. . . .

She had been in the schoolroom at Bellevue, for instance, where the vine hung over the balcony making a peaceful green light over the little boys and girls. Madame Chastel said, "*Écrivez la moitié, jusqu'à: 'Hannibal était parti pour les Alpes. . . .'*" when the alarm went and Madame stood up, her dark moustache trembling slightly above her lips, and cried, "*Attention. Marchons!*" And they marched between the desks across the parquet in the hall into the panelled cupboard that led under the stairs to the cellar.

Emily had been in the cellar. The concrete reinforcements made twisting shapes on the walls, there were dim piles of sandbags, and benches where they sat. Once the light went out and it had been quite dark. Emily sat on her bench and felt a sliding trickle run behind her ears. Somewhere a little girl began to sob, a little girl that might be Binnie. "We are not afraid," said Madame, "we think of our brave airmen, of our soldiers and our nurses and our ships — we are not afraid." . . .

("Mother, need we, need we go to school?")

("Why?")

("Because of — raids.")

("Why, Emily, you ought to be ashamed, *everyone* is carrying on their work! You mustn't be afraid of raids.")

("I'm not afraid of raids, I'm afraid of the cellar." But it was no use telling that to Louise.)

Louise approved of the cellar. "There is no immediate danger," said Louise; but she hurried them into the cellar and she snatched them away in one push from Paris to Louvain. "No danger" — in that clear and perfectly toneless voice, when she laid out in the cabin every night their warm coats and their life-belts; when with trembling fingers she tied the life-belts on them up on the deck.

("What is it? Is it a wreck? Is it a mine, or a submarine? Have we been hit?")

("Nothing. Only a practice.")

("*What?* In the middle of the night?")

It was a submarine, Emily heard that afterwards. The submarine had missed them. Why couldn't Louise have said it was a submarine?

Emily stirred and turned impatiently in bed. . . . Whenever I start to think, said Emily, I come back to Louise. Now — I shall teach myself to stop thinking of you, Mother. I am here, now, safe, away in this place, away from the world, with Charles. Soon, soon I shall think of myself and not of you, and I shall be free. I shall stay here and you cannot touch me here. Nothing, nothing shall happen here. . . . .

She lay and listened to the noise coming up from the bazaar where the day was well upon its way. . . . I see the bazaar, said Emily as she lay; it is interesting and exciting. The first shop you come to is the shop where they make kites; you can buy twelve kites for three annas in colours of pink and green and white and red, and a wicker spool to fly them with, and a pound of thread. The thread is glassed, and — only don't tell Mother — we fly them with Shah off our roof and challenge other kites and cross strings with them and cut them adrift and then we can put another bob on our kite's tail.

The front of the money-changer's shop is barred,

and he sits on a red cloth quilted with black and white flowers — and he is a Marwari with a small orange turban like a doughnut twisted on his head. He has nothing in his shop but a safe, a pair of scales and a table a few inches high. In India jewellery is sold by weight, and the jewellery is made of silver threads woven into patterns and flowers. The moneylender tests every piece of money he is given by weighing it before he takes it, and I think that that is sense. Shah does it too, only he bites the money instead.

The cloth-shop is inviting with rolls of cloth on the shelves all open to the street; cottons and prints with patterns, and new crisp sari cloth, and children's dresses with low waists, cut square and flat like paper dresses, hanging outside in the street. The grain-shops have grain set out in different colours in black wicker baskets, and with them are sold great purple roots and knots of ginger and chiles and spice. The sweet-shops have balls like American popcorn and other balls that are like marshmallows, and clear toffee sweets that are made in beautiful spiralled rings. Mother says we must never taste them but we have.

The temple is very clever and interesting because its outside walls and its floor are mosaic made from broken pieces of china. In one little patch on the floor we counted a hundred and seventeen pieces; the banyan tree grows right down through the roof of the temple; a banyan tree grows out of the earth and sends some of its branches back into the earth again — it sounds like dust to dust — and the walls of the temple are tiled with the same sort of tiles that we had in the bathroom at Bellevue. On the platform are the images of Rada and Krishna, made of two jointed dolls with tinselled clothes, and in front of them a table with offerings of sweets and flowers. A woman came to pray — on the brass tray she put a little powdered sugar and with her thumb she made on it the pattern of the sun for luck.

There is a mosque in the bazaar too, and it has a minaret shaped like a lighthouse beside it, only instead of a light, the priest goes there to call the people when it is time to come and pray.

There is such a good idea in the bazaar. There are rickshaws, but instead of men to pull them they are joined to bicycles and pulled along like that.

We buy bangles in the bazaar, glass ones, and the shop is full of their clear glass goblin colours. Mother forbids us to wear them because she says they are dangerous. They are dangerous; Binnie cut herself to the bone wearing hers — she had to have three stitches in her wrist.

("That's your fault, Emily. You take no care of Binnie. You are the eldest but you never think of her. You never think of anybody but yourself.")

Now Emily called across to Binnie's bed to see if she were awake.

The morning did not break for Binnie; there were simply the morning and evening of the next day.

"What are you going to do to-day, Bin?"

Binnie answered promptly. "I shall go fishing for pearls."

This was not such an incredible pastime as it sounded. On the edges of the river, in certain places, were beds of a curious deep-blue river-shellfish, more like a mussel than an oyster, and they could be dislodged and floated up by a hook on a string, sometimes — not very often. The native divers went down for them, naked and unprotected, and they could walk about below the water for minutes together without anything to help them but their muscles. Sometimes, not very often, just occasionally, the shells held a pearl, a real pearl with a gold sheen that was almost apricot. Charles had two in a pillbox on his desk. . . . Why doesn't he give them to Louise? . . . Don't think of that. We shall go fishing for pearls. . . .

"We'll take Shah and a fisherman," said Emily. "We'll take the fisherman's boat — "

("We shall float down on the sun-green water, trailing our hooks past little bays and promontories in the hard white sand; there will be no sound but the sounds of the boat and the voices of Shah and the fisherman.'') Other boats, the same as theirs, crescent-shaped with a wicker cowl in the middle, would float down past them with dark-skinned crews who did not know their language and could not speak to them any more than the floating clumps of water hyacinth could speak. No one would talk to them or ask them questions; there would be nothing to listen to or to watch, everything would be wrapped in sun and silence, quietness and sun.

Binnie sat up in bed. "Why, where's Don?" she said.

At that moment Louise came lightly down the verandah. "Children! Children! You have been asked to go to breakfast with the Nikolides."

Chapter IV

FOR EMILY, the Nikolides were as desirable and nearly as distant as on the first day she had seen them. She had met them; they had come; and the Pools had been to their house for tea and to spend the day; but Louise did not approve of Mrs. Nikolides nor Mrs. Nikolides of Louise.

("Mother, can't we go and see the Nikolides?")

("Every time you go there you are upset. Their food is so ridiculously rich." And when they did go Mrs. Nikolides would feel their elbows and shoulders bare in their sun-dresses and say, "You'll catch a chill, poor children. I wonder your mother can let you out in the river breeze, without so much as a coat on, or a vest.")

Now, direct visits were rare, but the children saw one another occasionally, passing in launches up- and downstream, or in cars on the road; but always they were separated, and in the presence of their mothers only sent small reserved smiles and the wave of a hand across the air or water. Emily did not know whether or not the Nikolides family would have sent more if they could; it was probable that their desires were as well schooled as themselves.

They were distinguished by their beauty, their obedience and their bravery. Emily felt that she and Binnie were not distinguished in any way at all.

Alexandra, the girl, was beautiful and dignified; there was beauty in her straight chiselled nose and curved chiselled mouth, and dignity even in the fall of her hair, curling black on a very white neck, and in her grave dark eyes; and her smile was like a queen's. She bore the weight of clothes with which her mother loaded her without complaining, only keeping still so that she should not feel their heat; and she was perfectly sweet-tempered with the ayahs and governess who followed her everywhere she went; she had beautiful unusual manners and once, when a car door was slammed upon her fingers, she had neither screamed nor cried, but simply fainted.

Her brother Jason was like her, but more sallow, completely stoical and biddable to the point of death. Binnie, in the rare moments when she had him to herself, liked to find out how far he would go; he had never yet refused her. He would, when she told him, climb out to the end of a branch of a tree, walk on the roof parapet, be pushed out in a tub on the tank — and was rescued each time, just in time, by Shah. It was fortunate perhaps for Jason that the friendship was not encouraged.

("No *wonder*," mourned Emily. "Why do you make him do it, Bin?")

("He never answers back," said Binnie with a slow smile. "He says nothing; he does it.")

So the Nikolides children remained as they first had looked for Emily, like those in a book, all that she herself was not, in another world, unattainable; and when Louise came down the verandah and said, "Breakfast with the Nikolides," surprise, excitement and delight swept every other thought out of her mind.

"Be quick. Hurry!" said Louise. "I've put your clean dresses ready, your spotted cottons and your sandals. The launch is waiting to take you."

They ought to have heard the smoothness in her voice, it was much too smooth to be natural; they ought to have seen her hands trembling against her dress; but they leapt out of bed, and cried "The Nikolides!" Without a look or thought they raced away to dress.

They met Charles on the steps downstairs. "Why haven't you gone riding?" asked Binnie in surprise.

Charles, as soon as it was daylight, went out riding — they were not often up early enough to catch him.

"Why do you go so early?" they had once asked him.

"Because that's the best of the morning."

"But it isn't really morning, it's hardly even day," Binnie objected.

"What is the day like then?" asked Emily.

"Like a violet," said Charles.

Binnie laughed, but Emily knew what he meant. She had seen the day opening as they came in on the river; the sky opening above the flat land in violet curves with a glimmer of that colour in the water and in the freshness of the dew. Charles said things like that and Emily knew what he meant when no one else did, and he was looking at her now in a way that made her pause.

"Why haven't you gone riding?" she asked, and the question made a rift for a moment in the excitement that filled her mind; but it was only for a moment, she did not even hear his answer.

"He is taking you to the jetty in the car," Louise said hurriedly.

"*That* little way?" said Binnie.

It arrested Emily too; it was strange that Charles should stay in to drive them a few hundred yards; it was out of order, but the morning was already and delightfully out of order and Binnie was in the car. Emily ran down the steps forgetting to say good-bye to Louise, and Charles silently followed her and drove them in a few minutes through the bazaar to the jetty where the launch was waiting.

"Emily, wait — " he said, but the launch had a feather of steam, like a breath blowing out of its funnel, and it rocked on the water as if it really were alive; and beyond it the green spaces of the river were bright with pin-points of sun. Emily could not possibly wait. She ran in front of Binnie down the jetty planks and jumped down on the deck; Shah saluted and walked down after them, and the loop of rope was lifted from the jetty post, the launch backed away into the stream and turned in a half-circle bearing them away. They saw Charles walk back to the car.

Something in the way he walked made Emily look again. "Binnie," she said, "there is something wrong."

"Oh, *Emily!*" cried Binnie impatiently; and after a moment she said, "If there were anything wrong, would Mother have let us go out? You know she wouldn't."

Emily longed to be convinced but she demurred. "Why did Charles take us down in the car?"

"I expect there is something she didn't want us to see in the bazaar," said Binnie practically. "Perhaps there is another leper. You remember the fuss she made about the last. . . . I remember him well," said Binnie with dispassionate interest, "he hadn't a nose. His nose had quite gone. Mother thought it was dreadful, but I didn't mind seeing him at all, did you?"

"Not in the least," said Emily proudly, but she had to press herself down in her chair and fortify herself by pushing out her ribs and making herself hard and strong, and a comfortable peace replaced the trouble in her mind.

The launch went on towards the Nikolides' house, which could be seen with the mill chimney and the sheds at a great distance down the river. The river traffic grew thinner; soon they were quite alone on the expanse of water, and it seemed that the house and the chimney were coming gradually and inevitably towards them while they on the launch were still; now they could see and separate the colours; the chimney and the sheds were red like the house roof, and the house walls were yellow; and presently they could see the line of trees and the fleet of launches moored there like grey ducks on the water. Emily was looking at them, excitement beating in her chest, but she still saw the figure of Charles walking away from the jetty and the sudden fear started up in her. . . . What is it? What can it be? . . . And immediately she asked, What has Mother done? and clearly she saw Louise. . . .

I see you, Mother. I cannot help it. Everything I know, I know from you. You have been there as long as I can remember. As soon as I come near you I am stupid and stiff and I cannot think properly and I cannot say even what I think. I can arrange words clearly in my mind so that they would astonish you, and as soon as I come to you to tell them, I cannot say any of them; but perhaps I am not quite as stupid over this as I used to be. You are so beautiful, so utterly quick and clever; your eyes are dark and your lashes make them look darker still and very very large, but I have discovered something: they are not as big as we think and they move quickly like a bird's; birds' eyes have no lashes and if yours had none, they would be exactly like a bird's, and your fingers are like your eyes, quick and busy. . . . Her mind broke into panic. . . . Mother, please be still. Don't do anything, don't let anything happen here! . . . And she grew angry. . . . I am warning you, Mother. I see you. One day, you will do more than you mean. . . .

"There they are," said Binnie, and on the edge of the jetty they could see far-away figures standing and waiting. "I should be jumping up and down," said Binnie, and she added, "but of course the Nikolides don't jump if they can help it."

Emily straightened herself. . . . I shall *not* think now. If anything has happened it can wait. . . . And replacing Louise in her mind came the figures of three little monkeys that Charles had given her. "They are Japanese," said Charles.

"Sensible people have them all over the world, not to emulate altogether, but there are times when it's good to be like them." "See nothing, hear nothing, say nothing," said the monkeys, and as Emily thought of them Louise seemed to dwindle back across the water; and the jetty and the Nikolides grew every moment larger and more clear.

Louise that very second was thinking of Emily. . . . I see you too. I see you, Emily. You always do all you possibly can to upset me. All this trouble has come from you and Charles. What did I say? What did I beg? "Don't give Emily a dog. Don't take Don into the bazaar." You never listen to me — you never think of me. When you went this morning you pushed and rushed into the car. You did not say good-bye to me like Binnie. You did not wave and smile. That was so like you. You forgot all about me. You forgot all about Don.

Don was shut up where you could not hear him cry. I need not have bothered. You never asked for Don. All that you thought of was yourself. You see I am right; I know you and I can turn your thoughts like the wind on a paper streamer. . . . And suddenly, into Louise's mind came a remembrance like a prick. Was she so sure? She remembered something that Emily had said a day or two ago. "Mother, if I have two children, do you know what I'm going to call them? Willy and Nilly,

Mother. Isn't that a good name for two children like us?"

Emily could not have thought of that for herself; it must have been coincidence — or Charles. She could not have thought that for herself. . . .

You have not improved, Emily, since I brought you out. You have gone unbecomingly sallow and you have grown too much, outgrown grace like a weed, though you have never been pretty like Binnie. You have a long face, not like a little girl's, with flattened cheek-bones that give your eyes a slant as if you were keeping a secret, and usually you are; you are deceitful and you have a way of keeping your elbows out defensively, and you are very very obstinate and you are one continual worry about your health. You looked well yesterday, to-day you are suddenly more sallow than ever. I have bought you so many ribbons for your hair, I like it plaited and turned up in coils, it makes your face look longer to have it hanging down like that; it is so fair and so limp it looks quite greenish, and when you shut your eyes it gives you the look of a girl that is drowned; it makes my heart turn over. But I am foolish to agonize over you, Emily. You think of nothing and no one but yourself. It is strange that I should have so insensitive a child. I am foolish to save your feelings, you have none to save. . . . A brisk stir filled Louise. . . . She has gone, gone to breakfast with the Nikolides;

she took that without one question. When she comes back it will all be over, and she will never know what has come near her. . . . And dramatically Louise cried, This threat will have been wiped out of their lives! . . . And then a small, familiar worry nagged her. . . . "I hope you will be careful what you eat, Emily. I have had to leave that to you. Charles is so odd, he refused to let me warn Mrs. Nikolides about your stomach."

"You shall not shame Emily like that," said Charles.

"Don't be absurd. You know how greedy she is. She will eat anything, and then she will be upset."

"Better to upset her stomach and save her face," said Charles.

* * * "We saw you from the distance," said Jason as the launch touched the jetty. "How do you do, Emily? How do you do, Binnie? What a long time you have taken in getting here!"

"How do you do? How do you do?" said Alexandra gravely. "No, you are not late. It's half-past ten. You are just in time for breakfast."

"What is there for breakfast?" asked Binnie as she stepped ashore.

There would be queer, rather greasy things for the breakfast that the Nikolides had at this enchanting hour; perhaps mulligatawny soup with rice, fish balls, stewed fruit and cake. Emily knew with certainty what would befall her later in the day. Never mind, "See nothing, hear nothing, say nothing."

A warm wind blew down the Nikolides' garden, bringing the smell not of breakfast, but of scent from the flowers on the row of trees that were champac trees — queer bare thick polished branches, no leaves and white chiselled cups of flowers touched with gold, as strange and exotic as the Nikolides themselves. Through the cracks in the jetty the water looked miraculously, clearly green, and Emily's stomach gave a delicious little rumble.

First Binnie, then Emily, then Shah, passed inside the house to breakfast with the Nikolides.

Chapter V

THE TELEPHONE rang in the Das house while Narayan was dressing; he called, "Shila, answer that."

Shila was dusting the study and when Narayan called she stayed there, rooted by his desk, the duster in her hand and a piteous expression on her face. The bell continued to ring. "Shila. Shila, where are you? Answer the phone."

She took one step towards it and, as if it knew she was coming, it gave another peremptory ring. "*Shila!*"

In a rush she took the receiver off and held it. There was a prolonged silence. Narayan came in fastening his collar. "Well, who is it?"

She shook her head and offered him the receiver.

"Who? Who is speaking?"

"I — don't know."

"You have taken it off and you have not answered it? What is the matter with you? Are you dumb?

Are you mad? . . . What have you been doing?"

"I have . . . not listened to it . . . Indro."

"Why not? Why not? All this time we have had the telephone and you are still afraid of it. Other girls use the telephone, why not you? What is the matter with you?" She twisted her fingers and said nothing, though her lips trembled.

"Answer. Answer me," shouted Narayan. "How many times have I told you to answer me?" He stopped, trying to control himself, and he said more gently, "You make me speak and behave to you in a way I have sworn not to speak or behave. Why are you afraid to answer the telephone, Shila?"

"Suppose — suppose it should be — Mr. Pool."

"And if it is — you can speak to him as well as I. Why should it be Mr. Pool? He has never telephoned me here, and at this hour he goes riding."

"Suppose he did not go. Suppose he has come back."

"Suppose! Suppose! I tell you, it won't be Mr. Pool. Answer it at once."

From the telephone impatient buzzing noises were coming; her eyes bright with tears, Shila held the receiver up and whispered down it, "Ah?"

"Louder. Much more louder than that."

"*Ah?*"

Narayan heard a second voice. It sounded impatient.

"Ah?"

The voice went on, a long speech, and her eyes slid to Narayan in anguish. "Ah?"

"Oh, give it to me," cried Narayan and seized it out of her hand. "Who is it? Who is it?" he barked.

"It — it is Mr. Pool . . . Indro."

He was intensely irritated. "And he will think I'm married to a fool," he cried bitterly. "You do not try, you do not care. You do nothing for me that I ask you. What use are you to me?" He turned his back on her and said, "Good morning, Mr. Pool. I am sorry I have kept you; my wife is an ignorant girl and not accustomed yet to answer the telephone."

Shamed to the quick Shila stood behind him; her head was bowed and her hands pressed together in an effort not to cry, but in spite of that two lines of tears slid down her cheeks and dropped onto her skirts; she was wearing a sari of white, dotted in a pattern of green; and between the green flowers the tear-drops fell and shone for a moment and sank away into the muslin. Narayan turned his head to make a note and she quickly bowed her head still lower and made the quick age-old gesture of drawing her sari across her face so that he should not see it, and ran out of the room; he heard her crying break as soon as she was outside the door.

He could not wait, he had to answer Charles's call, and he hurried off on his bicycle — but as he went, the sound of his voice, not Shila's, came back to his ears; and it sounded unnecessarily violent and a little pedantic, and from that violence came a sense of shame; he felt jarred, out of content, and though he tried to blame Shila the blame fastened on him and the sound of his angry voice seemed to follow him as he rode along the road. "*A woman's tears in the morning bring bad luck.*" That was superstition, told by old women like Tarala; but he almost turned and rode back to tell Shila — What could he tell her? Only that he was sorry and she would not understand that; she thought only that she had offended and that his right to punish was divine; besides, Charles had already been kept waiting and Narayan bicycled on, though he knew it would not have been necessary to say a word: to go back was enough. . . . Later, later. I will comfort her later, said Narayan, and turned in through the Pools' gate.

He was riding up the drive where the poinsettias dipped their scarlet beads when Charles, riding the little mare, passed him almost at a gallop and flashed out of the gate with nothing to show they had gone but a cloud of dust and kicked gravel, the servants who had run out of the house at the noise, and the noise of hoof-beats dying away on the road.

"What in the world?" cried Narayan, who had

fallen off his bicycle. He was furious. "He nearly rode me down. I shall certainly go away." He did not mean that; he was far too curious, and when the servants salaamed him with a civility that came from important happenings, he followed them at once to the stables. "What is up? Something is very much up." He was ushered through the stables to a loose-box, and there was Mrs. Pool in tears.

* * * This morning will never pass, Louise had said dramatically. . . . Days may be all the same in the sight of God but for us some are over before they have come, some go on for ever; the days of misery and suspense go on, days like this. . . .

(And interrupting her was a voice that was like Charles's, like all the unsympathetic people in the world: "You invented a dream for yourself . . .")

("I did not invent it. I dreamt it.")

("You invented a dream for yourself," said the inexorable voice. "Take care. You started more than you knew.")

("I can't stop it. I can't stop it!" screamed Louise.)

("You could have stopped it. Why didn't you look at the rider's face?")

Louise shut her eyes and her ears and turned her head away. . . .

She was in the long line of stables behind the

house where Delilah and a Bhutia pony and the pigeons lived. In an empty stall Don lay on the floor and Louise watched beside him, and Charles stayed there watching Louise. "Why don't you go away," said Charles, "and leave the poor little brute alone?"

"I want to be *sure*."

"You have made up your mind already. Why do you have to pretend?"

She did not deny it and he could have predicted the justification she made — "With children we must not take the faintest risk."

"Not we — you," said Charles. "I will take risks — in proportion — even for them. But you have no sense of proportion. You won't; not if Don and I and everyone in Amorra have to die for it."

"Oh, why don't you go away?" cried Louise.

Why did he stay? Why did he stay there, still and gloomy, watching her? The truth was that it was no good Charles's going away; in the day and in the night and the next day and every day Charles was conscious of Louise and Louise was conscious of Charles.

In the evening he worked late in his office and he could hear Louise in the drawing-room above; her heels made a tattoo on the stone floor, a tattoo that filtered down through the thick ceiling so lightly that he had to listen for it. He listened for her playing too, and it was either so restless or so passionate that it was infuriating; she played too softly, beginning something, wandering off into something else, or else she filled the whole house with a torrent of sound.

"Surely Mrs. Pool plays the piano a great deal," said the resident professors in the evening. "Is Mr. Pool so fond of music?" asked another. The students laughed and said, "She gets from the piano what she can't get from Charlie." There were rude rumours current in the College because Charles had lived eight years in Amorra and kept alone.

In the evenings when he came upstairs he would not find Louise playing; she was silent, usually embroidering a small canvas on a frame. Charles hated fine useless work.

"That is bad for your eyes, and for you. It's too fine."

"I don't find it fine."

It gave her hands something to do. Charles smoked cigarettes which he disliked and poured out drinks. Each time he touched the bottles on the tray he saw her watching.

"I don't get drunk, you know," said Charles. "That wasn't one of my failings."

Louise did not answer; her needle went a little more quickly in and out.

"Don't say you have forgotten."

She lifted her head and said with the direct

intentness of a little coiled snake, "I shall never forget."

But Charles was not stung. He smiled and looked down at her easily, as if she were a small, pretty thing, harmless to him. She was very pretty; she was dressed as if it might have been a party, her wide spreading skirts were chiffon, dead-leaf brown with a tinge of squirrel colour in the folds, and the brilliant colour of her hair with its knot shadowing her neck made her skin look cream and warm, and she wore two studs of earrings, tortoise-shell, that had all the colours of her dress, her eyes, her hair. "You always did know how to dress, didn't you?" said Charles.

Her look was almost a glare and he laughed and said, "Don't be afraid. I mean nothing more than I say. I do admire — the dress."

The evenings passed in silence and constraint until one night when Charles came up in an old pair of shorts stained with oil and chemicals and a shirt frayed, with all its buttons gone, and bare legs, native sandals and an old checked coat.

Louise stared. "I'm not going to dine with you like that."

"I fail to see your objection."

"In those clothes — "

"I put them on to match you."

"What do you mean?"

"You put on your worst mind to dine with me," said Charles mildly, "so I put on my worst clothes to dine with you."

She gave in with a sudden grace, and on the rare occasions that Louise chose to do that she could be very graceful indeed; and she found, now that she had allowed herself to talk to Charles, that it was a relief, it was even a pleasure; the evenings wound away smoothly with sudden little surprises of unexpected thought, like islands in a river. Charles was unusual, Louise found herself remembering and thinking of the things he said. He had changed; he was courteous and cultured; and another question came up in her mind with the uneasiness of one of Emily's pricks — had Charles always been courteous and cultured? Could it be — Louise who had changed?

I think about him because I am homesick and lonely, she told herself. It is because he is the only person here — that makes him seem important. . . . Louise, quite naturally, did not count eleven thousand Indians. To her an Indian was not a person. She tried not to think of Charles, but she was so much alone. Everyone else in Amorra seemed to lead a teeming busy life; Charles had his work; the children had their lessons, and for the rest of the day they were curiously absent. They had always some perfect plan of their own and, even when they were with her, they talked of things she could not talk of. They were immersed in their own occupations, trust Emily for that, and Louise was left alone.

Charles had a picture in the drawing-room, a new one that she had not seen; it was Chinese, of flake-white pigeons on a green background the colour of poppy stems. Most Chinese pictures are still, but this was full of movement, full of white wings beating upon the green, beating out of the picture. . . . Does Charles know the feeling of that? asked Louise. Is that why he bought it? . . . She would look at it with her hands pressed down on the keys of the piano, staring at it while the notes, held down, vibrated on and on until the room was full of them; they would not escape until they died, and the pigeons could not escape however they beat their wings. Did Charles feel that? No, probably not.

It was probable that he had not even bought the picture, it had probably been given to him by one of his Indian friends.

("Graft," said Louise scornfully.)

("Gifts," corrected Charles.)

They quarrelled over Charles's Indian friends. Louise could not understand how an Indian could be a real friend. "Naturally," said Louise, "we must be prepared to meet them in society now, and in the cities and larger places there are cultured Westernized people, like Sir Monmatha Ghose — "

"Monmatha isn't Westernized, thank God," said Charles. "He adopts certain customs and manners that are now more universal than Western, but he keeps himself quite integrate."

Louise did not understand what he meant. She hardly saw Sir Monmatha, though she had met and dined with him often. The students who worked and played and lived next door to her were quite unnoticeable unless they made too much noise; when, if Charles were out, she would send Shah to stop them as if they were street boys. If one of them had spoken to her she would have called it impertinence and she would not leave the children alone even with the venerable Professor Dutt. She hated it that Charles refused to have an ayah for them but sent them out attended by Mahomed Shah. She had a peculiar, distorted, almost diseased idea of the Indian, of his life and his religion, particularly if he were a Hindu. Nothing Charles could say would shake her.

They quarrelled over many things. They seemed to make a point of quarrelling; in Amorra that was easy; they were like two people on a stage — as they had been from that first moment on the deck of the steamer — held there in the limelight as husband and wife, with all that the audience did not know between them; and the situation was complicated by two of the audience being there on the stage with them, Emily and Binnie. They would not keep an armistice for long. . . . We have not quarrelled for two whole days, they said. I was forgetting. I am being far too amiable. I must start a quarrel at once. . . . If it was not Louise it was Charles. If it was not Charles it was Louise.

("Why don't you ride, Louise?")

("Isn't there only one horse?")

("I can use the Bhutia more. You can have Delilah in the mornings.")

("Thank you. I prefer not to share your horse.")

She regretted that. The days were still long and empty and though they were empty they were oppressive; she felt herself crushed under them, shut away from a world that was up and vitally alive. When I go back, said Louise, I shall now be a stranger. I shall be foreign for ever and ever. I have lived out of time. . . . She could only read and listen and ponder and wonder; but the wireless news reports had the unreality that they might have had for a child, a little voice speaking out of a box, and the daily paper by the time it reached Amorra was thirty hours old; papers from Europe came far apart in a deluge of deliveries held up together, sometimes three months old; books and letters were rare and precious; and from Paris, from Bellevue, was silence. . . . I have no mother or father, said Louise, no one nearer than my old governess, though she is very dear. Grief for a people is sharp, grief for a place is sharper and has a peculiar bitterness that can never be wiped away. It is the place I mourn most — and that, at this time,

I should be shut away, a prisoner. That is what I am — a prisoner. ("Nothing of the sort," the voice answered clearly and precisely. "You chose to come — you came. What did you expect?")

Louise did not listen. She asked aloud, "But what can I do? How can I keep with them at home — what can I do?"

"What everyone else is doing," said Charles, "go on."

But Louise only felt herself crushed, a prisoner dulled and tormented by loneliness and fear. She was afraid; she was in danger of dying, of losing herself — Louise. ("And it has taken you such a long time to build yourself up, hasn't it? No wonder you can't bear to knock it all down.") And two lines of newsprint that she had seen in some paper came inexplicably into her mind: *There are some preposterous edifices,* said the paper, *that the war has brought to light. . . . At least these will be better cleared away.* Louise checked herself sharply. Where was she drifting? And she tried to break free in paroxysms of temper that were not temper, but fear.

It was worst in the evenings, after the children were in bed; Emily went to bed with Binnie. Even in her loneliness and need Louise would not allow her to stay up; Emily because of her health must be sent to bed early.

"But I'm nearly twelve," Emily protested.

"You are still only a little girl."

"Indian girls can be mothers at my age."

"You are not an Indian girl."

"I'm not a little girl either," muttered Emily rebelliously; but she was still young enough to be sent to bed and she was sent to bed! Louise was left alone.

And as she sat alone Charles was working, she could see him, imperturbable and cheerfully busy. . . . There are two worlds, said Louise. There is one — reasonable, positive; some people are lucky, they live only in that. There is another, the limitless height of the first, like a mirage, a mad distorted mirage, and sometimes it blots out the other and the sky. You don't know what it is like, Charles. You have never seen it. You think I invent it, to bend the first world to my will, but it is there — it is there. I try to be reasonable — but it is there. You think I invent it, but I don't. . . .

Charles had very little time to think, to reason or to talk; he had to act, and arrange and settle; he had to create. The lights fell till late from the office windows across the lawn below, and there was a continual coming and going on the drive; white figures disappeared into the dusk, there were continuous bright stars of light from bicycles coming, and red stars of light from bicycles going away. Did everyone in Amorra have a bicycle? Did everyone in Amorra come and see Charles on business in the evening? It looked, she had to admit from the loneliness of the drawing-room, strangely attractive — friendly — busy and important.

Once she went as far as to say, "You work from five in the morning, Charles, till nine or ten at night."

"There is all that work to do," he said defensively.

"I — I know. Would it help you — Charles — if someone took part of — the correspondence for instance — from you? There must be a great many letters to write — someone with English at least that you need not supervise . . ."

"Meaning you?" asked Charles. For a moment she thought he was pleased, eager to accept; then he said, "No, thank you. My work belongs to me. That is one thing you won't get your hands on."

Now, this morning, they were violently opposed; Louise refused to leave Don, Charles sat and watched her, miserable and angry.

Don lay on the floor and all the exhibits were there: the bed with the gnawed wooden sides, the leash bitten through; and he had had a sudden choking fit like a convulsion, and he lay panting quietly on the floor.

"You did send for the vet?"

"I told you so."

"Why doesn't he come? Oh, why doesn't he come?"

"Because he can't fly," said Charles irritably. "He has to bicycle."

The Pekingese pressed their faces against the netting that had been nailed across the door and uneasily moved their tails; their tails were their barometers, they went down as they watched Don, up as Louise spoke or stirred; they made questioning marmoset noises in their throats, while the same question was going round and round in Louise's mind. . . . What am I going to do? What else is there to be done? This is hydrophobia. Hydrophobia. The whispered word is like a spark, a tongue of fear licks up from it and runs and flames and flares into a conflagration. That is no exaggeration, Charles. . . . In her mind Louise perpetually defended herself against Charles. . . . Hydrophobia is like that; it starts, no one knows where, it spreads and spreads away from its spark — anyone can get it — you, Charles; Emily, Binnie, the Pekingese, the servants; any of them, anyone outside them. We don't know if Don has been out of the grounds, we don't know where he has been. Did he go out? Where would he be likely to go if he had? Anywhere. Nowhere. Everywhere. He has shown no sign of biting but he is affectionate — to be more than usually affectionate is a symptom — he jumps up and fawns like all spaniels, he might lick, he might scratch. Affection can become a horror — I, who worship dogs, have to steel myself not to recoil from him. The virus runs from the spark of the bite, along the nerves, to the brain — sometimes it is quick, sometimes it can smoulder and smoulder along — and it is madness that kills in agony, for which there is no cure. Madness . . .

"If it is hydrophobia — " said Charles suddenly.

"You think it is. You think so yourself."

"I think it is — but it might be hysteria."

"Hysteria! Do you think I would not recognize hysteria?"

"I don't see why you should," said Charles, and he added quietly, "I have mistaken it for truth myself."

She turned her back on him. . . . It is like a plague, her thought raced on, we don't know where it will break out next. Don has been brought up with children, he may have jumped up and licked a child's face, a hand that had a scratch on it; I can examine Emily and Binnie for scratches — I am powerless to find and save those children. . . . And at the thought of the children, a sob rose in her throat.

("Why is it worse for children to die than grown-ups, Mother?")

("They are at the very beginning of things — they are little — unprotected.")

("Yes, but it's easy to make them again. It takes ages to make a grown-up.")

Louise moved impatiently. Why must she think

of Emily's arguments now? Emily was a perpetual annoyance. They had questioned the servants that morning — "Who has been near Don in the last few days? Who has been to the house?"

"No one but the men who come to the office."

"The Babu shall warn them. Anyone else?"

"The man with the cows — "

"The peon with the letters — "

"And — " Kokil the sweeper shifted his feet — "yesterday, the monkey man was here."

"The *monkey man?* You know I have given orders never to let him in!"

The monkey man had a drum, a miniature tom-tom with weighted strings, that beat as he twirled it in a little rattling rhythm; it sounded like the chattering of a monkey. He had a large male monkey and a little female dressed in patchwork clothes, and they all sat down together in the hot shade of a tree and the monkeys did their acts and dances, which towards the end of the performance grew candidly obscene.

"Why did you let him in?"

"Emily baba said — "

"Whose orders do you take, Emily baba's or mine?"

They were silent; they took Emily baba's. It was easier. Louise cried, "You must go into the bazaar and tell everyone. Everyone! Do you understand? Charles, you must see — you must insist — "

But there was no answering certainty on Charles's face.

"You must. You must."

"I'll try."

Charles was not at all helpful. Now he said, looking down at Don, "Louise, you must wait."

"We dare not risk it. He might escape — suppose he did? We shouldn't know where he had been or what he had done. Think of the havoc he might cause."

"He couldn't cause havoc, he wouldn't have a chance."

"He might. He might easily."

"The moon might turn to cheese," said Charles rudely.

"I don't understand you. How can you hesitate? No one else would wait a minute."

"Oh, I know. There are plenty of good fellows who will let down their dogs," said Charles with venom. "Deserters. Judases."

"Charles! Don't. Please don't."

"Why worry? You'll have your bloody way," said Charles and then he said more quietly, "Louise, at least don't do it while Emily's away."

"But that's why I sent her out. What do you mean?"

"Don't do it. Wait for her. Tell her and then do it."

"But why?"

"Because I ask it. Please, Louise."

"She's only a child. Charles, how could I let her go through this?" Charles's voice was usually light and faintly mocking when he spoke to her, unless he was angry; now its earnestness intrigued her. "But why?" she asked again.

"It would be better, Louise."

"You know nothing whatever about children."

"I know about Emily," said Charles. . . . I like my daughter Emily, said Charles, but he did not say it aloud. If only Louise would not get in the way I should like her very much. Binnie reassures me too, she is the answer to a question that has troubled me for years, but I have a peculiar faith in Emily. There is something vagabond about her, especially the way she moves her elbows and her head, that shows me she is tough and gay and sufficiently hard, while her eyes and her hands and her stomach, poor brat, show that she is duly sensitive. She is capable of taking proper treatment, she deserves it; but Louise will keep a hand across her eyes, and for Emily that means a struggle and fear — a misunderstanding, needless fear. Emily would rather suffer and understand, not at the time perhaps, but afterwards. Presently she would understand; however tragic and deep the suffering, presently she would digest it; digest is the perfect word, Emily could absorb and take what she needs from it, mix it with her own philosophy and discard the rest. It could become an integral part of her. I am acquainted with death, she could say, and death is the other side of life — together they are complete, the two sides of a coin, light and darkness, good and evil, death and life. Necessarily I must know both, or I cannot know either. Emily would presently understand. I, Charles her father, am certain of that; but I am not allowed to help you, Emily. I cannot reach you while you are beyond Louise. How could I help you if I reached you? I would remind you of the little words I could not teach Louise; you know them already but I should continually remind you of them: — *I am — It is — I see — I am*. And those, said Charles, are the first and the only things you can ever learn of life — learn them in a minute — go on learning them always — That is truth. . . . He did not say any of this aloud to Louise, he stared at the bricks of the floor silently, until he said, "Let me fetch her when Das has been. Let me fetch her and you can tell her yourself what you think it best to do."

"No," said Louise.

"Very well," said Charles, standing up, and she could see that he was passionately angry and moved. "Very well. Take the power of the angels if you must but, by God, you can do it alone." He flung over the netting, scattering the Pekingese, and shouted for the groom to bring Delilah.

Louise stayed, smitten into silence with a chill of superstitious shock.

Don lay on the ground at her feet, pressed down on the bricks that were cooler than the air, pressing his throat down on them and then getting up, stretching his head out as if something were in his throat, moving his head, hanging it down so that the shadow of his ears hid his face; when he looked down his face fell into its customary soft peaceful puppy folds, but when he stretched out his neck there was a staring panic look in his eyes and his body seemed wild and strained. He stood up stretching out again, his feet slipped on the floor and he staggered and fell, and choked, his claws scrabbling wildly on the bricks, and Louise stepped quickly out of his way, waiting till he lay still again. The Pekingese stirred and whined.

She picked up the thermometer that Charles had not let her use; in the hot air the mercury had gone up. She shook it down and at once, in her hand, it ran up to 105°. . . . No wonder in this country we cannot be reasonable; even the weather is unbalanced, a parabola outside normality. The hot sun beats sense and resistance out of us, there is another virus in it that attacks us all, nothing is normal. . . . There was nothing friendly and nothing normal to her, the country was a hyperbole of heat and terror and disease, she found only per-

petual enmity, abnormality, perpetual strain. . . .
But if we have to be inoculated for this, we shall
surely have to go away — and we must. I must. I
can't bear it any longer, cried Louise. I hate it, it
hates me. It is destroying me. It hates me. . . .

The back of the stable had brick holes for venti-
lators, and a pigeon came through one and looked
at her. Its neck was a deep glistening green, its eyes
bright and gentle; it bobbed its head two or three
times in surprise to find her there and murmured
"Coo."

Louise had to laugh and immediately began to
cry.

At the sight of her tears Narayan stopped aghast.
Tears. Nothing but tears. What was the meaning
of so many tears? Anil had been in tears last night,
Narayan had left Shila weeping; now, here was
Mrs. Pool with tears running down her cheeks and
they seemed a continuation, a culmination of the
tears of Shila and Anil. He stood, not knowing
whether he had better go away or stay, and superstitions chased one another through his mind. . . .
Three times tears! Oh, what is going to happen?
. . . Tears, very very painful tears — What did
they mean? A warning? An omen? He was sure that
something had happened and from that happening
rings of other happenings would spread out and
out from it. He was ominously certain of it.

Mrs. Pool was graceful in her crying. Her face

was not reddened or made ugly by her tears, it remained pale and her hair and her skin in the shadowless light of the stable reminded him of pictures he had seen of the Mother of Christ; perhaps it was the stable that put that into his head, but he found himself thinking it was a pity she was crying over a dog, not a baby. Still she disturbed him; with her eyes drenched in tears she seemed to him too much like Shila, and Shila herself was not unlike Anil; they were each a sad echo of the other. He wished they would not cry; but for him, if not for them, there was, he began to think, good in those tears; they seemed to be washing a throng of previous conceptions, old carelessness, and impossible illusions from his mind; Anil, perhaps, could not be perfect as Narayan would have him, his bright, other, wished-for self; perhaps he was simply Anil, an exasperating, intensely human and delightful friend. And Shila? Perhaps he had never seen Shila properly, she was his wife whom presently he might discover, with all the loves and frailties of a wife. And Mrs. Pool was not a species apart from him, with an insurmountable impossible difference; she was Shila's sister crying her eyes out as Shila had cried. His life had a promise as if it would soon be washed clean, and though he was a little uneasy because he had up to then preferred it coated in mystery, he was immensely cheered.

He walked steadily up to the stable door, snapping his fingers at the Pekingese to announce his presence. The Pekingese burst into short affronted barks. "Mrs. Pool?" said Narayan above the din. He stepped over the netting and came in; he saw Don, and came at once to him and bent down. "Is this the patient?" he asked jauntily.

"Don't touch him!" cried Louise.

"But what is the matter?" said Narayan, ruffled. "Please. You must have confidence in me. I am a qualified veterinary surgeon and will not hurt your dog." His dignity was touched. Don had made no movement and he bent down again.

"I shouldn't be so hasty, Maharaj," said Kokil sarcastically over the stall front. "Don't be in such a hurry. He is mad."

"Mad!" Narayan stayed where he was for a moment, his hand out, stiff, where it had been ready to touch Don, his eyes suddenly, intensely fixed on the panting black heap below him; he could not have moved, half for pride and half for fear; the inside of his collar was suddenly wet but his mouth and his throat were horribly dry.

"You needn't be afraid." He felt scorn in Louise's voice. "I don't want you to do anything for him. I want you simply to give him an injection and put him to sleep. I will muzzle him and hold him myself. You need not touch him." She spoke as if she were not sure he understood English and the effect of that was slightly insulting, but in his new-found understanding Narayan did not take umbrage. "You have only to put him to sleep," said Louise.

"Without examination? I could not do that."

She was surprised. "I have been watching him all morning; so has my — husband. It is quite obvious what is wrong."

"All the same I prefer to make an examination. I must do so, in fact."

"I tell you it isn't necessary. There can be no doubt."

He found the courage to be obdurate, though it was hard. "Madam, you may be wrong," and he said without meaning any offence: "You are not qualified, I think, to know exactly what the matter is."

She answered curtly, "Mr. Das, if you are rude to me I shall report you to my husband."

She could. She could also give to her report any complexion she chose; he was helpless to stop her and his confidence in Charles did not go as far as thinking that Charles would believe him, Narayan, against his own wife; but still he held firm. He put his bag down on the shelf and opened it with a click. Don started up, but Narayan compelled himself to stay still though the backs of his knees were damp against his trousers and his fingers trembled. "I do not intend any rudeness," he said, "but Madam, you must kindly allow me to examine the dog."

That succeeded; she swept aside and he went up to Don, pulling on a pair of gloves. Don sprang up to bark but before a sound came he gave a silent choke; he stood on all fours but his tail and hindquarters were down, his head was strained and his eyes rolled back showing the whites. He seemed fighting to swallow something, he panted and saliva frothed on his jaw; he made a dragging movement and collapsed back on the floor. Narayan stood there looking.

"Well?" asked Louise. "Do you have to see any more?" He did not answer and she asked, "What else is that but rabies?"

"The symptoms are of rabies, but — I am not sure."

"What else could it be?"

"He should be kept a day or so for observation," said Narayan. "In these cases we can never be sure until death approaches. It may be that it is not rabies — "

"Nonsense." Don was up again staggering round. "Isn't that enough?" cried Louise. "Must you torture him any more? Damn you. Can't you be quick?"

That was as real as a shaft — it quivered through him; it hurt like fire. He turned his back and went to the table setting out his things from his bag. He could see nothing, only a confused silvered shine of instruments and the glass shine of his bottles, and his hands were shaking so that the things chinked against each other as he took them out. In his ears were other sounds, the dry rustling of the banana leaves outside the stable, the whispering rustle of the little dogs behind the netting, the sound of water dripping gently, gently into the trough; and then, across them all, the hooting of the morning mail steamer and answering it, close beside him, a pigeon, and nearer than all of these the sound of the dog panting and the low sound of sobbing. The doctor in him told him that she did not know what she had said, she was hysterical and overwrought; he should treat her firmly and resolutely, but still he smarted and stung. He had only one thought now; he longed to end it and get away . . . Anything — anything to be away. "*Damn you. Can't you be quick?*"

The words seemed to creep down through him; through his heart into his blood, into every fibre, and he gave up. He went on quietly working but the whole of him felt cursed, and Louise looked at him surprised by his sudden quietness. "Please, please — hurry," she said.

He did not answer. His hands were doing their work; here was cotton-wool, here the phials; this was the metal case of the syringe; with care his fingers opened it, unpacking it, unrolling the barrel

[137]

from its protecting gauze, fitting in the needle. Presently he turned. "Stand aside, please," he said.

"What are you going to do?"

"I have something here which is instantaneous," he said, and once he had spoken he could not stop. "It was used in the last war; it cannot last but a second, one prick and it is over. Please do not cry. It shall not be so very terrible. It is not terrible at all, it is most humane, I promise you he shall not suffer at all."

Louise only bowed her head and said, "Be quick," as if her teeth were clenched.

He was instantly silent again, running the drops off the syringe. Then he repeated curtly, "Please stand aside. I have to bandage his jaws."

"No!"

"I do not wish to risk a snap."

"You needn't. I shall hold him."

"I mean that he may snap at you even, whom he knows so well."

"I have on gloves." There was a fanatical determination in her voice.

"When he feels the needle he may reach your arm."

Louise went down on both her knees on the ground and lifted Don across her and twisted her handkerchief tightly round his muzzle. "Get on," she said. Narayan shrugged and then he knelt beside her with the syringe; he took a loose fold of

Don's loose skin and ran the needle in and pressed the plunger, a hideous long prick. Don gave a sudden surprised groan and died.

There was a moment to wait. Narayan kept his finger on the plunger looking down past the white of Louise's sleeve to the dog; it was all out of perspective and for a moment the dog looked bigger than them both, and he was seized with terror at what he had done — as if this prick were an unwarrantable presumption; the moment went on and on, blasted by his usurpation, filling him with fear. He put his fingers on Don's side and, pressing, pulled out the needle; and under his fingers he felt the heart-beats lessen — lessen. They died while his own were sounding loudly in his ears. Then the heart under his fingers was still; he had done something he had no right to do; he would have given anything to start that heart again.

He stood up with the syringe dangling in his hand. "I shall go now," he said. "I shall wait for you in the house."

When he had gone the stable was quiet. The Pekingese, who had decided there was nothing more to wait for, were tumbling on the lawn with their balls; the grass shone under the sun, the sky was perfectly serenely blue; nothing had changed or moved an iota. Nothing had changed; only Don had died. He was gone though he was here in the stable. A calm cloud, glossily white, sailed across the sky and its shadow passed over the lawn and over the Pekingese and left them in the sun again.

Don was heavy on her lap and she knelt up and lifted him onto his bed, where he lay most naturally, his legs still curled from the way she had held him in her arms, his ears fallen forward, his face in heavy sleepy lines; but his eyes were open. She sat back to look at him. He looked perfectly alive, but his eyes were more surprised than she had ever seen them. With a rise of horror she tried to close them and at last he lay peacefully, his eyes shut, laid down on his bed. She knelt beside him, absently stroking him, chiefly because she was too tired to get up and leave him. She was terribly tired, and soon, when Emily came in, there would be so much — so much to wrestle with, and fight. . . . Emily is getting too much for me. How absurd. She is only a child; but I am so tired. . . .

Kokil stole out to look at her and stole away to report; all the servants waited, not daring to interrupt, longing for Charles to come in, and order the dog to be taken away.

After a time he began to stiffen, but he still stayed remarkably warm.

* * * Narayan pedalled furiously all the way home. Dust whizzed from his wheels and hens ran shrieking to the shelter of the house steps; babies rolled over and sat up in surprise and small naked

children shouted "Wah!" and pelted him with little stones and flew away in terror. For all these signs of his power, the feeling persisted. Why? He had done nothing wrong, but he felt that he had done something unforgivable, infinitely in the wrong. The sound of Louise's crying was in his ears and as he came nearer his own house the crying seemed to be Shila's. Why must he listen to this perpetual crying? He had had it all the way there, now he must have it all the way back. Why must this feeling stab him and nag him and threaten to rise from nagging into a pain that filled his soul? He rode faster and faster as if he could outride the crying and the wrong and the pain.

When he reached home he left his bicycle by the gate and no one heard him come in. The house was empty, even the kitchen was empty; on a slab were a row of little rice-flour cakes, his favourites, pressed into shapes, a pannikin of chopped vegetables and a little curry powder ground on a stone. They were for his morning meal. He went into the study. The first thing that met his eye was the telephone, scrupulously dusted and silent on his desk; and he looked gloomily at it, for it increased his sense of wrong, and he thought suddenly and inexplicably of Anil's father.

Why should Anil's father come to his mind, of all people? He saw him as clearly as if he were in a little mirror inset into the room, quite quiet and still in the mirror, prisoned into quietness on his wooden bed on the terrace above the fields, sitting in that posture for hours, while only the light changed on the fields and the folds of his shawl lost the gleaming whiteness of midday and took the deeper colours of the sunset. On the wall of Narayan's study was a real mirror with oil flowers painted on the glass and now he saw that someone had stuck a flower that was real too in the corner of the frame; it was a small rosy spray of oleander, the kind that is deep dark rose, and looking at it a tinge of peace crept into his mind.

He had now only a soft reflection of his trouble and he was filled with tenderness for all of them: himself, Louise, Anil, and Shila. He sat down at his desk and wrote a note to Anil on the paper put clean and ready for him, with a blotter from the Asiatic Gas Company, with which he had no connection. He wrote it and finding Tarala in the kitchen told her to send it off.

"Where is your mistress?"

She pointed to the window, and he saw that Shila was in the little court outside; thinking he was away she had gone there where the sun was very hot, to dry her hair. She was sitting on a low stool, not moving, a book in her hands; but she was not reading, she was dreaming, looking at the river, her posture stupid and soft with dreams. Immediately the old irritation rose in him and he put his head out of the window and called energetically, "Shila! Shila! What are you doing?"

Her voice answered him from far away, "Nothing."

It was lazily indifferent and it felt to him almost impolite. She always sprang up at his voice and came to him, or waited, standing silently to hear what he would say; but for the first time he was near her and felt that she was not thinking of him and he was startled and a little shocked.

He immediately went out to her. The sun had baked the walls of the little court to a flaky whiteness and the house tree, a pipal, made leaf patterns on it; sharply they fell over the light muslin that Shila wore, damp and clinging, nothing else but its thinness to hide her body. Her hair lay in wet strands, so black that they had a blue polished gleam. As soon as he touched her she started and the face she turned up to him was damp too, the temples exposed from the weight of her hair dragging back; her eyes were ringed and looked up at him wide and startled, the whole of her face seemed suddenly alive, brittle with life, vulnerable.

"Shila — " he began. She gathered up her things to go.

"Wait. Don't go. Why do you run away?" She did not answer and he looked at her book. "What is it?"

"*Ramayana*." Her answer was a whisper.

"And you don't read it. You sit with it and dream."

She looked down so that he could not see her face and shook her head. He asked gently, "Do you want our son to grow up a woolly head? Couldn't you read a little every day for him?"

She looked up at him and her eyes glowed with delight.

"Did you put the flowers in the mirror?"

Her lips parted in apprehension. "I am sorry."

"Why should you be sorry? They were very nice." And the little court and the house, the field where his cow was tethered, the garden and the jetty above the water seemed to him very nice as well. He forgot the sense of wrong that had filled him; he had left it with the outside world, away from this intimate and suddenly precious one of kitchen cakes and drying blue-black hair and oleander flowers and whispered confidence. He stood there with Shila, watching the patterns of the leaf-shadows, warmed by the sun, and he was soothed by the gentleness that was the core of the house, that the running of the river seemed to tell, and wondered why he had missed feeling it before. . . . I was too busy, said Narayan. . . . How often had he himself violated it? And how often had Shila said nothing and patiently put it together again? . . . I must grow more thoughtful. . . . And he had again, more strongly, that sense of promise for himself. . . . I shall begin again and differently, said Narayan. . . . "Shila!"

He did not know he had spoken until she looked up again questioning. Now he could not remember what it was that he wanted to say. He asked, "If Anil Banerjee comes to-night, have you something good for us?"

Her eyes fell and the happiness was wiped out of her face.

* * * Anil came. The house was waiting clean and fresh for him; Tarala had swept even the paths and courtyard and, while Narayan was not looking, sprinkled them with cow-dung. About Shila was an air of implicit obedience without a tinge of welcome in it; she had cooked the dinner herself, platters of crisp, light *luchis* that were a kind of puffed biscuit used instead of bread, a lentil curry, and sweets; sugar balls and sweet dumplings and diamond-shaped cream toffee, glittering with gold and silver sugar paper; she had even cut up mutton to make a second curry when Narayan stopped her. "Don't give him flesh. He will not eat it." She looked at him, in surprise. "Yes, yes. I know. It amused me to try to make him eat it, but I don't wish to force him any more." She dressed herself, putting a fine gauze sari over a petticoat and bodice of red, edged with lace, and pinned a line of jasmine flower heads round the knot of her hair, and

went into the study to meet Anil as Narayan liked her to do, quite resolved that she would neither smile nor speak all evening.

As Anil came in she lifted her hands, pressed together palm to palm and finger-tips to finger-tips, in front of her face in salutation, bending her head without a smile but he did not notice that. He said perfunctorily, "Good evening. I hope you are well. Where is Indro?" He thought it strange of Narayan to try to make a companion of his wife — strange and rather embarrassing and, anyhow, useless; and without waiting for her answer he passed her, filling the room with his young lordliness, and called, "Indro, are you there? Or are you out?"

"I am out," called Narayan gaily. "You are at any rate early. Shila, don't you ask our friend to sit down?" But Anil waited standing, calling out remarks at his ease.

"Where have you been all day, Anil?"

"I have been fishing."

"*Fishing*? And it is three weeks only to the Examination?"

"Three weeks — three years — what does it matter?"

Anil had always seemed laconic about the Finals, but Narayan knew how he had seethed and fussed and worried with the rest of them; now in his voice there was a genuine lightness as if he truly did not care.

"What made you go fishing?"

"I don't know."

Like Binnie he had waked and thought he would go fishing, even though his tutor was coming to coach him that day. He thought he would go fishing, not for pearls but for the *rui* that breed in tanks, and taste a little of tank mud when they are caught.

He knew Professor Dutt was waiting in his room, but once he had started to fish the hours were lost to him; he had to borrow a rod and line from the headman of the village that he knew outside of Amorra. The tank was quite deserted. It was in leafy green shade, the water a sleepy sunlit green, and dragon flies hovered still in one place above it. With his rod out he sat in a dream and a king-fisher sat opposite him on a post. It had beautiful feathers, but what he liked better was its knowing head and its eye that it kept all the time on him; it had a cheeky, gypsy knowing look for all its beauty.

They spent the day together. Anil did not catch a fish but the kingfisher caught three and swallowed them immediately and whole.

Anil thought of nothing all day, but as he stood up to go he said to the kingfisher almost mechanically, "Your feathers are as bright as my dreams," and as soon as he said it, it flew away. Was that an omen? "Perhaps I shall not pass after all," he said, and he said it again now to Narayan as Narayan came out of his room.

"Perhaps you will not if you take your time off to go fishing." And Narayan put his arm across Anil's shoulders. "Seriously, you shouldn't do that now. You must not only pass. You must pass with honours."

"And why?"

"I am ambitious for you."

"Thank you. But why? Why for me?"

"You are your father's son," said Narayan. He said that but he did not mean to say it in the least.

"Indro, why do you have this notion of my father?"

Narayan did not answer at once, but the evening was flawed; into the light bantering smile on his face came a remembrance — Anil did not know what else to call it — and a look of worry, almost fear. He said suddenly, "Anil, your father would not kill — any form of life."

It was a statement, not a question. Anil was quick. "Ho! Who have you murdered now? I thought you were a veterinary, not a doctor."

Narayan did not laugh. He said again, "No. He would not take life, I think."

"You know he would not."

"But why?" cried Narayan. "Why? What is his reason? There must be a reason."

Anil did not know the reason but he answered

in the oblique way of which he was so fond, "Perhaps, because each time you kill, you kill yourself." He said it at random but it struck a look of dread in Narayan.

"Supposing — death would occur in any case."

"Then why interfere? If it is fate let it be fate. You need not upset it. You should not upset it. There is poetry in fate. I like fate very much. It is cruel but the world would not balance without it. I heartily agree with it."

"Even when — it is yourself who are caught in its workings?"

"What could I then do?" Anil barely hid a small yawn. "So very British, my dear Indro, this mania for interference." Even that did not draw Narayan, and Anil went further. "If you interfere you are a cog. Yes, a cog in a wheel. Have you been a cog, Indro? I believe you have."

"I am not a cog." Narayan's face and voice were fiercer than the words and Anil looked at him in surprise.

"You are not angry? I was only bantering."

"Formerly — " said Narayan, and his lips trembled. He broke off and then said as if he were justifying himself, "I work. I only do my work." He tried to speak more lightly. "I am — not a cog. I am like oil in the wheels. Anyone who truly works is that." He could not help a little spite in the last words.

"The oil of life?" Anil countered it.

"Are you not thinking of the salt?" But under his apparent easiness Narayan was still troubled. Later he said, "You do not strictly follow your father, Anil. Is it against your principles to kill? I myself belong to the world to-day —"

"But all the same you do not like to kill," said Anil shrewdly. "What is this, Narayan? Before you had no interest in principles."

"I had no time," said Narayan slowly. "I was not you — I had to work." And as always when he talked of the difference between them, his voice grew disagreeable. "Everything I did I had to do. There was no time for anything else. That is the difference between us. You quibble — Shall I pass my Final? Shall I not pass? — it doesn't matter to you, I dare say, but to me it was death, and it was life. There was always too much, too much to be done."

"There is always too much to be done," agreed Anil, and another yawn came up to his throat. He did not think he could talk of Narayan and his principles any more. "Always too much. That is why I am not sure that I have time to pass the Examination." To his surprise, instead of pouncing on him Narayan said slowly, "That might perhaps be so."

"You were cross at me just now for wasting time. I was benefited by that waste," said Anil, and he said prettily, "I spent the day with a kingfisher, Indro," but even this did not produce the little shock, or the smile, for which he was waiting.

Narayan only nodded. "Once — do you remember?" he said — "we went for a walk. I did not want to walk but you said it would be jolly. We went off the road down into the fields . . ." But Anil was bored. He went to the window, and now it was dark and there was the night mail steamer passing upstream, her jewel red light showing, her searchlight stretching out before her, another yellow light in her nose, and below the garden came the sound of her wash breaking in a wave along the bank. . . .

We went off the road down into the fields. . . . There had been no path; the little rutted fields were hard as clay, dried with rotting weeds, but among them were patches of mustard. They came near a village where a path of beaten mud sprang up and led through a mustard field and Narayan, walking behind Anil, picked a head of mustard. Naturally, Anil was talking and Narayan listening, and as he listened he began idly to examine the flowers he had picked. He had seen the mustard fields in flower only as a whole, deep spreading yellow, in fact he did not remember ever really looking at a flower in his life. Now he looked at the mustard flowers; they were a dozen on a spray, spread in a shape like a parachute, each flower with five flat yellow petals, and in its centre a green seeded heart; each flower was perfectly mounted on its stem and as he held it nearer his eyes, it blotted out its own whole field, in fact it blotted out the earth; behind the flowers he could see only a glimpse of sky. . . .

And I had too much to do, said Narayan, ever to look at a flower before. What a shocking thing! And I have been so busy that I have not looked at one since — unless you can count the oleander that Shila brought . . . And beginning with the oleander, his thoughts went away on a small trail of peace. He jerked himself back. "It is shocking. It is disgraceful," he said aloud.

"What is?"

"Not to have time to live."

"It's your own fault."

. . . Well, who has the wisdom to save his own soul? Hardly anyone. It is not sense. Is it sense to retire as Anil's father has done, to give up business and politics and friends and opportunity and go apart to a lonely country village? No it is not sense, but it is most divinely wise. Since there is nothing divine in me I shall do nothing of the sort. I shall get a better job, as I have said before. I shall buy myself in, and reimburse myself, I shall batten on others and they on me, I shall go on until I reach the top; and then what shall I have gained? Nothing. Nothing at all. But that will not stop me doing it. . . . And silently he cried: I do not want to be divine. I want nothing divine in me. And still in front of him came that tiresome picture of Anil's father, sitting in his shawl; and he felt suddenly and extremely tired. . . . I can't help it, said Narayan wearily, there is God in the flower, and in the folds of the shawl, and in me — in all things, animate — inanimate — whether I like it or not. I cannot help it! . . . And aloud he cried: "I shall give it all up and go away."

The steamer had passed, the waves were dying down along the bank. "What did you say?" asked Anil.

"I shall give it all up and go away." But, said a second time, it merely sounded peevish.

"Now what has upset you?" said Anil, more interested. "Are you really in trouble? What have you done?"

"Nothing."

"All this talk of life and killing — you must have done something." Shila came in carrying a tray with betel leaves she had prepared on it, and Anil spoke to her. "Indro has committed a crime and will not tell us what it is."

Narayan flamed. "Will you be quiet?" he shouted. "You are driving me mad. Leave me alone!" And he cried, "I wish never — never — to be reminded of this again." And as he said it, there was a reminder knocking in his brain. Something — something in this affair which he ought to remember — something he knew but could not think of. Impatiently he put it out of his mind.

Chapter VI

"DON! Don! Don! Don!"

Emily's voice floated in from the garden, shrill and persistent. "Don. Don. Don. Don!" And Binnie's dutifully echoed behind it, "Hullo, Don. Hullo!"

Louise went on writing, but her pen bit a little deeper on the paper than before, wavered, jerked, made a blot, and stopped; she threw it down and it rolled with a shower of blots across her letter, spoiling it. Furious, she went out on the verandah to chasten the children, but the quick words did not leave her lips; Emily was coming across the grass with Don's lead in her hand and it swung heavily, at just above the level that a small spaniel's neck might be. It danced up and down as she walked.

"Don't jump up, Don. Bad dog! Down. Down. Down!"

"Hullo! Hullo, Don."

It was silly, babyish, stupid, clumsy, but it was ghostly. Even in the bright sunlight it was macabre and a little indecent. Louise held the verandah rail and the warmth of it creeping up her arms told her that she was cold. "How *ridiculous* and absurd!" she cried indignantly. . . . But — but — Why did Emily do it? Why did she keep it up? How could she keep it up? It had been going on for three weeks now, persistently, never stopping, never resting. It was not the game or the trick that Emily was playing that upset Louise — that was merely childish, absurd; it was the way she persisted — and that was neither childish, nor absurd; it was beginning to be diabolical. . . . I mean that, cried Louise, it *is* diabolical, devilish in the way she has thought it all out. . . . It was much too pat to be accidental.

Last Sunday . . .

("Read about Noah's Ark, Mother.")

(". . . *And they went in unto Noah in the ark, two and two, of all flesh wherein is the breath of life.*")

("Charles says that is God," Emily had interrupted.)

("What is?")

("The Breath of Life.")

("I suppose it is — in a way.")

("Charles say it is. Charles says, God is in me — See?" She blew on the palm of her hand. "That's my breath of life. God is in me, in everyone. Professor Dutt says if we kill anything, we kill God. You could kill God in me and in Binnie and in you and in Delilah and — " Her eyes, unblinking, fixed themselves on Louise's face. "And — in Don.")

Unwillingly Louise had to speak of it to Charles. Charles looked at her and said, "I know nothing about children."

"Charles. Please."

"Nor do you. Nor does anyone. They are unfathomable." And he added, "If you are wise you will ignore it."

That was easy to say. It was impossible to ignore it. It was even beginning to disturb the servants. They were adopting an exceedingly respectful, propitiating way of speaking to Emily baba.

Why did she do it? Why?

Emily herself did not know. At the beginning it had been done too quickly for her to realize it, and for a day or two she had kept it up blindly, covering her hurt; then gradually, as that hurt began to be felt harder and deeper, she had grown angry; and this was not rage or temper, it was angry, adequate, revengeful reason; it was even more than that, it was an inspired campaign. Very clearly and persistently Emily seemed to know what she should do next. . . . I am not like a child now, thought Emily, I am grown up . . . And she remembered the tales she had heard of people whose hair had turned white in a night. . . . I have turned old, said Emily . . . and the drama in that helped to bolster her up; her sense of drama was completely as strong as Louise's.

I have turned old. . . . It was true, she felt infinitely removed from the Emily who had gone out to breakfast with the Nikolides. . . . Something left off being in me then. I put on my clean clothes — and she remembered them, her spotted sundress, her sun-hat and sandals — and I went out to breakfast. Mother was clever. She knew how I felt about the Nikolides, she knew I would forget everything for them. . . . And it seemed to Emily sheer treachery that Louise should have used them against her. One thing — said Emily — I shall never go blind like that again. I shall never be blind. . . . And even to so young a girl as Emily there was something pitiable in the loss of that heedlessness. Breakfast with the Nikolides was always to be the last hour of her childhood.

In the first few days, in spite of the way she clung to his name, she almost succeeded in shutting Don out of her mind. . . . I will not believe it, she said, I will not believe it. I will not have trouble here. Don shall not be dead. . . . Slowly, from that, began the second stage: If Don is dead, and — Oh! he is beginning to be dead — it is somebody's fault. I put my hand out on him in the night and he was there and he was beating, quite alive. What did they do to him? They did something. I know he did not die in this — *untruthful* way. (That is what Louise would say to me: "*Emily, why do you have to answer me in this untruthful way? You are telling me a lie.*") Now that is what I say to you, Louise. You are telling me a lie. He did not die in this untruthful way. Somebody had a hand in it, and I think it was you, Louise.

You had no right to do it!

Don is mine. Mine. Even if he is dead — if he is dead, still he is mine. You cannot take him from me like this. You do it because you think I am a child. I shall keep him alive until I choose to agree he is dead. I asked for him. I wanted him, even if he were dead, to hold in my arms, but you said he had been taken away. Where? You would not tell me. I ought to know, he is mine. He disappeared while we were out. . . . You sent me out of the way, you used the Nikolides as a — a — Emily could not think of the word, and then it came — as a *decoy*. You have spoilt them. You have changed them from a private lovely thing to a decoy, and I shall never forgive you for that; and I will not accept it that he has disappeared and I shall not let Binnie accept it either. I shall go on and on and on until I have found out the truth; I shall not give up and I shall not forget. However difficult it is I promise I shall not forget, and Binnie shall help me whether she likes it or not. She says it frightens her; let it frighten her. I shall say to myself in the day and in the night, "Pay attention, Emily," and I have taken a book to my private place in the tomato bed where I shall write everything down in truthful writing. . . .

Emily sat in the tomato bed with an exercise book and a concentrated expression on her face; this made her look very ugly, her face was quite tied into knots with thinking, her hair was stuck to her forehead, which shone sticky and white in the heat, her sun-hat was pushed back and its billiard-green lining sent a sickly reflection down to her chin. She knelt, her dress above her knees, and with one hand she wrote and with the other she picked at the earth, picking it up in lumps, crumbling it and letting it run away between her fingers. The tomato plants made a malodorous forest round and above her, with their yellow five-pointed flowers and balls of unripe fruit hanging down; the ripe ones, poppy red, shone between; some had burst and lay rotting on the ground.

Her knees hurt pressed into the lumpy earth, her back ached, but she would not move. She longed to stretch out and lie flat in the sun, making the whole of her warm. For days she had had this curious coldness all over her body, in her legs and arms, even in her breath, a cold uncertain feeling that made her partly sick and partly tired. . . . The sun makes me feel better. I feel the sun through my clothes and my bare legs and behind my eyes and after a time in the sun I cannot think of anything, I can only feel sleepy; I like the sun but I am going to stay out of it, I am going to stay here until I have written this all down in my book, in truthful writing.

The most difficult part is to pay attention; the sicker I feel the less attention I pay. Well, they always told me I was bad at paying attention, now I am tasting that for myself. The first thing I shall write in my book is: *Pay attention, Emily. Pay attention, Emily.* . . . It was difficult to write. She was feeling so sick. . . . Huh, that's nothing. Think what happened to me after the Nikolides! . . . But thinking of that she immediately threatened to be sick again.

It was better to think of things from the outside; better really not to think, but only to see, to put the pictures on one after the other, like pictures in magic lantern slides. There was a magic lantern in the College with slides of insect pests and . . . Pay attention, Emily. See, here we are coming back from the Nikolides': *Binnie and I came back from the Nikolides' — in time for lunch. It was hot.* . . . I remember I thought what a pity it was that

[161]

we had lunch at one o'clock and the Nikolides only finished breakfast at eleven. . . . That was trying a stomach more than it could bear, and a plate of soup had kept reappearing to Emily all the way home, the soup they had had instead of mulligatawny: a kind of sausage of spiced mince in a soup of dark thick gravy, with strings of macaroni, ham and onion. The feeling of it stayed in her mouth.

"You are not going to be sick, are you?" said Binnie.

Silence.

"If you are, Mother will never let us go again."

Emily did not answer. The launch went buoyantly along bouncing her gently in her chair; she had thought that delightful on the way out. The sun on the water sent blinding diamond sparks into her eyes and from the engine and the lascars' galley came whiffs of hot oil and curry smells and garlic.

"You're sure you're not going to be sick?"

"If I am I can manage."

"You had better," said Binnie. She was not really severe, but so many things had gone from their lives because of Emily, because of her bilious attacks and her head and stomach aches; as she grew older Emily had become magnificent in concealing them. "If you can only not look too yellow," sighed Binnie. "I thought you would be sick. When I saw that soup, I thought you would be."

"Don't."

"I brought one of Charles's handkerchiefs," said Binnie.

She offered it. It had holes in it, and it had been starched almost stiff, but Binnie had dosed it with Eau-de-Cologne and Emily held it to her face. Immediately a wind rose from offshore and blew coolness across her and the launch turned to the jetty so that the deck was in shade. She was better, and they were jubilant as they walked home. Inside the gate the Pekingese came tumbling and barking to meet them, and it was then — then — that . . .

The pencil stopped. Emily's thumb dug into a hard lump of earth, pounding it, breaking it, spoiling her nail; she blinked her eyes; the lids were smarting, and she had to press her lips firmly together before she could go on.

"Kokil, where is Don?"

"The Memsahib says I'm not to tell you."

The answer had been so unexpected that at first they did not take it in. Then Emily's heart and Emily's face went still, but Binnie asked gaily, "Why? What is the matter with him?" No one answered. Kokil's stillness, like Emily's, penetrated even to Binnie. "What is the matter?" she asked again, but this time it was a real question. "Is he ill? Is he hurt?" Kokil was silent, moving the dust with his toe, not looking at them, and Binnie gave a sharp anguished howl. "He's dead. Emily! Emily! He's dead!"

Kokil looked at them, quite haggard with distress. "My orders are not to tell you. I'm not to tell you, but — Don dog is dead."

"No he is not," said Emily crisply. She could not have told why she said it, but she said it clearly and loudly. "Don dog will never die," and she walked straight upstairs to Louise. Outside Louise's door she jerked Binnie to a stand.

"You always like to do what I tell you, don't you, Bin?"

"Y — es."

"You always will do what I say?"

Binnie nodded. Her eyes, wet and blue, were fixed steadily on Emily.

"Then listen," said Emily austerely. "Whatever they tell you, whatever they say, Don is not dead. He — is — not — dead."

Binnie seldom asked questions in words, but she had a singular power of making her whole body ask them for her.

" — ?" said Binnie.

"He met us just now when we came in."

" —— ?"

"He is here now and he is always with us. Don! Down, Don!" Emily brushed down her dress. "Do you see? Come out of that corner, Don. He thinks there's a rat. Come out, you naughty dog. You can't dig there. *Come out*, I say."

" ———— ?"

"He's invisible now you see," said Emily.

Light began to break on Binnie's face.

"Say, 'Hullo, Don.' "

"H — hullo."

"Louder."

"*Hullo — Don.*"

"And if you want to be any help to me," said Emily, "you will go on saying that whenever you can remember. We have to give him all the encouragement we can while he's invisible, you see."

Louise was sitting at her dressing-table, picking up the brushes and putting them down again, taking the tops of her jars and bottles off and putting them back unused. She said in her careful voice, "Is that you, children? Did you have a nice time? Emily, I hope you were careful what you ate."

There were bright patches on her cheeks and in her voice, and a dead cold weight sank in Emily. Up to that moment she had had a little hope that it was not to be true; up to that time there was even a feeling that it could not be true, there would be — must be — a miracle — It was not to be true. Now that died. It was dead as soon as she saw Louise.

"Emily, come here."

Her track across the room came to a full stop at

the back of a chair. She stood there waiting, her eyes on Louise, and she put her arms up defensively on the chair back.

"Emily — and Binnie, there is something I have to tell you. You must be brave."

They did not answer. They only stared.

"Emily — Don was killed — this morning."

"No he was not."

"We did everything we could. The vet came — but he died."

"He didn't. He met us just now as we came in."

"Emily, you have just heard me say he is dead."

"You say it, but it isn't true." She and Louise exchanged stares. "Go on," said Emily. "Tell us how he died."

"He — was very badly bitten — by another dog."

"In a fight?"

"Yes. In a fight."

"Don doesn't fight," said Emily scornfully. "He never fights, he always runs away. He's one of the greatest cowards that have ever been" — and she asked desperately: "Where is Charles?"

"He is out." And there was a hesitating, painful pause.

"Stand up and don't fidget with your mouth," said Louise sharply. "Emily — " she controlled her voice — "I tell you — Don is dead. I am very very sorry about it, more sorry than I can say, but it's no use being angry — "

"Wouldn't you be angry if someone said that about one of your dogs?" demanded Emily, and suddenly her anger choked her; but it was not only anger, it was the soup as well, come back at this most inconvenient hour.

There was no hiding that bout of sickness. She was most mortally sick; she knew that point was reached when everyone gave in to her, when Louise ceased to scold or cajole and became suspiciously reasonable.

Emily did not know then what she was saying, but they told her she had cried all the time, "I want — Don — by my bed. Tell — them — to bring his bed — and — put it — by mine."

"Very well, darling. We will. We will."

"So that — I can touch him." And, "Where is Charles? I want him — badly."

"Yes — yes. But don't talk now."

And so the day went on until the evening, dragging through the familiar misery of all such days: the bursting pain in her head and eyes, the thick yellow taste of her mouth and the burning unhealthiness of her body; even her skin hurt. There was the smell of Eau-de-Cologne, the basin beside her, the towel spread under her . . . But the misery then was not as bad as the misery now. All the time she was so sick she was numb . . . *And, wrote Emily, it was days before I could feel again and I am not sure that I can feel properly now, I still have the feeling in my head of being sick and very tired and still not feeling properly. So one day I shall feel it even worse than this, probably.*

At the beginning, in the first shock, she was laid low — and she came very near then to an armistice with Louise.

I woke from a doze . . . And there was Louise sewing by her bed, with her needle glinting in and out of a thread of light that came from a chink in the shutters; Louise looked up and caught her eyes; Louise was pale, hollowed with pity, and her eyes as they met Emily's were anxious, almost timid.

"If you sew in that light," croaked Emily, "you will hurt your eyes."

It was a terrible effort to say that and it was not wise; at once she began miserably to retch again. Louise held her head as she leant over the side of the bed, and Louise's hands were cool and slim and their skin was faintly scented. Luxuriously Emily let them put her back on the pillow and smooth her hair and stroke her forehead. "Poor — little girl," said Louise. "Poor little girl."

Emily gave a small fluttering sigh and pressed Louise's fingers under her own. ("Why can't you always be like this?" asked Louise's fingers as clearly as if they had spoken. "Why can't you?" And

Emily's answered, "I can. I can.") And immediately and clearly she said aloud, "Mother, if you put your hands round Don's chest from behind you can feel his heart beating. It's like a little engine."

After that she lay alone.

She closed her eyes and presently she was sick again, but this time she had to manage by herself.

While she was reaching over the side of the bed, Charles came in and stood there looking at her. . . .

Charles came in and looked at me . . .

Again Emily dug and twisted her thumb in the earth. What had she expected of Charles? She did not quite know, but she had waited all day for him to come in, reaching out for that moment, certain of relief, and then . . . The tomatoes were hanging absolutely still but they seemed to be swaying and shimmering dangerously.

Charles came in to see her after he had changed, not straight up; she heard him ride in and waited for the curtain to lift and for him to appear, but she went on waiting. He came upstairs, she heard his voice, he was talking to Louise and then he went downstairs again. When at last he did come to her he walked up to her bed, and did not speak. He looked ashamed. Emily lay there dumbly, looking at him, and he still looked ashamed, and she, at once, became embarrassed, almost prim. It was a pity — after all that waiting there did not seem anything to say. Why did he look ashamed?

She made an effort. "Charles — " but she could not go on. Tears of weakness filled her eyes; she closed them trying to prevent the tears escaping under her lids; she succeeded and presently she asked the question she wanted to ask. "How do — you — say Don died?"

He did not answer at once but she felt him change and he said, as if he were angry, "Your mother has told you — he was killed in a fight." Emily knew he was not angry with her.

Charles did not lie — if you asked him a question he answered it; he did not lie. Charles said, "Your mother has told you — he was killed in a fight." Charles did not say, "He was killed in a fight."

She looked at him. "Don didn't fight. He ran away."

Charles did not answer.

"Don isn't dead," she said.

"Yes he is," answered Charles promptly, and suddenly he added, "Emily, if I were you, I should be quiet over this. Don't worry Louise."

Emily turned over and lay with her back to him. He knew it was a lie? . . . Charles does not tell lies, but he is going to be with Louise against me, in this. Why? I don't know. . . . What mysterious power had Louise over Charles to make him join in a lie with her like this — to make him uphold her? . . .

I don't care. I don't care, — wrote Emily, proudly, though her lids were smarting, — *I will be by myself.*

She knew now that was going to be true for her. She was to be alone — not even with Binnie. Binnie and Emily were sisters, children of Charles and Louise, but there was something in Binnie that made her especial to them, something that left Emily out.

Binnie was loyal, but Binnie was no one's ally. Binnie was like a sea-anemone, she took in as much as she could digest and spat out the rest into life; she made no attempt to retain anything more than she comfortably could. *She will help me just as far as she can, and then leave off helping; but she is a help. I met her on the stairs just now with Louise. "Hullo Don, Don," said Binnie as I passed and I saw Louise set her lips.* Binnie was useful as a machine gun, she sent in a stream of identical little bullets all on the same spot.

And mark you, Louise, wrote Emily and liked it, *mark you, I shall get what I want in the end. . . .* There is no escape for you. This time I shall win. I am learning to pay attention. I am thinking of this even in my sleep. You think I shall forget, but I shall not forget and I shall not give up even if I am alone. . . . And she thought of the Jerusalem song that Charles sang on the steps in the morning. *I have no bows and arrows, I have no sword or a spear, but I shall not cease from mental fight till I have found out everything, Louise.*

The next page was headed: *Inoculations!*

Now this was a very curious part of the affair, and that it was a part of the affair Emily was convinced. The children had been inoculated before, on board ship for typhoid fever; they had been vaccinated; now it seemed that there was a new disease and they were to be inoculated for that.

"What is it?"

"You would not understand."

They would not understand but they were to have seven ghastly inoculations that were done in the side of the stomach.

Even Charles protested. "But are they necessary, Louise?"

"Dare *you* take the risk?"

"If we examine them carefully for bites and scratches . . ." What could bites and scratches have to do with a disease?

"It doesn't harm you if they are done. Especially," she said with an edge of resentment in her voice, "as they can be done here. It isn't worth the risk, just for a few little pricks."

Little pricks. As Emily thought of them the whole of her seemed to recede leaving only her stomach, and her stomach seemed round and flat like the side of a tambourine with a brittle stretched thin skin across it. The Doctor Babu was frightened of the needle himself, he approached it towards them with his hand trembling and once he missed and had to start again; and then there was the long moment to stand with the needle quivering in and the plunger going down before he started all over again on the other side.

"O Mother, let me take the risk," begged Emily.

"Emily, how can you be such a coward? Think of Binnie. It isn't as terrible as all that."

"It is. It's simply dreadful," cried Emily, "and it isn't necessary, either."

"Would I ask you to have it done if it were not necessary?"

"Yes, you would. Don't you believe anything she says, Binnie!" shouted Emily, and from an overheard tag she cried: "It's just a form of propaganda."

Charles walked hastily away. If the disease were so bad, why was Charles not done? Emily counted up the people. Louise, she herself, Binnie, Kokil the sweeper, and the Pekingese. Such a curious and peculiar choice.

"Shah, will you be done?"

"Not I!" said Shah, and laughed.

"Why not?"

Shah was evasive. He shrugged.

"Have you ever been inoculated?"

"Inoculated? Wah! When I was a soldier — for plague, for typhoid — and *langwana* — vaccination."

"But dogs can't get any of those diseases, can they, Shah?"

That was the most mysterious of all. Why were the Pekingese inoculated? She had discovered that they were done — only by accident. Every morning, very early, they left with Kokil in the car. Where to go? To Dr. Das's house and Dr. Das was the vet. He was in the telephone book, the only Dr. Das. Dr. N. C. Das, Vet. Surgeon.

"Charles, why do Picotee and Sun go to the vet?"

"To be inoculated," said Charles incautiously.

"Like us?" pounced Emily.

"Yes." And then he added sharply, "What did you say? Well, yes, as a matter of fact, like you."

"For the same thing?"

Charles stared at her, but under his scrutiny she kept a bland, inquiring face.

"Yes, for the same thing," said Charles. "And I'm too busy to answer any more questions."

What diseases do people and dogs get? . . . i have to find out that.

Can people get distemper? Can dogs get malaria? What disease do dogs and people get? . . .

All these things Emily wrote down and conned over in the tomato bed, and every day she held a session there and every day she had garnered a

little and achieved a little more; the sessions grew
longer and longer.

"Emily, what have you been doing to your
knees?"

"Kneeling on them."

"Kneeling on them? They are filthy and stained
with something green. Kneeling? Why?"

"To pray," said Emily pertly.

"For whom?"

"Not for *whom?* — for *what?*" said Emily, and
she fixed her eyes on Louise. Their ordinary hazel
glowed with a yellow-green light and she looked
like a young tiger cat. "I'm praying for something
I mean to have, and I shall get it. I shall get it soon,"
said Emily.

War had opened between Emily and Louise.

"Kokil," said Emily in the evening, "why haven't
you brought Don's food?"

"*Don's food?*"

"Yes. Don's food. He's hungry. Go and get it at
once. Bring it."

Kokil hesitated, looking at her. "Emily baba, the
Memsahib told you. Don dog is dead."

"She says he is dead but he is not."

"With my own eyes I saw him dead, Emily baba."

"With my own eyes I see him alive. Don't talk
to me. Go and fetch his food."

He did not know whether to go or to stay. Emily's

nerve broke and she screamed, "Fetch it! Fetch it at once!"

To placate her he brought it, and Louise, coming down the stairs, saw three empty bowls where only the two Pekingese had fed.

"Why three?"

She could not understand his answer. "Why three?" she asked again.

"Don dog," said Kokil simply.

"Don't be so stupid!" cried Louise angrily, but next day they were there again.

("Mother, don't you think Don's *sweet?* Do you know what he did . . .")

("Hullo, Don. Hullo, Don. Hullo, Don.")

("Good night, Mother. Good night, Binnie. Good night, Don.")

"Emily. Stop it!"

"Stop what?"

"You know very well."

"I don't. What do you mean?"

"Emily, once and for all, will you stop this clowning?"

"I don't know what you mean."

"I forbid you — either of you — to mention Don's name again."

Silence. They were lying on their backs looking at her.

"Why?" said Emily.

"Don is dead, Emily. This — this — playacting is senseless and — horrid."

"Not as horrid as being dead," said Emily.

Louise caught her breath. She was standing between them and in front of her was Don's small empty *charpoy,* its rug folded, a bowl of drinking water beside it, and his lead coiled on the bed.

"You are not to say it. Not to. Understand! You are not to say his name again."

"We shall have to learn to whistle then," said Emily.

After Louise had gone and Binnie was asleep she had another fit of crying; as she lay exhausted after it she looked up at the sky through her net and wondered for the first time where Don had really gone. . . . Where did he go? I know they put him away somewhere; buried him; but where is he, the breathing part of him? That made a gap of terror in her, and she hastily put a thought over it, an anodyne. "There has been so much dying lately," she said, "that anyhow he won't be lonely." But the stars all slid together in the blur of tears.

Chapter VII

CHARLES, I must speak to you."

Louise was standing by the piano looking out of the window as he came in. He thought she must have been standing there for a long time, she looked so strained and white and her handkerchief was twisted into a string in her hand. There was only one lamp lit in the room, a lamp with a deep shade that made a circle of light on the floor round it and left the rest of the room in dusk; only the flaky shapes of the pigeons in Charles's picture shone on a background that had sunk away into the wall. The sky outside the windows in relief was a clear deep blue, the blue of blue flowers; the stars were still small and fresh in the sky, and the tops of palms showed indistinct and feathery in their blackness. A chatter of sounds came from the bazaar, not loud but shrill and never ceasing, and with it nearer, in the garden, were a dozen indescribable sounds of an Indian night: lizards, crickets and an owl, a flute from the servants' houses, but more than anything else Louise listened to the tom-toms and the cymbals from the temple in the bazaar and beyond them — somewhere, the sharp yapping of a dog.

"Noise. Always, always noise. Never for one moment is it quiet." The handkerchief twisted and jerked. "It never stops. It goes on all day; it is worse at night. It's driving me mad. I have nothing to do but listen to the noise."

"It isn't a bad one to be listening to as noises go just now," said Charles quietly. "Don't forget that, Louise." But Charles knew himself how the noise came into every corner of the house. He knew how the high vaults of the ceilings gave back every drum-beat as they gave back the piano notes, with an empty mocking echo. Every room had its grey lizard with an incessant *tck tck* in its throat, and just outside the window on the cork tree woodpeckers and cockatoos hammered and squawked all day and at night a cricket scraped in a Chinese whisper. "That cricket has sent me nearly mad quite often," said Charles gently. "Come and sit down and I will get you a drink."

"That's your cure for everything, not mine," Louise lashed suddenly at him. "You know it isn't only the noise . . . Charles, let me go away. It isn't any use my staying. I hate it, I loathe it. I can't bear it any longer. You don't know what it is doing

[179]

to me, I don't know what is happening to me, and I'm afraid. Sometimes I think it is I who am going mad. I'm always alone — always. You don't know . . ."

"Why shouldn't I know?" asked Charles. "I was alone for eight years. Quite alone." He did not sound in the least sorry or bitter about it. "There is one thing I can promise, to comfort you: it gets better after about three years. The longer you stay, the better it gets. In the end you may decide to stay for ever."

"I would die first."

"You would have to," said Charles pleasantly. "It happens quite naturally. When you are alone, you grow — you alter completely. You are changing, Louise."

That was true. Something of Louise was struggling to live but giving itself up slowly to die. She was angry. She was being killed by them all, by Charles and Emily and the remembrance of Don, by the silence and the noise of the place, by the heaviness of the sky and the stretch of water and the empty dusty plain, by the nearness and the cruelty and noise and stench of the bazaar. . . . Who would not die? cried Louise. No one could be herself here. No one could exist here and remain herself. I am dying, dying, dying, cried Louise, and I do not want to die.

Charles watched the struggle in her face, the

tense nervousness of the way she stood, with set shoulders and quick fingers, plucking at her handkerchief; and he said, "Why don't you give in, Louise?"

"To Emily?"

"I was not talking of Emily."

She turned, suddenly and dramatically appealing, her eyes dark with tears. "Let me go away, Charles —"

Charles waited a moment before he answered, watching her, "You can go, but — I shall keep the children."

"Keep the children!" That had not for one moment occurred to her. "*But you can't*. They can't stay here with you."

"Why not? All these years I have worked honestly for them, faithful to them — and to you; and I think that is more than you can say — isn't it, Louise?"

"I — It doesn't matter to you what I do. That is nothing to do with it."

"Isn't it? It most certainly is. I am very particular and fastidious about my children and — Emily is getting older."

Slowly Louise's face was stained with a sudden deep painful red.

"That matters, doesn't it?" said Charles.

He wondered why she always wore these soft falling-away colours that he hardly noticed at the time and could not forget afterwards. He wondered why her hair shone so deeply in the light that it had all the shades of gold in it, ending with the brilliance of dark wallflower gold in its knot. He wondered why he still could not keep himself from the thought of touching her hair — and her skin; he could not forget the touch of her skin, he could not be satisfied until he touched it again. But she was talking of Emily.

"Emily!" she cried. "You are obsessed with Emily."

"I would be if I had any sense," said Charles.

"Why are you helping Emily against me?"

"I'm not," said Charles. "She doesn't need me. She doesn't need help. She is fighting a large-sized battle, not only against you — and I should like to see her win. I hope she doesn't hurt herself too badly in the course of it, but I can't help her. I think she will win," said Charles; "she is remarkably full of power, poor brat."

"Nonsense."

"She is a very tenacious person," he said. His lips twitched; he was thinking of Emily's attack that morning. . . .

("Charles, what diseases do people get besides whooping cough and measles, mumps, scarlet fever, dysentery, malaria, and chicken pox and smallpox and plague?")

("Quite a lot more," said Charles.)

("Tell me some.")

("Here in India — tuberculosis.")

("Do dogs get tuberculosis?")

("I believe they can, but it's not common.")

("Is it terribly dangerous and catching?")

("It can be dangerous and it can be caught, but not all in a minute like that.")

("Oh! Have you ever heard of people getting distemper? Or worms? They don't get tick-fever, do they?")

(Emily!)

"She is only a child," said Louise.

"That is no reason why her powers of tenacity should be smaller than mine — or even yours. She is fighting you, Louise — "

"I know. That is what I can't understand. How can she keep this up — for so long against me — as if she hated me?"

"Perhaps she does," said Charles.

"She couldn't, Charles."

"It's against all tradition, isn't it?" And he asked, "What are you going to do about it?"

"What can I do? What can I do? I try to ignore it, but after a time — it's ridiculous to say it — but it's becoming — eerie."

Charles said nothing and in the pause the cricket's scrape seemed to rise a notch higher. Above the drums the dog still yapped.

"Charles — the servants don't like it."

"No, they don't."

"Things are happening. That is the odd part. Things that Emily could not possibly have thought of. Have you heard — about the footmarks at the washing *ghat*, for instance?"

At the northern end of the College tank, the washerman had his *ghat*. The College was walled on all sides, its gates kept shut, but the washerman told this story, and it spread quickly through the College servants to the bazaar: —

"The only dogs in the place are the small cat-dogs of Pool Memsahib and cat-dogs have paws with little pads that print small shapes when they run. It was not the cat-dogs. Well, we carry the clothes from the boiling and they are dipped and beaten and then spread on the grass for bleaching, but now — if we leave them to turn our heads or go inside — all over them are lines of footprints, a dog's footprints — too small to be confused with anything else, a leopard or a cow — too large to be the cat-dogs' — footprints the exact size of the black dog that used to run on them before, the black dog who is dead, the black dog that the Missy Sahib says is still alive.

"It could not be the black dog. The black dog is dead. Well, who has seen another dog? What other dog is there? How could a dog come into the

[184]

College grounds? No one has seen it, no one has heard it, but the prints are there."

Only the washerman's wife, sitting by the clothes at the verge of the tank and eating what her husband left for her in the pot, had heard the English children calling and whispering in the garden next door and felt something go by her like a clap of wind that sent coldness into her stomach so that she retched and the food fell out of her mouth.

After this it was alleged that Kokil had caused the body to be tied to a brick and thrown into the tank and that anyone who chose to come there at night would see the *bhût,* the ghost, rise from the water and drag the brick across to a certain tree. Now nobody swept leaves up under that tree and a little lime was put on the trunk and a few rags tied along the branches; and everyone was very careful not to look at Emily, the familiar of the ghost, if they should chance to meet her.

She noticed a curious falling away from her wherever she went. "They don't seem to like me any more," said Emily; "but you don't mind me, do you Shah?"

"I don't mind," said Shah amiably. "I had an uncle possessed of a devil myself."

That shook Emily. It was flattering but it was frightening. Frightening . . . When she saw the paw marks on the sheets, her eyes went bright with fear.

"Do you know anything about this?" Louise was peremptory.

Silence.

"Answer my question."

At that moment Emily could not answer the question, her throat and her tongue were dry.

"Emily. Answer me."

She licked her lips. "It's Don."

"Don't be absurd."

"It's just like Don," she argued. "He was always doing it."

"You did this yourself."

"*I?* How could I?"

"That is what I want to know."

"I couldn't do that. Could I? Could I?" Even Louise caught the appeal, and the perplexity and doubt in her voice.

"She has started something that she can't stop," said Louise, and suddenly she cried, "Why doesn't that dog stop its yapping?"

"Now you are being ridiculous."

"I know I am. Do you think I don't know that? I know I am — and I can't stop it! I can't help it. It's this house and this place — and all of you. All of you!"

"That is a *pai*-dog tied up on the other side of

the bazaar," said Charles; "and a *pai* must get in and run over the washing too. You know that, Louise."

She answered slowly, "I think — I'm beginning to be haunted. Everything is worse since this started. Something dreadful is going to come from it; it will fall on someone, somewhere. I know it will. I'm haunted by it. Why? I *think,* I truly think that Don was mad."

"And you wanted to get away, didn't you?" said Charles.

"You mean I used Don — "

"I mean Don was convenient."

"That is an abominable thing to say." Charles shrugged. "You will see," she cried, "you will see. I shall prove to be right in the end."

"I expect you will," said Charles wearily. "It doesn't matter much. In the end there must be such a small difference between being right and being wrong — "

"And what of the risks?" asked Louise.

"I am not denying the risks."

"What would you have done then?"

"I should have recognized the risks," said Charles slowly. "I should have pointed them out, particularly to Emily. We should have treated them with the dignity they deserved, because they are grave risks. We should have given Don every possible chance; and then we should have carried him to his appointed end. It would have been appointed then, you know," said Charles.

"You are even beginning to think like an Indian."

"That is no bad thing in a way," said Charles, and he asked, "Why don't you give in? Tell Emily, Louise."

"That is what she wants me to do. What she is trying to make me say."

"Well, why not? It is true."

"No. You must speak to her," said Louise. "I shall not give in to her. She must learn she is not her own master. She would listen to you." She tried to speak lightly but there was anger in her voice. "She has always been fickle, perhaps because her feelings are not very deep, and she forms these — these attachments for people — the Nikolides for instance; I remember at Bellevue she was ridiculously fond of Félix, the cook, for a little while."

"And now she has a ridiculous attachment for me," said Charles drily. "Well, as it happens, I rather value that and I won't do anything to harm it. You can speak to her yourself."

"I can't — " and she cried, "I seem to have lost her since I came here."

"What makes you think you ever had her?" asked Charles.

Louise was stung. "If you had seen her in Paris — "

"I did not see her in Paris. Nor did you," said Charles. "You have never seen Emily in your life, not Emily as she is. Come to that, you have never seen anything as it is in your life. I am warning you, Louise. You are doing something unforgivable. One day you will do more than you mean — some serious damage. If you don't take care. If you don't take care, Louise . . ."

Chapter VIII

IT WAS easier for Narayan to wish to forget than to forget. To begin with, every morning the Pool car drew up at the gate and Kokil came in with the Pekingese. They delighted and interested Shila very much.

"What kind of dogs are those?" she asked, "or are they cats?"

"Of course they are not cats. They are poodles," said Narayan. "Moreover, they are very valuable."

Shila knew that already. They were sent in a car, Tarala for instance had never been in a car; they were having injections, costly ones from Calcutta as if they were humans; Tarala had asked Kokil how they were fed — they were fed on mutton and chicken and fish; and they had come in a steamer from England.

"And meanwhile there is starvation and famine and war on every side," said Narayan.

The injections given these rare and valuable dogs that had never been heard of in Amorra gave him a certain prestige, but at the same time it offended him. Again he felt as if he were interfering. . . . But if I go on like this, I shall have to give up practice, he said. If I am interfering with fate by giving an anti-rabic injection, I interfere by giving a drench to a horse or a cow. Pool is interfering with fate by teaching the people to fertilize their lands. That is not sense . . . And it seemed to him in that depressed moment that it was unspiritual to have any sense at all. He said this aloud to Shila simply because he had to say it aloud.

She offered timidly, "Perhaps you are fate, you and Mr. Pool."

That salved him for a moment but his conscience was so tender that anything that reminded him of the morning at the Pools' made him wince. Yet all the time he was trying to remember . . . what? Why should he need to remember when he wished, so much, to forget? What could have happened in this affair that he ought to remember? He could not think of it. He gave the Pekingese injections each morning as soon as the serum arrived from the Pasteur Institute. With it came a yellow paper that he had seen before.

Under no circumstances, said the paper, *should the dog be destroyed — for by doing so one of the most important signs of rabies, viz. the short duration of life, is lost and proof cannot be obtained.* . . . You see, you see, the thought that was haunting him burst out, there is no proof. I am sure, now I am sure, he was not mad. . . . And he longed, would have given anything, for a proof — a proof. If one of the Pekingese died of hydrophobia, that would be tantamount to proof, but as he looked at them — even for that relief — he could not wish death on them. So he continued gloomily to give them injections.

"I don't know if it is necessary," said Charles, "I don't suppose it is, but my wife wants them to be done."

"I see."

"You have no objection to doing them?"

"No, no. I shall be glad." He did not sound at all glad.

Charles looked at him and paused. "Das — I know my wife is — nervous. You had no doubt, had you — in your own mind — that the dog was mad?"

That was the question Narayan had been dreading, but while he was still wincing he answered, "None whatever."

No bites or scratches were found on Sun and Picotee. He gave them seven injections each.

Sun stood without a sound, his forelegs braced, his head turned thrown back and his face drawn into lines of acute silent suffering, every hair stiff; Picotee's tail dropped between her legs in a hopeless trailing, and she would not stand up. She lay limp and abandoned to her fate on the table and every morning she gave a piercing cry as the needle went in. All the same Narayan would rather have injected her than Sun. Sun's silence was unnerving, but after it was over every day they both went into rhapsodies of relief and joy, leaping and dancing and barking.

"They are nearly human," cried Shila in delight, but Narayan found this study in character disturbing; character in a Pekingese, character worth respecting, like Sun's? He was glad when the injections came to an end and they need come no more.

"Send me the bill," said Charles. Narayan did not want to send it, but Charles insisted.

"But — what shall I charge you?"

"I don't know. Charge by the visit."

He wrote out the bill: —

> *To seven visits from Mrs. Pool's*
> *poodle dog* . . . . *Rs 7.*
> *To seven visits from Mrs. Pool's*
> *poodle slut* . . . . *Rs 7.*

He did not charge for Don.

The money came by return and with it, **in**

Charles's writing, a postscript *Attending a dog at my house, Rs 4*. It lay on the desk untouched. Narayan kept looking at it all day.

He would have liked to confide in Anil. No, he could not possibly have confided in Anil, and anyway Anil was curiously elusive at the moment. . . . I have not seen him for days. He does not come near me, grumbled Narayan. Soon it will be the end of term. . . . He recalled himself sharply, he had forgotten the Examination. . . . Of course I have not seen Anil. How could I? He is working every moment . . . but his vision of the end of term refused to be of Anil sitting in the Examination Hall, pinned to his papers; it was of Anil going home for the Durga *puja* holidays, where all the ritual of the *puja* fortnight would be prepared.

They will have Durga *puja* in their own house, said Narayan. They will have ornaments for the Goddess, of real gold — all the rapacious and idle and greedy will gather there to be fed. Money will be poured out on a ceremony that has no reality at all. Ceremony is the curse of this land. . . . But in spite of his scornful and sensible words his mind was already following the story of the *puja* and it seemed to him simple and beautiful. Nearly all the Hindu festivals have a quality of naïveté, and it is this that keeps them fresh; they come with a piquant shock of promise and surprise each year. It does not matter how many Durga and Lakshmi *pujas* are lived through, the *puja* is perpetually new.

The Goddess Durga is the consort of Siva; she keeps house for him, but once a year she too goes back to her father's house; the festival celebrates her visit and in her wake all the sons and daughters of Hindu Bengal go back to their homes. Durga ends her holiday on the fourth day and her spirit is returned to her husband by the immersion of her image in the river; but the sadness of her leaving is healed in the worship of her daughter Lakshmi, the Goddess of Good Fortune, on the day and night of the full moon. . . . Childish nonsense! cried Narayan, but suddenly he called Shila.

"It is getting near the holidays," he said. She did not answer but he knew by the sudden constraint on her face, the trembling of the edges of her lips and nostrils, what she was waiting for. The festivals start with the autumn new moon, and last, with a short break, through the nights when the moon grows, until the full moon. Last year Narayan had forbidden Shila to keep the sacred days; nothing was allowed into the house, not a gift or an extra cake, or the smallest image. "It is silly superstition," said Narayan.

Shila's heart had been hot with shame; in every Hindu house the festival had the significance of Christmas; the chief and most joyful days of the year; the Government observed it, offices were shut, universities and schools closed, everyone went home on holiday, everyone joined in worship — except Narayan; and Shila's shame was sharpened by fear for him; goddesses were easily offended. If arrows of fire, shot from an invisible bow, had pierced him now as he sat at his desk, she would not have been surprised.

But instead, Narayan was handing her a small pile of notes. "Take this money," he said, "and buy whatever is necessary. You can use it and more. Make a list of the presents we should give, for Tarala and whomever it is suitable."

She did not move. He had to open her hand and put the money into it.

"But last year . . ." She was mystified, trying to find out from his face why he had changed. "Last year, we did not have — anything. . . ."

"Is that any reason why this year we should not?"

He saw himself beneficent, a patriarch, as if his family were twenty and not two. Then he was aware that a delicate struggle was filling Shila.

"What is it?" he said. "What is it you want to ask me?" and with a return of his old irritation he cried, "Well, ask. Ask. Ask."

"Indro . . ." she asked. "Shall you . . . go to the temple?"

He hesitated. "I may go to take you" — and he said magnificently: "It is necessary that I should inform myself of these things from time to time."

He stood up and went to the doorway, where the steps led to the verandah, and he looked down past them to the river and the bank stretching out of sight. Everything he could see was either green or blue or white; the flat blue-white of the water, repeating the sky, the green of the bank and the foliage in his garden and the floating water weeds, and sharp touches of white, the clouds, a water-lily that had opened under the jetty, and along the banks, the tossing white heads of the pampas bushes.

"Wherever I see pampas I know it is autumn," said Narayan.

"And when it is autumn the festival time is here," whispered Shila. "We shall keep it in our house. We shall make Durga *puja* at the temple — we shall have our tiny *Sree* — we shall have gifts . . ." and she began to plan them.

"Tarala shall have new clothes — I shall make cakes for the children. Indro — you need new shoes, and new shirts."

"Not from that money," cried Narayan; "that is the condition. All, all of it is to be spent on festival only. It is not for gifts. Spend it for worship. Give it for the feeding of the beggars. Take it and make it good. Give nothing of it to me." And he said, as he had said before, "Do not remind me of it ever again."

Chapter IX

THERE was nothing of autumn in the night. It was hot with the heat of September that is deadly and stifling, as if all the months of stifling nights and days had culminated for the end of summer. The moon was old, nearly gone, the stars seemed to shine for themselves without shedding their light, there were clouds, and the heat was manifested in the blackness, that was still and black and hot, pressing down upon the town and on the houses; pressing round the beds where some people lay in an exhausted slumber, where some people could not sleep.

The College was silent, without a light; it was possible only to make out the darker buildings against the dark sky; on the tree that wept into the tank, the flowers were dying with a sick heavy smell. The watchman's lantern was on the drive but the watchman had disappeared, he had gone into the shadows and lain down to sleep, with his stomach pressed into the cool verandah stones. Shah had sensibly gone to bed in nothing but a loincloth, and his stiff-cut starched and polished uniform was left by itself in his house, where it could be seen by the light of his oil lamp, looking strangely more like Shah himself than the thin dark sleeper on the bed.

In the bazaar the unknown dog was still yapping, and Louise was awake in her room. It seemed to her now that she had not slept through a night since she came; and the endless void of dark wakeful hours culminated, like the heat, in these tonight. She heard Charles downstairs, she heard him get up and go into the garden; once she thought he came upstairs and she lay, tense, waiting, and held her face down into her pillow so that she would not call out to him in her loneliness: "I am awake — and bitterly lonely — lonely. Lonely — " But the pillow muffled the words.

Once she heard Emily turn, and move her bed. What did she want? Louise was not alone in the night; Emily was awake too; but Louise shrank from speaking to her; Emily still had Don's bed beside her.

It was dark; she longed for a light but lay perversely in the dark. There was a sound on the stairs that might have been a rat. A lizard slid down the wall near her bed with a *tck* that sounded loudly in her ear, and outside with the babel of night sounds, jackals began to howl; they howled like all the lost souls and banshees and ghosts in the world wailing together. The wind stirred in the sides of her mosquito-net and the blown-in sides touched her bed with a slurring animal sound that made her catch her breath, and she screamed for Charles.

She held her hand across her mouth struggling to hold that scream. She wanted Charles. She wanted his actual physical presence here beside her, she wanted to feel him and to touch him. . . . How can I? she cried. She must be shocked at herself; she tingled. What are you thinking of, Louise!

It is only the night, she reasoned; it was the night and the heat and her sleeplessness and the worry over Emily. It was only Emily that made her think of Charles. . . . Emily, I blame you for everything that has happened . . . I see you, Emily . . . And exasperation swept up in a storm at the way she had to see Emily now. For days Emily had worn a blind and wooden face, blind with obstinacy, wooden with determination, chalk-white; even her hair had a toneless look. Emily was so plain these days that the sight of her gave a pull to Louise's heart; and she was taller, grown long in the legs, even her hair had outgrown its little-girl length; she had begun to look adolescent. . . . Nonsense, she is only a child, said Louise; but Emily was exhibiting every sign of developing into a girl, with new glimpses of grace under her gawkiness, and soft swellings round her nipples of which she was secretly conscious and ashamed. . . .

It's the country, cried Louise; I hate it. Look what it has done to Emily. I don't want her to grow up. She is still a child. She shall be a child . . . And she had a vision of Emily as she had been when she was a baby, between her and Charles, a baby girl, precious as a nest, bright as a star, with yellow silky fluff standing out from her head, in that sentimental glance, like a Holy Child's halo. . . . What has happened to her since? asked Louise. What has happened in between? I don't know. What have we been doing? . . . And the answer came back to her: *What have you been doing?* That question seemed to be asked her again, with a deafening loudness: *What have you been doing?*

It sounded through Louise, loudly, accusingly, and she sat up in bed, shaking, pushing off the darkness. The whole of her body was wet, and she felt as if she were suffocating with blackness and heat and remorse and fear. . . .

Emily, stop. Please, please stop it, Emily. I am coming to tell you: This cannot go on any longer. It must be stopped. I will give in to you for ever if only you will stop it; if only you will take that look off your face, try and be more natural and more childish, grow more flesh on your bones, show life in your hair. I did kill Don. You guessed it and you were right. I did lie to you. Yes, I did. I did. I did. I did it all so swiftly that it happened in one impulse. I was caught in it even before it was done and that is why I did it; under the laudable, plausible motives, that is why I did it. Panic comes like blood to my brain — you cannot understand that. Of course not, you are too young. . . . Charles was the only one who did understand! Charles! Only Charles — and at the thought of him she began to cry.

She swung her feet down off the bed to the floor, the solid stone floor checked her crying and she groped in the darkness for the switch of the light. The light hurt her eyes, smarting with tiredness and tears, and she sobbed again, calling Emily and Charles confusedly — "Charles — but I must talk to Emily. I have to tell her what I did to Don. . . ." And she knew, surely and certainly then, that Don had not been mad. . . . I killed him. . . . She saw the doubtful, unwilling face of the veterinary doctor. . . . I made him do it, I made him guilty too. . . . And she listened and heard, still, clearly, across the night noises, the yapping of the dog.

"Emily," she cried, "Emily! Emily!"

She ran down the verandah to Emily's bed. She stopped and there was a long silence.

Emily's bed was empty.

Chapter X

IDLENESS stayed with Anil. "What has happened to your work, Banerjee?" Everyone asked him that, angrily, sternly or reproachfully, with curiosity from the other students, without surprise from Professor Dutt. "Young men are folly. All, all of them," the Professor would often say, and he gave Anil back his books without a scolding. "You have not made up your notes. Why do you hand them to me?"

"He will not get his pass, will he, Sir?"

"I expect that he will not," the Professor said mildly and Anil looked back at him with a smile so sweet and brilliant that the old man stayed, his breath caught, staring until he picked up his ancient umbrella that sheltered him across the quadrangle, and scurried off the dais out of the room.

"What is the matter with you, Anil?" His friends crowded round him, but Anil pushed them away.

"I am engaged on an idyll of idleness." They

thought he was being humorous, but it was true. In Anil's room was a little glazed image of Saraswati, the Goddess of Learning, and now she was wreathed in jasmine flowers though Anil did no work. It was reported that he lay on his bed and looked at her, and sometimes he sauntered alone in the garden, holding her on the palm of his hand. This quixotic behaviour violently confirmed public opinion that he would take all the prizes, and other aspirants grew sulky; it was awkward for them, they dared not copy Anil and leave off their studies abandoning themselves to Saraswati, they needed every hour for study, and they were forced to appear to their admirers as neither so clever nor so pious as Anil. Naturally Anil had more adherents than they.

He did not want them. He spent his days alone. He sat through his lectures in a veritable fortress of thought, it was so impregnable; or else he cut them and lay on his bed in his room, not answering when anyone knocked at his door. In the evening he went out walking, so far and so fast that in such weather not even the most devoted cared to follow him. He left Narayan's letters unanswered and did not go to his house.

People began to stare at him. He looked different; there was an elation about him and his eyes were excited though he was usually quiet, but sometimes they would hear him singing loudly and nasally and when they asked him, he did not know he had been singing. A rumour began that Anil Krishna Banerjee was drinking.

His walks were long and solitary. He walked by the river, far beyond the easy trodden paths where the students walked to get the breeze; he left the houses and the path behind, until the only path was a narrow deep-pitted one where the men who towed the boats put their feet; he had seen them, when the breeze fell, drop out from the boat near the land with a rope, and putting the loop of it round their chests, strain on it and draw boat and cargo and family along. Anil would have liked to try it but he was shy of the narrowness of his chest and his lightness; probably the boat would pull him off into the river.

On the low ground, when the river had receded after the rains, it had left great shallow lakes; and there he found water-lilies, and hyacinths and grasses of a bright surprising green, and villages built out of the water on stilts; once a flight of duck lifted out of the water almost over his head with a flash of their white breasts; a feather drifted down, it was the same white as the tufts of pampas grass.

He went into the fields and here the water had dried and the earth had a richness it had only at this season; paddy birds, white and long in leg and bill as little cranes, pecked in it and the farmers were finishing their ploughing; all across the plain they could be seen over and over again — in a repeating pattern of a little man, a yoke of oxen, and the earth turned up in dark lines on the fields. Weeds were stacked in the fields and these made, on the pattern, round purplish dots — some of them were fired in the evening and then the pattern altered: the chequered lines of the field walls were lost in the rising mist, the men and the oxen had gone and in their place the dark bone shape of the plough was left alone, and one after the other the fires burnt red and a spiral of white smoke went up into the evening.

With his power of bribing, Anil stayed out late. When he came home he wrote poems, he sat up writing them most of the night and with unusual reticence he did not show them to everyone. He showed them only to Narayan.

Narayan was always enthusiastic over Anil's work. That meant nothing. "I want you to show them to Sir Monmatha Ghose," said Anil, "I want you to show them even to Mr. Pool."

Narayan showed them to Professor Dutt. "But these are good!" said Professor Dutt in unflattering surprise. "I must show these to the Principal," but before he could do this, Anil asked Narayan to get them back. "I can't spare them," he said, "I want to finish them first."

"There is no hurry. Let him show one or two for an opinion."

"I don't want an opinion," said Anil crossly. "I know what they are like for myself. I want to finish them first."

"But Anil, it is to your interest — "

"Let me finish them first."

That was the only thing that spoiled these days for Anil. He was oppressed by a feeling of hurry; nothing else mattered but the finishing of the poems. He must finish them. He must get them done and he did not know how many there would be nor even what they would be; he knew they would follow one after the other, but to achieve them took a great deal of idling and dreaming and moving about. He had to shut himself away. Often, now, he went out at dawn and slept out under a tree at midday and walked on in the evening.

Often he missed the evening meal at the Hostel and then he would ask the villagers for food. One night, at dusk, when he had been out all day, he asked an old man sitting on his house step, where his and his son's supper was laid out on plantain leaves; he had a little rice and vegetables and sauce and a brass *lota* of pepper-water.

"May I eat with you?"

"How can you eat with us? You are a Brahmin."

"I can eat with anyone," said Anil happily and

he joined them, but when supper was over and the women had taken away their share, the father began to scold. The supper had been too small to stop his hunger and he wished he had not given any of it away.

"You are a Brahmin. You should not say the things you say, let alone do them," he scolded Anil.

"It does not matter what I do," said Anil dreamily.

"You are not yourself. You are your caste!" said the old man. "What would they say?"

"I shall not be there to hear it," answered Anil as he drifted away.

It was dark. The moon was over and ready to rise again. As he followed the dark path only the dried jute stick stack, white and brittle, piled in the branches of a tree, showed him when he had come to the edge of the village, and it was difficult to find his way across the fields though some of the weed piles were still smoking. As he came through the back streets of the town where the electric light had not yet been taken, every doorway was filled with the warm soft light of wicks in oil, except where a more wealthy family had the roaring glare of petrol lamps. He passed those quickly and looked in at the door of the huts where the earth walls were turned to gold, for they looked attractive and a little romantic. Sometimes a woman came to the door with a light in her hand, a bowl with a single wick floating in it that lit her neck and chin and left her face in darkness; the effect of that seen over and over again was mysterious and quickening. Outside the men were talking and smoking a hookah or cheap cigarettes, and their voices followed Anil down the road. He knew they all looked after him. The bicycles passed continuously and some, like those of the clerks who went to Charles's house, had bicycle lights and others had none and their riders carried wicks with shields made of paper bags. They passed him and whizzed into the night. . . .

Why do they go so fast? Why do they all hurry? . . . One of them seemed to recognize him. A voice cried out of the darkness, "Good de luck, good de luck," as it went by. Why should it call "good luck"? And suddenly he remembered with a jar that to-morrow was Examination Day. For a moment he was startled, but the Examination seemed oddly remote and he discarded the thought of it; but it had given him a small shock. . . .

How quickly time has gone, he said. What have I been doing? I have so much to do. . . . And a nervous tension filled him over the finishing of his poems. On a verandah as he passed, women were working, rolling betel leaves for the festival; one had a tray of round cakes made of coconut and sugar, *puja* cakes . . . And soon I must go home, cried Anil in dismay. I cannot go till I have finished my poems. . . .

He walked on and on, out of the town and into it again, thinking, composing, thinking. He sat down on a door-step under a street light and wrote down his poem with a pencil he had in his pocket and a piece of paper he found in the road, the side of a torn paper bag. It was the best he had done and when it was written, safely caught, fixed on the paper, he was tired, very tired. The tiredness was perfection. He was sure it was the best poem he had written, he felt it was very near the best poems in the world, and it had been as difficult as if he had caught something as wild and terrific as a star and induced it to lie pulsing in his torn piece of paper. Very tired, he stood up to go home.

As he walked a mood of bliss lapped him; he discovered that he was gently drunk with it. The spirit of festival was already in him. . . . I feel excited, full of undercurrents of excitement. . . . And the undercurrents threatened to well up and swamp him. . . . What is the matter with me? I feel — too much. . . . That was the only way he could describe it and for a moment he felt alarmed, but he answered himself. . . . It is the poem. The whole of me is full of my poem. At the moment I am my poem. What a good thing I wrote it down quickly. If I had not written it down it might have choked me. I should have been choked by my own poem. I must be quieter. I must distil — yes, distil my poems — as the moon distils itself, surely and certainly. The moon . . . And he stumbled in the dark and stubbed his toe.

Slightly chastened, he arrived limping at the gates of the College and gave a gentle double knock and the porter in his sleep let him in and sank on to his bed again.

Anil walked across the grass where the trees made thickets of blackness in the dark. The tank lay dark and opaque with only a faint spread reflection from the stars. Suddenly Anil stopped. At the top of the steps was a figure, sitting with its back towards him. After a moment he went on towards it and now he saw in the uncertain starlight that it was small, very pale in the darkness, with a fall of colourless hair. He had almost believed it was an apparition when it heard him and he saw it jump. It put up its hand and said in clear imperious English, "Hush!" He saw it was a child of Charlie Chang's.

If Anil had met Emily or any of her kind in everyday life he would have been nonplussed, but in this mood of exaltation under the darkness, he came up to her and asked, "Why hush?"

In her ordinary senses Emily would have been paralyzed with meeting a stranger, Indian or English, suddenly and alone in the dark; but she would also have been terrified of going out alone, even as far as Shah's house at the gate, and she was particularly afraid of jackals. She was exalted like Anil but it was an exaltation of ecstatic bravery, almost hysterical, brought on by fear and misery and amazement at herself. Anil's voice reassured her; she could only see his white clothes blown a little by the night wind that had started in the garden, and the flickering movement of his hand as he held down the tails of his tunic, but she could see he was an Indian.

"How do you do?" she said. "I suppose you are a student at the College."

Anil became equally formal. "Yes, I am a student, and you must be Miss Pool."

"I am Emily Pool."

"My name is Anil Krishna Banerjee." He began to have the slight joviality of a grown-up speaking to a child and Emily became immediately more distant.

"How do you do," she said, and Anil knew at once that she was displeased, just as he knew at once that he liked her. He could not see more of her than her shape and the fall of her hair but he liked the way her voice came back to him in the darkness like a bell with a clear certain tone. She quieted him; he felt that he was meant to meet her, that she was bound in with his destiny, and he hated to offend her. He wanted to amend what he had said but he did not know how to and there began a stilted social conversation between them.

"Do you like it here in India?"

"Yes, thank you."

"I expect that you find it hot."

"Very hot."

"You came from France in the war, I think."

"Yes."

"Was the war then bad?"

"Very bad," said Emily briefly; it was plain she did not want to talk about it. Anil could think of nothing more to say though he wanted to say more and the silence grew longer and longer between them. Then Emily, feeling it was her turn, asked the only question she could think of, "Do you like being a student?"

"I have enjoyed it, yes."

He did not know he had answered in the past until she asked, "You are not a student any more then?"

He said suddenly, "Miss Pool, I ceased to be a student about three weeks since."

"Oh. What are you now?"

He answered at once because he knew exactly, "I am a poet."

"Oh," said Emily again.

"You think that is a pity?"

"Yes."

"But why? It is very nice to be a poet. Shouldn't you like it? Shouldn't you like to be a poet?"

"No I should not," said Emily decidedly. "Poets die young."

Anil laughed. "What a funny girl you are."

"They do. There was Shelley, and Keats and Chatterton. They all died young."

"You learn that in your books. It is not necessarily true. I am happy as a poet. I will sit no more in class. I will not study in books when I can study in the world. All these years I have been glued to work. I wonder that I let them make a fool of me so long."

Emily objected. "When you are young you have to do lessons."

"Yes, that is so. When I was a boy, for instance, we had a very disagreeable schoolmaster; besides our lessons we had to wait on him, we even had to press his legs and rub them when he was resting and he had very skinny legs."

For some reason that soothed Emily and pleased her; she laughed. Anil felt success spreading through him and he said, "Now I am wondering what you do here for lessons."

"I do lessons with Professor Dutt."

"Old Granny Dutt? This is a link between us. He is my tutor too, at least formerly I was with him." He was surprised that so small a girl could be so advanced. "I thought you would learn with your mother."

"No." There was an edge to that and he did not miss it. Anil, who did not really listen to any voice but his own, was curiously alive to Emily's.

"Miss Pool — no, I shall call you Emily — what would your mother say if she knew you were here to-night?"

There was no answer.

"I think you should not have come here by yourself. Would she not be angry if you were to be seen?"

"No one will see me. No one will come here now when it is dark."

"I am not surprised," said Anil. "It is very spooky. When first I saw you I thought you were a ghost."

"Did you?" asked Emily breathlessly. "That is — odd." And she said as if she was surprised at herself for telling him, "I came — to see a ghost." And she added quickly, "Of course I know it isn't here."

"Then why did you come to see it?"

"Because — " reluctantly she said — "it is something to do with me."

"A ghost and you?" But they did not seem such odd companions.

"I heard them talking and I came to see. It's

my ghost." And she said a little defiantly, "It is the ghost of my dog."

"Then the dog is dead?" said Anil gently.

"Perhaps he is dead," said Emily in a still flat voice.

That was the best of talking to Indians. They asked you questions without limit but they would never press you for any particular answer; they understood perfectly how to slide from one thing to another. "Come — he is, or is not, dead?" Anil might have asked her, but instead he told her, "My father used to keep dogs when I was a boy. They were great Danes and they were very costly, but he gave them up; my mother used to make him take them and feed them outside the house."

"Why?"

"Because we are of Hindu faith; we are Brahmin; and the dogs of course ate meat. That we do not allow and my mother was extremely orthodox. My father also is orthodox now, more so than my mother. Before I left they asked of me a vow that I would not take anything forbidden, not even eggs — but milk of course I take."

"But don't you like eggs?"

"I don't know. I have not tasted them."

"But you are grown up," said Emily with yearning in her voice, "you can do what you like."

"No. Still I cannot. I have taken this vow and it would be wicked of me to eat these things."

"In France," said Emily thoughtfully, "it was wicked not to eat," and she thought of Madame Souviens and how she would kiss her fingers when she spoke of her onion and cheese-cake, and the voice in which she said, "*une bonne soupe*," and she remembered the soup at the Nikolides'. "Can you eat soup?" she asked.

"There are certain soups . . ." but Emily had gone from Madame Souviens to the morning with the Nikolides; through the cracks of the jetty the water looked miraculously clearly blue, and she saw first Binnie then herself pass inside the house to breakfast and she smelled the champac flowers as she went . . . And all the time — all the time — while I was away . . .

"Your ghost does not come," said Anil.

"I didn't think he would." He heard the same bright-edged break in the words and he tried again to see her face. What kind of child was this that could have such grief and contain it? Anil was profoundly stirred. "But you hoped?" he said gently.

He felt a tremor go through her. Though she was sitting only on the step beside him, even her hand not touching him, he felt the tremor clearly. She gave a little cry like a choke and hid her face in her hands. He could only catch one or two words dropped from the confusion of crying. "No one . . . gone . . . in the night . . . tell them . . . no one . . . no one . . . Mother . . . no one . . ."

Anil could not bear it. He put his arm round her and drew her close and through the thin muslin of his shirt he could feel the wet heat of her cheeks and eyes, and the movement of her lashes and the shaking of her body; the whole of her was throbbing with sorrow and emotion, trying to escape, beating its way out in a tumult of words and tears. Anil did not know what to do, so he simply held her, and from her an unaccustomed smell rose to his nostrils that made her even more incomprehensible, — the mild fresh smell of a well-kept English child, — and it disconcerted Anil; he held her and muttered small cajoling words that he did not know he remembered and that he had not heard since he left his nurse; gradually they penetrated to Emily. She could not understand them but she was comforted by them; they were friendly and his shoulder was slight but firm and she too was arrested by the unfamiliar smell of him; she began to cry a little less and sniff a little more.

"Have you no handkerchief?"

Emily shook her head and wiped her nose on the back of her hand; Anil appeared to think that would do as well. He did not like to ask her any more questions in case she began again, but he tightened his arm and said: "Let us talk of this a little more, perhaps to talk may make it better.

Truly I am very much concerned in this — " As he said that, very earnestly, a tremor like Emily's, but not like Emily's, seemed to run through him too — not of grief but of something even more solemn. It surprised him. He went on quickly, "Suppose you were to see this ghost — now," and he pointed dramatically, "there — "

She turned sharply and quailed and looked across the tank as if she expected to see a devil, but there was nothing there but the still black tank, the few stars in it, the few fireflies above it.

"Now, now. You will not see it," Anil comforted her. "I think you will never see it. Once I heard of the spirit of a tiger, but not of any other animal. See, we watch for him to come. No. No. He does not come."

There was no answer, only a grateful small rustle.

"And there is another thing," said Anil, "and why should you not do this? We, of Hindu religion, when we wish for the repose of a soul — that it shall rest in peace for instance — we make a small *puja* . . ."

"*Puja?*" asked Emily.

"Worship — celebration," said Anil. "In the month there are two periods, '*devipaksha*' when the moon is growing, and '*Krishnapaksha*' when the moon is going away; light nights and black nights; and the black nights are the times for ghosts. You will do your *puja* then. You can take, in some place — under this tree for instance — a few good things: some fruit, or sweets, some good sugar or rice or cakes, even some vegetables; and you will place them on a little table or platform that you have made look pretty, and if possible you will have flowers and a small light — and you will offer these things with prayers to the spirit for whom you wish to make peace, though by offering to one soul you offer to all, and for one year he will gain rest. It would not be irreverent for this especial dog, I think. Why should you not do that, please Emily?"

Emily considered it. "Soon — not yet." But there was a distinct relief in her tone. She gave a sigh that came from the bottom of her heart.

Presently she asked, laying her hand on his knee, "You are not a medical student, are you?"

"No. There are no medical students here. Why? Is there some question you wanted to know?"

"I wanted," said Emily, and her voice was alert again, "I wanted to know what diseases there are that people and dogs can get the same."

"You should ask Das, my friend."

"Dr. Das, the vet?"

"He is a vet, he is also a very nice fellow." Anil yawned. It was tiresome of Emily to turn this suddenly into a definite conversation; and then he looked down at her head below his shoulder — in the brightening starlight it looked pale, ruffled and worried; he could see one hand clenched against her cheek, she was thinking, and in front of her the dim spaces of the tank shone empty, and paler now there were more stars.

"Come," he said, "you should not be out at this time. Come, you must let me take you back to the house. We will ask for your spirit another night. When the moon is over — though I shall not be there —" and again that brimming of extraordinary excitement rose in him so that he caught his breath. "Come," he said when he could speak, and helped her to her feet. They walked across the grass; his stubbed toe hurt him abominably.

"Why do you limp?" asked Emily.

"I hurt my foot."

"Lean on my shoulder."

Anil smiled, and very lightly put his arm across her shoulders. They came in at the gate, past Shah sleeping soundly on his bed, and went up the drive between the dark shapes of the poinsettias to the house, where a light showed a width of railings on the top verandah and the shapes of two mosquito-nets. Anil looked curiously around him, he had not been so near a European house before. "Who sleeps on the verandah?" he asked.

"That is where I sleep. That is my bed."

They were pinned and held in a circle of light, they were blinded, their eyelids fluttered like moths' wings as they stood there fixed. Emily's shoulders jerked under Anil's arm and she shrank back against him. "It's Mother," she said.

Anil's stomach made a surprising movement on its own, totally unrelated to him; it gave a sudden terrified rumble; between shame and his premonition of fright he almost decided to go, but pride ran down his legs and stiffened them. He knew that he ought to go straight to Emily's mother and speak to her, but he could not bring himself to do quite that. Instead, he shook Emily's hand and said, "Good night. You will be safe now. Someone is coming to find you, I think."

"Wait! You are not to go."

Louise's voice startled and shocked them, especially Emily. Anil was a visitor, even though it was the middle of the night. She said in rebuke, "Mother, Mr. — Anil is here."

Louise brushed her aside and behind her and said to Anil in a suppressed icy voice, "I cannot speak to you. You must wait for my husband."

"Certainly." Anil's own voice was high with dismay and the beginning of serious fright. "Certainly I will wait, Mrs. —— Mrs. —— " He could think of nothing at all to call her but Mrs. Chang.

"Don't speak to me."

"Moth — er."

"Emily, go and wait for me in my room. You are not to go near Binnie."

Emily was really frightened. Louise looked like an apparition of herself, her hair streaming down, her face blenched, and the strong porch light made odd shiny planes and shadows in it; why did her skin look so queer? And then Emily saw with a shock that Louise's face was wet, and immediately Emily broke out into a cold wetness too. It was a relief, it took some of her fright away.

"Mother," she said boldly, "don't be so angry. Did you think I was lost? I'm sorry — Mother."

"Go upstairs. Don't speak to me. I will deal with you later." Emily put out a hand and Louise screamed, "Don't touch me! Get away — upstairs." The scream and recoil were so dreadful that Emily was struck dumb.

Anil at last began to speak. "I demand explanation," said Anil. "I am a student at this College and as such am not under your authority, Madam." The "Madam" came trippingly to his tongue but his surprise and hurt swamped it. His voice grew shrill with indignation. "I was just now returning from an evening's excursion — "

"That is a lie," said Louise, and her voice was low after his; breathless and rapid. She was beside herself. "The College is closed at eleven o'clock." Anil, from sheer fright, smiled, and that drove Louise on to dramatic fury. "If I were a man I should horsewhip you. That is what they would do to you in England. Flog you so that you should never forget. Don't try and defend yourself. I saw you. I heard you. How long has this been going on? Emily has been queer for days — "

And suddenly Emily could bear no more. She burst into loud terrified wails like a baby and fled up the steps. Charles was standing in the doorway and he caught her just inside the door.

"Look at me," said Charles. Trying to hold her sobbing she looked back at him from a tear-sodden face, ugly and swollen with crying, from tired tear-red eyes. He noticed that she was tidy, her hair was still held back from her face by her narrow white night ribbon, and she wore her old checked coat buttoned over blue and white pyjamas; except for her slippers that were wet and stained with grass, and her face that was wet and stained with tears, there was nothing to show for her expedition. Charles's face, very serious, relaxed as he looked at her. "Go upstairs," he said gently. "Dry your feet and wait for me. I shan't be long."

He went quickly down the steps. Anil and Louise were still there, Louise still fanatically speaking, Anil with his back to the darkness. The light threw their shadows a long way on the grass, Anil's was still but Louise's was exaggerated, mocking her movements, making them into antics and melodrama. Charles came up behind her and put his hands on her elbows holding them against her sides as if he wanted to crush them together. Louise screamed, but the ugly poisonous words finished abruptly; she struggled; he held her rigid in his grip, while his voice came over her head, quite politely: "I think you had better go in, Louise. Emily is not hurt. She is quite all right," and to Anil he said, "Will you wait and talk to me for a few minutes? Don't go."

Anil was a long way from going — or speaking. He was so absolutely shocked that he could not speak or move or think.

Charles was bruising Louise; the soft flesh of her arms was pinched under the hardness of his and his fingers pressed her down and back against him. "Charles! Let me go! Let me go!" but he turned her towards the house and impelled her up the steps. He loosened his hands and the blood flowing back into the bruises made her cry out again and she fell back against him, faint and sick. He lifted her and carried her upstairs, where Emily had already gone.

But, for Louise, neither Emily nor Anil was there.

She was in another night, in another house; it was another flight of stairs. The pain was the same and she remembered the flash of the enamels on the shelf, the last flash of reality as Charles swept her up past them, crushed and giddy and sick, in his arms. She remembered the night outside the window when he had torn the curtains down ("Damme, we must have gala stars!") and she remembered the sound of her sobs coming in breathless gasps as they were coming now. She remembered how she had escaped over the side of the bed and he had put out a hand and thrown her savagely back. It was always his strength that was in her mind, the force of his strength. ("Don't provoke me too far, Louise. You don't know how strong I am.")

Suddenly, at dinner, he had stood up and thrown his whiskey in her face and pulled the cloth off the table and thrown the candles down on it. Emily was there too; she remembered how helplessly the baby Emily had woken up and cried, and how the frightened little Anglo-Indian nurse had popped her head in at the door. "Don't be afraid, Nancy, I am only mad, not drunk," said Charles, and he bellowed, "Go into your room and shut the door." He drove the servants out of the house and locked the doors and windows. "I wish I could shoot out the lights," he said, "but I haven't a gun"; he looked at the Dutch axe over the fireplace: "But I have an axe and by God you shan't miss anything!" And then he had smashed up the house.

She remembered the nightmare of broken wood and glass, the shrieking of the nurse and Emily — and she remembered the struggle when Charles caught her by the stairs. She remembered the dreadful, mingled taste of whiskey and blood in her mouth where her lips had bled, and her clothes torn off her on the floor and her struggles with the softness of her bed muffling her cries, and the naked heat of Charles pressing down on her when at last she gave in and lay still. Now, powerless against his strength, in his arms again, she knew what she knew then and had known ever since — that secret moment would never be lost between them, between Charles and Louise, whatever they did to it, whatever it did to them; the flow from his body to hers, from hers uprising to his, had a fire that could never be put out, that burnt them still. That night, stretched on her back, she had lifted her hands to him in ultimate surrender when she forced them down again.

But now she clung to him as he put her down at the head of the stairs. "Can you stand up?"

"Don't go. Don't go," she moaned.

He steadied her sharply. "I must go. That wretched boy is waiting."

"Let him wait."

"You have done enough damage already. I must stop it if I can."

"Charles. Please. Come back. I want you. I want you, Charles — "

Charles had gone downstairs.

For a long time she stood where he had left her.

The colour came back into her face. She looked at her arms where the bruise marks were already turning dark, and she clenched her hands and gave an angry pitiful sob. Then a sound struck her, an exhausted dreary sound, and it had been going on all the time. It was Emily crying unheeded, as she had cried when she was a baby in the broken house.

Emily . . .

* * * Anil was obediently waiting. In fact he had not moved. He had dimly seen how Charles had taken Louise away, but her voice seemed to go on still — though long before Charles had come he had lost the sense of the words. He was numb, and when Charles touched him he only looked up dully.

"Will you come into my office? We can't talk here."

"Thank you," but as he walked up the steps and heard his own shoes on the stone, it grew real and he started back and cried, "No. I prefer not."

"We can't talk outside — in the dark," said Charles reasonably. "You must come in." Anil hesitated and walked in after Charles, who was turning over and over in his mind what he possibly could say.

"Sit down."

"No" — but a nervous whimper shook Anil like

a hiccough and he had to sit down, on the edge of a chair, his head bent. He was shivering.

"You are exhausted," said Charles, and he looked at him puzzled. Could Louise have done all that? And then he saw that Anil's shoes were caked in mud; there were splashes of mud on his legs, and on his *dhoti* that was not white any longer but bedraggled and limp as if it had been soaked and dried and worn a long time. "Where have you been? What have you been doing?" Another shivering hiccough. "If I give you a drink," said Charles, "will you take it?"

Anil only shook his head. He wiped his hand and his thumb across his forehead and the sweat dropped off on his shirt; his shirt was soaked to his body on his shoulders and chest. He shivered in silence, looking at his shoes — and then he choked, suddenly and painfully.

"You are ill," said Charles.

Anil shook his head again. "I have had," he said, "a small swelling in the throat, and I am very tired." As he spoke he lifted his head and Charles recognized him. He could not remember his name, but he remembered him from his lectures, at the debates, at the meetings, and his heart sank. This was a difficult boy to deal with, a turbulent popular student, a ringleader, one of the College bloods, and then he looked at Anil again and was struck by the look of peculiar excitement on his face; it was more than immediate excitement or misery, it was unearthly, and Charles was nonplussed. Now he had Anil here, more than ever he did not know what he could say.

Anil said it first. "I have done nothing. Nothing," he repeated. "Why does she accuse me? I have done nothing."

Charles tried to cover his confusion and growing dismay by asking businesslike questions. Anil was in no state to resist them.

"Why were you out so late?"

"I — had been walking."

"So late?"

"Yes — I had been out a long time — "

"You know the College rules, you were breaking them — "

"Yes."

"Have you done this before?"

"Yes."

"You bribed the porter, I suppose. Anyone else?"

"No."

"Didn't the Superintendent know?"

"Sometimes — I have given him present — "

"I see. Where did you find my daughter?"

"She was there by the tank. She was afraid. I comforted her and brought her in because I thought you would not like that she was out alone, but I did nothing to her — nothing, nothing, Mr. Pool," and he shouted, "Why does she accuse me then?"

The sound of his own voice, loud in this room, terrified him, and he sank into frightened silence, shivering again and wetting his lips which were suddenly dry.

"My wife should not have accused you," said Charles; "I can see that, and she will apologize. She found the little girl missing from her bed and she was naturally upset. I am sure she did not know what she was saying — "

"No — " Anil agreed; and he looked up and cried, "But she insulted me — "

"She did not know what she was saying. I have told you, she will apologize — "

"She was most cruel and wicked to me, when I had befriended her child."

"Meanwhile, it appears that you have been breaking College rules for some time," said Charles thoughtfully, and he picked up a pencil. "To-morrow is Examination day and you, I am told, have a great chance. It would be a pity to spoil it — wouldn't it? Listen to me. We do not want to make a fuss. If you will promise me that you will go straight to bed and say nothing of this to anyone, I shall see Sir Monmatha Ghose in the morning and tell him the whole of the story, and I under-take that he will overlook your breaking of the rules this time. You shall see him too, if you wish, and you will get your apology."

Anil's fingers, working nervously, had found his

poem in his pocket, the poem that was a star caught on a dirty piece of paper; he thought of the night with Narayan when he had seen the firefly. . . . It was not a shooting star but an insect. . . . A desolation filled him and he nearly threw the poem down in Charles's wastepaper basket, but something even in the feel of the paper it was written on contradicted him, its words seemed to run from his fingers into his soul. . . . But there can never be another like it. My freedom is ended. I can stay out no more . . . And it burst from him in despair, "You must report it? Oh, Sir!"

Charles was puzzled again and he was tempted. There was something here that mattered deeply to the boy. More than his chances in the Examination, more than the fear of being found out. Charles was tempted but he sighed and said, "I am afraid I must."

"And they will not take action against me? Or against them?"

"Not this time, but probably they will be warned."

Anil said nothing.

"Otherwise I must send a servant for the Superintendent now. That will be very unpleasant for you." Anil still said nothing but his tongue came out and wet his lips and his eyes were on Charles, pleading and oddly bright. Charles felt an increasing distaste for the whole of it but he forced himself to insist. "Do you promise?"

"Yes — " . . . It is all over now. What does it matter?

"You understand. Not a word to anyone."

"Yes."

Charles asked, "What is your name?"

Anil was startled. "But I know you. Why don't you know me?" his look said, and Charles answered the look. "There are hundreds of students," he said, "you will have to tell me your full name."

"Hundreds," said Anil. The word seemed to sink into him in the silence.

"What is your name?"

"My name is Anil Krishna Banerjee."

"Das's friend?"

"Yes."

"You will get your apology in the morning," said Charles, but Anil hardly heard him. "Remember you have given your promise," said Charles — but he had the feeling already that he was speaking to an Anil that changed as quickly as the ripples on the river. It was impossible to catch or fix him. Anil had given him a promise; was that Anil here any more?

He hesitated. Almost, he decided to ring up the Principal. After a moment he let the boy go.

* * * Emily waited for Louise. She knew Louise would come before Charles and the waiting was very long. She stood at the foot of the bed and though she was shaking with tiredness she did not

attempt to sit down. She could not even approach Louise as far as that and she stood taking in as little of the room as possible. Her mind would not think about Louise, it refused to; it froze itself into terror; now and again it dodged this way and that, then crouched again and was frozenly still.

What had she done this time? What could she have done? It was more than going out of bed. ("You are not to go near Binnie.") . . .

I know your voice, Louise, your coaxing voice, your charming voice, your angry voice, your cutting voice and your frightened voice, but I don't know this one. There is a tone in it I have never heard before and it makes me shake and shrink and freeze, but I don't know what it is. I don't know what I have done, except what I have done, and this is something worse than that. What have I done? What have I done? . . .

She looked up at the high vaulted roof where the stucco of the pale walls glimmered up into darkness; outside the windows the sky seemed to swing a little with its panoply of stars, but that may have been because she was swaying on her feet. The sky was luminous with starlight, lit and blue, why had the earth been so dark then? The walls and the windows seemed to fall away, opening Emily to that marauding darkness, darkness where she had escaped from what dreadful thing? Or done what dreadful thing? . . . But what, but what, Louise?

Now I am beginning to be afraid. What happened to me out there in the dark? What did I see? A man? A ghost? A dreadful bogie? What? When? Where? When? Where? That was my shriek going up to the stars, bursting my chest, hurting me, hurting the whole of me, but there was no sound; the scream was too high for anyone to hear, tearing through me, cutting its way out of me. Now I am afraid. I am afraid. I am afraid. . . .

A puff of wind moved a shutter; the slats of it creaked and in the wind she smelled the garden outside, the earth cooling, the smell of dew and nightstrong plants; it blew reasonably and coolly on her hot forehead and it seemed to blow into her head. ("You went out and sat by the tank to see Don," said the wind, "nothing else, nothing more. You talked to the student who was kind and brought you home but you told him nothing that was not your own to tell. That is all you have done. Nothing more. Nothing else.") The moment passed. She was calm. . . . I am glad, said Emily, I am glad Louise did not catch me then . . . and, as always when she had those moments by herself and kept them to herself, she felt strong.

Presently Louise came in; she took no notice of Emily but sat down on the bed as if her knees had given way, and hid her eyes with her hand. Emily was not as frightened; Louise looked angry and miserable but she did not look strange any more.

"Come here," she said, with her eyes still blinded.

Emily advanced an inch.

"Closer." That was reassuringly like Louise, imperious and impatient.

"I'm sorry I went out, Mother — " At the sound of Emily's voice Louise took her hand away from her eyes and that expression came back into her face. "What have I done, Mother?" cried Emily in panic. "What have I done?"

Louise did not answer. Emily and something else seemed to be fighting for importance in her mind. "Where did you go to-night?"

"I went to the tank. I heard what the servants — the people — are saying about — about Don. I wanted to show it was not true."

"Of course it's not true. You know that," cried Louise. "You are using that as an excuse. You are so sly and deceitful that nothing is beyond you. I don't believe you. Do you hear? I don't believe you," and Emily had the feeling again that Louise's anger was not only for her, and Louise seemed to sense that too. She stopped and, as if she meant to make herself pay attention to Emily, she took her hand, and Emily knew she forced herself to do it and that she did not want to touch her and again Emily cried despairingly, "Mother, what have I done?"

"Emily, you wouldn't be afraid to tell me the truth, would you?"

Her mind ducked and froze.

"You wouldn't, would you?"

Emily shook her head.

"*Would you?*" A good human exasperation overcame the falseness in Louise's voice. It gave Emily a breath as if she had come up into the air.

"I wouldn't."

"Emily, I want you to tell me: what did that man talk to you about there in the garden?"

"Man?" Emily wrinkled her nose trying to think. Anil had passed out of her mind. Then she remembered. "Mother, you *were* rude to him."

"You are getting to be a big girl now, a girl not a child." As she said it Emily seemed to sink into smallness; to Louise who had wanted to keep her a child she now seemed aggressively childlike. "Get bigger. Get bigger," said Louise's hand and Emily sank faster and faster into little-girl stupidity. "You are old enough to know that you must never speak to strangers — strange men," said Louise with that same breathlessness. "And if they speak to you you must go away from them at once. At once," repeated Louise sharply. "You know that, don't you?"

A flicker of curiosity ran through Emily. She wanted to ask why, but she only said, "Yes, Mother."

"Do you understand what I mean?"

"Yes," said Emily hopelessly and she cried out miserably, "Why can't I go near Binnie?"

"Of course you can go near Binnie."

"You said I couldn't. Why not? What have I done?"

"Emily, be quiet. You're not trying — to be sensible. Now listen. You went out to-night — "

"I told you I did. Punish me. Punish me if you like."

"I don't want to punish you. I'm trying to make you understand."

"I *don't* understand. First you are angry with me. Then you are not. What do you want? What do you want me to say?"

"You are deliberately trying to provoke me, Emily." Louise sprang up from the bed. "I don't want to lose my temper with you but you make me do it." She came close to Emily, who shrank back until the edge of the bed was pressing into her legs. Louise seemed to tower over her with the power of a giant, but again she stopped herself. "Emily — " Her voice altered, it was coaxing and cajoling. "Try and tell me what happened to-night. What did he say? What did he do? How did he come? Can't you tell me anything he said to you to-night? Anything you talked about at all?"

Emily felt a touch of understanding and pity that was not childlike but completely mature. . . . How old I am now, she thought, and then she lost it. . . . Her eyes looked this way and that, searching for inspiration.

"Emily?"

She shut her eyes. Her mind went backwards and forwards trying to remember. She felt a wave of sickness coming over her.

"What did you talk about?"

(You are not going to be sick, are you? Emily asked herself. The words rang in her head and they brought back the breakfast with the Nikolides and joined it to this trouble to-night; it began then — with the Nikolides; it has been getting bigger ever since. . . . "What did you talk about?")

"Soup," said Emily suddenly.

Louise gave a sharp breath like a hiss and slapped her cheek.

Emily jumped and all the colour went away from her face except from that one mark. She did not cry. She looked at Louise quite silently, her eyes brimming with dignity and hurt.

"You are impossible. Impossible!" cried Louise. "I try. I do try, but you are impossible. What am I to do? What am I to do?" She walked up and down, as if the pain were too bad to keep still, and she said, as if a repellent little snake had crept into her room, "Get away. Go away to bed."

Still with those baleful eyes on Louise, Emily crept out and away along the verandah. She was cold. Cold. Charles did not come. The coldness numbed her. Her pyjamas were wet, but she was burning, and in spite of the burning she was cold and she lay shivering, sick and dry with a brittle cold dryness. How can you be wet and dry, burning and cold? There was no warmth or live feeling left in her, only her head felt hot and her eyes burnt with shock, and her cheek where Louise had hit her.

She heard Charles come up. She waited, trying not to cry. She waited. Charles went into Louise's room and after a while he closed the door.

She put out her hand and rubbed the edges of Don's bed; the wooden edge was still rough with his biting, the rug was there that he had scraped up into a nest before he lay down on it, and the lead that he had broken. The lead dangled limply in her fingers, nothing at the end of it. Before, there was a pull, warmth, sturdiness. Now only limpness, emptiness. There was no one. No one. In a rush of despair she thought, This is what it feels like to be dead.

* * * Charles came upstairs to go to Emily but Louise's door was open and he saw Louise. She was walking up and down the room, up and down, until she turned and faced him; her hair was on her shoulders and with heat and anger she had a flush of colour in her cheeks and the heavy white folds of her dressing-gown swung in round her feet as she turned, showing the shape of her hips and thighs and legs in folded slender lines. "You are always right," she cried. "Always! You are hateful. Hateful."

"And you, even when you have been as poisonous as you were to-night, still remain so beautiful," said Charles, and he leaned against the door surveying her. "Why is it? More than beautiful. You have an angelic face, Louise, the face of an angel; you ought to be so kind. I wonder why you are not. By the way," he asked, "what have you done to Emily?"

"Can't you hear her? She is crying in her bed," and she said defiantly, "I slapped her face."

"Charming," said Charles, but he made no move to go to Emily.

"Well — what are you going to do now?"

"What can I do — except what I have always done? Take the consequences. I expect there will be consequences," said Charles. "I don't think that boy will hold his tongue. I told him you would apologize."

"I won't apologize."

"You will have to. God knows what you have smashed this time — " and he said softly, his eyes on her, "Last time it was a house — "

"You smashed that . . ."

"No, you," he corrected. "You had made a mistake. You see, you married a man, when all you wanted was a money-box."

"That isn't fair."

"Of course it isn't. I find it hard to be fair to you, Louise. You call me hateful. For years you have made me feel hateful, and I shall never forgive you for that."

"You were hateful," said Louise hotly, "you didn't trust me."

"Were you to be trusted?" asked Charles. Louise did not answer. "That was it," said Charles, "you were not reasonable. You did not want something — you wanted everything. You wanted to spend all your money and be rich, you wanted to have a child and have no worry and pain, you wanted to marry and not be married; and when it naturally didn't fall out like that you made an outcry and a moan. You wanted to be trusted and have the fun of being untrustworthy — you did have fun, didn't you, Louise? And you wanted me to be jealous — without being inconvenient."

"You forced yourself on me."

"What a villain. Go on."

"You behaved abominably."

"I behaved like a fool. Look at the statistics," said Charles. "You stayed with me for nearly three years — say a thousand nights, Louise; on one night out of a thousand I lost my temper with you. Why was it only one?"

"It isn't a joke," said Louise icily.

"No. Nor was it then," said Charles, and his eyes grew hard. "Can a man assault his own wife? Apparently he can — if she chooses to make a scandal of it . . . and, incidentally, make it impossible for herself to see him again — for eight years, Louise?"

"I had no wish to see you again. You were bestial."

"And the result of that was Binnie," said Charles thoughtfully; "and Binnie, the child of violence, is very nearly perfect. That doesn't make sense, does it?" His voice was not steady, he had forgotten his bantering. "I tortured myself over Binnie. You knew that, didn't you, Louise? That is why you never wrote and were so careful not to let them tell me anything. *Dear Sir,*" he mocked bitterly: "*Mrs. Pool has instructed us to inform you that a daughter was born on the 4th April.* I thought she might be abnormal. I thought I might have made her blind or ill. I believed all the old wives' stories. When I walked up on that steamer I was shaking — and then she came across the deck and put out her hand and made me look . . ." He did not go on.

"Why didn't you ask?" said Louise.

"Because you wouldn't have told me. You were very angry, Louise. You did everything you could. You separated me from Emily — finally. I shall never have Emily again. You refused to see me."

"I couldn't bear to see you."

"You didn't dare. There was one thing you could not forgive me about that night, Louise," said Charles, "and that was that you liked it."

"That isn't true."

"Isn't it? Why didn't you ask me for a divorce? Why wouldn't you take it when I offered it to you? Why didn't I divorce you?" — He came closer — "Why, when you were frightened to death, did you come back, Louise — "

"You didn't want me. You don't want me now."

"Who in their senses could want you?" shouted Charles. "You make nothing but trouble wherever you go. I can't escape it, and neither can you." He looked at the bruises on her arms. "I hurt you to-night, the first time I have touched you for eight years. It seems I'm beginning where I left off — because I touched you to-night I can't go away," and he said, "You are eight years older, Louise. This time are you going to run away?"

* * * Anil was so tired that he walked out of Charles's room, across the garden and across the grounds, up to the stairs of the Hostel and into his room without feeling anything at all. He did not wait to take off his clothes, he simply dropped his shoes on the floor and fell over on his bed asleep. He must have slept only a little while when he woke up choking. . . . I have caught cold, he thought again, and it seemed to his tired, over-tired brain that this nuisance of catching cold was something terrible, an accident that might finish by exterminating Anil. . . . I hope it doesn't hurt me too much, he said, and jerked himself back to sense. . . . I must be sensible . . . But to wake with a dry choking throat is a peculiar kind of terror, worse when the arms and legs are so deadened with sleep that they cannot rise off the bed and fetch a drink of water.

He fell asleep again and dreamed that Mrs. Pool was suffocating him.

This time he woke by sitting violently up on his bed, literally tearing himself out of the dream. Sitting up, presently he began to breathe properly. . . . I cannot lie down, my throat is too uneasy . . . and he leaned against the wall and went to sleep in that position; but every few minutes he woke.

Chapter XI

CHARLES called early at the Principal's house. It was outside the town and remarkable because it was three storeys high and looked all the higher for the flat land round it. He left Delilah by the steps and was asked to come up, past the first floor, past the second and onto the roof, where he saw a small marquee built into the sky with a top that was lined inside with a quilting of patchwork flowers. Sir Monmatha Ghose sat under it, his legs folded neatly into each other, on a bed with a mattress tied down with a cotton sheet and two of the enormous bolsters called "Dutch wives." Sitting as he was, on a cloud, between two clouds, with the real clouds rolling slowly past him, he was like a god being carried in his palanquin of flowers through the air; he could see his domain, all the College, Charles's house, the Farm, the new houses, the road to the river, and the river; and in the very distance, the Nikolides' chimney smoking against the sky.

"Welcome to my seat in heaven," he said. "Now you see how I spy on my students. It is truly heavenly. From up here I can see just how big they are — so small that they are not important at all. Down there they are sometimes so important that they blot out everything else. Then I come up here to readjust my eyes."

"And I have come to drag you down again," said Charles. "Monmatha, something very unpleasant has happened — "

"Not on Examination day," pleaded Sir Monmatha as he sat up and unfolded his legs. "What is it?"

Charles told him.

"Anil Krishna Banerjee?" said Sir Monmatha Ghose. "Yes, I know him. Yes, he might do it and he might just as easily not. It is impossible to predict. You are quite satisfied, of course, that he did not; but I do not think he can keep it to himself. He will make a fuss, undoubtedly, and they are ripe for trouble to-day. They will probably go on strike. Well, it has happened before." He sighed. "Troubles in College are not usually sexual ones, though the authorities make arrangements for all foods of mind and body except that." He looked at Charles and it struck him that Charles had singularly the look of a man who has been fed; he had lost a haggardness that he used to have, most noticeably for instance on that night when he had come to listen to the news. "You have heard the news?" said Sir

Monmatha. "I think Greece will be next. The Nikolides were going home to Athens for the winter. Now they are not going." He sighed again. "Yes, I am afraid it will make a stir. I am sorry, Charles."

"I am sorry too." Charles did not go on.

"Does the little girl know?"

"Not so far. I shall tell my wife to keep her in. I left them asleep."

"Das may be able to help. He can influence the boy. I shall be going down to the College, could you have a word with him?"

"I will go now. If we can stop it at the beginning . . ."

"The beginning." Sir Monmatha pointed down. "My dear Charles, it has begun!"

* * * When Anil woke for the last time he was sitting in his chair with his arms on the table and his head on his arms. This time he woke completely; he had a dry electric wakefulness and his throat refused to swallow. He took off his shirt and took his drinking cup and went outside; after a drink it was better and he washed out his throat and cleared it with noisy spittings.

"Who is it who makes such filthy noise?" He did not answer. The water had eased him and he splashed his face and chest and arms. It was beginning to be light; the darkness was raftered by light, but in between were mammoth wedges of blackness, and Anil had a sense of heaviness as if the darkness would never lift; but the birds knew that it was morning, they were beginning their earliest sounds in the trees and then, far over their heads, dropped from the minaret into the College grounds, came the first call of the Muezzin from the mosque in the bazaar. The lights were on in the Moslem Students' Hostel.

Anil splashed himself as if he would never finish in the cool water; he could feel his body burning through his soaked waistcloth. . . . I think I have some fever, he said.

As he went back along the verandah the daylight was growing; voices spoke to him, on the beds a white mosquito-net was lifted, a bolster thrown out, arms stretched; there were yawns, hawkings, spits over the verandah rail, laughter, the opening noises of the day. Anil was revived by the cold water, and as he passed among his friends, he began to smart with remembrance.

There was the tank, turning green in the growing light, the cool glimmer of water, the shadows, still liquid, of the trees. That was where he had sat with Emily and there was the slumbering outline of the house, and one after the other, smarting bitterly, came those moments, there in the porch, when Mrs. Pool had lacerated him. *Mrs. Pool. Mrs. Pool. Mrs. Pool.* Her name was repeated, hammering in his brain, throbbing with bitterness and injustice and wounded pride. *Mrs. Pool* — and soon it was running in a whisper down the colonnaded verandah of the Hostel.

The students gathered. They leaped from their beds, they came up from the privy, they left their washing. The whisper passed from tongue to tongue — *Mrs. Pool. Mrs. Pool. . . . Miss Pool. . . . Mrs. Pool.*

They all knew Emily and none of them admired her; they all admired Louise; that did not prevent them conveniently overlaying both with their own inventions: Louise was a hag, a siren, a malefactor; Anil could not see anything else but Mrs. Pool, Charles was blotted quite out of his mind and Emily was a figment who altered as he wished.

She grew and waned also according to the rumours that were now rushing about the College and changing in the same surprising manner. . . . Anil Krishna Banerjee had rescued the child Pool and Mrs. Pool had accused him . . . Anil had accused Mrs. Pool of cruelty and Mrs. Pool said she would flog him. . . . Mrs. Pool had flogged him. . . . Anil, who had rescued a little child from assault, was to be flogged and sent to prison and forbidden to sit for his Examination. . . . Mrs. Pool had hit Anil with a horsewhip. . . . Mrs. Pool had made improper advances to Anil. . . . Anil had made improper advances to Mrs. Pool. . . . Anil had made improper advances to Mrs. Pool and Charlie Chang had flogged them both — with a horsewhip. . . . Anil (but no one really believed this) had flogged Charlie Chang. . . . That monster, the girl Pool, had assaulted Anil. . . . Anil was to be expelled. . . .

They flew from mouth to mouth, and the quadrangles filled with students; groups of them gathered and surged round corners of the buildings, where on ledges or pediments other students harangued them; where one came down, another sprang up; Moslems joined with Hindus. The Superintendent of Anil's Hostel, attempting to telephone the Principal's house, had been bodily placed on his bed and advised to stay there; and one young Hindu, with cheers, climbed out along the first-floor balcony and cut the wires; only he cut the wires of the electric extension instead, and all the fans went off and it was necessary to cut the telephone cable on the inside, which might more prudently have been done in the first place.

The morning meal at the Hostel was carried round the square, and a procession started with it to the Principal's house. *We shall not eat injustice* — a banner was scrawled; there were other banners, — banners of the League, the Onward Movement, — and someone had made a straw figure and dressed it in a frock and given it long dangling legs and a head of straight jute hair. It was really not at all unlike Emily. They had garlanded Anil and put a white cap on his head and painted his forehead and he was in the middle of them, but before the procession could start a car was reported to be coming from the Principal's house.

The procession shrieked and swayed. "They are coming to arrest him!" And the shriek passed down its length: "Hide him. Hide him. Hide him."

Anil was passed from one set of hands to another, he was hustled and bundled and pushed, his cap was knocked off and the garlands pulled off his neck, until at last he reached the fringes of the crowd, where nobody knew who he was or why they were passing him along or what they were to do with him and they left him to pass himself; they were all pressing in the other direction, watching a party of students who were daringly preparing to surround and halt the car.

Anil found himself in Charles's mango grove at the back of the College; through it a path led to the river road. Anil stood there panting, leaning against a tree, his face against the bank. He felt very ill. . . . I have much fever. What is it? Perhaps it is tonsillitis. Perhaps it is diphtheria . . . But he had no pain in his throat, only the sensation of blockage, of swelling; it made him swallow nervously and continually, but he was frightened by a strange feeling in his head. He had had it all morning; for moments together he had no head at all, he had only a gap . . . I suppose where my neck is left . . . in which was a noise and a hot light . . . as if the sun had sat down in my eyes; but how could the sun sit in my eyes if my head is not there? . . . I am quite sensible, you see.

It was very quiet in among the young trees. The hubbub seemed to be moving away from him, there was no one now near the grove but one old woman picking dung off the road and putting it in her basket. The bark of the tree scratched Anil's forehead and he had one thing that seemed to him to need most urgent atention; his toe where he had knocked it on the stone last night was sore and swollen. . . . It is most dangerous, a swollen toe, thought Anil; I must have it seen to. . . . And then he remembered that this path led out towards the river. . . . Indro's house is by the river. Indro will put it right for me. I shall go and see Indro. . . .

He started limping down the path and presently he began to run, but every few moments he would stop and say, "Excuse me. I am not to be interrupted. I am going to see Indro."

* * * When Professor Dutt came down to assist at the Examination Hall he could not get in. The students were lying down in the road outside and on the steps.

He did not attempt to insist. He turned round and went home and put his umbrella away.

* * * Narayan's house was preparing for the *puja*. Each side of the door were fresh plantain trees standing in pitchers of Ganges water with green coconut; mango leaves were strung across the lintel. Tarala was busy with rituals of her own in the courtyard, but most of the work had to be done by Shila; there were many things that Tarala as a widow must not touch. Shila loved to do them; she had made the platter of ball-cakes, molasses rolled with coconut, that stood cooking near the window; she had folded innumerable betel leaves, and now she had chosen her best Benares sari to wind below the dais of the *Sree*. Now she went into the garden room where the materials were ready, and loosening the folds of her sari a little because she found it hard to kneel now, she went down upon her knees to make the *Sree*.

It was modelled of rice-flour and Ganges water and it needed clever fingers; she took a lump of the paste to knead in her hand and rolled it on her palm, round and round with the other, her thumbs held back; the movement grew into a rhythm, and the rhythm grew into a song and presently she began to sing.

The tuneless happy sound carried to Narayan in the study, and he began to draw it in shapes on his blotting paper. He was writing an account of what he had spent on *puja* presents and it was far too much, but as his pen went round and round his gloom left him and he tore the sheet out of his account book and threw it on the floor. Shila heard him and, taking it for impatience, stopped singing at once.

Narayan was sorry. Now he liked to hear Shila in the house; he liked the feeling of festivity. Here, on the river, the morning had signs of the cold weather, there had been mist on the river, and mist in the dew. Already, before the *pujas* had come, the wind said, "After the *pujas* are over — after the *pujas* are over we shall start again. . . . After the *pujas* my son will be born — " and he was intensely and superstitiously glad, in spite of his extra expenses, that he had given that money to Shila to spend.

Attending a dog at my house . . . (Destroying a dog at my house.)

Until that day I worked to save life, never to destroy. My cases have died, but that was in spite of me — not because of me. . . . What a fuss! What a fuss to make about a dog when men were dying, men and women and children, crushed from existence, hundreds at a time. . . . But it is the same — even if it is one dog and a hundred men. It is *against,* not for; it is *counter* — an offence against life. By my guilt I have laid more guilt upon mankind overlaid with guilt already; and this, when each one of us should be a rock against evil. Each of us — soldier, sailor, tinker, thief, black man, white man, nigger-boy, Chink. . . . I have done violence, and the stain is deepened because of me . . . And he passed to the thought of himself (and he cried, "Don't let it bring bad luck!" and he shut his eyes and prayed from the bottom of his heart).

He opened his eyes; and as if he had been dropped from the ceiling, there was Anil in his room.

"Anil . . . you!"

"Indro — give me some water. Some water, Indro, please."

He was terribly out of breath, gasping painfully, with sweat running down from his neck from his hair, in which were caught a few dishevelled jasmine flowers; his shirt was torn across the shoulder, but it was his face that most startled Narayan; under its dust and sweat, and the vermilion that had run from the mark on his forehead, was a look of the wildest excitement that Narayan had ever seen, his nostrils and his eyes were dilated and his eyeballs were red, bloodshot.

"Anil — are you very ill?" Anil shook his head, too out of breath to speak. "Where have you been? What has happened?" A suspicion crossed his mind. "Are you drunk?"

"Water. Water, please."

On the desk was the tray that Shila always put ready with water and a dish of nuts; he poured out water and Anil drank in gulps, but Narayan was looking at the clock. "Anil, look at the time. What in the world has happened? Look at the time."

Anil wiped his face in his sleeve and spat, clearing his throat. He did not go outside but spat untidily on the floor, and sat looking dully at the stain.

"What — time? Why?"

"The Examination. Have you forgotten the Examination?"

Anil lifted his head and the excitement came back into his eyes. "That is exactly what I came here to tell you. I remember now. There will be no Examination held to-day."

"Why? For God — why?"

"We are on strike," said Anil and he said it with a kind of primness that had such pride and wanton mischief behind it that Narayan cried out: "You are behind this — you!"

"Yes. It is all because of me."

"You fool. You worse than fool. What has possessed you? You have everything and then you throw it away. Why have you done this, you fool boy?"

"Wait till you hear the reason."

"I don't care for the reason."

"Listen. Listen." His voice was uneven, high

with excitement, then husky. "Indro — last night I was out — I came in late — and — "

"And? And? Go on then."

"I met — one of Charlie Chang's daughters."

" —— ?" said Narayan.

"No. I tell you it is not what you think," cried Anil violently.

"Then why is the trouble . . . ?"

"Wait. Listen." He became rhetorical. "She was a child. She wept. I comforted her."

"How comforted her?"

That put Anil out of his flow. He said uncertainly, "I — don't remember."

"Did you touch her?"

"And what if I did? I am not poison, am I?"

"How old was she?" Anil was picking at the nuts, shelling them and throwing them on the floor. "Big? Little? Perhaps thirteen?"

"Perhaps, but listen, Indro — "

"Why was she out?" Narayan demanded angrily. "What were they doing to let her out alone?"

"She was searching for her dog." Narayan flinched, but Anil said, puzzled, "And yet I think she said her dog was dead; then why was she searching for it? It hurts in my head if I have to think of these things. Don't ask me questions. Listen, Indro — "

"Tell me what is true. Tell me what really has happened."

"But listen, but listen." Anil could not remember in the least what had happened. He could only repeat what they had shouted in the College, what now they said he said had happened. "I comforted this frightened child, so small and so afraid. I took her in and then — the woman, Mrs. Pool, abused me — in a most beastly fashion. She insulted me. She is my worst enemy. I brought the child to her. She would not listen. I was not permitted to explain — her husband came — he threatened me —"

"Is all this true?" Narayan was dazed.

"True? They came to arrest me. I am to be flogged. Incarcerated."

"This is disgraceful." Narayan was catching fire.

"Think of my father and my name. I am ruined —"

"But who — who has done this to you? The Principal? The Police? Mr. Pool? He has not the power, I think. Has he lodged information about you? Whose orders are these? Who gave them?"

Anil's excitement snapped, his voice dropped to an odd dull languor as if he could hardly speak. "No one."

"No one? *No one!* Then why, for God, have you done all this?"

"I don't know."

Narayan stared at him in amazed silence. Anil's eyes were shut, his hands were round his throat, his lips fixed open, and between them a bright round bubble of saliva winked in the light like a third eye come from the inside of Anil to look at him while his eyes were shut; it trembled and exploded, leaving a smear of spittle on his chin. "Why are you in this state?" cried Narayan.

Then the gate closed with a wooden thud and someone came down the path to the door. Anil sat up with open eyes. Facing them at the bottom of the steps was Emily.

Her sudden apparition seemed to surprise her as much as themselves. She had come to see this Dr. Das; she was forbidden to go out alone but she did not think it mattered now what she did. She had been waiting outside trying to make up her mind to go in and at last she had precipitated herself in at the gate. Now her entry disconcerted her as much as it disconcerted them and they stared at one another in surprised silence. Then — "This is the girl," said Narayan in vernacular. He said it as a fact, not as a question, and Anil nodded, staring at Emily.

It was obvious that she did not recognize him. Anil's heart gave a pang. . . . I thought she was pretty — how ugly she is! At least he wanted her to be pretty and he could see from Narayan's face that to him she looked ugly too: tall and lanky, all knees and elbows, and her hair was no colour and her white face glistened with sweat. Where was his graceful little ghost? She had been small, light-boned in his arms. Now he barked at this gawky stranger: "Why do you come here? What do you want?"

She opened her lips. They were dry and for a moment nothing came through them. Then she said, "I want to see Dr. Das." Her voice was the same, with the same clear, slightly imperious bell-like tone, a way in which no Indian girl would ever speak; the voice that had told him at once she was English in the darkness by the tank. In spite of himself he softened. "Mr. Das? There he is."

"Oh no! Oh no! No!" said Narayan unexpectedly; he had retreated behind his desk.

"Come in," said Anil to Emily.

"In — my shoes?" asked Emily. She had never been in an Indian house before.

"Certainly," said Anil rudely. "Mr. Das is Westernized. He does not mind what dirt you bring into his house."

Neither Narayan nor Emily heard his rudeness. Emily came in gingerly as if she were treading on unfamiliar ground and Narayan watched her helplessly. She came straight up to his desk and said seriously to him, "I want to ask you a question, Dr. Das."

"Not just now. Not just now," said Narayan. "You must excuse me. I have no time to answer now, Miss Pool."

"It won't take you a minute."

Her eyes examined him with a child's particular searching-out gaze, quite unabashed; her eyes were some years younger than her voice and he looked back into their foreign green-flecked clearness and the feeling of wrong and shame came up in him so that he said as if she had spoken, "I am sorry."

"Dr. Das, my mother's Pekingese have been coming to you here for injections?"

The question moved his attention from her eyes to her.

"What disease did you inject them for?"

"Hydrophobia." She looked puzzled and he said, jocose in his nervousness, "You don't know what that is, I bet you."

"No."

"Hydrophobia. That is rabies. That is madness."

The eyes flinched, then they came back to him more searchingly than ever. "Were they mad?"

"No, no. It was prevention — against the bite of mad dog."

"Had they been bitten by a mad dog?"

"No. I do not think so."

"Then why did you inject them?"

"Your mother asked for it."

"My mother." Again Anil heard the edge to that; even now he was sensitive to her.

"Dr. Das, you came to our house the day — that my dog died."

Narayan answered carefully, "Yes, I did."

"Did you — bandage up his wounds?"

"He had no wounds."

"No wounds!" In her surprise the word hung on her lips.

"It did not hurt him," said Narayan. "It was all over in a matter of seconds."

"As quick as that?" Her voice was incredulous.

"Yes. I tell you, he did not feel anything at all."

"Then — why did he die?"

Narayan stopped and looked at her. "Don't you know?"

"They told me he died in a fight."

"And what did you think?"

"After you said hydrophobia, I thought he died in a fight with a mad dog."

"Perhaps, in a way, he did."

"What do you mean?"

"Well you see," said Narayan slowly, and he picked up a pencil and tapped it so that he need not look at her eyes, "we had to put him down, put him to sleep, because we were afraid that he had been so bitten."

"Had he?"

"He . showed certain signs. Your mother thought — "

"Did you think so?"

"I don't know. Still, I do not know. She would not wait for proof . . . proof," said Narayan, and once more something was ringing in his mind, pressing to be remembered. He grew angry. "No one can tell what the outcome of this will be, but there has been nothing but trouble and loss. Your mother gave no time for reason or sense. . . ." He grew angrier. "Your mother is very difficult and headstrong. You should ask her to answer you for this — "

Emily was still and into her face came an expression of shock and with it of triumph. "Mother!" she said in a long whisper. "Mother!" She remembered her manners. "Thank you," she said to Narayan, "I think I will go home now," but Narayan was looking over her head at someone behind her.

"May I come in?" said Charles.

The whole of Anil's body gave a quick nervous start. He glared at Charles; he stood on the edge of the verandah, clenching and unclenching his hands.

"Good morning, Das. . . . Good morning," said Charles to Anil.

"Really, really," said Anil offensively, "it seems, Indro, that your house is to be turned into a rendez-vous of Pools."

Charles's hand came inside Emily's arm — "I

came to see you, Das. I did not know that Emily was here."

"So you take no better care of her than formerly," said Anil.

Charles propelled Emily away. "Wait for me in the garden." And he said, "You are not to go home without me." Emily had not even heard him. He ignored Anil and said, "Das, I have come from Sir Monmatha Ghose — to speak to you."

Narayan was trembling, but he stood up with his hands on the desk; it was easier to stand up to Charles if he had his hands steady. "I also would like to speak to you. Most shocking things are reported to me, Mr. Pool. A most shocking thing has been said to this boy." His voice, now that he had achieved it, was over-blustering.

"And you have believed everything he told you?"

"Unfortunately it is only too likely," said Narayan bitterly. "I too have had experience of Mrs. Pool. Because he was Indian the worst suspicion came into her mind. Without waiting, he is convicted — "

"He is not convicted." Charles was sharp.

"This may very well go to law," said Narayan, taking refuge in a side issue. "There is libel. There is defamation — "

"Don't be absurd. You let this boy run away with you, Das. I have come to you — "

"You thought that I should help against my friend? You thought that I should hush him up?" Narayan was now truly run away. "Or did you track up your own daughter who came following him here?"

"You are not to speak to me like that — "

Narayan buried his face in his hands. It was not in this way that he had meant Charles to come. Everything was loud, noisy, rude and untidy; the room was a litter of nutshells and stains where Anil had spat. He cried, "It is horrible. Horrible."

"It has been made so," said Charles. "The College is in an uproar. Four students are under arrest — I had hoped — " He asked wearily, wonderingly, "How did it have to grow into this?" And he asked Anil, "Why couldn't you keep your promise?"

But all this while Anil had been struggling, searching, struggling to find his head. It was necessary for him to find it because he could not breathe without it; the noise of the pain in the gap took all breath; there was hurt in the noise now, agony that blinded him. He screamed.

"My God! What is the matter with him?"

They caught him and held him between them. He felt their hands, gripping him in every place and doing nothing to help his head. He tore away from them, beating at his throat with his hands, screaming without a sound coming from his lips. How could there be a sound? He had no lips —

because he had no head. . . . They were there. With a rush of air into his throat, his head was back again. He lay sucking in air, and his lips were wet — and curiously stiff.

"*Anil.*" Narayan was bending over him and he said to someone behind him, "Water." A hand passed a glass of water and with those odd, stiff-feeling lips Anil drank. "That is better." Narayan's face was anxiously looking into his. "Anil, can you speak to me? Have you pain? Where is trouble? Tell."

Anil wanted to tell. He wanted to complain of his head that had come back to him with those strange lips, of his mouth that felt so stiff, and of his throat, and the noise, and the pain in the noise, but all he could do with his mouth that would not move properly was to croak, "My toe. My toe is swollen."

"Your *toe?*" But Narayan went down on one knee to examine it; though he tweaked it and pulled it Anil did not feel it and he cried again querulously, "My toe."

"Nothing is the matter here except the toe is bruised." Narayan examined the foot and the ankle and then he saw at the side of the shin a small pale scar. He saw it; he looked at it; at Anil; back to it. His face changed, into a dreadful silent stare. He had remembered.

Chapter XII

EMILY, sent away by Charles, went round the corner of the house. The sun striking off the river blinded her; she stood still, holding on to the plaster, and the red hurting glare of her eyes exactly suited her. She was angry; angry with a good right anger; it was in her legs and in her face and stomach and hot in her heart, but it would not overflow until she meant it to overflow. She was compact with rage, dangerous, ready. . . . I am coming, Mother. I have found out everything I wanted to know. This time you are going down to me, not I to you. I am up. I am right. There is no mystery left. All of it has been cleared away from you. I see you, Louise. I see you exactly as you are. You are larger than I am and powerful, but you cannot crush me now. . . .

This garden was beginning to be adjusted to her eyes. She saw it as a small sunbaked spot, bright with green and a few brilliant heads of marigold against the white sandy soil; and in front of it was the river, a shimmering width of brightness. She liked it. She liked the way the garden was shut in on three sides and open to the river on the fourth, she liked to stand there hidden, not tall enough to see over the walls, and see the sweep of the river and the plain and the huge domed shape of sky. . . . It matches me; the hot sun matches me, and the water running past. I am hot and I am strong and I can see a great way. I see what I could not see before. I shall call you names Mother, I shall call you a cheat because you cheated me and a liar because you lied and a coward because you were afraid to tell me the truth, and I shall call you a murderess because you murdered Don. You killed him. You, not Dr. Das. I know how you made him do it. I know only too well. I hate Dr. Das but I do not blame him Mother, I blame you. I don't care who takes your part. I shall never have anything to do with you again. You can take Charles and you can take Binnie. I prefer to be by myself. . . . And all at once there was a crack in her anger and desolation seeped through. Hastily she closed it again. . . . Don't let my anger go. Emily, stay as angry as this till you get home. Stay as angry as this.

Don was once alive. He felt the sun on his back; his legs, if he sat down for a moment, were up at once to run again. He liked gardens and sun and grass and sticks and leaves; he used to play with them; now all these things are still because he is not here. He loved other things too — cool floors to lie on, his own bed; best of all, food; second best, toys. I don't know which were his balls because the Pekingese have taken them; I let them take them, a ball is a silly thing alone. I shall not cry; I only feel like crying because I have been tired. Now I am not tired any longer. It is nearly over and I am coming, Mother. I am coming now. I shall come straight to you and I shall say, "Mother, I know all about it now. Liar. Cheat. Coward. *Murderer*." That is what I shall say, "Liar. Cheat. Coward. Murderer." Now, whenever I need to say Mother I shall say one of these. . . .

She was turning to go when she looked in at a door near her. She had been standing near the doorway of a room, built into the house, and in spite of her hurry, once she had looked in Emily stayed there. There was nothing in the room but a young Indian woman making a little white image on a stand. It was like the clay images Emily saw nowadays in the bazaar, of a Goddess with a crown and ten arms, but this particular Goddess had four.

Emily had seen this phenomenon too often to be very astounded. From her own bed at night she could hear the sound of four religions, the bell from the Mission Church, the muezzin calling from the mosque, the gongs that were rung by the nomad Buddhist priests, and the tom-tom and cymbals and bell from the temple. Charles said, from the *Gita, "Howsoever men approach me, so do I accept them; for on all sides the path they choose leads them to me."* Emily liked that. It made God sound big.

Shila had finished the figure; it was both delicate and firm and she was pleased; now she had made the rest of her rice-flour more liquid and was decorating the stand with patterns. With nothing to guide it the pattern came quickly and Emily watched her fascinated; neither of them heard Anil's scream. Emily's eyes followed Shila's hand and, as if there were something soothing in those even loops and circles, she grew quieter. She was more comfortably angry. She leaned against the doorpost and asked, "How does your hand know where to go?"

Shila did nothing so jerky as to start; she pressed her fingers together so that the flow of liquid stopped and looked up with surprise in her eyes. To look from the dark room to the garden was a little dazzling and she could see only the black outline of Emily, but like Anil she knew from her voice that she was English and she answered in English though Emily had attempted the vernacular, "What did you say?"

Now Emily was surprised. Shila's English was

not clipped like Anil's or Narayan's, she gave her words a musical lilt. "What did you say?"

"How do you know the pattern?"

"I know it. My mother knew it and her mother. Even my mother's mother's mother," and she knelt up a little. Emily saw at once that she was going to have a baby.

"If you have a daughter she will know them too," said Emily.

"One day I shall have a daughter. First I shall have a son," said Shila quite positively and she ended her pattern. Then her eyes came back to Emily. "How did you come here?"

"I am sorry. Do you mind?"

"Not at all, but how did it happen?"

Emily evaded that. "My father is talking to Dr. Das."

"My husband?"

"Is he your husband?" Emily saw Narayan in his European coat and trousers, with his desk, his book-cases and his charts, and then this empty room and Shila on the floor, in her single cotton sari that left her arms and part of her back bare. At her face, Shila laughed. "You have come to the back of the house, you see. Here we are domestic in the Indian way. Won't you come in?"

Emily asked again, "Oughtn't I to take off my shoes? Your husband said he did not mind, but — "

"You are nice," Shila said softly, "but you need

not. Often my husband comes in, even into the kitchen, with his shoes."

"But you would like him to take them off," said the shrewd Emily.

"In this part of the house, yes."

"I will stay here," said Emily, and then she remembered. "At least, I have to go." Still she stayed. "What are you making her for?"

"It is our *Sree*. It means grace, and as that is an attribute of our Goddess Lakshmi, we make an emblem of her. We will offer her flowers, and fruit and rice, all through our holy days." She smiled at Emily. "She is the Goddess of Good Fortune."

"I am glad I have seen her," said Emily gravely, "I am glad I have seen how you do it," and she hesitated and asked, "Do you think — an English girl could make a *puja*?"

"Anyone can — if they believe in it."

"I should believe," said Emily, "but there is something I have to do first." And she said goodbye and turned to go home.

* * * The procession had been round the town. It went to the Principal's house to make a demonstration, but when it arrived there was no one to see it; the Principal had left for the College in his car and Lady Ghose was in Darjeeling. Someone suggested they should throw stones, but it was no part of their programme to be undignified and the procession returned through the bazaar. Here among the lanes and side-roads it was forced to split up and many little processions went wandering off by themselves and remained lost for the rest of the day.

The staff and Sir Monmatha Ghose were in conference in the College Hall, where all was prepared for the examination of the B. Ag. candidates. There was something reproachful in the rows of small tables, each with its pile of foolscap, a piece of pink blotting paper, a clean pen and inkwell and an empty chair; along the aisles between them, where the monitor should have paced with a watchful eye, messengers scurried up and down; outside the windows the students were singing.

They had been singing for a long time; the conference had been in session for a long time. No one knew what to do next. There was a hitch.

"We will return to work if you reinstate Anil Krishna Banerjee."

"But he has never been dispossessed."

"Has he not? Has he not? He is imprisoned at this moment."

"You have hidden him yourselves."

"That is a lie — a lie to cover your actions."

"Listen to me — "

"Until you release him we shall listen to no one — to nothing."

"I tell you, we have not got him."

"And neither have we — where then is he? Is he thin air?"

* * * It was quite a long way from the Das house to the College and Emily wanted to get in before Charles, and Charles was riding; she had seen Delilah held by a boy in the road. It was very hot, even though the road was planted all the way with trees, and the people she passed turned round to look at her curiously. She began rather to wish she had not come out alone.

Charles was a long time talking to Dr. Das; Emily was certain she had made slow progress though she hurried; every moment she expected to hear Delilah on the road behind her; but there was no sign of Charles as she came within sight of the College.

Then she gave a little hiss of dismay and annoyance. She had come up with the tail end of a procession that was filing in through the College gates, completely blocking the road. She could see a press of people — students, she thought from their white-clad shoulders — and she could hear a hubbub and shouts and the beating of a tom-tom, and far ahead she could see a figure, a stuffed doll on a pole swinging above the heads of the crowd. . . . What are they doing now? groaned Emily. She tried to edge her way through. It was impossible. The people were pressing against the gate, trying to push their way through.

Here in the vanguard, Emily was among the beggars who had clustered round the College gates; they hopped on sticks or were dragged in wooden boxes on wooden wheels, or pulled themselves along on one another's shoulders; there were armless ones, and legless ones; one with no nose, one with his teeth growing through his cheek; they ran with sores, and from their rags came a putrid old dead smell; and Emily, shuddering and sick, hurled herself away from them into the crowd.

Now she was forced to go with it; step by step, she found herself walking in her own procession though she had no idea whose effigy it was that swung from the pole ahead. The crowd were shouting on all sides of her but she had no idea what they said. She walked, trying to move sideways as she advanced, to reach the farther edges of the crowd by her own gate; she was banged and pushed, flung sideways, in the press of taller people; they could not see her face, hidden by her sunhat, or realize her difference. The crowd smelled almost as badly as the beggars; a stale smell of sweat, another almost lavatory smell, and mixed with it a sweetness that was like flowers and scented oil; she was astonished that she did not mind it more though the heat was unbearable. She pushed and pushed until the people thinned and she reached the farther side.

She knocked against a woman who carried a water-jar on her hip and the water spilled over and the woman turned to look. She looked at Emily's face, and for a moment she did not take it in, then she shrieked a stream of vernacular and caught Emily by the arm. She was immediately ringed with people, but before they could touch her Shah was there.

He had no more authority than his uniform and a pair of boots could give him, but the ring broke. Shah seized Emily and dragged her to the gate. The moment his back was turned his temporary prestige was over and he had just time to pull Emily inside and shut the gate, on which excited hands began to batter and pound.

Emily did not in the least understand what had happened. She smoothed herself down. "Why did you touch me? What made you do a thing like that?" she said severely. "It was only a procession. I shall report you to the Sahib." Deeply affronted, she walked up the drive to find Louise.

The crowd began to pelt the gate with stones. Someone threw a brick. Then a police sergeant swept round the corner on a motor bicycle and there was immediately a miraculously cleared space along the road. Shah opened the gate.

"Have you a *lathee?*" the sergeant asked. "You can use it if necessary."

Shah smiled and spat on his hands.

* * * Louise was not in her room; she was in the drawing-room, sitting at the piano, but she was not playing. She was pressing the notes thoughtfully down with one finger and letting them spring up again. Binnie was looking from the window at the massed students in the College grounds.

Louise did not appear to hear them, or Binnie who was reporting everything they did; she just touched the notes softly and let them spring up again, and there was a small new smile at the corners of her lips.

It was extraordinary how loud those quiet notes sounded after the hubbub and the heat that Emily had been through; they came winging across the room to her and each one was like a very clear, round full-stop.

Emily stood outside and looked into the room; Louise looked up and saw her and she stayed, her finger holding down a note, and while the sound of the note went on nobody moved. Emily stood outside; she saw the room, she saw Louise, and it was a clear completed picture. Everything was in it; the sky was in it, reflected on the walls of the room, held in light between the windows; the shadows of the trees fell across them in clear green patches, moving and fretting; there was noise in it, sustained with the vibration of the note — distant shouts and cries and singing; there was dust rising in the light of a sunbeam; simplicity in the exposed backs of Binnie's thighs as she stood on tiptoe to see; there was sleep in the sleeping shapes of the Pekingese, curled head to tail on the rug, and business in the wings of a bee searching with her honey-bags in the flowers; the honey was food and drink; and there were colours wherever Emily's eyes rested. All the colours, and thoughts and shapes and sizes — everything was in the room; and what had happened to Louise?

Louise was suddenly quite small.

Even when she let the note go and stood up, she did not seem so large to Emily, and as Emily went across the room to her she said, "Emily, how tall you are! How tall you are getting," said Louise. She stepped back from Emily against the piano.

"Did you go out with Charles?" sang Binnie without turning her head. "When we woke up both of you were gone. What *is* happening, Emily? Is it what they call a riot?"

Louise did not ask any questions. She seemed to accept the fact that she and Emily were now and henceforth different. She said, "Emily, I shouldn't have hit you last night." She said it in an unaccustomed way, stiffly and politely, but with a quietude that Emily had not heard before. Louise was new. "I am sorry," said Louise.

"It doesn't matter," said Emily. It did not matter. She had touched extremity in the night. Charles had shut the door and she was left alone. Now she was Emily — Emily alone — Emily walking by herself. No, decidedly it did not matter now. She said quite softly, "I know — what you did to Don."

For a long time Louise did not answer. Then, "He is dead," said Louise. "It's no good wishing."

"He is dead," agreed Emily.

"Will you kiss me, Emily?"

. . . Kiss you or not kiss you, it does not matter now. I am Emily who walks by herself. . . . For a moment she had a sense of being cheated; it was her victory and it had flagged, it had brought her nothing — only Emily who was to be alone. As she said that, she was conscious of a new feeling — like stretching, as if she had the power to stretch herself out and touch, with her finger-tips, the sides of a new world. There was no limit to this power — what was it? It was freedom; and though it was a little giddy, headlong in its possibilities of loneliness, there was strength and satisfaction in it. . . . I was right to have fought, said Emily, I was right. . . . A sigh that she could not escape from rose to her lips, but even as she sighed she was saying *I am free*, and she kissed Louise.

"It isn't finished yet," cried Binnie from the window. "They are all shouting. Listen. They are starting again."

* * * It was past noon when a rumour began to circulate that Anil was not in jail, not captive in the Principal's house, not hidden in the Police Quarters or in the Hostel: he was in hospital. Before this had time to grow or change it was confirmed.

Sir Monmatha Ghose came out on the balcony of the hall and asked the students to disperse as Anil Krishna Banerjee was ill. There was a momentary effect, they were stilled, hundreds of dark faces and heads turned up on a sea of white towards the balcony; but before he could go on, one cried, "How — ill?" — another, more boldly, "He was not ill!" — and a babel broke out, "What have you done to him? What have you done?"

Sir Monmatha held up his hand, he shouted, and his words were tossed back to him on whistles and cat-calls. He went inside. "Sir, why not send for the Police?"

"I shall not have the Police in my College," he said. "Presently they will hear reason."

They showed no sign of it. The insane ugly noise went on. Then there was an ebb. Another rumour was filtering through the crowd, more than agitating it; a pall of perplexity and doubt hung over it. . . . Anil was not ill. Not ill? No. He had been stricken dumb.

It came from an orderly in the Hospital itself, who had seen Anil. Small inside hairs of superstition lifted in every student's head. Dumb! It spread through the bazaar, gaining heat as it ran; but another came to meet it, and this came from Tarala, who also had seen Anil; Tarala said that he was visited, speaking in every extraordinary tongue with demons' voices. The two rumours became tangled and for ever, in Amorra, there persisted a tale of a dumb boy who in trances spoke with the voice of God.

The students poured out of the College to the Hospital. The little hospital at Amorra stood in waste ground, railed off with neat railings on a knoll and shaded with trees. It looked innocent and unprotected as they marched down on it, and there at the railings was Charles Pool.

There was a minute of intense stillness and then a shout of anger went up from everyone; some could not remember now what exactly Charlie Chang had to do with this, but they shouted with the rest. Their cries rolled forward as they surged towards the Hospital. "We — want — Banerjee. We — want — Anil — Banerjee — Where — is — Banerjee? We — want — Anil."

Charles stood perfectly still behind the railings, two small spick-and-span white ones that reached to his waist; and because of the knoll and his height, he seemed very high to the oncoming students; the sun struck flashes of light from his monocle into their eyes as if, now that Anil was smitten dumb, he would smite them blind. They were moving, he was still; they were shouting, he was quiet; but the power had changed from them to him. He took out his monocle and the students in front stopped as if their feet had gone into the ground.

It was the first time any of them had seen him without it; they had always looked at the glass in his eye, never at his face. Now, suddenly, he emerged before them, a Charles they had never seen. He looked at them with tired naked eyes, and they felt his look pitiful and stern as if he had something to tell them that was grim and sad.

The front ranks had stopped and stood waiting perfectly silent, but those at the back, who were not near enough to see him, booed and called and whistled. "Pits! Pits! Pits!" they cried. "Where is your beastly daughter, Charlie?" And rising into a clamour, "We want — Anil Banerjee. We — want — Anil."

They pushed themselves against that immovable front line until it could hold no longer and broke and was swept forward against Charles. Legs and thighs and stomachs were bruised and crushed against the railings; some were trodden upon, some thrown over; there were screams and shrieks of pain; and tumult broke, those in front trying to push back and those at the back pushing insanely on, still with their shout, "We — want — Anil — Banerjee. Anil — Banerjee!"

Charles's head and shoulders were still above the crowd; he could still be seen, the figurehead of the turmoil, with a space behind him; the railings had not given — yet; and suddenly, he filled his lungs and with all the measure of his enormous voice he bellowed "Hush!"

They were quiet from sheer surprise. It was an extraordinary word to use to a mob, an extraordinary word to bellow in that shattering voice, — a child's word in a tumult, — but it was right. There was an instant stillness as if even the wind had been put out; they waited and into that hush climbed not Charles, not authority, but the young veterinary surgeon, Dr. Narayan Das.

He was Anil's friend, and the sight of him brought more silence and surprise. He climbed up on the railings, hiding Charlie Chang who was supporting him, and there was a look on his face of such woe that a murmur broke out again. "Speak to them. Speak to them quickly — Indro," said Charles.

Narayan's lips trembled; the whole of his body, his feet balanced on the thin rail, his hands on Charles's shoulder, trembled; he quivered from head to foot. He saw the crowd as Sir Monmatha

Ghose had seen it: the young black heads, the faces, hundreds it seemed to him, on white shoulders, turned to him; only he was not much above them, he was close to them; close; and his lips suddenly opened, and his heart, with all his grief, and his reproach, and his anger and his love; and what did he say?

His voice sounded very large to him; the whole of him was in it, it seemed to break the sky and come back to him, but it sounded very little to the students after Charles's — little but very clear. It reached even to their outskirts. They all heard it. "You — must — be — quiet," said the little voice, "Anil — is — dead."

Chapter XIII

THE HOLIDAYS were over, the queer exotic *puja* fortnight was gone, with the things of which it held so many in its span. It was like Emily's room, everything was in it, but now it was gone; only, washed up by the river on the banks and round the *ghats,* were small fragmentary remains, the straw inside body of the Goddess when the clay had washed away, pieces of coloured paper, flowers like a farewell garland on the water.

The strange light nights were over, when villagers, who went to bed soon after the sun, stayed up and visited from village to village, when their songs could be heard going home across the fields in the dawn; the bazaar had sunk back into its customary clamour: there were no more processions of students or of *pujas* in its streets.

The College was shut and Sir Monmatha Ghose spent his mornings and his evenings on his roof. In the College life a seal had been quite firmly and immediately pressed on the break in it where Anil had been; "There can be no break in the continuity of our lives," said Sir Monmatha Ghose, "we must not make it so." The students had gone into the Examination Hall next day. There had been no demonstrations.

Anil's brother and the family priest had come on the train. They had taken his body to the river for burning, bound on a narrow litter that was decorated with cloth and green leaves and flowers. He lay with a white cloth up to his chin, his face turned sideways into his necklace of flowers, the red mark of sandalwood, which he had worn so often in life, on his forehead; and presently his friends came and carried him away.

Narayan was not asked to be present at the funeral rites, neither the brother nor the priest would have allowed his presence there, but after they had gone Narayan asked permission to go to Anil's room and it was opened for him.

"I think I can do that for you," said the Superintendent. "Besides," he added, "there is nothing of value there."

Narayan found the poems in an old exercise book among the papers on the table. He took them and hid them under his coat. He was ready to go when he turned and looked round the small room. It was just as Anil had left it, no servant had been in to clean and tidy it; the bed was still creased where Anil had lain and tossed, his *lota* was still half full of water, on the floor lay a dirty crumpled shirt. With suddenly blinded eyes Narayan bent down to pick it up.

Something rustled in the pocket as he turned it right side out; he pulled out a piece of paper, dirty but carefully smoothed and covered with a few distinct lines. It was another poem.

It was more than another poem. As Narayan read it, Anil was not on his pyre by the river; it did not matter where he was, he had not died. After a while Narayan folded it and carried it away with the others.

"The brother would not have known what they were," he said to Charles. He copied them carefully and sent them to Sir Monmatha Ghose. . . . He had come, this evening, to hear his opinion. Like Charles, he was shown up on the roof.

There was one more feast that had not come into the larger *pujas* — the Kali *puja,* Diwali, the Feast of Lights. Already, as Narayan bicycled through the streets, there were signs of it in the town; now, as he waited anxiously for the Principal's verdict, first one light, then another, came out like pinpricks, and a firework sizzled into the blue.

"You are as high as the rockets here. It is barely dusk and they are out already."

"They are a little previous — like these poems," said Sir Monmatha.

"You mean they are no good?" Narayan was stung with bitter disappointment.

"On the contrary, they are very good indeed. What a pity he could not have waited longer! But there is one — "

"I found that in his pocket, after he was dead," said Narayan. "It seemed very much alive."

"It is," said Sir Monmatha, and he promised to see that they were published, in a book after Anil's heart, printed and published in India on Indian paper, bound in *khuddar*, with a hand-made Indian design. "Naturally, if his father permits," said Sir Monmatha.

Narayan had written to Anil's father already but he had had no answer. At first he had been offended, then grieved, then glad; Anil's death belonged to that period of violence in which he had been caught, that he perhaps had caused. He and Charles had not left Anil, and the horror and the helplessness of those struggles would be on him all his life; but it was over. Over. Anil's father had receded into a little figure away over countless fields and peasant huts and sunset skies. Now something much more interesting was to happen; something that would not stop for grief; that would, in its mysterious fashion, balance grief. He could not at present think too much about Anil. At the moment he was thinking of a row of houses, far too tall and close together, in a street of noise and garbage smells; and he looked down from Sir Monmatha Ghose's roof, and far away, over the lights, he could see his little house set down beside the river; and as he looked he saw a line of lights, tiny as beads, break out there too, along his wall.

"I must go home," he said.

"How is your wife? She keeps well, I hope."

"Very well."

"Are you so modern that you will be disappointed if it is a son?"

Narayan had nowadays a quick friendly smile. "I shall not be disappointed," said Narayan.

On the way home, in the Farm road, he met the Pools; winter work had started on the Farm, ploughing and planting for sugar-cane and wheat, the pulses and mustard were planted already, and the rice was growing high. Charles was out early and late, and here he was, walking down the road with Mrs. Pool. Narayan heard their voices before he saw them in the dusk and he stiffened; he still could not forgive Mrs. Pool. His guilt went beyond him into her and he could not wipe this last trace of violence from his mind. . . . That is the meaning of religion now to me — non-violence — to be completely without violence to any. . . . Still he could not accomplish it with Mrs. Pool. He passed them without stopping, with a bow of his head that was too quick and clumsy and came only from his neck.

Charles smiled at him and Mrs. Pool opened her lips; they just parted and closed again, it was not even a smile, and she tilted her chin. . . . She is not altogether changed either, said Narayan, and that cheered him and gave him an affinity with Louise that he had not dreamed of. He looked back at her; yes, she had the same ridiculous elegance, for walking on the deserted Farm road: a light full-skirted dress, a parasol; she was leaning on Charles's arm and before them Binnie danced backwards, speaking to them and walking at the same time. Charles lifted his hand in salutation. They and Narayan passed on down the road.

* * * Where was Emily? Emily was in the deserted College garden by the tank, and she had a small decorated table on which was laid a saucer-light burning in butter, some rice, a collar of flowers, and a paper ball.

She had made it of paper because she did not want anything of her *puja* to be discovered. This was her last secret; and her table was the lid of a cardboard box and she had decided to put it on the water where presently the cardboard would soften and sink and carry everything away; if the flowers floated they would not be noticed. There was *puja* in the air.

Now, in the last light, she placed her table on the water and pushed it out from the steps. With its little flame reflected in the dark water, it eddied round and round, gently blowing across to the shades beyond; but however hard Emily looked there was nothing there.

The student boy had said that. *And if you offer for one you offer for all. . . .* I wonder what has happened to him, said Emily; but of course all the students have gone home.

A rocket leapt into the sky close beside the wall and curved over her head into blue and red stars. There would be nearly as many lights on earth to-night as there were in the sky.

Emily's burned steadily as it floated away.

THE END

FIELDS OF BATTLE

Kate Alexander

In the romantic tradition of THE FLOWERS OF THE FIELD, an irresistible new novel of conflict and heartbreak, love and loss.

Rilla Grey would never have met Barney Wainwright if the outbreak of war in September 1939 hadn't seen him posted to her home town. Ill-matched in background and worldiness, Rilla is dazzled by the attractive, young officer until a hasty marriage based on necessity ends a charming interlude. Neither is prepared for the ravages of war, the equally intense battlefield of their fateful marriage nor the gnawing loneliness of long separation.

When they meet again, after the war, they are strangers with unshared memories and uncertain of their future together. But bearing the visible scars of hard won maturity they are to make a decision you will never forget.

Futura Publications
Fiction
0 7088 2154 5

LOVE AND HONOUR

Leslie Arlen

THE FIRST VOLUME OF THE MAGNIFICENT BORODINS
DYNASTY

LOVE AND HONOUR is the first novel in a powerful saga
of love, survival and courage, surging across the turbulent
heart of revolutionary Russia.

THE BORODINS — for years they had carved Russia's
destiny beside the Tsars. Now the twentieth century
heralds a new era of turmoil and social upheaval.

As the foundations of the dynasty crumble relentlessly,
the story of Ilona Borodin and the American George
Hayman mirrors the turmoil of the age. For Ilona is trapped
by marriage to a Russian prince who demands her total
submission. At the mercy of a passion which shatters
family loyalties, she must look beyond the Russian
heartland to a thriving America to find the freedom to
love.

Futura Publications
Fiction
0 7088 1935 4

THE BLACK DUCHESS

Alanna Knight

Magnificent, proud, with a seabird's grace, the BLACK DUCHESS glides out of the harbour's still waters to join the Holy Armada.

Her captain, Don Felipe — half Spanish, half Scot — is confident of victory over Queen Elizabeth of England. But the future holds many unsuspected perils, unknown hazards. He knows nothing of the seductive stowaway, Maeve, who will teach him the meaning of love . . . and loss. He is ignorant of the secrets of the Orkneys — the islands at the edge of the world, home of the trolls, seal women and mermaids — where he will feel the yoke of sweet bondage to the desperate, beautiful Lady Sibella. Least of all does he expect to see, through the clearing smoke of battle, across the shining waters of time, a face that exactly mirrors his own . . .

Futura Publications
Fiction
0 7088 2299 1

All Futura Books are available at your bookshop or newsagent, or can be ordered from the following address:
Futura Books, Cash Sales Department,
P.O. Box 11, Falmouth, Cornwall.

Please send cheque or postal order (no currency), and allow 55p for postage and packing for the first book plus 22p for the second book and 14p for each additional book ordered up to a maximum charge of £1.75 in U.K.

Customers in Eire and B.F.P.O. please allow 55p for the first book, 22p for the second book plus 14p per copy for the next 7 books, thereafter 8p per book.

Overseas customers please allow £1 for postage and packing for the first book and 25p per copy for each additional book.

CLARA & OLIVIA

LUCY ASHE

MAGPIE

A Magpie Book

First published in Great Britain, Australia and the Republic of Ireland by Magpie,
an imprint of Oneworld Publications, 2023
This mass market paperback edition published 2023

ISBN 978-0-86154-410-3
ISBN 978-0-86154-409-7 (ebook)

Typeset by Geethik Technologies
Printed and bound in Great Britain by Clays Ltd, Elcograf S.p.A.

Oneworld Publications
10 Bloomsbury Street
London WC1B 3SR
England

Stay up to date with the latest books,
special offers, and exclusive content from
Oneworld with our newsletter

Sign up on our website
oneworld-publications.com

For my sisters, Jo and Suzie

GLOSSARY

adagio – the opening dance of a traditional *pas de deux*, e.g. the 'Rose Adagio' from *Sleeping Beauty*.

Ballets Russes – one of the most influential ballet companies of the twentieth century, led by the impresario Serge Diaghilev. The Ballets Russes performed across Europe, North and South America between 1909 and 1929.

Cecchetti method – a rigorous style of ballet training devised by the Italian ballet master Enrico Cecchetti.

character shoes – heeled shoes used for dancing based on folk or national dances, for example the 'Mazurka' in *Coppélia*. The heel protects the dancers' feet from the frequent stamping movements in character dancing.

Coppélia – a comic ballet originally choreographed by Arthur Saint-Léon with music by Léo Delibes. The production staged by the Vic-Wells in 1933 was the Petipa version, with just the first two of the three acts performed.

corps de ballet – a group of dancers performing non-leading roles; literally 'the ballet company'.

Diaghilev, Serge (1872–1929) – the founder of the Ballets Russes.

rosin – a powder by-product of turpentine used by dancers on their shoes to prevent them from slipping.

Sergeyev, Nicholas (1876–1951) – regisseur of the Imperial Ballet at the Mariinsky Theatre, he fled Russia after the 1917 Revolution. He took with him trunks containing the written records of many of the great ballets of Marius Petipa and Lev Ivanov. The classical repertoire of ballets, including *Coppélia, Giselle, Swan Lake, The Nutcracker* and *The Sleeping Princess,* is known as the Sergeyev Collection.

Sleeping Princess, The – a classical ballet choreographed by Marius Petipa in 1890, now known as *The Sleeping Beauty.*

Stepanov notation – a notation system for recording dance movements, named after the Russian dancer Vladimir Stepanov. His book *The Alphabet of Movements of the Human Body* was published in 1892. The notebooks that Sergeyev smuggled out of Russia recorded ballets notated using the Stepanov method.

de Valois, Dame Ninette (1898–2001) – the founder of the Vic-Wells Ballet, which evolved into Sadler's Wells Ballet, then the Royal Ballet and Birmingham Royal Ballet. She is known in the ballet world simply as 'Madame'.

Ballet movements

adage – section of a ballet class with slow movements of the legs to improve balance, extension and coordination.

allegro – section of a ballet class with jumping steps.

arabesque – one leg extended behind the body with the knee straight and the foot pointed. In *arabesque allongée,* the line of the body is almost horizontal to the ground.

attitude – the working leg is lifted either in front (*devant*), side (*à la seconde*), or back (*derrière*), with the knee bent.

balancé – a swaying, rocking step in any direction to a waltz rhythm.

barre exercises – in the first part of a ballet class, dancers run through a series of exercises. These take place at the barre, a bar on which the dancer places their hand while dancing. These exercises include, in the order in which they are carried out:

pliés – to bend and stretch both legs at the same time;

battements tendus – one foot slides out smoothly along the floor to a full pointe of the toe;

battements jetés or *glissés* – as with *tendu* but with the toe just lifting off the floor;

ronds de jambe – the leg makes a circle, front, side, then back, either on the ground (*à terre*) or lifted off the ground (*en l'air*);

battements fondus – smoothly unfolding the leg into the air, with the supporting leg bending and then extending;

battements frappés – a raised, flexed foot touches the ankle then springs out with great energy to a pointed position;

petits battements – the foot moves quickly around the ankle with the knee bent;

développés – drawing one foot up to the knee and then unfolding the leg into the air; and

grands battements – exercises that usually finish the barre work; throwing the leg high and controlling the movement as it lowers. For *grands battements en cloche*, the leg is thrown forward then back alternately.

brisé – a small travelling jump in which legs assemble (*assemblé*) and beat together.

chaînés – quick, travelling half turns with the feet in a tight first position.

demi-bras – arms held low, extended either side of the body.

échappé – the legs spring out at the same time to either the side, front or back. *Sur les pointes* is on to the toes.

en pointe – dancing on the tips of the toes while wearing pointe shoes.

épaulement – turning the body from the waist so that one shoulder comes forward and the other goes back.

grand jeté – a large jump with the legs split in the air.

pas de bourrée – steps en pointe in tiny movements that make the dancer appear to float or glide.

pas de deux – partner dancing, traditionally where the female dancer is supported or lifted by the male dancer.

pirouette – a full turn on one leg. They can be performed *en dedans* (inwards) or *en dehors* (outwards).

port de bras – arm movements, literally meaning 'carriage of the arms'.

relevé retiré – drawing one foot up to the opposite knee, the supporting foot rising to the toes, the heel coming off the ground.

PROLOGUE

He wheels her out into the road. He should stay hidden, but part of him wants to be seen: he deserves her. He has waited long enough, worked hard enough. She belongs to him, dressed forever in the same red skirt with the same pink shoes tied around her ankles. Lace and net graze against her motionless thighs. Her skin is smooth porcelain and her lips are pink. Never has there been a lovelier figure, unchanging, unbroken by the pace of time. Her sightless eyes will not fade. A beautiful statue, preserved forever. He has watched her for so long, holding her in his gaze, locking her into position like a photograph.

He imagines dancing with her, the two of them arm in arm under the stars. Silent, of course, but that is no matter. It is better that way. She is a dancing doll, his Coppélia, created at last. He can finally believe it, now that he has her in the wheelchair. Pausing at the end of the street, he reaches down to her wrist and lifts her arm above her as if she is waving to a crowd. Ice-cold. He drops her arm in fright. Life lingers, like a promise; but he is afraid of what will happen when she wakes.

He needs to move quickly.

LONDON, 1933

ACT ONE

1

SAMUEL

It is Thursday, the day Samuel Steward delivers the pointe shoes to the theatre. He has been looking forward to it all week, even as he sits at his workbench, stills his mind, focuses his eyes on every stitch of satin and leather. Now, he walks hurriedly up through Covent Garden to Clerkenwell. His arms ache under the weight of those pale pink shoes, the satin smooth over the paper, hessian, paste, wax thread, all hidden of course when he stretches it right side out and inserts the sole. A perfect arc of a shoe. Arched like her feet when she rises up, weightless. Olivia Marionetta. He whispers her name, his voice too human, too rough, for a name that dances above him.

Familiar piano notes guide him up the stairs towards the ballet studio. He can hear the dancers' feet, their tapping across the floor, lighter now that the ballet mistress has been granted her wish, a wooden floor rather than the cold concrete that made the shoes echo through the room. It was the proudest day of his life when Mr Frederick touched his shoulder, nodded his approval and knocked against the workbench the shoe that he, Samuel, had made. An entire shoe made from start to finish with his own hands. He has worked steadily these past two years, making the progress from mixing the paste to cutting the leather, from labelling the regular customers' shoe lasts to stamping the latticework across the sole of the shoe. He has mastered each stage, perfecting the shaping, the moulding, the stitching, the exact number of hard hits needed on the shoe jack to produce the pointe shoe's mesmerising arch.

He imagines his rose, that tiny engraving he has cut into the bottom of her shoes. When he realised that his shoes were going to Olivia Marionetta, he knew he needed to honour this privilege. Writing her name in pen across the sole of the shoe was not enough; he did that for all the dancers. He needed something more for her. And of course he chose the rose. There was nothing else he could see when he closed his eyes, felt the smooth block of the shoe, imagined his mark. Her face, her eyes, the perfect bun she wears at the nape of her neck, her hair parted at the side. And the little white rose she pins into the top of the bun.

Samuel reaches the studio, his bags heavy with the shoes. The door is open, a small window into an imaginary world, a world he would like to trap forever in his mind, transcribe to his sketchbook, mark on paper with pencil, chalk, charcoal, his forever. But he knows he is not welcome. He is for the shadows, basements with dusty workbenches, his hands moving strong and fast over satin and paste, moulding the shoes that these dancers from another world will take from him. The turn-shoe method, all the work and sweat hidden inside. When he strains his muscles to wrench the shoe into shape, all that love is tucked away, out of sight. The dancers, they will make them their own. They will stitch them, cut them, wrap ribbons around their ankles, break the shoes, soften them, pummel them against hard concrete steps until they can move silently, softly, like butterflies across the stage. They do not even know he exists.

He knows how to make himself invisible. From the dark, where the shaft of light through the high windows of the studio cannot reach, he watches. He doesn't know what any of the steps are called and cannot keep up with the music of those names when the ballet mistress sings out the words in French, the dancers mimicking them with their hands until the music starts again and they fly across the floor.

And there she is. She flies higher than the others, he thinks. A vision in a bright white leotard, a thin skirt tied around her waist. She wears his shoes, the ones he has crafted with extra special care, adjusting the width, the length, the vamp of the toe box as she needs it. When he pencils her name onto the paper note that he pins onto her bag of shoes, it feels like a love letter. *For Olivia Marionetta.*

The dancers travel across the floor on a diagonal, ending their routine with a spin, their heads whipping around, their eyes steady. Olivia rises up on her toes, his shoes holding her strong. Her body is perfectly poised, and yet she turns and turns, one more rotation, and then a moment of stillness, before running to the side of the room. She watches the next set of dancers repeat the steps. Samuel realises he is holding his breath.

He looks again. There she is, her legs strong as she jumps. But no, it is not her, not this time. He looks away, steps back further into the shadows. Clara Marionetta scares him. At first glance she is her sister's double. She has the same face, same dark brown hair with the shimmer of red, same long sloping neck, same thin body with strength that defies its suppleness. The same feet, with those high arches that seem to command his shoes to dance. But in every other way they are different. He can tell them apart instantly; he just needs to see their eyes, the edges of their mouths. Clara looks in the mirror as she dances, with a fierce flame in her eyes: she owes the world nothing. She wears her shoes with a careless ease, the soles black and worn, a streak of dirt rising up from her heel. When she finishes her turn, she directs her gaze right at the ballet mistress and smiles; she knows she is beautiful, worthy, outshining the other girls. The ballet mistress calls out a correction; Clara turns away and rolls her eyes.

But Olivia does not dare meet the teacher's eye, hardly glances at herself in the mirror, leaves the dance floor with a little frown. Samuel wishes he could go to her, like he has seen those men do who wait at the stage door after performances. He would tell her how beautiful she is, how perfect, how the whole world must adore her. But of course he could never do that.

The teacher calls for them all to come to the centre, for the reverence, he thinks she says. The chords from the piano are familiar, like an ending. He watches the dancers step sideways, their arms wide, and he knows he must hurry. He doesn't want them to find him lingering. Mrs Dora gave him clear instructions to place all the shoes in the correct pigeonholes in Wardrobe before the class ended. For those ballerinas not yet converted to Freed shoes, he is to leave a little postcard, hand-signed by Frederick Freed himself: *We make shoes bespoke to you, the perfect shape and size for your foot.*

Wardrobe, as he has heard the dancers call it, is a chaotic room with no windows. It has none of the order of Mrs Dora's shop, the neat cubbyholes of pale pink pointe shoes all paired and ordered by size. Samuel likes to be in and out before the wardrobe manager, Mr Jack Healey, arrives. He has heard Mr Healey nagging the ballerinas to remove their piles of pointe shoes, reams of ribbons, the leotards and practice skirts that spill from every corner.

Samuel pushes aside a row of long white skirts, the net catching on his coat. It is quiet here, just the faint hammering from the carpenter's workshop where the set is being prepared for the next ballet. He stands in front of the rows of pigeonholes, the names of the dancers and actors and opera singers chalked in lightly on little slate boards. He places his bag at his feet and lifts out the shoes, protected in their cloth sacks. Scanning the chalk names, it is easy to tell which are the dancers, their names transformed into Russian, French, Italian words, exotic, beautiful sounds that elevate them far from the likes of him, plain and simple Samuel Steward. Beatrice Appleyard, Anton Dolin, Stanislas Idzikowski, Lydia Lopokova, Clara Marionetta, Olivia Marionetta, Alicia Markova, Toni Repetto, Antony Tudor, Ninette de Valois. He would like to know if these are their real names. Perhaps that would make them more tangible, more human; perhaps that would give him the courage to speak to her: Olivia Marionetta. He leaves her shoes until last. Taking them out of the cloth bag, he checks each shoe, rubbing his thumb over the little rose he has engraved into the sole. Each one is perfect.

With his heart beating fast, he lifts out of his deep coat pocket the white rose that he bought for threepence on his way out of Covent Garden that morning. He had almost been too nervous to buy it, the flower seller's smirk following him as he lingered by the stall. But he had been determined and now here he is, a rose in his hand, slightly crumpled but still flawless, smooth silky petals. He places it in Olivia Marionetta's pigeonhole, on top of her new pointe shoes. She does not know the hand that crafted them, but maybe she will feel herself dance lighter, taller, brighter, and she will know that she is adored.

2

OLIVIA

I look for luck everywhere. Today, I need to calm my nerves, soothe the anxieties that keep jumping to the front of my mind, refusing to be kept at bay. My porridge stares at me this morning; I can't eat it. It would be unlucky, a curse, to fill my belly with such ordinary, heavy-looking food. Today I need to shine.

We are all superstitious. We thrive on routines and good luck charms. They give us certainty, focus the mind, take us to a magical place where we can leave the real world and become the dancing apparitions the audience want us to be. We need our muse, our Terpsichore, to lead us onto the stage. Changing our names was the first step. Clara and I used to be plain old Olivia and Clara Smith. But we changed it to Marionetta when we left ballet school and ascended to the ranks of the company, joining Miss de Valois at her brand-new Vic-Wells ballet company, rebranding ourselves to match. It was our mother's idea to take her name, Marion, and weave it into something better than Smith. Clara was reluctant, but I persuaded her that Mother needed this, some recognition of the role she had played in getting us this far.

At Sadler's Wells Theatre, the home to our Vic-Wells Ballet, we have a specific dwelling for our superstition: an old monastic well that lurks in the centre of a dark and shadowy storage room underneath the auditorium. We traipse down there when we need luck, our visits punctuating the rhythm of our lives. Each day starts with morning ballet class, those essential ninety minutes that keep our bodies supple and strong. No one is allowed to miss class, though the principal dancers often do, somehow avoiding Miss de Valois's disapproval. If we have time, we hide ourselves in the gloom of the well room for a few minutes before afternoon rehearsals, finding a dark spot to massage our feet. We visit it before performances, at least three shows a week in the October to May season now that our company's reputation is growing. And then finally, if there is no post-show party to dress for in a mad, ecstatic rush, we reach down and dip our fingers into the well before we go home to sleep, to recover. My sister will always choose the party, while I prefer the quiet of home. I like to rest my aching limbs for the next day's work.

I spend longer than usual at the well this morning. There is a cool darkness to the room, lit faintly by a single light that hangs beneath green enamel and wire frame from the low ceiling. The well sits in the centre, a stone rectangle three feet wide and rising a couple of feet off the ground. I like to sit on the stone edging, my feet pressed into the cool stone wall. Towards the corners of the room, four steel beams rise up from the concrete floor, giving the room a cramped tightness. If there are more than a few of us down here at once, it is easy to bump into something, or even someone, lurking quietly in the privacy of the shadows. The old stone well cover rests against the side wall of the room, a dust sheet draped over the curious carvings that I like to run my finger along when I have the room to myself. It has a long history, dating back to when a monastery must have stood on the site, perhaps as far back as the twelfth century, surrounded by fields and gardens. It is hard to imagine now, with the New River closed over and buildings springing up all over Islington. Our theatre is number five of all the Sadler's Wells that have drawn the London audiences. Miss Moreton, in the rare moments we can distract her from her relentless pace through class, tells us about the theatre, how when Richard Sadler built the first one back in the seventeenth century, he made it popular by playing on this watery attraction. The wells were closed over, but the superstitions remained. We have gladly rebirthed them, all of us dancers ready to pounce on the first sign of magic and mystery.

The stone well cover, found by builders nearly three hundred years ago, has been preserved, protected from destruction every time the theatre is pulled down and built again, emerging from the ashes with new ideas for new entertainments. Even the builders, it seems, were superstitious. Our theatre isn't perfect. But I still love it, despite the tiny dressing rooms and the terrible acoustics in the auditorium.

It seems darker than usual this morning, shadows dancing slowly between the steel beams and the low, still water of the well. I can barely see to the end of the room where a storage cupboard is hidden in the corner and a wooden crate of stage props gathers dust. I looked inside the cupboard once, only to be confronted with mops and ropes, as well as a strange display of tennis balls and cricket bats. The theatre is gradually filling with the debris of productions, each show leaving behind its mark. A stack of photographs that didn't quite make the walls of the theatre foyer is leaning against the back wall, frozen moments of *Les Sylphides*, *Narcisse et Echo*, *Les Rendezvous*, *Nursery Suite*, the monochromatic figures blurred and faded. It is wonderful to be part of Ninette de Valois's growing company, the ballets we put on works of art to rival even the legendary days of the Ballets Russes. I do not miss those long nights that Clara and I have spent shivering in cold dressing rooms waiting for our performance in variety shows and revues, squashed between singers, comedians, even Cochran's pretty young ladies who gave us no space in the mirror to do our make-up. Our little ballet numbers were divertissements, instantly forgotten. But not any more, not with our Ninette de Valois and Lilian Baylis and the Camargo Society propelling us forwards.

With cold and frigid air, this is not a place to linger before class. Coming here alone, without the sweat and heat of the other dancers' bodies to fill the space, the room smells damp, like laundry that has been left wet too long. But I have wishing to do this morning. I need some luck. Nicholas Sergeyev is coming to class today.

His arrival has sent whispers around the theatre corridors for weeks, and I am sure the cafés of Bloomsbury and Covent Garden are spreading our excitement even further. Regisseur of the Mariinsky Ballet, Nicholas Sergeyev escaped in the aftermath of the 1917 October Revolution. Somehow, amongst all the panic, he smuggled out tin trunks holding all his notation books. The records of the great Russian ballets were preserved.

And now he is coming to us. He is to teach us the ballets that made Russian dance so famous. There is to be *Coppélia*, *Lac des Cygnes*, *Giselle* and even *Casse-Noisette*. I have heard so much about these ballets. I long to learn the choreography, to lift the notations off the pages of those old books and transform them into living dance. It would be wonderful to see the notebooks, to see the steps Petipa and Ivanov marked onto the page using that devilishly difficult Stepanov notation. There is no way I could understand a single symbol, but I will learn the steps faster and more accurately than anyone. Even my sister, I think. Clara is not very good at sticking to the choreography. It drives Miss Moreton mad. Me too, to be honest. It is one of the reasons I always wear my hair in a low bun, in the romantic style. It sets me apart from Clara, who always wears her hair high: one small difference to help people see us as two distinct dancers.

I perch on the stone edging and lean over into the well, dipping my hand into the water. I have to stretch as far as my arm will go, my fingers just breaking the surface. My knees press against the wall of the well but the distance is too far and I slip, my ribs hitting hard against the stone. Then I find my balance again, blinking as I watch the water moving and rippling like a kaleidoscope of greys and blacks, hiding whatever lurks beneath the surface. I lift my arm out, my fingers wet, and let the little drops of water fall onto my pointe shoes. The sharp pain of the stone against my ribs has startled me awake, reminding me of what I need to do today. Without pain, how do we know we are working hard enough? I said that to Clara once and she laughed at me. She didn't understand what I meant.

But this is the luck I need, or at least a gesture to give me the clear focus I want for ballet class. I know it is just a superstition, but this little drop of luck is my counterbalance to something strange that happened last week. It makes me shudder when I think of it, red staining my vision when I close my eyes. The blood remains, like an evil curse. When I went to collect my new pointe shoes from my pigeonhole in Wardrobe, there was a white rose in there, resting on top of my shoes. I picked it up, surprised. I turned to Clara, asking her if she'd put it there. She shook her head, refusing responsibility. I think she was a little bored by it, didn't see it as worthy of her attention. An admirer, perhaps; we all have them, men who come to every show, who linger outside the stage door, who deliver buckets of flowers that irritate the stagehands that have to carry them to our dressing rooms, choking on the strong scents and sprays of pollen. But this was just a single rose, no note or signature. When I turned it over in my hand, my finger caught on a thorn. I pulled it away fast, but the thorn had buried itself too deep inside me and I ripped my skin, a tiny bead of blood spilling out. I sucked it clean, but the blood kept rising to the surface in relentless bubbles. Eventually I thought I had made it stop, but I was wrong; it must have continued to bleed as I packed my pointe shoes into my bag. When I started sewing the ribbons onto my shoes that evening, I saw that I had left a dirty smear of blood across the satin of the shoe. It made me nervous, that blood, like a bad omen, a stain that could not be removed. Even once I had frantically rubbed on a paste of baking soda and water, I could still see the red darkening the satin like a ghostly palimpsest.

This water, our well famed for centuries as cleansing and heal-ing, has set my mind at rest. I run up to the studio to prepare for class. As usual, I am one of the first to arrive. Clara always teases me about getting everywhere so early, but I can't help it. I don't see the point in leaving everything to the last minute, as she does. The Company doesn't share my opinion, I know. They think it terribly unfashionable to show too much effort at anything and would never let themselves be seen actually prac-tising outside of class and rehearsal. Of course they all do, they must, these goddesses who laugh and joke but still manage to perform the perfect triple pirouette, their legs rising to their shoulders.

Today is the perfect day to be early, because just as I am knot-ting the ribbons on my soft-block ballet shoes, who should walk in but Nicholas Sergeyev himself. Miss de Valois travelled to Paris to persuade him over to London. The rumours are that she found him in a tiny studio *appartement* in a run-down part of the city, another Russian ballet teacher sharing the room. Seeing him now, taking small erect steps into the room with Miss de Valois at his side, makes me jump to my feet. I feel I should curtsy or something, but he ignores me, instead looking about him in a perplexed and rather lost way. I don't know what he expected, perhaps a corps de ballet to welcome him.

But as the Company gradually arrives, there is a very different mood to usual morning class, an energy and excitement that shows in the way we all warm up, the girls throwing their legs higher than ever, the boys jumping up and down at the barre, their muscles firing. We all watch Nicholas Sergeyev. He refuses to smile, the faint ghost of a grey moustache twitching as he looks anxiously around the room. He is small and upright, his cheeks drawn and thin with age, though he is not yet sixty. His travels, the stress of leaving his home country, seem to have lined his face like the contours of a map. I like his presence here, even though it terrifies me; he brings Russia and the old-style ways of ballet with him. Even Clara seems a little nervous. She stands with me at the barre, which I am glad about. It is easier for teachers to tell us apart if we are right next to each other, the small differences in our dancing and our appearance more obvious.

The class begins and Miss de Valois is at her most fierce. From the very first exercise at the barre, she seems to be performing a role, her terrifying eccentricities exposed. We have all heard stories of the Russian ballet masters with their sticks and their anger and their sharp eyes noticing every finger a millimetre out of place. Sergeyev is nodding as she bangs her stick on the floor. This is how he likes classes to run, with everyone a little scared, the adrenaline keeping our legs high and our toes pointed.

Every dancer in the Company has turned up today, and all on time. Even the new and exciting Helpmann is here. The star dancers have taken the best positions at the barre, where the line of their legs and arms will be shown off to advantage. Lydia Lopokova, Alicia Markova, Anton Dolin, they are all here. Markova's is a rare appearance; usually she just appears onstage, barely even warming up. Her diary is always packed with engagements: dancing with the Vic-Wells, for the Camargo Society, for Marie Rambert's Ballet Club. The Wells Room, as our studio is called, is bursting with dancers, the steam from our bodies misting the windows. Strong smells of sweat and rosin and the leather of our shoes pack the air. Even some of Miss de Valois's favoured girls from the school have managed to sneak in, squeezing into the corners where there is hardly space for them to stretch their arms. We all know that this Russian man has the power to elevate us to the top, to cast us in the best roles or to leave our names off the list entirely for the ballets he is reviving. For a moment, at the barre, dancing the slow adage that Miss de Valois calls out, I imagine myself as Aurora, Odette, Swanilda, Giselle. But a hard whack on my calf from Miss de Valois's stick wakes me up and reminds me to stand stronger, keep my leg extending away, in *arabesque*.

We take a few minutes' break after the barre work, the girls changing from soft-toe shoes into pointe shoes. Usually for ballet class we wear shoes that are nearly ready to throw out, saving our fresh ones for performances. They are expensive, and the company allowance for pointe shoes doesn't even come close to covering how many we need each month. I get through five pairs every four weeks, eking out those last few days with my muscles straining to keep my arches lifted and my ankles strong. But this is our chance, finally, to show what we can do. It is worth the expense. We all want to catch his eye. It is surreal, really, that this tiny man, in a suit that falls from his limbs like those costumes hanging from the rail in Wardrobe, has our full attention, he and Miss de Valois, who has transformed into a demon for the morning.

I go into the corridor and collect my bag, settling down in a corner to change my shoes. Clara is with me, massaging her feet through the pink silk of her tights. There is a ladder under her foot, just starting to spread up the heel, which is grey and stained from hours of dancing on dusty floors. She needs to scrub her tights with a bar of soap, like I do, but I know she's unlikely to bother. The corridor is quieter than normal, despite the crush of sweaty bodies; we all fight for space to stretch our legs in amongst the medley of warm-up clothes and shoes. Hushed whispers spread through us, punctuated by the quiet tap of pointe shoes as girls stand and press their feet into the floor. From inside the Wells Room, we can hear Nathan, the pianist, playing out some tunes while Miss de Valois stands next to him, beating out the pace with her stick.

I reach into my bag.

I know immediately that there is something wrong, something missing. I can't breathe. Both hands now search through the bag, my body tense as I rise up on my knees, hunched over the too-dark cavern of its opening. One of my pointe shoes has disappeared.

'What's wrong?' my sister whispers.

'I've lost a shoe.' I try to keep my voice low, holding down the panic threatening to bubble to the surface.

'Let me look,' she says, taking my bag from me. I realise that my hands are shaking. I can't go back in there without my pointe shoes. That would be it for me, my chance at being cast in one of his ballets gone forever.

'I've got a spare pair,' I hear Clara say, nudging me back from the abyss my mind has drifted towards. I had got as far as Ninette de Valois refusing to have me back in class, sacking me from the company, not being able to pay the rent and ending up dancing for drunk old men on a cruise ship. But Clara saves me from that nightmare with the offer of her shoes. They are an old pair she hasn't cleared from her bag, far from perfect condition, but better than nothing. I will just have to dance my best, rising out of my hips to stay tall in the shoes. Knowing Clara, she's already worn these for a class longer than she should have done. They are a little torn under the toe, but they will do.

Clara squeezes my hand as we go back into the Wells Room, before fighting her way to the front row and dragging me with her. We line up next to each other, waiting for Miss de Valois's instructions. I feel a hit of remorse for thinking so badly of my sister this morning, her lateness and sloppiness, her carefree attitude to everything. But she is the one who is prepared for class, with her spare pair of shoes. I try not to get distracted as we go through the *adage*, then *grands battements*, *pirouettes en dehors*, *petit allegro*. It is difficult, though, with my mind drifting back to the well, trying to remember if I left my shoe down there in the darkness of the basement storage room.

When class ends, I gather up my belongings as quickly as I can. I run down the corridor that follows the edge of the building towards the pit and wings until I reach the entrance to the basement room, that flimsy door that the stage manager has given up trying to keep locked. The light is off and I have to fumble around the wall by the door to find the switch. I walk down the steps, my eyes adjusting to the gloom. All is quiet, just as it was before, and there is no sign of my shoe. I walk to the well and kneel down by its thick stone wall. The famous waters have not given me the luck I asked for today, it seems. I am cross with myself for being so careless. I lean over the edge, my eyes finding shapes in the dark.

There, floating on top of the water, is a pointe shoe. The ribbons are tangled like weeds. And next to the shoe, its petals drifting across the surface, is a single white rose.

3

SAMUEL

Samuel has all the parts of the shoes lined up neatly on his workbench, a deconstructed artwork. Hessian, paper, satin, glue, the sole. The welting machine is across the room, where Mr Frederick is standing in his overalls, his hands working fast, his head down in concentration. Samuel can make more than ten pairs of shoes a day now and is getting faster. The work is physically exhausting, each shoe demanding arm, wrist and shoulder strength to wrestle and bang it into the perfect shape. And then there is the tiny rose he stamps into the soles of Olivia Marionetta's shoe, finding a quiet moment when Mr Frederick is on the other side of the workshop, preoccupied with his own craft. He has finally finished his rose cutter stamp, which makes it faster, a quick press, done in an instant. He dedicates one day a month to making her shoes, ten at a time as well as another five soft-toe shoes. He loves those days. Every stitch feels like a caress. He took his stamp home with him to finish, working under the little lamp on his desk in his tiny one-room flat off Exmouth Market. At least it's the top floor, and bright in the mornings, unlike the gloom of the basement where he works beneath Cecil Court.

He does love the workshop though, the chance to create and shape and fashion something beautiful out of all those malleable, simple ingredients. Sometimes he feels like he could be an artist himself, but then he remembers these designs are not his. He does have his own designs, piles and piles of his sketches of shoes, clothes, hats, all scattered about his room, some in the drawers, some pinned up on the walls. Around his bed, his chest of drawers, his desk, are his pencil and chalk sketches in all the colours of the rainbow, scraps of material pinned against them, velvet, silk, satin, lace. He can't share them with anyone. It would be too revealing, too exposing. Sometimes he imagines himself going up to Mr Frederick with a handful of his designs, maybe the high-heeled boots he is so proud of, with the soft soles for dancing character roles. But it's no use; they are probably worthless, unoriginal, no good to anyone. He should just be grateful for this job, he knows, and keep making these beautiful pointe shoes day after day. As his father always said, stick to what you know and you won't go wrong. Don't give anyone a chance to laugh at you. His father had laughed at him, though, Samuel remembers so vividly, that day he showed him his sketch of a pair of winter boots, the green leather football buttons running down the ankle, the fur trim topping the lining. He had spent days over that sketch, perfecting the shapes and proportions, searching through his chalks for the exact green he wanted. He never showed his father another sketch, not after his loud mocking laugh followed him out of the living room door, back up the narrow stairs to his bedroom. The silence of his mother, her downcast eyes at the dinner table, he remembers it all. It was easier for her to say nothing, a patient sufferance. His parents still live in that dark, gloomy house in Clapham, his father going out every day to the railway where he works as an engineer, his mother waiting for him at home in a freezing house that he refuses to heat during the day. Samuel will never go back there, not if he can help it.

Mrs Dora has left the door open up to the shop, a little pool of light spilling down the steps to the basement. Samuel likes hearing the murmuring of the dancers who come in to be fitted, the strong tones of Mrs Dora as she advises them and instructs them. You'd think she knows their feet better than they do themselves. Perhaps she does.

Mr Frederick asks him to take some finished shoes up to the shop. It is a brilliantly bright morning, still a little frosty, the cold air drifting in through the front door as it opens and closes. On his walk to work he had sunk his feet into the hard white grass in the little parks that he weaves his way through, enjoying the sound of the crisp crackle of the frost. He likes avoiding the main roads that teem with noisy, impatient people, instead finding small havens of quiet.

They are busy this morning. The fame of these shoes grows through the city. No one notices Samuel as he stocks the shelves, ordering the shoes exactly as Mrs Dora likes them. Two young girls from Miss de Valois's school are laughing as they raise themselves up and down, pressing the arches of their feet forwards, pointing their toes, extending their legs. Everyone likes these shoes, how they seem to meld to the feet, exactly the right support without being too hard, too unyielding.

The door opens again, the little bell above the door tinkling invitingly. Samuel hears two voices, both identical in note and pitch. They call good morning to Mrs Dora. Samuel recognises them instantly. Even with his back turned, his whole body frozen as he reaches up to the top shelves of pointe shoes, he knows which voice belongs to Clara and which to his Olivia.

'Samuel, get me two pairs of your shoes, size four,' Mrs Dora calls to him, barely turning towards him as she greets the twins.

He moves quickly, pulling himself into action, and nods, pointlessly; no one is looking at him. He reaches for the shoes, knowing instinctively which are his. The shoes he has made for Olivia are ready for his next delivery, so he takes a pair of these, as well as a pair from Clara's pile. He is ahead of his work, the shoes ready earlier than Mrs Dora expected.

'Oh no, don't worry about that,' Clara says, smiling, but a little impatiently, Samuel thinks. 'We love the shoes we have from you already, no need to change anything about them. We just want to put in another order.'

'And buy some ribbon,' adds Olivia, 'and see if you've decided yet about adding to your range. We're all desperate for some character shoes that won't give us blisters.'

'Give us time,' replies Mrs Dora gently, gesturing them to the counter, where she will put in the repeat order. 'Are you sure you don't want me to check the shoes on you again, while you are here? I would so love to see how they fit you.' She pauses and looks to Samuel, who is holding the shoes she requested out to her. He doesn't dare glance at Olivia, even though he is desperate to look. She is so close, the closest he has ever been to her. One quick look, and that is all, then. He takes in everything with one little flick of his eyes: her low-heeled boots so snug around her slim ankles, her thick navy coat that she buttons high, a cream scarf wrapped around her neck. Her hair is in the bun she always wears, but without the rose. He has always thought that seeing her dressed as a normal woman, not in her leotard and dance skirt, would make her more real. But it hasn't had that effect at all. If anything she seems even less real, as though if he closes his eyes she will disappear.

'All right,' he hears her say. 'It will be fun to try them on with you, in your beautiful shop.' Mrs Dora looks delighted, emerging from behind the counter in an almost youthful burst. She rarely shows such lightness, her authority and experience making her seem far older than her real age, barely thirty. To Samuel she seems ancient, infinitely wise, despite being just ten years older than him.

The twin sisters peel off their coats, draping them over the wooden and velvet stools that Samuel helped Mr Frederick to build last year. They unlace their boots, Clara flinging them to the side, Olivia placing hers neatly to the left of the stool. Samuel watches as Mrs Dora kneels, placing Clara's right foot onto the little ramp. She slides on the shoe, feeling around the width. She repeats this with the left foot before moving to Olivia, gently rubbing the satin around the heel and toe. The sisters stand and turn to each other. They take each other's hands and rise onto their toes, their feet strong in the shoes. They draw their feet together into a tight position, legs crossed from the top. Samuel watches, staying as close as he can to the edge of the room. He looks down at his own feet, large and heavy in his boots. He is not delicate or dainty; his feet cannot move like theirs, fast and light little pitter-patters into the ground. Samuel is not graceful, but he is strong. He has to be to make these shoes. Since working at Freed his muscles have grown, his shoulders broadened. Even Mrs Dora commented the other day, marvelling at how he'd changed, his forearms thickened from all the bending and banging. But still no one notices him, standing there in his overalls, grey and brown against the glowing pink of the shoes behind him.

Olivia is bending and stretching her legs. He's heard Mrs Dora request a plié over and over to the girls she fits, her commanding voice matching that of the terrifying ballet mistresses he encounters at Sadler's Wells. Now *plié*, and stretch, she says as the girls try out the different shapes and sizes of shoe.

'They feel wonderful,' says Olivia, sitting back down on the stool and stretching her feet away to admire the shape of the shoe. Samuel stares as she brings one leg up towards herself, twisting her foot so she can see the sole. She rubs the pale leather with her finger, tracing a line from toe to heel. For an instant he thinks she is looking at his rose, his symbol that marks the shoes as just for her. He feels a sudden panic, deep in his stomach. What if she realises he put the white rose in her pigeonhole; what if she is offended, or worse, laughs at him for daring to make such a gesture? If he moves now, he can get down to the workshop before she turns to see him. But Mrs Dora is in the way, blocking his exit route.

Samuel feels his heart beating fast, his face starting to burn. He tries to imagine what he will say if Mrs Dora reveals him to be their pointe shoe maker. His hands are clammy. What if they want to shake his hand, he thinks, panicking, trying to wipe them on his overalls.

'They are perfect shoes,' Clara says, smiling down at her feet. She does a little turn, spinning on one foot then the other until she comes back around to face Mrs Dora. 'You make us dance like swans.' She laughs, throwing her hands above her head and crossing her wrists.

Olivia stands and looks about her, taking in the walls of shoes stacked neatly on the shelves. She has taken off the shoes and is holding them in her hands. Her feet are bare, the long thin bones that stretch from her toes to her ankle pressing against mottled pearl skin. Finally she notices him, his large mass blocking a column of shelves. 'Do you help Mr Freed make the pointe shoes?' he hears her say.

He doesn't trust himself to speak. All he can do is nod.

'Well, they are lovely, as Clara says.' She turns them over in her hands. 'I get through them very quickly, so you'll have to work hard to keep us in our shoes.' She is teasing him, he realises. But all he can do is nod again, pressing his hands against his thighs. She waits a moment, looking up at him. In her bare feet, he sees how small she is, at least a foot shorter than him. He reached six foot when he was sixteen, six foot three when he was eighteen, and over the last two years his body has been slowly catching up and filling out.

He doesn't know why she is still standing there, smiling. Maybe he has paste on his face from making the glue, or maybe she can't believe that someone as large and inelegant as him could work in a shop that makes such a shoe. But then he realises she isn't looking at him. She is looking behind him at the rows and rows of shoes and the spools of ribbons that Mrs Dora measures out and cuts with such precision.

'The perfect colour of shoe,' she says, almost a whisper. She looks like she is in a dream, imagining herself onstage, that burst of applause when the curtain rises.

She finally gathers herself and glides back to join her sister. He is fascinated by how thin and sinewy her feet are, every step revealing muscles, tendons, bones he has never noticed in his own.

And then they are gone. They disappear around the corner, the bell sending out its ripple, like an orchestra has suddenly packed away leaving just a triangle whispering its final notes. That is how he feels, with her gone. It is as though an imaginary world has vanished, leaving him awake and staring at his large, sweaty hands.

4

CLARA

My sister is asleep when I get in, later than I should. She rolls over in bed, murmuring. I reach down and gently ease her hair out of that tight ponytail she insists on keeping in at night. It isn't good for her, all that tension. She almost wakes, but I rest my hand on her shoulder until she is calm. I like to look at her, the smooth skin of her neck that she always manages to carry with such elegance, even in Miss Moreton's most painful *petit allegro*. I catch myself staring and feel a little guilty, vain, seeing myself mirrored in her face.

In the bathroom are the bowls of water she has left out for me, two deep china toilet bowls we found in an antique shop behind Sadler's Wells when we moved here and tried to make these tiny Bloomsbury rooms our home. I refuse the cold salt water, not tonight with a freezing wind seeping in through the walls and windows. And the water is no longer hot. My feet will have to cope, even if they are tired. Hours of dancing in those pointe shoes straight into an evening of dancing through the clubs of Fitzrovia has not been kind.

Olivia will be cross with me in the morning, asking lots of questions which I shall not want to answer. I suppose I should regret not pressing her more determinedly to come with us, but it would have been no use. Nathan always tells me not to bother; he prefers having me all to himself. And besides, Olivia has no time for frivolities that take her away from soaking her feet, stretching her muscles, sewing the ribbons on her shoes, darning the ends with that long, curved needle that I always manage to prick myself with. And sure enough, her shoes are ready, piled neatly on top of her bag. Mine is next to hers, the contents spilling out as usual, in a mess. I know I will find a dozen hairpins scattered amongst my tights. As I peel off my dress, which is sticking to me with a sour sweat from the heat of the tavern, I catch sight of my own pointe shoes piled against the wall. The top pair has been prepared exactly as I like them, the ribbons angled back towards my heel, the toes darned just around the edge. Olivia. She did this for me, tonight, while I was out dancing, drinking, flirting with Constant, Bobby, Pat, Nathan, a crowd of us wild, restless girls from the company. If only I had her discipline, or even her kindness, though sometimes I think she does these kind things for me in case someone mistakes me for her; she has to work doubly hard, keeping me up to the standards she expects of herself. It must be frustrating for her, especially when she sees me with rips in my tights or cheating the Cecchetti footwork: she is always whispering to me to get my heels down, as if it is her own feet I am somehow neglecting to use with the precision she always manages to achieve.

I return to the bathroom and scrub my face with cold water, feeling even more guilty now. I splash water hard against my skin, shivering as it drips down my arms. I look up into the mirror and stare. Ballet dancers are surrounded by endless mirrors: all morning in ballet class and rehearsals, in the dressing rooms, our bodies and faces straining to match each other's. We train to become identical, perfect, classical, while all at once trying to shine brighter than the others. But me even more so than most. I am mirrored every time I turn to Olivia, every time we follow the instructions of the ballet mistress, our feet moving in time. Sometimes I think I am seeing my sister; sometimes I wish I was more like her, that I could work hard, return home for a good night's sleep, rest my body, save the money that I know she is so determined to bank up for better rooms, warmer walls, a proper kitchen perhaps rather than the sink and stove that are tucked away in the alcove behind the curtain. But I would prefer to dance and party and live my life everywhere, not only when the curtain lifts and the audience applauds, when Constant lifts that baton and the orchestra begins. I love those moments, of course I do, but they are not enough.

Tonight, when Miss de Valois and Miss Moreton left the Café Royal, it was as though a layer of respectability had been stripped from our little group, leaving us raw and ready for misbehaviour. We adore them both, but it is adoration tinged with fear. I couldn't face our ballet mistresses in the morning class if they saw what I really get up to after a few drinks.

Constant had us all roaring with laughter. I joined in the drinking and the incessant chatter as I always do, though I could sense Nathan's disapproval when my laugh spilled out too loud. Constant commandeered the piano, blasting out loud notes of jazz, glasses glowing with Tokay wine never far from his side. We ended up, finally, in the Fitzroy Tavern on Charlotte Street, dancers, musicians, even the stunning young Florence Lambert with her perfectly arched eyebrows and those huge eyes. I still remember the day they married, Constant and Florence, two years ago. It was a hot August day with Florence clutching carnations still wrapped in their paper. She was a child, really, just sixteen, though she claimed to be eighteen. Two years with Constant has sophisticated her, lost her that wide-eyed doe look, that innocence. Now she has a permanent look of mischievous disapproval, enjoying her husband's loud drinking and storytelling so she can hit him playfully over the shoulder. And he had a lot of stories to tell tonight, gossip elevated to myth. He can spin a simple encounter into a legend, and reduce a hero to ridicule. He takes great artists and makes them human: Pavel Tchelitchew's painting looks like a *Daily Mail* exhibit for the best design in the sand at Margate; the ballet mistress's love of Schubert worse than listening to a hyena screeching; and so on. It is only when, after too many drinks, he starts his lampooning of the great Diaghilev that Miss de Valois gives a little shake of her head and he clams up with a naughty expression on that childlike face of his.

We exploded into the tavern, full of wine and a little food, ready for music and more drinks to fuel our loud, fast laughter. It was busy, a wall of sweat and steam rising against the bitter February weather outside. Right then I felt like a film star, slipping my coat from my shoulders, my backless dress revealed to the room. Nathan bought the coat for me; he insisted on it one day in October last year when we were roaming the streets of Fitzrovia. I remember it had started to rain, a misty, autumnal drizzle that settled onto our skin like dew. Nathan pulled me into a crowded little shop on Percy Street and rummaged along the rails until he found it, holding it up against me and pressing the fur against my cheek. Second-hand, of course, and rather ragged, but it is still the most glamorous coat I have ever owned. It is dark green, long, nipped in at the waist with a belt, and has a huge fur collar that rises high around my neck. I felt awkward taking it home that night, knowing Olivia would look at it with envy. We share everything, exchanging dresses, blouses, hats, even our bandeau brassieres that Olivia somehow manages to keep in perfect crisp white condition. It's cheaper to share, giving ourselves new outfits by delving into each other's half of the wardrobe. But Olivia never comes out with us, and I have to work hard to convince her she can wear the coat too. She always blushes when I suggest it, changing the conversation as fast as she can.

At first I loved seeing it hanging next to all the other beautiful coats in the cloakrooms of the cafés and restaurants and bars, its velvety thickness, its collar pressing against the others to establish its place, its belonging. But gradually over the past few months it has started to sit differently, weighing heavier on my shoulders. Every time Nathan wraps his arm around my waist, pressing the belt into my stomach, I want to shake him off. I want to throw the coat into the dirty puddles in the road, walk into the restaurant alone, free. But I can't do it; every time I meet him in the theatre foyer, I take his arm and let him lead me to the party, the café, the exhibition, the concert that he has chosen.

Tonight we played silly word games, huddled as we were around a corner table in the already heaving tavern. Nathan was next to me; he was next to me all night in fact, finding the seat right beside me before the others could claim their places around the many different tables we soaked in wine and whisky. At each one, Nathan was a little closer, his shoulder touching mine, his hand brushing against my back as I reached forward for my wine glass, his leg pressed against my thigh under the table. The ballerina and the piano player, all of London ours to charm; I smiled all night.

Nathan Howell is our company pianist. He plays for our lessons, relieving Constant of a duty he can only fit in once or twice a week now that our Vic-Wells Ballet is starting to grow. Constant found him. Or so his story goes, a story that he repeats regularly on our post-performance nights out. Nathan doesn't really like it, I think, though he pretends to laugh along with the rest of them. I have learnt not to laugh, not any more. Attending a concert the other side of the river, Constant walked in late, exhausted from a busy day, fully prepared to leave after five minutes, to head home and fall into a deep sleep. But there on the stage was a boy playing the piano with such skill. When the concert ended he marched up to the front, pressing against the shirt fronts and fur collars of the departing crowd. In fact, the performer was twenty-one years old, an accomplished pianist with years of childhood experience playing for packed crowds, a child prodigy, rushed from one concert to the next. But that night when Constant found him, Nathan had very little money left, the concerts were running out, and he needed to pay the mooring fee for the boat where he lived on the canal in Islington, a narrowboat loaned to him by a retired boatman who could not bring himself to sell up. And it was Constant Lambert standing before him. Who could resist the man who had been commissioned by Diaghilev, himself barely an adult when he composed his *Romeo and Juliet*? Nathan said yes immediately. The next day he was perched on a piano stool in the barely finished studio at Sadler's Wells, learning the difference between *pliés* and *grands battements* as fast as he could. It was that or giving up his strange home on the canal, a lifestyle that turns the heads of the radicals and bohemians and undergraduates he tries to emulate. Nathan, it seems, will do anything to avoid succumbing to a life of dreary ordinariness.

I get into bed at last, stretching my legs away from myself and flexing my feet. Olivia's bed is pressed against the wall, barely two feet away from me, but she sleeps so silently and still that I have to check she is there. My calves are tight from the heels I wore tonight and the walk home across cobbled streets behind the British Museum. Nathan walked me home, waiting until I was safely inside before he continued the journey up to his boat on the canal. I am very curious to see it one day. Olivia and I have walked along the towpath a few times, but we get strange looks from the men who heave crates in and out of their barges and the workmen who lean lazily against the large doors of the warehouses, cigarette smoke drifting towards the water. I have never known anyone who has lived on a boat before, but I can imagine Nathan there, the cramped walls decorated no doubt with his piles of sheet music, the programmes from all those concerts he has performed in since he was a little boy. But on a night like tonight it is probably freezing. Though maybe no more freezing than our rooms, I think, pulling the blanket higher around my neck.

I close my eyes, but sleep doesn't come easily. I remember those scraps of paper that littered the table, sticky with wine. It was Constant's idea. He loves games, especially word games where he can build nonsensical epics and ballads. Nathan insisted we play together, and we tried our best to come up with something that made sense. Pat chose the words we were to use for our heroic verses, confounding us all with his wicked wit. He winked at me as he read out the words: doll, phantom, alcohol, crawl, annum. Nothing any of us wrote made much sense, but Nathan used the distraction to turn the paper and scribble out a note, a line of verse. *A lovely apparition, sent to be a moment's ornament.* I felt a little lost by it, confused, like I was reading something familiar but with the meaning just out of reach. Nathan does this sometimes, his mind going somewhere I don't quite understand. Sometimes it makes me feel stupid, unable to match his genius, whatever that word really means. But tonight it was as though the words were dripping on to me like candle wax, catching me in the romance he knows how to spin, a secret, intimate gesture. I couldn't place his meaning, but I knew that the words somehow bound me to him against the noise and chaos of the others. I turned to him and smiled, shifting as I untucked my foot from between his shins.

The note is inside my coat pocket. Maybe one day, if I have the courage, I will ask him about it, what he really meant. But for now I am exhausted. And a long day of ballet class and rehearsals is not too many hours away, topped off with a triple bill of performances in the evening. Olivia will be furious if I make us late.

ACT TWO

5

CLARA

The theatre is silent tonight. There is no show, no audience driving up in their loud motor cars, no rustle of silks and furs, velvet and tulle. Outside, Rosebery Avenue is quiet, as though London has forgotten we are here. Tonight, dressing rooms that are usually packed with dancers have fallen still. It is just me and Nathan, with the lights on low in the Wells Room. We will be thrown out soon, the theatre caretaker doing his nightly rounds to check none of us are sleeping in our tutus, dreaming of tomorrow's class.

We have been rehearsing *Coppélia* for several weeks, Nicholas Sergeyev banging his stick, somehow deciphering the chaotic notations in his books, calling out the steps, the mime, the rhythm. When he finally realised that there were two Marionetta girls, he couldn't get enough of us, searching through his notation books and character lists to see how he could spin the illusion of two identical ballerinas onto the stage. But Olivia looked disappointed when the cast list went up. We are to dance two of Swanilda's friends, good roles certainly, but not what she wanted. But I don't know what she expected. Swanilda was bound to go to the top. Lydia Lopokova and Miss de Valois will be sharing the role. Though when Lopokova arrived at the studio for the first rehearsal, dressed in comically out-of-fashion rehearsal clothes, a little woollen shawl around her shoulders, a baby pink cross-over cardigan making her look even smaller and rounder than she already is, we had to work hard to lower our raised eyebrows. But it didn't take long to see how suited she was to the role, comic, brilliantly expressive, a burst of energy. It's hard to believe she is forty-two. In Act Two, teasing Dr Coppélius into thinking she is his doll come to life, she had us all in hysterics. Even Nicholas Sergeyev gave in to a brief smile.

Miss de Valois was a more obvious choice, we all felt. It always amazes me how she can go from business all day, running the school, rehearsing us, to then changing into her ballet shoes and practising at the barre. Then, to top it all, giving a wonderful performance onstage at night. She is a beautiful dancer, with strong, fast legs and an even stronger sense of character. She can bring a part alive, transporting the audience to the dreamland of the stage. Perhaps it is the glass of sherry we know she sneaks in before every performance that helps her to move so easily from all the papers on her office desk to the lights of the stage.

Nathan plays the notes of Delibes's waltz from Act One on the piano and I dance what I can remember of Swanilda's variation. It is not my role, of course, but we all learn everything, just in case we get called up, someone breaks an ankle or there is a sickness that spreads through the principal dancers. Highly unlikely, but we can all dream. I know Olivia has learnt every step of every role. She could be Swanilda tomorrow.

I am tired and don't really want to still be dancing. Every rise en pointe is an effort, my legs slow in the *pas de bourrée*, the *relevé retiré* sluggish and low. The air in the studio lingers with the smell of sweat and rosin and the strong cheap perfumes of the dancers; I want to leave it all behind for the night, escape into the streets. I long to be at a café with the other girls, a glass of cold cheap wine in my hand, but Nathan insisted on rehearsing. He, too, is a little afraid of Nicholas Sergeyev. They argue over the score like children fighting over sweets. When it doesn't fit in with his notations, Sergeyev simply deletes bars of notes from the score that Nathan and Constant have to squeeze back in the next day. Temperaments are fragile, these grand masters shooting each other sharp looks across the studio.

Nathan must feel playing for ballet class is a little beneath him, the child prodigy now banging out tunes for *pliés* and *battements tendus*. Playing for Sergeyev was to be his big break, I expect he thought, a chance to ascend out of the daily grind of the Wells Room. But it is usually Constant Lambert who plays for rehearsals, or Ippolit Motcholov, Sergeyev's own pianist, who is always happy to make the musical score fit the notations. I rather like Motcholov, the faraway look in his eyes and his gentle manners. But I'll never admit this to Nathan, who sees him as a direct threat to his success. The dancers like him, though, and we find many opportunities to draw him into conversation at the end of rehearsals. He brings us memorabilia of Russia, always carrying a photograph of the Czar, Czarina and their daughters in his coat pocket. It is romantic, like we are recreating the past.

Finally, I flop to the floor, my legs stretched wide. My eyes graze tiredly over the photographs that line the walls as I rest back on my hands, opening out my ribs in a vast yawn. Nathan stops, mid-bar, and looks over to me.

'Had enough?' He sounds a little impatient. He knows I have been rehearsing all day, that my feet will be killing me, my muscles aching, my stomach empty.

'Definitely,' I reply. I don't need him to be another ballet master right now. I need him to say that we've been here long enough, that we can leave, go home. I am desperate to get out of here. But I know even then it won't be over. He'll want to find a café, drink wine, talk and talk until I can barely keep my eyes open.

'Let's do Swanilda's solo one more time,' he says, looking back at the score. I sigh and pull myself to my feet. I've had enough and I don't see why I should perform for him, rehearsing a dance I will probably never have the chance to do onstage. He starts playing, the music suddenly irritating and fussy, like a fly buzzing around my ears. I refuse to dance, instead walking up to him and putting my hands on his shoulders. Leaning down, I press my head against his, one hand sliding down his chest. His hands falter, missing a note. I kiss his cheek.

'Just one more time, Clara,' he repeats, moving his head away from mine. I stand straight and take a step back, looking down from his golden hair to his long, elegant fingers that stretch over the keys. My tiredness is starting to rise inside me, a little hysterically, tears just held at bay. This is what happens when we dance for too long without enough rest. And I haven't eaten for hours. I hate feeling this way, like my body is slipping from my control.

I pick up my clothes and shoes from the corner and head to the door. I just need to get out and home before I say something I regret, my nerves itching with irritation. Even the thought of food has faded from my mind.

The notes fall away and the piano is silent. I turn and he is right there, his arms catching me.

'I'm sorry,' he says, pulling me towards him. 'You're right. We've been here long enough.' I don't want to give in to him, to forgive him so quickly, but I am exhausted and can feel myself letting go. It is not only rehearsals for *Coppélia*; we are in the midst of a busy season of performances with *Pomona*, *The Lord of Burleigh* and *The Birthday of Oberon*, the latter being a huge production with a chorus of forty, Miss de Valois's first choral production. We have to wear masks, which some of the critics objected to, and I have to say I agree. Dancing with my face sweating under a mask only adds to the exhaustion. And a one-act version of *Le Lac des Cygnes* keeps finding its way into triple bills, the exacting precision of the choreography demanding that we stand for what seems like hours in swanlike poses, our necks and backs stiff. Our days are packed with class, rehearsals, performance, on repeat.

I don't want to cry. It is not the version of myself I let anyone know. Only Olivia sees me cry, but I've been hiding tears even from her recently. She is so self-absorbed, focused only on class and rehearsals, sewing ribbons on her shoes, exercising her feet every night before bed. Sometimes I want to shake her, convince her to come out with us after performances and let herself relax, just for an evening.

But I don't know why I am thinking about Olivia right now. Perhaps because when I catch sight of myself in the mirror that runs along the edge of the room I see her staring back at me. It startles me, a cold breath of air rushing around my ears. I don't like it, this stern, determined young woman who will give up anything to dance on that stage. That isn't me, and I refuse to let Nathan push me more. Perhaps he should be with Olivia, I think, as I pull away from him, twisting my arm out of his hand. In the corner of my eye I can see myself reflected in the mirror. For a moment, my reflection seems to stay entirely still, a ghostly statue with her arm still gripped by Nathan. Then time speeds up again and she finds me, matching my fast march through the door.

He follows me to the dressing rooms and waits while I get changed. The roots of my hair ache as I release the tight knot on top of my head. It feels glorious to massage my scalp, reversing the direction of my hair. A headache that has been brewing for hours, just under the surface, starts to disperse.

I can see him in the doorway through the reflection of the mirror; he is looking around him with a curious expression, as if this chaotic mess of costumes, hairpins, greasepaint, ribbons, is a toyshop. My eyes narrow as I watch him move through the room, picking up objects we have left on the dressing tables: a brush, a make-up sponge, a lipstick, a tiara made of cardboard and sequins that should have been cleared away to Wardrobe. A layer of powder coats the bottom of the mirrors, transforming the reflection into the impasto strokes of an impressionist painting. It is a little figurine that holds him. A tiny ballerina, the type you might find in a music box. The legs are in *arabesque*, a long romantic tutu stiff in porcelain. That doll could turn forever and ever and still her skirt would never droop, her arms would never dip with tiredness, her feet would never blister.

He doesn't think I notice when he slips the dancer into his pocket. She is not my dancer; I won't miss her. It probably belongs to one of Miss de Valois's students from the school, who try to tiptoe in here to spy on our costumes. They have so many trinkets and good luck charms. Dolls, jewellery, photographs they have persuaded the goddess Alicia Markova to sign, feathers fallen from costumes that they sneak into their bags, a discarded pointe shoe worn by the leading dancers, as if placing these shoes on their feet will conjure talent and fame. Olivia and I, we just have the well, that shadowy water that promises us nothing. I have found Olivia down in that gloomy basement too much recently, staring into the water as if there is something hidden under the surface. I shouldn't encourage her, but I like the routine too much, dipping my hand into the water before each performance. We all have our obsessions.

As we get out onto the street, the lights in the theatre thud dark behind us. I can breathe easier now we are outside, the sound of a bus slowing at the end of the road a comfort after the echoing silence of the empty theatre. But as Nathan walks with me on my way home, I can't stop thinking about that little doll hidden inside his pocket. When he leans against me, I can feel the sharpness of her legs digging into my hip. He adjusts his coat, moving his pocket so she doesn't press into me any more. He must realise I felt her tiny foot prodding me through the leather.

We walk quickly, fighting off the cold and the dark. I have refused the offer of a meal, but Nathan persuades me to let him walk with me just as far as Great Ormond Street. We cut along Exmouth Market, the stalls empty and still, just a few tired men in overalls glugging back the last of their pints before they stumble home to bed. A woman sweeps outside the public house, calling out angrily as a man pushes past her, his legs wobbling as he finds his path home. The only lights spilling out on the street are above the shops in those tiny flats that must be noisy from before dawn until the pubs close late at night. I have walked this route so many times, but I find I am glad of Nathan right now. The darkness is unsettling tonight, deep and wide, as though it might swallow me whole.

Something makes me stop, a sudden change in the light.

'What is it?' Nathan says, pulling on my arm. I look up at the row of windows that line the street. A light has vanished on the top floor, leaving a gaping hole like in a smile of broken teeth. I stare up, focusing my eyes. In the darkness of the window, I am sure I can see a man. He is standing very still, almost hidden by the shadows. But I can see him. And I know he is looking right at me.

6

OLIVIA

Ballet class ends with Sergeyev appearing clutching a notation book, his pianist Ippolit Motcholov trailing behind him. The pianist winks at pretty little Molly Brown, one of the young dancers who has just made the transition from the school to the corps de ballet, before ushering a scowling Nathan off the piano stool. Miss de Valois cuts the *allegro* short, the men falling away to the sides of the room, sweat staining the cotton fabric of the shirts that they tuck into their black tights.

'*Le Lac des Cygnes* rehearsal, swans only,' calls out Miss de Valois as Sergeyev impatiently taps his cane at the front of the room. Already Motcholov is playing the notes of Tchaikovsky's Act Two and already we feel ourselves transforming into one unit, a perfect corps de ballet. The boys slowly leave the studio and the girls line up, our bodies finding the exact alignment mirrored by the others. When I glance up into the wide mirror that wraps around the room, it strikes me how we could be one long paper doll chain, every angle and curve the same. We cross our arms above our heads, holding them there. It is a relief when we step out into an *arabesque*, returning in a *balancé*, our aching arms now lowered. We *bourrée* en pointe, our legs striking fast into the ground with our bodies still and serene. We can feel every detail of each other, the slant of our necks, the quiet pace of our breath. We must not stray out of line. Sergeyev watches us with a tight glare, his eyes narrow. He keeps shaking his head, the black frame of his round glasses sliding dangerously down his nose.

The moments of stillness are the hardest. We stand in *attitude à terre*, our eyes gazing at a point on the ground away from us on a diagonal. I can feel my toes pressing uncomfortably inside my shoes and the back of my legs are starting to cramp with tiredness. Clara is in the row to the right of me and I look up, finding her reflection in the mirror. She seems to feel my eyes on her and she looks up too, a smile floating over her lips. We hold each other's gaze for just an instant before Sergeyev bangs his stick, spitting out a torrent of angry Russian exclamations. The music cuts mid-bar and we start again, the tension spreading. I can see the strain in our necks, the muscles around the sharp shoulder blades of the girl in front of me tight with nerves. No one wants to be noticed. In the corps de ballet, to be different is to fail.

It is Miss de Valois who stops us this time, her voice sharp in the sudden silence.

'Hermione, your knees are flabby in *arabesque*. Start putting in some effort.' She walks amongst us and I instinctively pull in my stomach and straighten my back. We are all holding our breath. 'And Joan, you aren't in line. I don't want to see you.' She turns back around and walks to the front. 'I do know you are pulling that face, Joan,' she calls out, her voice accusing. 'You'll need more talent if you want to get away with an attitude.' I turn to see Joan blushing bright red, her eyes fighting back tears.

We repeat the opening five times before finally being allowed to reach the end of the dance. All expression has been beaten out of us until we dance as one, even the set of our faces frozen into an unreadable blank. When, at last, Miss de Valois and Nicholas Sergeyev leave the studio, we collapse onto the floor, a low murmur of sighs spreading through us. No one wants to speak, at least not until we are in the safety of the dressing room. I untie my ribbons and gingerly pull off my shoes. My toes are painful to touch, bruising spreading along the joints.

Alicia Markova and Anton Dolin appear in the doorway. Two stars. They don't have time for us.

'We need the room,' Anton announces, marching in and throwing his bag under the barre at the front. They will be rehearsing the *pas de deux*: Odette, the swan princess, and Prince Siegfried. Usually I would want to stay to watch. But not today. I can't hear that music again.

Morning class and rehearsals finally over, and no performance tonight, I have an afternoon to myself. The dressing rooms empty out quickly, the girls stripping off leotards and taking down their hair. The differences between us seem to reveal themselves as we wipe down our glowing skin: the shapes of our naked calves, the curve of our breasts, the thickness of our hair as we brush out the kinks. A palette of reds and pinks and burgundies is smudged across our lips. By the time we are dressed again, it is only me and Clara who are still trapped in the repeated image of our face.

The corps de ballet is important, essential even. Especially in *Le Lac des Cygnes*, where the swans drive the entire movement of the dance. But I want more. I don't want to become invisible, an exact replica of everyone around me. Even the direction of our gaze must be identical, which is especially hard for me, I think, for already I am denied absolute uniqueness, Clara sharing my every feature. And so today I am going to do something for me, just me. I have an important mission, a journey across London that may bring me one step closer to principal dancer, prima ballerina; perhaps the assoluta part is a dream too far. Sometimes, if I try very hard, I can imagine myself back in time as one of Marius Petipa's ballerinas, dancing for the Mariinsky Ballet, wrapped in fur that tickles my nose as I leave the theatre, surrounded through Theatre Square by admirers.

I need something to set me apart from the others in ballet class. I want to be noticed, and not only because my mirror image is dancing alongside me. There is such a fascination with identical twins, even more so identical twin performers. It is as though we are a trick, an illusion. Sometimes, though, I worry that if Clara didn't exist, then I wouldn't be enough. I really would be entirely invisible at the back row of the corps de ballet, uninteresting without a double.

The practice tutus we wear for rehearsals are cheap and itchy. They rustle and scratch, hardly the illusion of ethereal magic we are striving to achieve. I look enviously at Alicia Markova, her perfect costumes made at her own expense, replacing the cheap, noisy taffeta for the lightest tulle. She even has two bodices for each costume, a matt one for performances and a shiny satin for press photographs. Of course, she has enough money. Unlike the rest of us, she is paid a proper salary for her performances, while we make do with just £2 per week. We need her, though, her reputation carrying us all with her at our fledgling Vic-Wells. There are rumours she is to be appointed prima ballerina any day now. It would be a sensible move for Miss de Valois, celebrating the fame of Markova.

Today I am going to find the costumier Madame Manya. If I can persuade her to make me my own practice tutu, I can stand out in rehearsals. I can be more than just a replica of my sister and the other girls in the chorus. And besides, I've earned it.

While Clara has been out spending her money on champagne and fancy meals across London, I have stayed in, saved up, darned the ladders in my tights rather than spending and spending on luxuries we cannot afford.

I was so nervous when I approached Markova in her dressing room last week. She was wiping make-up from her eyes with cold cream, leaving greasy smears across her cheeks. Even like this she looked beautiful, her eyes shining like a creature from another world. I pretended that Miss de Valois had asked me to collect a package from Madame Manya but that she'd forgotten to give me the address. Although Markova narrowed her eyes at me in the mirror, she scribbled it down all the same, thoughtfully adding some instructions and road names along the way. This is the best way to get there, she told me. Don't risk the back streets; don't go through Regent's Park in the dark.

It may as well be dark, I think, as I make my way through London to Maida Vale. The day started with a heavy mist that refused to lift and by now the sun has entirely given up, a thick fog settling over everything. I have to keep stopping to check the little scrap of paper, a smear of cold cream and blusher from Markova's finger colouring the words. Street signs are not easy to see, but I know where I am for the most part, Regent's Park just to my right. Buses crawl past, their lights struggling to break through the gloom. The light is slow and treacly, like our legs in *battement fondu* when we rise up out of the *plié*. Pausing as I cross over the wide road above the canal, I peer over the black iron railings into the water, watching as a dirty cloud of smoke swirls below me, ghostly fingers beckoning from under the bridge. They creep into my lungs and I shudder, speeding on along the pavement. Eventually I find the road I need, Markova's light scrawl on the piece of paper matching the street sign that appears and vanishes as the fog floats by. I walk slowly along, counting the houses, the fog so dense with smoke that the numbers are hard to read. Aware that I am a strange woman lingering outside homes, I try not to get too close to each door, but soon I think I must be about there.

I stand in the street for a moment to compose myself. The whole walk here, over an hour of marching through the damp fog, has made me anxious, as though I am being watched and scrutinised. As though someone might jump out at me and demand to know what I am doing. Why do I think the great Madame Manya would make a costume for me?

Madame Manya isn't expecting me, which makes me nervous. I have practised what I will say, how I will introduce myself: a dancer at the Vic-Wells, a colleague of Alicia Markova. I think about saying she is my friend, but that is simply not true and therefore a risk. I will have to rely on my own credentials and hope Madame Manya is willing to create a tutu for me. She is retired, but I know she still takes on occasional work for deserving dancers.

There is a light net curtain in the window of the front room; it makes me think of the white gauze of our practice skirts, just revealing the shadow of our legs beneath the fabric. I blink, trying to decipher the shapes and colours hidden inside. It is too faint, smudged like a spoiled painting. I squeeze my eyes shut and then open them again. There is something there, a woman, white skin, black lace, her arms held out by her thighs in *demi-bras*. Suddenly, the fog seems to fade in front of me and I see her more clearly, her eyes locking sightlessly into mine. A scream escapes my lips, a weak whimper that is immediately drowned in the rolling, persistent fog. There, through the mist and the glass and the gauze, is my face. I can see myself inside the room, dressed in the velvet and tulle of a deep black tutu. I take a step back, grabbing onto a dark unlit street lamp. I watch, horrified.

The face, my face, is changing, blotting itself out into a white blank. I blink and it has gone, just an oval shape, featureless and bland. It is barely there at all.

Just my reflection in the glass, I tell myself firmly, finding the courage I need to step towards the front door. My knock sounds timid, dulled by the fog, and I shift anxiously from foot to foot as I consider trying again. But just as I reach up to the brass knocker, a young woman opens the door, dressed in an elegantly cut black dress. Her hair is sleek, pressed down at her temples. It is only a white apron, tied at the side, that softens her. A maid perhaps, or a secretary.

'Can I help you?' she says, looking at me sharply. I must look damp and cold, the grey fog drifting behind me.

'I am here to see Madame Manya,' I reply, forcing out the words and a smile that I know is far from convincing. 'I would like to commission a tutu.'

'I see.' She waits, looking me up and down. Finally, she says, 'Well, you had better come in then.'

She leads me through to a small parlour. It is the room I saw from the road. She goes to the window and draws closed heavy red curtains, shutting out the street. Just a small slither of pavement still shows, like the dark shapes of the auditorium in those first few minutes of a stage call. 'Wait here, please. I will see if Madame Manya can see you.'

The woman leaves me, closing the door behind her. I hear the echo of her heels as she moves down the hallway into the back of the house. I am too afraid to look about me, to see if the woman I saw from the street is still there, watching me with her blank face. I glance quickly to my left. There is a double sofa, old-fashioned but in good condition, the fabric soft and plush. I don't sit. I am too anxious. Slowing my breathing, I listen for any sign of movement. There is nothing, so I try to relax, looking up at the muddle of memorabilia, paintings, sketches, photographs, costumes, that crowd the room. I am surprised the woman has left me alone. There must be a fortune of treasures in here, a delicious temptation for a young ballet girl.

When I see it, I laugh. A mannequin with a featureless white face poses in the corner, dressed in a black tutu with a velvet bodice. A motif of gold thread dances across the skirt and the neckline is woven with a delicate sprig of golden wire. Jewels hover around the hips. They look bold and bright, but I know they will be as light as lace, the dancer never even knowing they are there as she twists and turns across the stage. The mannequin is oblivious to her costume, arms stuck at jaunty angles. The tutu is wasted on her.

I turn, brushing my coat over my hips, imagining wearing such opulent black netting. My fear has gone now, and just a longing remains. Then, surely, Nicholas Sergeyev would notice me, Olivia Marionetta, not just one of those pretty identical twins.

And that is when I see it, arranged with a fascinating mix of care and chaos. There is no mannequin for this, just a pole and a base, no doubt with a fabric torso hidden within. White feathers are layered over tulle, a light sparkle shimmering from the tiers of the skirt. I reach out, my fingers hovering by the bodice, the white and cream goose feathers in perfect condition. A green glass stone centres the costume, like the eye of a swan gazing sorrowfully back at me.

'She never wore it more than twice,' a voice behind me says. 'Then, she'd be back to me, weighed down by the tulle and tarlatan, demanding the skirt to be renewed. A dying swan, brought back to life.'

I turn, my heart beating fast, pulling my hand back from the tutu. Madame Manya is older than I expected, frail too. I suddenly feel a fool, barging in here and asking for my own tutu. Especially now that I am faced with this: Anna Pavlova's costume for her famous dying swan. We have all danced the solo, on our own in dark empty studios, in our imaginations, in our sleep. Saint-Saëns's haunting music hovers at the edge of our consciousness every time we see a white dress, a feathered tutu, a swan arching its long, graceful neck. Before Pavlova died two years ago, Clara and I would creep up to her garden in Hampstead, desperate for a peek at the swans that she kept in her ornamental lake. Ivy House was a beacon for us when we were children; whenever we walked on the Heath and out to Golders Hill, we were drawn to it. Our feet took us in one direction only. We imagined the dancers she auditioned and coached in her studio, the productions she discussed for the Ballets Russes, the costumes she had delivered and prepared. Once, we had been certain we'd seen Enrico Cecchetti appearing at her door in black tie, but really it could have been any white-haired old man with a terrifying look in his eye. We heard that he died not long after, collapsing in the middle of a ballet class. All that ghastly *épaulement* finally did away with him, I remember Clara said, shockingly, when our ballet teacher told us. We were just fourteen then, all of us little girls putting on the perfect expression of loss for the passing of the great ballet master. Not Clara, though. Nothing and no one were too big for her to joke and prod, make a little human.

'Four thousand performances, can you believe,' Madame Manya says, her eyes moving quickly over the costume, as though searching for snags and tears.

I take a step back, suddenly feeling trapped in the crowded room. Signed photographs of ballerinas loom down at me from their frames, their smiles too sleek and poised. Madame Manya has reluctantly turned her attention to me, dragging her eyes away from her shrine to Pavlova. She must find me lacking, a dancer that no one has heard of standing amongst her museum to the greats.

'Thank you for seeing me,' I mumble. 'I dance at the Vic-Wells Ballet. With Ninette de Valois and Alicia Markova,' I add, pointlessly. Of course she knows about the Vic-Wells. She gives nothing back, her hands clasped and still at her waist. I grapple for something that may impress her. 'We are rehearsing for *Coppélia*. Nicholas Sergeyev is here in London.'

A small smile appears at the edges of her lips, the wrinkles around her cheeks deepening. Her collar is high, little scallops edged in white embroidery, and it makes her head look as though it is floating above her dress. There is more material than there is woman, I think. Maybe this is what happens when you create costumes for ballerinas.

'And you don't think the practice tutus at Sadler's Wells Theatre are good enough for you,' she says, tilting her head to one side as if to get a better look at me. I don't know what to say. She is right, of course. But I can't say it out loud. 'What did you say your name was, dear?' she asks, moving to the sofa and taking out a little notepad from a drawer in the low table at the centre of the room. She keeps the drawer open and I can see inside. A treasure chest of ribbon, buttons, threads, a measuring tape, pins, pencils. It gives me a little confidence, as if this might not to be so strange a request, that she is, perhaps, still working.

'Olivia Marionetta,' I reply, relieved at my balletic name, far better than Olivia Smith. 'I would love to commission a tutu from you. Nothing too elaborate, just a white practice tutu that will be a little quieter and firmer than the skirts we wear for rehearsals.'

I hold my bag close to me. I have the money I have saved up with me, but I have no idea if it will be enough. Surely £3 will buy a tutu; it has taken so long to save it up and I have agonised over whether to spend it. Our salary is so unstable. We are only paid for the season, and there are weeks on end when we have no regular income.

Madame Manya, too, seems hesitant. She takes a notecard from a small pile on the table and hands it to me. There is a sketch of a romantic-style tutu on the front, the end of the long skirt disappearing into the page in light pencil strokes. I turn it to see a list of prices. They start with the most basic practice tutu, no bodice, just the skirt that ties at the back. The list has eight options, the most expensive being a specially designed costume, complete with ornamentation. I don't need that, and besides, it is £20. I run my finger up the list, scanning the prices. The practice tutu is £5. It is a shock, how expensive they all are. It would take me months more to save up another £2. I can feel my cheeks start to burn, the colour rising uncontrollably. I feel stupid, turning up here with such high expectations, and now I will leave with nothing. There will be a long walk home through the fog to our cold, draughty flat. And tomorrow I will pull on the same scratchy tutu with no hope of setting myself apart from the others.

The dressmaker is watching me. For a moment I have an insane vision of her asking me to dance for her; I perform the dying swan, my feet *bourrée*ing around the room, my arms wrapping around me in those poignant final breaths. A tear comes to her eye; it falls down her cheek like a drop of rain, and she thinks of her Pavlova, how much she misses her, how Pavlova would have wanted her to make this tutu for this special girl, lovingly cutting and sewing the twelve layers of tulle.

Neither of us moves. Eventually she stands, gesturing to the door. 'Why don't you have a think, and come back to me next week if you want to go ahead?' She is kind, saving me from the embarrassment of explaining that I cannot afford her.

Of course she wasn't going to ask me to dance for her. Sometimes I think I live in a fantasy world.

She disappears without saying goodbye, and I am let out by the woman in black. Her apron has gone, revealing a long thin body stiff inside her dress. She says nothing, closing the door firmly behind me. Just like that, I am shut out of their world, Pavlova's dying swan costume safe and hidden.

I walk quickly to the end of the road, pulling up my coat collar around my neck. What little light there was has now been consumed by the fog. I am grateful, in a way, my face dissolving into tears. I bump face first into the chest of a large man as I turn the corner too fast, which makes me cry out. The shock of it is what I need to pull me back into reality. I apologise without looking up.

Following the same route home, my spirit is a little crushed, like that feeling after a cast list goes up and I am, once again, in the corps. But I am no longer anxious, and as I walk back I feel a strange sense of safety, as though those judging eyes that were watching me on the way here have turned into guardian angels, following me home and back to where I feel safe. When I really think about it, I don't know if I would have the courage to appear before the company in a practice tutu made by Madame Manya. It would be too bold, too real, too self-assured. Perhaps, after all, I am better off without it.

7

SAMUEL

He must speak to her. Something, anything. He feels his cheeks redden right up to his temples when he thinks of how he just stood there, like a dumb oaf, in the shop that morning three weeks ago. They could have so much in common, if he were just able to find the courage to start a conversation. He knows she loves dancing and costumes and ballet shoes. Perhaps she would like to see his sketches. Perhaps he could even design a costume for her. He lets himself daydream, there at his workbench, imagining her running onstage dressed in the lace and net that he has created.

Thursday again. He plans every moment he will spend in Sadler's Wells, how he will go straight to Wardrobe, rushing to get in and out before the dancers or Mr Healey need the room. Just before he makes his daily commute to the Freeds' workshop, the morning light still reluctant to creep in from the waking street, he writes a note. He is going to put it in Olivia's pigeonhole, just under the shoes so it is hidden from anyone but herself. He hasn't signed it. That would be a step too far. He considers drawing a small sketch of a rose in the corner of the page, but even that feels too much. What if she realises it is the same as the imprint marked onto the bottom of her shoe? What if she takes the note to Mr Frederick, demands to know what it means?

Dear Olivia Marionetta, he writes, his hand hovering before the *M*. Should he just write her first name? Would that be too informal, too presumptuous? In the end, he decides it would be. *I am writing to express my admiration, not only for your perfect, beautiful dancing, but also for you. I love your kind smile. I just wanted to write to tell you this. I love watching you.* (Samuel crosses out the sentence and starts afresh, carefully tearing a new square of paper. He tries again.) *I love the moments when I am able to watch you, and one day I hope I will be able to tell you in person.*

Just as he is about to press the note into his pocket, he changes his mind. She doesn't know what the rose means on the bottom of her shoe; surely it will be safe. And so, with a faint hand, hardly there at all, he signs with a rose, drawn carefully in pencil then filled in with a light pink chalk.

He delivers the shoes before lunch, listening out for the familiar sounds of piano music punctuated by the tap of the pointe shoes on the studio floor. The music stops and starts, angry striking of a stick on the floor accompanying the heavy silences. He doesn't go near the Wells Room, not today when he can feel the tension spreading out through the corridors of the theatre. When he leaves, he walks down the road to the little stretch of garden further along Rosebery Avenue. He feels exhausted, as though he's just accomplished some great feat. He hardly notices the group of boys who chase each other through the garden, their breath transforming into mist. It is cold, a fog settling over London like a thick pall, claustrophobic and chilling. His hair is damp from the air. He gets out from his coat pocket the sandwiches he made that morning. White bread with cheese and the pickle his mother gave him last month, one of the occasional gifts she delivers when she feels a pang of guilt at how long it is since she's seen him, the house in Clapham too cold and quiet all day.

Mrs Dora has given him the rest of the day off. He is ahead of his targets, and they are waiting for a delivery of satin before they can begin the next order. With the thick fog creeping around him, his first idea of walking to the river seems less appealing. He doesn't know what he would like to do to fill this rare time off. He should have asked Mrs Dora if she knows of any free exhibitions, or any art classes he might be able to attend. But he'd been afraid she'd look at him strangely, or laugh at him. Why would an apprentice like himself want to go to such things, she'd think.

Just as Samuel is about to give up and go home, he sees a woman speed past him, her head held still, her arms wrapping her coat tight around herself. Olivia. She walks with purpose, her feet making small, fast steps along the pavement. He gets up from the bench, rewrapping his remaining sandwich.

He follows her. The fog threatens to eclipse her, so he stays close. He panics as she turns the corner onto Euston Road, a cloud of dirty fog swirling before him. Samuel thinks he has lost her into the noise of the road, the people in their dark coats and scarves who weave in and out of one another, appearing and disappearing like ghosts. But then a bus groans past, its lights on and sending murky spotlights ahead. She appears again, a dark wool hat fitting closely, just revealing her signature low bun at the nape of her neck. Olivia, he thinks, has no problem dancing between people, sidestepping with hardly a change in her posture. It is harder for Samuel, whose large shoulders take up half the pavement. They walk in tandem for over an hour, Olivia occasionally stopping and taking out a scrap of paper before starting on her way again, peering at street signs through the haze.

They are in Maida Vale, having walked far along Euston Road, Regent's Park lingering to their right, surrounded in ghostly mist. When they cross over the canal, the water is hidden in dull clouds of fog. He watches from the corner as she stands outside a house, a slender figure moving lightly from foot to foot. Eventually she takes a step forward and rings the bell.

He creeps a little closer to the house she has entered. The curtains to the front room are ajar, leaving a small gap of low, warm light that spills out before it is submerged by the fog. Crouching down on the pavement, he looks through the gap. A low hedge of holly pricks him through his trousers, but he is oblivious to the pain.

The room inside is like a vision from one of his dreams, where his mind drifts as he measures, cuts, stitches the shoes. It is exactly what he wants in his own room, his dark room with the cracked plaster walls above Exmouth Market. His sketches, postcards, scraps of materials: they are all replicated here but on a much grander scale. In this room, lit up like the stage on Sadler's Wells as the curtain rises, there are full costumes, mannequins, framed photographs, not the faded scraps that he has stuck into the wall with pins. Just two nights ago he finished a design of a tutu, a rough sketch chalked in midnight blue and gold. He had, however, been precise with the measurements, writing in the amount of tulle, satin and ribbon it would require. It was a pointless task, really, as he could never afford even half of the material it would need. He'd enjoyed it, though, imagining Olivia's face as he presented it to her. The tutu she is gazing at now is not too dissimilar to his design. And yet the distance between his sketch and the life-size mannequin's costume in there is an insurmountable gulf.

Olivia is back outside far quicker than he expected. Samuel just has time to run to the end of the street. He turns back once he is around the corner, lingering for a moment. Building up courage, he thinks he could speak to her, as if in surprise at finding her here, a coincidence that they are both on the same street at the same time in this eerie London fog. He has just decided to do it when she flies around the corner, colliding with him heavily. She seems to bounce off his chest with a cry. He is about to speak, but she is too quick for him. She doesn't look up, muttering a quick sorry before continuing along the pavement.

Samuel follows. He waits until she arrives at her flat and the little light from her window illuminates a small square of the night sky before he turns north to his own rooms.

At his desk, he stares at his sketch, willing it to lift from the page, transform into twelve layers of tulle. Of course, it does nothing of the sort. He crumples it up in one hand, disappointed in himself. He resents his cowardice, his timidity and his doubt that holds back his ambitions, his fear of being scorned. Olivia had been crying when she left that house. And he could do nothing about it. More than anything he longs to deliver a tutu to her door, handcrafted by himself. But it is not to be. They are both alone in their small, cold rooms. And nothing can be done to bring them together.

8

CLARA

We must visit Mother. It is our penance, the last Sunday of every month. Sunday, 26 February 1933. I have lost count of how many times we have visited. This must be almost the fortieth time. It never gets any easier, and today is one of the worst sorts of days to visit. There is heavy cloud cover, an endless drizzle. We will be stuck inside in a claustrophobic visitors' room the colour of puce. We will be suffocated by it on the walls, floors, sofas that sink worryingly low. There will be no chance of a walk through the gardens.

Colney Hatch mental hospital, in certain lights, looks like a palace. But today the sky is a slate board that weighs on the towers and brick of the hospital. Olivia tells me off when I call it an asylum, but that's what it is. We are quiet on the short train journey, getting out reluctantly at the little station in Friern Barnet. We have gifts, as usual, but we know not to bring food. Once, Olivia made little cakes, carefully iced with pink ballet shoe shapes. Mother stared at them in horror. She turned to me and asked, spitefully, how many I'd eaten on the way here. So now we stick to flowers, a card, a photograph from our latest show, an old pointe shoe of Markova or Lopokova that we manage to sneak out of the dressing rooms before they throw them away. Mother likes the flowers best. She gathers them in her arms, drawing them to her and smelling them with a look of utter delight on her thin face. The nurse always tells us off. We are only exacerbating the depths of her delusions.

Mother is waiting for us in the visitor room. She is draped in a navy shawl dotted with silver thread that sparkles a little in the bland light. Her long grey hair is wrapped above her head with a silk scarf that trails down over her shoulder.

'My girls,' she calls to us as the nurse shows us in. She holds out her arms and we go to her, forcing smiles on our cheeks. It comes a little more naturally to Olivia, Mother's favourite. We sit either side of her, all three of our foreheads pressed close together as she squeezes us to her. I can feel her hands, her long, thin fingers, grappling and digging into my skin. This is her way, feeling our collarbones and scapulas, testing out the boniness of our spines. I know Olivia can't eat in those few days before we visit Mother. She stares at herself anxiously in the mirror, terrified she won't be thin enough for Mother's discerning grip. But Olivia is always thin enough, and Mother strokes her cheek gently.

'The perfect ballerina,' Mother sighs as she turns away from me, Olivia still held in her arms. I sit back, the sofa sinking under my weight. I will wait for Mother to talk to me, I think stubbornly. I know I should be more understanding; she is unwell, anxious, depressed, on heavy medication that just about keeps her on the edge of sanity. But she infuriates me, and if I could I would leave her here and never visit again. It is Olivia who always gets us to the train station on time, collecting up the little parcel of gifts, putting on the smile Mother requires.

'A little bird tells me Nicholas Sergeyev is in London,' she says, a sly smile creeping around her eyes. She grabs both our hands. 'And what roles has he given you? When am I to see my girls as Giselle, Odette, Aurora?' She is getting carried away, her imagination taking her to the only place where she can cope with reality. When Olivia and I started showing talent after those early years of ballet classes, she threw all her energies into our dancing careers. She lived for our classes, signing us up with the best ballet mistresses in London. She forced her way into the lessons when she could, watching us dance with hawk-like eyes. She lectured us on the bus journeys home: our legs had been dull, our heels weren't touching the ground in *petit allegro*, our elbows had drooped in pirouettes. Or, when her mood was vicious and triumphant, snarling about how terribly another girl danced, how much better we were, how she couldn't tear her eyes away from us. She seemed to know more about ballet than we did, following the reviews of the Ballets Russes like a religion, knowing exactly who was to be cast for each role, the choreographers, the new dancers rising up the ranks. She hunted down retired ballerinas who could teach us privately, giving over vast portions of our father's salary as a bank clerk to pay for the lessons. When we joined Ninette de Valois's school in 1927, we were thirteen years old and already very accomplished dancers, thanks to our mother's relentless pursuit of the best teachers in London.

Those two years before de Valois opened her school had been challenging for all of us. Our father died when we were eleven, a slow and painful cancer that dominated our non-dancing lives, Mother moving frantically between hospital appointments and ballet classes. When he died, she filled those free hours with more ballet, setting up the front room as a studio for us to practise, taking us to shows, writing charts on the wall of our progressions. Father had known he was dying for months and had prudently organised his finances so that we could cope without him. He knew Olivia and I would become dancers and could make a little money that way, but Mother would never be able to get a job. The few jobs she could be qualified to do would be beneath her. But even so, money once Father died was always tight, and the little we earned dancing small roles in operas at the Old Vic theatre barely covered our costs of pointe shoes and tights.

Colney Hatch costs us very little. But the money Father left behind has nearly run out, and Olivia and I try to avoid drawing down any of those few remaining pounds. I don't like to think of how sad he would be to think that the money he saved for us so carefully has been spent on keeping Mother in comfort at a county asylum. She has a small allowance which she spends on trinkets and worthless jewellery when, on her calmer days, she is allowed to join a supervised group of patients on shopping trips to the local town. She is wearing some of her purchases now, bracelets clinking against each other as she moves her long, wiry arms.

Olivia is telling her about Sergeyev and the rehearsals, spinning it out into a magical tale. Mother is enjoying it, closing her eyes as Olivia hums the music. She opens them again, sharply, when Olivia pauses.

'So which one of you is Swanilda?' she demands. Olivia pauses. I don't care if we tell the truth or lie. Olivia can decide whether it is easier to pretend one of us has the role, or to persuade Mother that Swanilda's friends are worthy, enviable roles.

'Well, Ninette de Valois and Lydia Lopokova are the first and second casts for Swanilda,' my sister replies. She sees the look on Mother's face change; quickly, she adds that we are both also learning the roles, as understudies. Not strictly true, but I suppose we do know every step.

'I remember dancing for Diaghilev,' she says, rising to her feet in what she must think is a graceful swoop. 'He wanted me to perform as the Firebird, but I was too petite. The costume nearly drowned me.' Here we go, I think, glancing at Olivia with a grimace. It has started earlier than usual. Every visit, we have to sit through her delusions, her fantastical version of her past where she was a ballerina in the Ballets Russes, dancing for Diaghilev, Fokine, Nijinsky. They all adored her, but she gave it up to have her twins. It is a complete fabrication, of course. She has never set foot on the stage, apart from when she used to linger too close to the edge of the wings at the Old Vic when we were dancing in an opera or play. The stories started after Father died. I think she must have been living them in her mind, fantastical escapism from all those awful hours she held his hand in the hospital bed. He was too ill to be looked after at home and so the small amount of money that his parents had left him when they died years ago was spent, tragically, on his own death. He was moved into a cottage hospital in Finchley and never left.

Once Father was gone, she couldn't resist repeating those inventions out loud, capturing us at the kitchen table while she went on and on about these strange, inconsistent, ridiculous stories.

She sways from side to side, her shoulders so delicate beneath the navy shawl. She has shrunk visibly these past three years. She could be blown away by a strong wind.

We were fifteen years old when Mother stopped eating. Our bodies were changing, both of us developing in mystical synchronicity. It happened so quickly. One day we were these tiny little waifs, our chests washboard flat, our hips narrow and straight. The next we were growing and shifting, our white cotton leotards no longer decent. It was Christmas Day 1929 when we started our periods. Both of us woke with tiny spots of blood in our knickers. Olivia looked terrified, but I hugged her and we laughed and crept into the bathroom to search through Mother's drawers for her Kotex sanitary napkins.

She found us in there, our bloody knickers from the night discarded on the bathroom floor. Her face was frozen, staring blankly at us. It was as if she'd forgotten we were normal girls. I think she wanted us to stay as we were forever, thin, delicate, androgynous nymphs who were immune to the changes of puberty.

I'll never forget that Christmas Day lunch. Olivia and I were in high spirits, giddy with the excitement of becoming adults. We were both piling food onto our plates, tomato soup then the slices of ham that Olivia and I had charmed the butcher into cutting extra thick, potatoes, bread sauce, plum pudding at the end. Mother had a headache that morning so had left us to cook, which was preferable as she never let us add enough cream to the soup. She was in her room, coming out every so often to fill up her glass with the brandy that we were adding lavishly to the butter. She joined us for lunch but picked at her food, occasionally bringing her fork to her lips then setting it down again with a sigh. We tried to ignore her, making our own conversation, laughing about a dance we'd seen the younger class do at Miss de Valois's school that made them look like ungraceful chickens.

Finally Mother snapped. She stood up, knocking into the table and making the lit candles shake ominously.

'You two continue filling your faces until you explode. See how you like it in the morning when your stomachs poke out of your leotards. And do not think I am going to sew another hook onto your skirts, young ladies.'

We watched her in silence, our mouths still full of food. My chewing sounded volcanic inside my head. She left us, retreating into her room with another glass of brandy. Olivia looked at me, uncertain. So I picked up my fork and kept eating. Olivia did the same.

And so, for the next three months, Mother shrank and shrank. She lost pound after pound, obsessively checking her ribs and hips in the mirror each day. One morning there was a delivery of weighing scales, far more expensive than we could afford, Mother ushering the man into her bedroom, where he set them up. It was a point of pride for her when she stepped off those scales each morning and announced her new, diminishing weight. She tried to make us get on them after her. She wanted to shame us, two slim and healthy ballerinas who weighed nearly a stone more than their mother. I watched Olivia carefully. It was contagious, this obsession with weight, and I refused to let it catch us.

When Mother fainted at Miss de Valois's studio, that was when we knew something had to be done. A nurse came to see us, then a doctor, then a psychiatrist. Nothing would help. Finally, she was deemed dangerous for us to be around. She had locked the kitchen and hidden the key. For a week we had to sneak out to eat, spending all our pocket money from the shows at the Old Vic on pastries and buns at cafés.

We were sixteen when she was admitted to Colney Hatch. Our house in Highgate was rented, so it had to go. With the returned deposit we moved into the rooms in Bloomsbury, gradually making them our own. Holidays, when there were no performances for us to audition for, were spent in Brighton with Aunt Alice and Uncle Cecil, who were appointed as our guardians, but we always escaped as fast we could, getting back to the busy schedule of class, rehearsals, small parts in revues in London. The Brighton house was noisy and chaotic and the only space to practise our *pliés* and *tendus* was in the garden. We did our pointe work on the tiny paved terrace, avoiding the white and green splats from passing birds, and we did *allegro* across the grass, scouting out the ground first to avoid the holes our cousin Benjamin had dug with his spade. A horrid little boy six years younger than us, he found great delight in pelting us with acorns, pine cones and twigs whenever we thought that we had found a quiet moment to dance. They were all happy to let us go when we asked to be driven to the station, to return to our lives in London. Our aunt and uncle would visit regularly to begin with, checking we had food, were paying the bills, were looking after ourselves. But the visits soon dwindled, the train journey in from their home in Brighton too long and inconvenient when they had their own children to look after. Mother's sister, Alice, did not get on with our mother. She agreed to keep an eye on us as a kind of penance, a self-imposed punishment to reassure herself that she had done enough. If she visited us, she could make herself feel better about never going to see Mother in Colney Hatch. Aunt Alice brought her son and daughter to watch us at the Savoy Theatre in June last year, but I think they were shocked by the performance, the jazz of Frederick Ashton and Buddy Bradley's choreography in *High Yellow*, far from their expectations of how ballet dancers moved. They left before we could come out from our dressing rooms at the end, leaving a brief note about needing to catch the last train home.

It is only these monthly trips that drag us back to the past. I long for the day when the doctor calls us in and tells us that it isn't good for our mother's mental stability for us to continue visiting. But he has not done so yet, and so here we are.

We leave when Mother starts shouting at us. She has a surprisingly loud voice for someone so tiny.

When we get home, I go straight to our miniature kitchen. I am prepared, as always after visits to Mother, with the ingredients for one of our favourite meals: cod with potatoes, in a butter and leek sauce. I bought the fish yesterday, so it is now swimming in melted ice, the skin glimmering in nacreous clouds in a bowl by the window. As I chop the potatoes, Olivia comes up to me and wraps her arms around me. I kiss her cheek and we stay like that, reminding ourselves how to love, until the vegetables are ready for cooking.

9

NATHAN

Nathan Howell likes to think he was one of the greatest child piano players of the first few decades of the twentieth century. He has kept all the programmes, his name in bold letters, followed by the titles of the most complex of piano solos and concertos. It was a point of pride that he could play anything, even Beethoven's *Hammerklavier* sonata, Ravel's *Gaspard de la nuit*. Stravinsky was easy for him, the rhythms bouncing through his child-size hands. It worried him, as he got older and he no longer looked like a strange little pixie barely able to reach the pedals, that his audiences would lose interest. And he was right. As soon as he reached adulthood, it was as though the enchantment he had conjured as a child had been switched off. The concerts dried up, one after the other, until he was grateful to accept the job with Constant Lambert at Sadler's Wells. Now, he plays in the orchestra when there is an opening, but usually he is in the Wells Room, hidden in the corner, subjected to the loud tapping of Miss Moreton's cane on the floor.

Clara Marionetta noticed him, though, when she came in to the studio to rehearse one day over a year ago, her pointe shoes flung carelessly over her back, held by the ribbons. Neither of them, in the end, had managed to rehearse anything that evening. Instead they found themselves talking for over an hour, drawn to each other, until the caretaker had kicked them out.

They found that they shared a love of exploring, finding out what was new and exciting in London. Together they have visited science exhibitions at museums, art galleries, jazz shows, clubs, tiny wine bars and loud cafés, fashion shows, the zoo, illusionists.

Nathan likes the way it feels to introduce Clara to places she would never go on her own; it reminds him of his importance, his status, the celebrity life of his youth, especially when someone recognises him from his concert days and comes over to reminisce about one of those great juvenile performances. Once, Clara's sister came with them to an art exhibition opening in Chelsea, but she drifted uneasily on her own, refusing the glasses of champagne that waiters in black tie balanced effortlessly on silver trays. She left early and didn't come with them again. It was just as well, Nathan thought; he did sometimes find it very difficult to tell the twin sisters apart. He always had to work out who was wearing which outfit and secure it to memory so he didn't muddle them up for the rest of the day. In ballet class it was easier, with Clara wearing her hair high and Olivia's in a low bun at the nape of her neck.

He waits for Clara outside Sadler's Wells. It is the first Saturday of March, and a brightness is appearing in the London sky. The opera is performing *Cavalleria Rusticana* and *Pagliacci* tonight, so the dancers have a free weekend now that ballet class and rehearsals are finished for the day. Nathan has decided they will visit the National Gallery. A new work is to be unveiled. Or rather, exposed from under a great sheet that has been hiding the art for weeks. For this is not the usual wall-hanging painting. This is a mosaic commissioned for the portico of the gallery.

At last Clara appears from the dressing room and Nathan takes her arm impatiently. He hurries them forward through the London streets, keen to arrive before the crowds get even heavier. It is busy, this first sighting of early spring sun drawing people from their homes. They pass through Covent Garden, weaving in and out of the bustling energy of men transporting crates, sacks, barrels, boxes, all labelled in the thick black letters of their trade name. The clatter of wheels and the shouts of the workmen ring out through the streets, and Nathan has to pull Clara to the side to avoid a tottering tower of onion bulbs that threatens to spill over into their path. Trafalgar Square is full of a different energy, couples and families parading around in the sun in their best outfits, the light spraying through the water of the fountain. Two little girls play under the translucent mist of the water, screeching joyfully as they find rainbows above their heads. Clara watches them, lingering to dip her hand into the twinkling water as they walk past, a crowd of fat pigeons parading territorially about her feet. Nathan turns to her impatiently, gesturing for her to stay close.

They climb the steps to the National Gallery, Clara readjusting her hat to stop her hair tumbling down around her shoulders. They have walked so fast that they are both breathless.

Inside, men and women move like dancers in slow motion across a ballroom floor. All eyes are down to the ground. 'It could be an exhibition of people's ugly brown shoes,' Clara whispers to Nathan.

'Shush,' he replies. 'Let's find a good spot.'

The portico has an air of studied quiet, calm and concentrated after the busy chaos of Trafalgar Square. Boris Anrep's mosaic is larger than Nathan expected. This is the second set, *The Awakening of the Muses*. The first set, *The Labours of Life*, was completed in 1928, but Nathan hardly remembers its opening.

It portrays so many of life's roles he simply knows nothing about: engineering, farming, science, family. Especially family. This new set of mosaics fires his imagination. Bacchus and Apollo stir the muses awake, revealing the faces of the celebrities of his youth. There is Osbert Sitwell, Clive Bell, Diana Mitford, Virginia Woolf as Clio, Greta Garbo as Melpomene. Anna Akhmatova, the great Russian poet, is Calliope. And then the one Clara is straining to see through the crowds of people: the ballerina Lydia Lopokova as Terpsichore, the goddess of dance and chorus.

When Nathan took the job at Sadler's Wells, he imagined he would be quickly snapped up to join the Camargo Society. He was young, talented, had performed at all the great concert halls of Europe. He knew what audiences wanted, where the Arts could go if they took the right steps. He could be an asset to the society, he thought, speaking at their committees and helping with the ambitious programmes of dance and music they financed in London. When he was a child, his parents told him daily that he was special, that he was talented, that the world was lucky to have him. They whispered this mantra to him in the green rooms before concerts, at his bedside when, exhausted, they tucked him up and he fell asleep dreaming of scales and chords, his own inner metronome sending him to sleep. He grew up believing the world owed him applause and gratitude, that he would be welcomed with open arms in any theatre or concert hall.

He looks over to the little crowd of people who peer down at Anrep's mosaic. The Camargo Society at large, he thinks enviously. They have a basket with them, tucked between their feet, which holds a bottle of champagne and glasses. Maynard Keynes reaches for it, laughing as a museum attendant rushes to him, shaking his head.

'But my wife is at our feet, cast forever in marble,' he objects, politely and indulgently. His wife smiles, dipping her chin a little, posing. She is Terpsichore, the great muse, her face etched in Byzantine colours on the ground, a vision of greens and pinks and ochre. Nathan watches them, Lopokova and Keynes admiring the art, the champagne bottle now returned unopened to the basket. Constant Lambert is there too, and Ninette de Valois. Edwin Evans arrives and joins their group. He is the Camargo Society's musical adviser and recently music critic for the *Daily Mail*. Nathan turns away, angry. He regularly encounters Evans in the corridors of Sadler's Wells, but he always avoids him. He doesn't trust himself around him, not after what happened all those years ago. He's convinced it is Evans's influence that is keeping him from the exclusive meeting rooms of the society.

Edwin Evans had followed his music career, writing up marvelling, exuberant reviews when Nathan was very young. The dazzling Nathan Howell was a child star, a musical genius, performing virtuoso piano work with extraordinary skills. Then, in 1925, when Nathan was fifteen, by now starting to look like an adult and playing the piano no differently to how he had played it for the past five years, Evans changed his tune. He came to see him in a concert of Elgar's piano music, a gala at the Philharmonic Hall that Elgar himself was attending. Nathan was still at his peak, astounding audiences and taking in a good salary. Of course, it was harder for him and his father by then, with his mother gone and his father struggling to keep up with Nathan's busy and complicated schedule, but this was a highlight, a concert they had both been looking forward to. Nathan's father still whispered the mantra: he was special, he was talented, the world was lucky to have him. He built Nathan's already inflated confidence with those encouraging words, but his heart was no longer in it. Since his wife had gone, some part of him had gone with her, and he could no longer quite find the enthusiasm to follow Nathan around Europe, waiting in gloomy green rooms, signing contracts in dusty offices and sending endless letters reminding producers that they were yet to pay his son for his performance. While his mother had looked for excitement in each new city they visited, his father was reliant on his little pot of sleeping pills, barbiturates that knocked him into a fast, deep sleep as soon as they returned to the hotel room.

The review that came out in the *Evening Standard* the day after the performance was cruel. It would have been cruel for anyone, but for a fifteen-year-old, even one as self-assured as Nathan, it was a blow. He read that he played with the emotion of a rock and the charisma of a fish. While his fingers performed all the right notes at the right tempo, there was nothing in his performance that couldn't have been performed by a diploma student who had diligently worked through their exams. In short, Nathan might have been a child prodigy, but now he was well on the way to becoming a mediocre adult.

Musicians, critics, audience members, they all rallied round to complain about the harshness of Evans's words. But the die had been cast and slowly, gradually, almost imperceptibly, Nathan's invitations to play dwindled. Over the next six years, he made a slowly declining living as a struggling concert pianist, his father too old and tired to help, until one day he was found by Constant Lambert and the new stage of his life began.

Clara returns to him, full of energy. 'What do you think of them?' she asks, putting her arm through his. She guides them around the mosaic, pointing out little details that Nathan hasn't even started to notice. 'Look at Woolf,' she demands. 'Her silver dress is so alive, like it might fall off her if she stands up. Let's hope it does,' Clara laughs, pulling Nathan in towards her. 'Clive Bell doesn't look like he's indulged in much wine, does he,' she continues. 'He's got grapes in his hair, but he's a very sombre Bacchus.'

'Is that Greta Garbo?' Nathan asks, pointing at a golden mosaic of Melpomene, her hand held out with a wreath of flowers suspended in the air above her. 'Isn't she supposed to be the muse of tragedy?' he continues. 'She looks far too happy for that. I rather like the idea, though, of her fixed forever in the ground. I didn't enjoy *Mata Hari*. All that crazed exotic dancing was vulgar.'

'Don't be ridiculous, Nathan,' Clara replies, digging her hand into his ribs and making him double over in unwilling laughter. 'Greta Garbo as Mata Hari is my absolute idol. An exotic dancer and a spy, entirely unafraid of her own desires. Why would you want to condemn her to a life of stone, being trampled on daily by all these visitors? One day, they'll hardly notice she is here.' She moves them on, pointing out details in the art that bring the figures to life, enjoying the strange contrast of stone and energy. 'And there is our Lydia,' she cries out at last. 'The muse of dance. How funny that she is holding a squirrel.'

'Surely you would like to be immortalised in art, fixed forever in perfection?' Nathan asks, more serious now, almost talking to himself instead of Clara, who is crouching at the edge of the mosaic. 'There is the great Lydia Lopokova, the perfect muse of dance, never changing, a goddess.'

'Like your mother, you mean?' says Clara, forgetting herself, letting a touch of resentment creep into the words. Nathan has told her many times about his mother and her tragic death when he was twelve. He has described his mother as perfection, shown Clara photographs of her, a stunning woman with bright blonde hair and a long, elegant neck. In one photograph, the one he carries with him always, she looks like a film star, glamorous and ethereal.

'What has my mother to do with this?' he replies.

'I'm sorry,' Clara says, seriously, standing up to face him. 'But don't you see what Boris Anrep has done here? This is not a fixed memorial of lifeless art. This is a conversation, a moment's breath, a celebration of all the varieties of life. These aren't gods in stone, they are people, alive and breathing, who reassure us we can find art and beauty in every corner of life.

'Look over there.' She points. 'Lydia Lopokova in the flesh, trying to persuade her husband to pour her a glass of champagne. And in three weeks she'll be onstage as Swanilda in *Coppélia*, teasing Dr Coppélius into thinking she is his precious doll come to life. And we can, forever, dance and run and skip over this mosaic. This makes me think of life, modern life, not memorials to perfection.'

'Well, let's agree to disagree on this one, my beautiful ballerina,' Nathan says, taking her arm again, finding control. 'Personally, I would like to be fixed in time at my most glorious. But for now, let's try to get a table at the Café Royal and drink far too much wine to art and beauty and to getting on Anrep's list for his next instalment of muses.'

He tightens his grip on Clara's arm and leads her to the exit. As they pass between the columns of the façade, Nathan looks back and casts a grim stare at Edwin Evans and the rest of the Camargo Group, desperate for them to notice him here, the once-famous child prodigy still in the midst of art and culture, still walking amongst them, this time with his very own ballerina. But none of them even notice he is there. Nathan Howell has been forgotten, a passing footnote in the records of the gazettes and journals of his childhood.

10

OLIVIA

The studio at the top of the theatre where Miss de Valois runs her school is empty this morning. The girls and boys are down at the Old Vic for the day to audition for chorus roles in a new opera. I take a step inside, at once remembering the relentless exhaustion of those ballet classes, the repetition of each exercise until Miss de Valois was satisfied. I remember standing in fifth position en pointe until my legs shook with the effort. A long mirror reflects my image back at me, my face thin and tired, my hair tied tight off my face.

I walk to the front of the room and place my bag down at my feet. Looking back at the door to check no one has followed me, I take out a pair of pointe shoes from the depths of my bag. They are not mine. Alicia Markova left them behind after a rehearsal for *Le Lac des Cygnes* yesterday, two discarded satin shoes in the corner. I stole them when she had left the Wells Room, tucking them away in my bag.

Turning them over in my hand, I try to find some secret clue as to her fame, her certain status as prima ballerina. The satin is scuffed more on the outside edge of the foot than the rest and the sole is soft and pliable with a sweet smell of glue and sweat and baking soda. She has burned the edges of the ribbon with a match to stop the fraying and her stitching is neat and even. I place them on the ground in front of me and reach again into my bag, a nervous thrill spreading through my toes.

It wasn't only her shoes that I took. She had tucked away a little make-up pouch in the corner of the studio, packed with cold cream, powder, lipstick, a stub of a kohl pencil. I stole the lipstick, hiding it within the folds of my warm-up layers until it was safe to transfer into my bag. Now I take it out, pulling off the lid with a satisfying pop. The end has been worn down into a smooth red round. Stepping towards the mirror, I lean in until I am just inches from the glass. It takes a few attempts to paint the colour onto my lips, dabbing with my finger to tidy the glow of red that threatens to dance outside the bounds of my mouth.

I put on her shoes, tying the ribbons securely around my ankles. They are too narrow around the toe, the wing soft but still pressing uncomfortably into the arch of my foot. When I stand they feel a little better, the supple satin and leather bending to me. I rise en pointe, drawing my feet into a tight fifth position. The shoes are far too soft and it takes all my strength to stay tall. With small shifts of my weight, I try to find balance. Taking my arms into a round first position in front of me, I start to turn, little *chaînés* that take me around the edge of the room. My head finds a spot in the direction I am travelling, whipping around fast every time I turn. The room becomes a broken collage of cubes, the black-and-white photographs on the walls, the hard straight back of the piano, the dark brown line of the barre. But then my vision starts to falter, the lines blurring and bleeding as I turn and turn, my balance breaking and the shoes unsupportive underneath me. They know I am not their mistress; they care nothing for me. I catch sight of my shape in the mirror but all that I can decipher is the red of my lips like a wound.

And then I see him. In the doorway a man is watching me, his body heavy and dark, with shoulders that threaten to break through into my space.

I fall, the shoes slipping and dragging me down to the ground. A bolt of pain shoots through my wrist and my hip smacks hard against the floor. But when I look up, there is no one there, just a gaping emptiness leading back out to the corridor. And yet I am sure I recognised him. A hulking man who lurks behind his bags of pointe shoes, his unsettling eyes following our feet as we dance.

When I take off the shoes, blood stains my tights, a red and brown mess that is wet and fresh. I gently feel through the tights, wincing at the raw skin on my toe. Seeing myself in the mirror, I shake my head angrily. This is what happens when I try to rise above my level, when I try to be someone I am not, overreaching myself and falling hard. Hurriedly, I pack away the shoes and the lipstick, wiping my mouth with the back of my hand. It looks like a rash, a red slash that has started spreading through my skin.

Downstairs, I quickly find my balance again. When I go to collect my new set of pointe shoes from Wardrobe, there is a frantic energy in the room, a frisson that spills out on fitting days despite the sharp pins that the costumiers fasten precariously around our ribs. My previous pointe shoe delivery is just start-ing to run out now, so I haven't been in here for over a week. After my trip to Maida Vale, I have been avoiding rooms that remind me of my misguided Promethean failure. Stealing Markova's shoes did nothing to help. Mr Healey is shouting at a girl from the school who has knocked into his stand of tutus, their frills poking up indecently into the air. Two women from the company are being measured for costumes, and a large pile of colourful shoes for the men in *Coppélia* is slowly collapsing into the middle of the room, a red heeled boot making a daring dash towards the door. I hover at the edges, keeping out of everyone's way. Miss de Valois is also in here, with a new girl I have only seen once, when she came for an audition. I had been walking past the Wells Room and was shocked to see that the girl hadn't even brought her practice clothes or shoes. Miss Moreton made her remove her outdoor shoes and stockings and stand at the barre in her bare feet. She must have had something special, because within days she was enrolled in the school, joining 'the bombs', as we liked to call them, in their makeshift changing room in the dress circle ladies' cloakroom. Clara and I had been there once, and yet we were all quick to forget how intimidating older, more established dancers could be.

When I reach into my pigeonhole and place my pointe shoes in my bag, a little square of paper falls to my feet. All theatre post is delivered to our Wardrobe pigeonholes, our pointe shoes stacked amongst letters from admirers, cuttings from newspaper reviews that one of the girls thinks we might like to read, the season's contracts. But this little note feels different, the edges of the paper thin as though torn from a larger sheet. I pick it up, turning it over twice.

Dear Olivia Marionetta, I am writing to express my admiration, not only for your perfect, beautiful dancing, but also for you. I love your kind smile. I just wanted to write to tell you this. I love the moments when I am able to watch you, and one day I hope I will be able to tell you in person.

It is signed with a rose. No name. On the other side is a simple sketch of a ballerina in a long white romantic-style tutu, little wings floating out from her arms.

Holding the note to me, I smile. I long to get out of Wardrobe and somewhere quiet where I can turn this over in my mind, work out who it is that has written this for me. It is too noisy in here, with Mr Healey shouting louder, the musical lilt of his accent ascending into hysterics. A headdress for an Act Two doll in *Coppélia* has disappeared from Wardrobe and he is furious. Even Miss de Valois is starting to look flustered, ushering the new girl out of the door. The girl looks terrified, her wide eyes staring at Mr Healey in amazement. Miss de Valois never brought me in here for a fitting when I joined the school, I think, a little resentfully. Clara and I had to be resourceful, begging older girls for their discarded leotards, resewing ribbons from worn-out shoes onto each new pair. I wish I had been adored by Miss de Valois, taken under her wing and protected. But there were two of us, two Marionetta girls who could look after each other. We carried our mother's name, Marion, and we carried her anxiety and stress and fear, but we left as much of her as we could in that hospital a train ride away. Perhaps wishing for a replacement mother in Miss de Valois is misguided. One mother hasn't helped us make a smooth transition into adulthood; why would a second be any better?

I go straight to the well, nodding politely at the new young stagehand I encounter on my way along the corridor. He looks back at me as I open the door leading down to the storage room: he is too new, I think, to realise how regularly we like to come here. I make my way down the steps, relieved to see that there is no one else here. It is cold, as usual, but the stillness of the water and the dim, quiet light is soothing. There are no shadows reaching their grey ribbons around the edges of the well, no whispers from the low chill that reaches up from the water. I feel safe in my isolation.

With my eyes straining in the low light, I read the note again. There is something wonderful about a note like this. The writing is round and firm, the words clear but artistic, as though the writer has taken care that every letter is beautiful as well as legible. I lower myself on to the stone wall surrounding the well, easing my legs out in front of me. My muscles ache, a dull tiredness that spreads all down my hamstrings and calves. I lean forwards, stretching luxuriously, the note balancing on my feet. Too many *brisés* today; I've been trying to match the same rhythm and energy as Lydia Lopokova, who seems to fly across the stage. She has a wobbly knee, as she calls it, an injury from overuse throughout her long career. I've seen her speaking firmly to herself, doing her funny little warm-ups before launching into the most bouncing and brilliant arrangements. But when rehearsals end she walks with a limp, the jarring bursts of pain streaked across her smooth, round face revealing her as human. I shouldn't be complaining about tired legs, the right sort of tiredness that signifies I will wake up stronger and faster in the morning. Getting old and injured feels so far away, like a tiny grey cloud hovering benignly on the horizon.

Bending forwards further, I press my hands into my thighs. I know exactly who I want the note to be from. And yet that would be impossible. Nathan Howell's affections are firmly fixed elsewhere. I have watched him with Clara. The two of them are always out together, exploring London, experiencing so much in a world that doesn't include me. I tried once to go with them, to visit an art exhibition. I hadn't realised it would be an opening, and I felt underdressed and uninteresting compared to everyone else there. They were all either glamorous or bohemian. I was neither, just a little tired and too nervous to approach anyone. Nathan and Clara hadn't wanted me there, not really. So I can cross Nathan off the list. Or maybe not, I think, turning the note once again and checking it really is addressed to me and not my sister. Yes, it is definitely to me. Perhaps it could be from him, a secret message to signal his desire. And I have, often, seen him staring at me, his gaze lingering as I finish a *grand allegro* right next to his piano.

I know it is the coat that makes me think more hopefully of Nathan today. When Clara got in from a day out with him this weekend, she threw off her coat, casting it in a crumpled green pile in the corner. Nathan bought it for her last year and she wears it whenever she goes out with him, the fur thick and elegant around her neck, her waist neat beneath the belt. I imagine him holding her there as he kisses her, his hands pressing into the soft green fabric. Picking the coat up off the floor, I gently smoothed out the creases as I hung it up.

'Just leave it,' she said, waving her hand dismissively. 'I'll deal with it later.' It was so strange, I remember thinking, to talk about the coat that way, as if it was a problem to be solved. 'In fact, why don't you wear it,' she said, a little tiredly. 'I'm sick of wearing the same thing every time I go out.' She paused and added, 'It'll look lovely on you.'

'Won't Nathan mind?' I asked anxiously. I was longing to wear it, the thrill of feeling the same wool against my skin that Nathan had touched and admired. It would make him feel closer, more mine. I could feel the heat rising in my cheeks as I imagined walking to the theatre in Clara's coat.

'He'll probably just think you're me, same as everyone else.' She turned to me, more focused now. 'Honestly, you'd be doing me a favour.'

I lean down, finding my faint reflection in the water. Perhaps he does admire me, not just as the mirror image of my twin. But of course I am her double, every contour of our faces replicated, captured in the other like a daguerreotype. Clara and I find it hard to avoid the stares of men when we walk together outside, two identical young women side by side. Sometimes, when we walk through Regent's Park, they call out to us, harmless admiration I suppose, but I hate it. It always feels like an attack, even though, technically, the words are kind. I fold into myself, moving closer to my sister, letting her laugh at the men, sending them away with a quick comment and a toss of her head.

There is a man who sends me flowers before every Tuesday night performance. But he is old, a regular patron who takes the same seat every week. And he would definitely sign his name on a note such as this. He is a lover of the ballet, the art of it, the music, the choreography. He doesn't hunt for pretty young dancers to seduce with rich gifts and generous payments. Mr Ilya Abelman is his name, a Russian émigré who now lives in Primrose Hill with his very bossy daughter, or so he tells me when he finds me in the foyer after a performance and talks until I am half asleep and longing for my bed. He always has a little box of Carson's fruit pastilles with him, sold for sixpence by attendants at the auditorium doors, that he takes home to his adult daughter. He moves from theatre to theatre each night of the week, never missing a ballet show. He told me once, when I found him waiting outside the theatre to present to me the most elegant box of chocolates, that he had followed the Ballets Russes across Europe – *Swan Lake* in Monte Carlo, *The Firebird* in Lisbon, even *The Rite of Spring* in Paris. He loves the ballet, purely and devotedly, and would never write a note like this. His words would be bold, indulgent, describing his favourite divertissement in a performance. I am fond of him, especially when he catches me leaving the theatre and folds my hand in his, kissing it chastely as though I am a princess. Clara has no time for him. But he is one of the few men that seems to be able to tell us apart, and I love him for it. Perhaps he can sense that I belong to another time, that I would be more suited to the glamour of Imperial Russia than this penniless London life where we have to search the audition lists for roles to occupy us out of season. Our Vic-Wells season runs from September to May, so there are three long summer months to find employment, and more importantly payment. It is an exhausting time, and I don't relish the hours spent standing in stiff poses for the opera or for plays, dressing the stage with my body. Some of the other girls have found themselves rich patrons, men who linger after each performance, pressing gifts into their hands: jewels, clothes, expensive meals at hotel restaurants. My Mr Abelman isn't like that; he never expects anything from me, never invites me out to late-night dinners in the corner of secluded bars. The girls come into class the morning after these dinners, a new fur stole on their coat, a new bracelet circling their wrist. They smirk and smile, but I don't believe them when they say they enjoyed themselves. If I catch them when they think no one is looking, I can see another look clouding their eyes. They stare down at their new jewels with a fascinated horror, as though struggling to comprehend what it was their body did to get it there.

Despite the first signs of spring, it is cold, especially down here by the well. Eventually, I stand, stretching my arms up to the low ceiling and rolling my neck. With stiff fingers, I release my hair from its bun, spreading it across my back. I hardly ever wear my hair down now. It feels exposing, like I am giving away a part of me that I prefer to tidy away and hide from sight. The note is a mystery and will have to stay that way for now.

As I walk back up to the Wells Room, I hear piano music trickling down from the top floor. It is coming from the board room, a small room at the top of the theatre that we use for solo rehearsing. It can barely fit a piano, a dancer and a teacher. Sergeyev has been coaching the leads in there, and we can hear him sometimes, even from the floor below, calling out instructions in broken medleys of French, Russian, English.

I make my way up the stairs, the warmer air of the top floor reaching me with its distinctive smell of damp, like wet fur. I avoid looking into the school studio, the rip of skin on my toe still too fresh, the humiliation too sharp. The door at the end of the corridor of offices and small rehearsal rooms is ajar, and I peer around to see who is rehearsing. The blood rises fast in my cheeks, colour spreading uncontrollably up from my neck. It is Nathan, his face fixed in concentration, his hands moving lightly over the keys as he plays the familiar notes of the bolero.

Before I can stop myself, I have taken a step into the room, propping myself up against the door frame. He looks up at the end of the piece, noticing me for the first time. His face softens into a smile.

'You sure you don't want to rehearse?' he says. 'I don't think Sergeyev needs this room for another hour.'

I am confused. He has never asked me to rehearse with him before. That has always been a privilege reserved for Clara, the two of them secreting themselves away whenever Nathan can find a piano free in an empty rehearsal room. It only takes me another second to realise that he thinks I am Clara. My hair is loose and I have the green coat over my arm. I had taken advantage of Clara's offer this morning. It might not be too long before she changes her mind and takes it back.

Our voices are similar, nearly identical, and to someone who doesn't know us well, they would be impossible to tell apart. I don't know if Nathan will be able to tell I am not Clara if I speak. Something makes me think not; he is not the sort of man that really listens to a woman when she speaks. And yet here I am, wishing he loved me, wishing he looked at me with the same admiring, even proud way he looks at my sister. Recently I've noticed her dismissing him at the end of rehearsals when he comes and puts his arm around her. She shrugs him off, making up an excuse about needing to cool down, to stretch, to get to a costume fitting. I wouldn't treat him like that, not if he looked at me with the same pride as he looks at Clara.

My heart beats hard as I take one step into the room. I want to go to him and kiss him. It would be like a dare, like when Clara and I were little and we would challenge each other to creep up to Pavlova's Ivy House, to touch the wall, to clamber up on the tree by her garden and look over at her pet swans.

I can't risk it. I am not prepared. Instead, I stop after just a few steps and smile at him, trying to mimic Clara's wide smile, showing her teeth, so different to mine, which is guarded, closed. 'I've got to get ready for the Act I rehearsal now,' I say. 'But maybe tomorrow.'

I turn quickly, almost running out of the room.

'See you later then, Clara,' I hear him call after me, more a question than anything else. And I don't correct him. This isn't new, being mistaken for my sister. But this time it feels thrilling, adventurous, like I've slipped into a role where I can do whatever I wish. I feel stronger, a little dangerous.

Later in rehearsal, my hair back in its low bun, I enjoy watching Nathan staring at my sister. This time it feels as though it is me he is looking at, that I too am the recipient of his gaze. It is an opportunity. And one that I will not let slip, wasted, through my fingers.

11

CLARA

Rehearsals for *Coppélia* are picking up pace. We are all excited about the first night, but it is still over two weeks away. Costume fittings are frantic and there is the constant sound of sawing and banging coming from the carpenter's workshop behind the stage. They are creating a set of an Austrian village, influenced by the tradition of the Bavarian harvest, complete with pretty flower displays, wooden benches, rustic door frames. And of course there is the workshop of Dr Coppélius, the eccentric doll-maker who makes a mechanical doll so lifelike that Franz, Swanilda's fiancé, is convinced she is a real woman, perpetually sitting in the window reading a book while lace frills sit stiffly around her neck. The perfect image of dull, idealised femininity. Franz is an idiot. He should be able to see that fun, lively, alive Swanilda is a much better choice. I am glad we are not performing Act III, in which Swanilda forgives Franz for preferring a lifeless doll to her. They marry, a joyful celebration with the whole village coming out to dance. I am not sure it is realistic. Would Swanilda really forgive him? It seems unlikely.

It is a wonderful ballet, full of comic energy and fun. Lydia Lopokova has become quite friendly with us all, enjoying our attentions, it seems, the opportunity to share little scraps of stories and choreography from her days at the Mariinsky, the Ballets Russes, touring in America, dancing with Fokine and Diaghilev. I watch Olivia hanging on her every word. If she could, my sister would transport herself back in time to the early twentieth century, to the dormitories of the Imperial Theatre School in St Petersburg. She would be entirely suited to the prison-like routine, a convent of precision and order. The chance to dance alongside Bronislava Nijinska and Tamara Karsavina would make it all entirely worth it.

I prefer listening to Lydia's stories of Fokine and Isadora Duncan, how they broke all the rules of classical ballet, determined that they could do something better than the rigid poise of the Russian school. Isadora Duncan is so entrenched in myth and magic that she barely seems real to me. I remember when the news of her death was plastered dramatically across the papers in 1927. It had seemed like the loss of a dream: how much I would have loved to have met her. But even her death was glamorous to me, her long silk scarf caught in the wheels of the motor car on the Riviera in Nice. She was thrown onto the road, strangled by the scarf. Her last words, *Adieu, mes amis. Je vais à la gloire*, seemed so romantic; but then I was just an impressionable child in love with the stage, desperate to find my own chance of glory.

It is the glamour of America and the experiments of dance, film and theatre that truly excite me. I long to be as bold and outrageous as Isadora Duncan, who shocked Russian audiences by dancing on the stage with her hair loose and flowing, her feet bare, once even exposing her naked breasts. I smile when I think of how shocked Mother would be if I got on a boat to America and broke from the traditions of classical ballet. But there is no chance of that happening, not when I have the comparative safety and security of the Vic-Wells, my sister by my side, Ninette de Valois steadily expanding our world, the promise of a growing British ballet. And yet I would love to leave London. The furthest I have ever travelled is on a ballet tour to Manchester.

Hanging back after rehearsal today, I linger at the barre with my pointe shoes still on. I feel restless and I don't want Olivia by my side. She is at her most intense right now, driven only by the ballet. She left the studio without me when she realised I had no plans to hurry. Nathan isn't here either, his absence giving me permission to dream and imagine, to feel lighter without his gaze fixed upon me. It was Ippolit Motcholov who played for the rehearsal today, Constant Lambert seething from his chair at the front as he tried to work out how he was supposed to reconcile Sergeyev and Motcholov's version of the score with the expectations of the orchestra. It is usually the dancers he has to worry about, grumbling when they refuse to keep up with the pace of his baton. Though to be honest these dress rehearsal altercations thrill me, ballerinas shaking their heads under the glowing light of the stage while Constant angrily throws his arms around from the orchestra pit.

Nathan isn't here today and I feel no guilt that I am glad. I need a rest from him and his constant watching and expecting. He always has to be doing, achieving, finding purpose in every stage of the day. So frequently, he makes me rehearse with him, which is tiresome, especially when I can tell that he is watching me as he plays the piano, stopping when he can sense me faltering. Let's start again, shall we, he'll say, waiting for me to get in position. Or we are out in London, searching for exhibitions and concerts, tracking down the best new restaurants, walking briskly through the cold night air to find the new wine he knows we absolutely must try. He always has to be first, fully immersed in London culture, shaking hands with composers and conductors, artists and actors, the top chefs and sommeliers. He is used to it, from his days as a child star, and I can tell he still yearns for that attention, to be the most admired person in the room. That is what attracted me to him at first, I suppose: this relentless drive and pursuit of the best. His unapologetic entitlement. Often I think he still achieves this attention, especially with me on his arm, a beautiful young ballerina in a backless silk dress. I know I look different to the other women, my glamour coming not from expensive jewels and furs but from the way I hold myself, my elegance, my ballerina poise. He introduces me as his ballerina from the Vic-Wells and men look at him enviously, their eyes grazing over me. It is easier to smile and shake their hand, but I don't know how much more of it I can take.

I tried to make it very clear to him the other night that I am tired of being treated like a prize, paraded in front of the men he wants to impress.

It was the night after the opening of Anrep's *The Awakening of the Muses*. We were on our way home from a Sunday night Ballet Club performance at the Mercury Theatre in Notting Hill. It had been a glorious evening of dance, with a triple bill of *Lysistrata*, *Les Masques* and *Le Spectre de la Rose*. With a trio of choreographers, Antony Tudor, Frederick Ashton and Michel Fokine respectively, this felt like we were at the centre of something exciting. Alicia Markova, Pearl Argyle, Walter Gore, even Ashton himself, were dancing. I loved *Les Masques*, the glorious costumes by Sophie Fedorovitch with Markova in a white chiffon ballgown with a long train, carrying a transparent mica muff, a white gardenia in her hair. The story is daring, sexually heightened: a wife and husband meet each other at a masked ball, each with their lover. After some changing of partners, the wife and husband are reconciled and the mistress and lover go off together.

'I prefer the Russian classics,' Nathan said on the way home, as we squeezed ourselves through the crowds leaving the packed Mercury Theatre. 'Petipa and Ivanov, they knew how to create a perfect line of corps de ballet. This was just an excuse to flaunt sexual promiscuity under the guise of art.'

'You're wrong,' I replied bluntly. 'There was more art and drama in *Les Masques* than in an entire row of *Lac des Cygnes* corps.' We walked in silence, a deep frustration building inside me. He had ruined the evening, somehow, by not understanding that ballet was so much more than lines of dancers standing in perfection across a large, open stage. Eventually, with the silence widening between us, I had to speak.

'If you don't want to see the new ballets, why do you agree to come to these Sunday nights at the Ballet Club? No one is forcing you to. I'd rather go alone than have you whining about the dancers being too expressive for you.'

'I don't have to like it to want to see it, Clara,' he said, a note of smug intellectualism creeping into his voice. This is how it always seemed to go when we disagreed. My enthusiasm was childish, undiscerning, whereas his critique was founded in knowledge and experience. I had thought, when we first met over a year ago, that I would enjoy having someone to talk with about art and dance and music, and maybe I did to begin with, when I thought I was in love with him, impressed by his past, his confidence, his certainty that he belonged. But now it grates with me; I find him supercilious, condescending. It is only when we are both a little drunk on wine and glamour that I find myself drawn to him now. There needs to be champagne flowing, a band playing, the loud laughter of friends, for me to find him attractive.

'I didn't like the way you introduced me to Charles Lynch,' I say, bolder now. I am in the mood to argue.

'What do you mean? The pianist? How did you want me to introduce you?'

'Not in that patronising way you always do it.'

'You're going to have to be more specific, Clara.'

'And this is my ballerina,' I mimic. 'It's as though you are offering me up on a plate. Can't you just say my name, or, even better, let me speak for once.'

'I didn't think you'd be interested in speaking to Charles.'

'And why not?' I demand. 'He's Marie Rambert's pianist. He set up the Ballet Club with her. I might want to talk to him about the performance, maybe even tell him how much I enjoyed *Les Masques*. You didn't say anything at all to him about how well he'd just played. You just wanted to show off your ballerina.'

'Don't be ridiculous, Clara.'

We were silent in the taxi home. I asked the driver to drop me at the end of my road. If Nathan had apologised to me then, I might have forgiven him. If he had invited me back to his boat, then the evening could have ended very differently. But he'd never asked me to come back there with him. I'd hinted, frequently, about how much I wanted to see his home, how romantic it must be living on the canal. I had visions of us wrapped in blankets, a candle burning, the water glistening in the moonlight. He never responded to my suggestions, though. At first I thought he was being chivalrous, protecting my honour. A year on and he still has not broken, no matter how much I want him to. All I get are kisses, his lips pressed against mine, his hands wrapping around my waist. We kiss in the dark behind Sadler's Wells, our bodies pressed into each other. I have felt him harden, my body responding, pulsing and wet. But even then he has resisted, turning away and returning home alone, leaving me frustrated, disappointed, frozen with longing.

Lydia Lopokova is still in the Wells Room, pulling on her pink cardigan again and rubbing her knee. She sees me by the barre and comes over.

'Are you all right?' she asks, her face kind. She has a wonderfully expressive face, with big eyes and smooth round cheeks. Lopokova is not at all sculpted with the angular sharpness of so many of the other great ballerinas. I nod and smile back. I like talking to her. She has so much personality, breaking the myth of the mysterious ballerina.

'I have watched you,' she says, putting her hand over mine on the barre. Her skin is warm, alive. I can see veins throbbing across her wrist. I have heard her playfully complain in the dressing room that hands are the first to betray a dancer's age. It is an insult to show veins in the theatre, she has said, laughing a little but also conscious of her age, forty-two compared with my nineteen.

'You remind me of myself when I was younger,' she says. 'You dance like an actor, full of passion and fire. You need to keep it, nurture it. Never let anyone take it away from you.' I feel a lump forming in my throat. No one has ever said this to me before. 'When I was at the Imperial Russian Ballet,' she continues, 'they tried to stifle us. At my graduation from the school to the company, I was told I should immediately divert myself from my overemphasised affectation and mannerism. Thank goodness I didn't listen. If I did, do you think I would have travelled the world, had roles created for me by the best choreographers, had my name splashed across the American and European newspapers?' She stops and looks at me, her eyes narrowed curiously.

'Come,' she says. 'Let me teach you one of my favourite moments of ballet from all my many years of dancing.' She smiles as she says this, hiding how she must really feel about her age behind a charming laugh.

Lopokova takes both my hands and pulls me into the middle of the room. 'Now, fold back your arms like this,' she instructs, throwing her head back. 'The Firebird. Diaghilev was worried I wouldn't be able to do it, but I proved them all wrong. I was just eighteen years old, and taking on the most challenging of Fokine's creations.'

She chants the music, its strange rhythms and beats, Stravinsky's clashing collage of wild sounds that make me feel on edge, at the precipice of some painful passion. Her voice is discordant and laboured, her uneven breathing a bass to the familiar tune.

'Imagine the red silk, the flames of your headdress, jewels flashing at your wrists.' She continues singing the music, her voice rising and falling in chaotic cries. I follow behind her, my arms fighting against imaginary chains, moving in and out of *arabesques* and jumps that shine and then hold, frozen like a bird watching, waiting.

'Use your eyes,' she calls to me. 'They must look down your arm, then up, sharply. Feel the anger of the bird, refusing to be entrapped by the prince. Resist him, find power in your arms.'

We dance, our legs fast, changing directions, jumping high *jetés* across the room, pirouettes in attitude that hardly end before we jump again. Every turn ends with a staccato pause, our heads moving in fierce stares. Finally, we both collapse, exhausted, onto the floor. We lie side by side, our breathing heavy. I can feel every nerve in my body tingling, alive and used. Awake. She turns her head to me, smiling.

'This can be you, always,' she says. 'Look outwards, beyond this room.' She gets up slowly, pushing herself to her feet with her hands. 'I'm going to pay for this tomorrow,' she laughs.

She is at the door before I can stand to join her. I call out to her, to thank her, but she is already gone.

12

SAMUEL

Samuel has had an idea. It is bold and potentially futile, but he has been working himself up to it all week, making himself promise that he will not let the weekend arrive without seeing it through. Finally, on Friday morning, he finds the courage.

The workshop feels alive this morning, the machines buzzing and the benches spilling over with tools and satin. Beauty stripped down to its first construction. Samuel has his sketches rolled up, tied with a piece of string. He has been carrying them around with him all week, in to work and then home again, a constant reminder of his promise to himself. And now they balance on the workbench, just clear of the shavings of leather and the dust of the paste flour that settles around him.

He eventually manages to speak when they are standing by the urn where they make their mid-morning tea.

'I heard some of the dancers talking about needing character shoes.'

He pauses. Mr Frederick nods, listening as he stirs the sugar into his cup. Samuel waits to see if Mr Frederick wants to speak. There is nothing, just another nod as he pulls the teaspoon out of the cup.

'I was delivering pointe shoes last week and caught the end of a rehearsal of Ashton's *Façade*, the tango I think it was, and I noticed that the heeled shoes Markova was wearing were not as well-made as our pointe shoes. Perhaps if we branched out, made character shoes as well, there might be some demand from the dancers.' Samuel shifts nervously from one foot to the other.

'I am not sure we can fit them in right now,' Mr Frederick answers. 'We have so many pointe shoe orders coming in. And I'd need to hire a designer for the shoes, which would take time.'

This is Samuel's moment. He takes a deep breath and unrolls the sketch, holding it out to Mr Frederick. 'I wondered if you might like to look at my designs.'

He waits as his employer takes the sketch, holding it open at the top and bottom. The drawing is neat and precise, measurements written around the edges with a list of materials pencilled in at the bottom of the paper. Samuel knows he only has one chance to make an impression, to convince the Freeds that he is serious. Mr Frederick reaches into the top pocket of his overalls and pulls out a pair of glasses. He doesn't laugh or grimace. He doesn't pass the paper back to Samuel with a shake of his head. He doesn't speak harsh, dismissive words, all the things that Samuel has imagined each morning when he runs through scenarios in his head.

'This is very interesting. Very interesting indeed.' He taps the paper lightly. 'Where did you learn to do this?' He doesn't wait for a reply. 'Why haven't you shown me this before?' Frederick Freed looks up then, his forehead dimpling with lines that speak real interest and real, unfeigned pleasure.

'I've been designing shoes and costumes since I was a little boy,' Samuel replies, a little louder now, strength coming into his voice. He surprises himself by being able to say the words he has practised; he didn't think it would be possible. But he doesn't tell Mr Frederick the full story, how it was his schoolteacher, Miss Frances Luck, who first showed him the women's magazines with the pages full of patterns and designs and haberdashery advice. There was *The Needlewoman*, *The Lady*, *Woman's Life*. Samuel was fascinated by them and his teacher let him flick through the pages each morning while he waited for the rest of the class to arrive. He was always the first one in, his father marching him out of the house far earlier than necessary every day. Then there was the school production of *Peter Pan*. Miss Luck asked him to help with the costumes and he spent many happy hours after school sewing a headdress for Tinker Bell and a little red smock for Peter. That was until he made the mistake of asking his father if he wanted tickets to the performance. There were no more afternoons staying late at school after that. His mother was given strict orders to collect him immediately after lessons. She was not to let him indulge in such frivolous nonsense ever again. Miss Luck had no opportunity to persuade his parents otherwise. She left the next term to get married, taking her pile of magazines with her.

He forces himself to stand still and firm. 'I love creating the sketches and the designs, imagining the materials that would work best. It's what drew me to applying for a job with you and Mrs Dora in the first place. But I've never actually created any of my designs, not the shoes anyway. I don't have the tools at home. I've created cheap versions of some of the costumes, but I don't have a sewing machine, so it's slow work. I've just made a few headdresses and ballet tunics, nothing special.'

Samuel has still not told his parents exactly what he does for a living. He doesn't like to think how his father would react if he knew he was creating pink satin pointe shoes, a far cry from the train engines and railway tracks his father maintains. They think he works in the bookkeeping department of Selfridges, still a disappointment but at least an acceptable employment. And he hasn't lied to them as such. He did have an interview at Selfridges; he just didn't mention to his parents that this was not the job that he ended up accepting.

'Well, these are certainly very special, lad,' Mr Frederick says, filling the silence that has replaced Samuel's words. The two of them look back down at the paper, Samuel tilting his head, seeing the sketch as though for the first time. The shoes are cream-coloured with a small heel and the shape is all curves and smooth lines, an embellishment of petals cut into the toe in a fan design. He can see them now on the stage, worn by a dancer, Olivia maybe, the debutante in Frederick Ashton's ballet *Façade*, the village dancers in the *Coppélia* mazurka.

'I'll talk to Mrs Freed about it, I promise you that,' Mr Frederick says, rolling up the sketch and placing it on the work-bench. 'We might not be able to get started on these right away, what with all the pointe shoe orders, but you can rest assured that we will come back to you for designs when we can.' He picks up his tea and starts to walk back to his stool by the welting machine. 'You've got talent, my lad. And make sure you remember that.'

Samuel finishes his order of shoes by lunchtime. Mr and Mrs Freed have a wedding to get to and are keen to close the shop early for the day so they send Samuel out, wishing him a happy weekend.

'And you'd better not be thinking of selling those sketches to anyone else,' Mr Frederick calls out cheerfully, as Samuel walks up the stairs from the basement workshop. 'I should make you sign a contract,' he laughs. It is the most animated Samuel has ever seen his employer, usually such a quiet, reserved man, reluctant to emerge from the privacy of his workshop.

Samuel laughs back. But inside he is overjoyed, too happy for mere laughter. This is serious, life-changing even, the first time he has ever been handed such praise. Praise for something that he and only he has created. His father's harsh, cruel laughter doesn't even enter his head. He knows he should be more understanding, that his father became a different man when he came back from France, how it affected every decision he made as a father, a husband, a man. But Samuel is glad he has left that house, even if he does worry every day about his mother, who has to manage those cruel dark moods alone.

When he delivered the pointe shoes to Sadler's Wells yesterday, there was a poster on the noticeboard reminding dancers of the *Coppélia* stage call. Someone, probably Miss de Valois, has scribbled across the bottom of the notice in thick black ink: 'Do not make dinner plans.' They all know these rehearsals can go on for hours. With just one week until the first night, the energy at Sadler's Wells is bubbling, a flurry of costumes arriving, the last parts of the set constructed, the props gradually building within the properties room. Wicker crates packed with lighting foils and new metal brackets for the sidelights pile on top of one another in the foyer, waiting for someone to clear them away to the correct department. Stage calls are exciting, and Samuel knows he will be able to sneak into the auditorium without any trouble. He is a regular, part of the scenery, accepted without being noticed. It is to the theatre that he will go on this unexpected Friday afternoon off.

Samuel walks fast, enjoying the early signs of spring. He notices everything today: the light on the grass, the bright yellow of the daffodils that have sprung up in the most unlikely places on the roadside, the blue gems of the grape hyacinth hiding amongst the base of trees. As he walks through Exmouth Market, he looks up at his rooms. Even they look less gloomy today, and he can just about make out one of the walls with its patchwork of sketches, designs, colours, tiny pieces of fabric. He is proud of that wall, a museum of his ideas. Even the people of London look less miserable today as they move briskly along the market stalls. There is a brightness to the noise as the sellers call out their prices: the market is full to the brim with breads, fruits, vegetables, cakes of soap made in the warehouse down by the canal, wooden figurines handcrafted by the old man on Meredith Street. Newspapers are packed together like stacks of ironed laundry, the mesh-covered news boards announcing horror in Germany, but no one seems to notice. Not today. A boy is selling white roses from a trough at the end of the market. He is calling out in a loud, high voice, like a song. Samuel cannot resist. He has some coins in his pocket, enough to buy one rose. The boy takes his money quickly, pocketing it away with fast hands, in case his customer changes his mind. Samuel carries it with him to Rosebery Avenue. He feels bold today, certain that nothing can happen to make this feeling go away. It reminds him of when he was very young and it was his birthday, the promise of the day's specialness acting as a barrier from the threat of sadness. His mother always made an extra-special effort on his birthday, baking a cake and cooking his favourite meal of sausages in batter. His father usually managed to make it through the day without saying anything cruel, once even taking him outside and playing a modified game of cricket until he grew tired and left Samuel alone to throw the ball up and down into the air.

He won't think about his father today. The theatre promises excitement, transportation to another world. Olivia will be dancing. He read the cast list; he knows she is one of Swanilda's friends, dancing in the square in Act One, sneaking into Dr Coppélius's workshop in Act Two. Entering by the pit door on Arlington Street, he moves solidly and silently through the dim light. The rehearsal has not started yet, but there is a quiet energy, a low murmur of activity, the set being adjusted into place, the orchestra gradually filling the pit and warming up their instruments, the muffled banging that he recognises as ballerinas pounding the noise out of their pointe shoes on a hard concrete step. He pauses, looking down the corridor that runs towards the pit and backstage; the door down to the well is open and he peers in to see nothing but a dark set of steps that fall steeply to the basement room. The light is too dim to make out who is down there but there are voices coming from below, the sound now growing and coming closer towards him. Suddenly, a group of six dancers, men and women, burst out, running in single file up and then along the corridor towards the entrance to the wings. He stands back against the wall, watching them as they fly past. They are not in full costume, just a few fragments that he has seen building up in Wardrobe: floral headdresses, colourful boots, bright sashes, wigs. Mostly they are in practice tutus, two in the long romantic style, one in a stiff, doll-like classical skirt that extends straight out from the hips. They have to practise in the more challenging costume elements, checking they can still dance the role with the addition of headpieces and bows. It is Olivia and Clara who are the last to appear up the steps. They are laughing together; Samuel feels a pang of envy at their intimacy.

Olivia stops at the top of the steps, turning back around in the dark of the doorway. 'You go on,' she says to her sister. 'I've left my cardigan down there.'

Samuel waits in the corridor, still pressed against the wall. He hears her feet tapping lightly, then silence, then they are tapping again on the way up. She is in her pointe shoes. He knows the sound of those blocks, the supple leather sole that he has formed with his hands.

'This is for you,' he hears himself say.

Olivia jumps, crying out. 'Goodness, you scared me.' She looks upset, irritated. He is imposing on her preparations, ruining the calm and control that comes from dipping her hand in the magical waters of the well, her good luck charm.

'I'm sorry,' he stammers, holding out the rose. A thorn is digging into his thumb.

'What's this for?' she says, looking at the rose suspiciously.

What is it for, thinks Samuel, panicking. This isn't working as he imagined it would. On the short walk from buying the rose and arriving at the theatre, he had visualised her drawing the rose to her and smelling it, perhaps rising up on her toes and kissing him on the cheek. Looking at her scowling face now, that doesn't seem very likely.

'It's to say good luck, for the stage call,' he comes up with. She takes the rose reluctantly, turning away from him immediately as she does so, her bag spilling open at her hip. Inside, he can see two more pairs of his shoes, both a little worn, the ends grey with the dust of the floor. Her darning is neat, small U-shaped patterns adorning the satin. 'I hope the pointe shoes are working out well for you,' he adds.

Her face softens a little but Samuel can sense distrust, a barrier she has fixed between them. 'Of course, you work for Mr Freed.' She is smiling politely, nodding to herself as she remembers where she has seen him, why he seemed familiar but distant, a face she simply couldn't place. 'Well, thank you. This is very kind of you. The shoes are marvellous, and I shall dance even better knowing I have the luck of Frederick Freed's magical pointe shoes.'

She is acting, he thinks, turning on the role of the gracious ballerina. He wants to mention the note, tell her it was from him, but he can't. It doesn't feel right.

'Goodbye then. Enjoy the rehearsal if you decide to stay,' she calls out as she turns and starts running along the corridor. Her bag is still open, ribbons and ballet shoes exposed. A soft-toe shoe balances precariously on the top and at the moment she starts to run it falls out, hitting the ground with no sound at all. She doesn't notice and keeps running away towards the stage.

Samuel waits, listening to her steps disappearing and merging with the growing moans of the orchestra. He walks towards where her shoe lies on the ground, the ribbons splayed wildly about the upturned leather sole. Kneeling, he picks it up, turning it over in his hand before going to the top of the steps. He has been down here before, to the sacred well that he knows the dancers obsess over, their good luck routine. It is cool and quiet, making him think of the Freed basement workshop at the start of the day, before the welting machines start up their whirring. Some of the same smells linger too: wood, dust, the musk of satin and leather. But there is something else drifting through the damp air, the salt of sweat, grit, passion. It had been strange to see the dancers emerge from here, their faces bright and their costumes sparkling as though sprinkled with a magical, unearthly dust. There is none of that brightness by the well: it is a monster's cave, the water shadowed like those gloomy children's books he remembers from school, with their illustrations of Hades dragging his victims across the river Styx. Kneeling by the stone that surrounds the well, he looks down into the water.

He holds it in his hands now, feeling the darned edges of the toe, the satin scuffed and stained from dancing on dusty floors. This is not the first time he has stolen one of her shoes, and it occurs to him that he is locked in a strange cycle of creation and destruction. It feels ritualistic to him, lowering the shoe into the water, spreading the ribbons out on the surface. The water darkens the satin, slowly filling the shoes and turning it on its front. She will need to return to him for more, and each shoe will give her luck, strength. He soaks her shoe in the water she trusts. She will come back here later; she will see her shoe dancing in the dark water; and she will believe, truly believe, that her luck can come true.

13

CLARA

I don't hang around after the stage call. It has gone on all afternoon, stopping and starting, constant readjustments of the placements of the corps de ballet on the stage, Miss de Valois calling out orders which are then reversed by Sergeyev, who creeps up onstage and twists props and furniture as he sees fit. They argue over the position of the dolls in Dr Coppélius's workshop in Act Two, and there is a tense silence after Miss de Valois absolutely refuses to let the hay bales from Act One stay visible onstage in the second half. And the orchestra is all over the place, having had not nearly enough rehearsal. It is such a musical ballet, every step working in a precise marriage with the music, that the pressure to get it right is immense. I thought Constant was going to explode during the mazurka. He isn't supposed to be conducting. It was going to be Geoffrey Toye. We rather depend on our Uncle Geoffrey, as Lambert affectionately calls him. He has an air of complete experience, which of course is entirely to be expected after his years working with Lilian Baylis at the Old Vic before she renovated our Sadler's Wells and expanded her management to these two theatres, each on opposite sides of the river. Uncle Geoffrey has been a governor at Sadler's Wells since its conception two years ago and there are rumours he is composing a wonderful ballet about a haunted ballroom for us, which Miss de Valois will create. But he was in a car accident last week, the news of which has shaken us: I overheard Constant say to one of the orchestra that he barely escaped with his life. So Constant is conducting, which is only increasing the tensions between the musicians and Sergeyev.

By the end of Act Two, we are all very relieved that we are only putting on the first two acts. I know I should stay and wait for all the notes, but I am exhausted; we all are. The ballet is held together by the corps de ballet, with some big dances in Act One that require strength in the legs and light smiles on the face. I have smiled enough for one day. Once I have changed out of my practice clothes, I join the rest of the cast in the auditorium. I take a seat at the back of the stalls, half hidden in darkness, hoping to find a moment to sneak out unseen. The other girls are huddled together near the front; a mistake, I think, but at least they can distract each other. I could go to join them, but I don't have any more energy left to move. Instead, I stare up at the ivory panel above the proscenium arch, staying awake by attempting to make out the features of the Finsbury coat of arms that glares down at us. A fish and a winged bull peer angrily at one another between *arabesques* of running water.

After the Act One notes, I have had enough. It is late and I just want to get home to bed. I catch Olivia's eye and gesture to the exit, but she shakes her head. She will wait, of course, committed to the bitter end. I have almost made it, my bag over my shoulder, my old woollen coat wrapped around me with a scarf right up to my chin. I leave via the Arlington Street exit, the cold air a shock after hours inside the busy theatre.

I feel a heavy hand on my shoulder. Turning abruptly, I pull myself away. It is Nathan. He doesn't have his coat, just the Delibes piano score under one arm.

'Where are you going?' he asks. I look at him blankly.

'Home. It's late and I'm done here.'

'They haven't given the notes for Act Two. You can't leave yet.'

'Nathan, it will be fine. Olivia will tell me if there is anything I need to know.'

'Are you going to walk home on your own?' he asks. He might be concerned about my safety, walking home late in the dark, but right now it just irritates me, a paternal pressure that goes beyond what I want from him.

'I'll see you in the morning, Nathan,' I give in answer, turning to walk away from him.

'There's the exhibition tomorrow, at Olympia,' he calls after me. 'Shall I meet you in the foyer after morning class?'

I stop, sigh, turn back to him. I had forgotten about the exhibition. I really want to go, and Nathan has already bought the tickets. There is a special dance sketch by Penelope Spencer that the Vic-Wells girls are all desperate to see, and I don't want to miss out. I just wish I hadn't agreed to go with Nathan. More than anything, I want to dress up for the outing with Olivia, meet the other girls after class, travel on the bus with Beatrice and Hermione, Sheila and Nadina, all of us graduates from Miss de Valois's school who have been working hard together all season. I have been spending so much time with Nathan that I've rather neglected my friends, and I realise how much I miss them. Right now I feel on the outskirts of their group. We are all village girls in *Coppélia*, rehearsing together, complaining about our sore feet together, laughing behind their backs about the strops our ballet masters and mistresses throw. But somehow I don't feel like I belong; I'm left out, not quite getting all the jokes. And it is because of Nathan. He takes so much from me, all my energy, everything I have to give.

'Yes, of course,' I reply. I do want to go, and Nathan has bought the tickets for us. 'I'll meet you after class, but I think lots of the others are coming too, so we can get the bus with everyone.' This is my attempt to prepare him, ease him into the fact that I do not want to spend the entire afternoon by his side. I want to watch Penelope Spencer's sketch with a laughing group of girls by my side; I want to enjoy the fashion parades and the garden shows without Nathan's commentary in my ear.

'See you then,' he calls out as I walk away. 'And I've got a surprise for us,' I hear him add. My heart sinks at that; this will be his way of getting me alone, a romantic gesture that I don't want, not when it takes me away from my friends and my sister.

The next morning, we all get changed after class with an excited buzz, the girls revealing new dresses and hats for the occasion. We add lipstick and rouge, all of us hustling for places in front of the mirrors, pinning our hair into place. Gradually, the familiar smells of sweat and powder sweeten into new perfumes of citrus and vanilla. When we left the flat this morning, Olivia asked if she could wear the green coat. I wish I could find the words to tell her that she really doesn't need to ask. She can keep it. When I wear it I feel trapped in its folds, the fur choking me. I feel the expectant weight of Nathan's eyes on me, transforming me into a woman I do not want to be any more. I have started trying to tell Olivia so many times, but I never get very far: I just don't think she would understand. We share everything, have experienced every moment of our lives together. That is until Nathan came along and made a little world for me that was mine alone. I know I shut Olivia out of my life with Nathan, presenting her with a curated and limited version of our relationship. The morning after an evening with him, all she wants to hear about is the music, the champagne, the dresses and jewellery of the women we encountered, the dancing, the walk home through a moonlit London. All she sees is romance.

Today, I manage to feel elegant in my new dress and stockings, a navy hat with a twisted knot at the side adding a modern look. These, I bought for myself, and I love them all the more for it. I have unpacked my old woollen coat out of its hibernation at the back of our wardrobe; I never thought I'd feel so pleased to wear it again. There is a copy of the latest *Woman's Own* on the dressing table, and Hermione flips through it as she waits for the rest of us to finish getting ready. Hermione Darnborough sets the style for all of us, bringing in her discarded blouses and skirts, leaving magazines for us girls to read with avid attention between rehearsals. She is a year younger than me but seems much more mature, helped of course by her wealthy family keeping her in the best new fashions. She looks like a model, tall and lithe, and leaves an absolute mess behind her wherever she goes: make-up, hairpins, tights, ribbons. Miss de Valois once shouted at her for being so slovenly. But she is very beautiful and we all rather look up to her. Though sometimes I feel she takes those matronly words of advice in magazines such as *Woman's Own* a little too seriously: I do not only look after my appearance as a duty towards myself and some hypothetical man I am to marry. All this talk of marriage and duty and creating the perfect home makes me wants to laugh, loudly and rudely. I remember an article in *Miss Modern* last year: 'When a man looks for a wife, she must have a nice taste in dress. Clothes are important to a man's success.' This secretly horrified me, the idea that what I wore was more relevant to a man's success than my own. But some of the girls read these magazines as gospel, hanging on to each word of advice.

The *Daily Mail* Ideal Home exhibition is not to be missed. We all love it and Olivia and I have been attending every year since Father died, dreaming up ways we too could transport the modern furniture and gardens and linens and fashions into our own little lives. The trick is not to take it too seriously, not to be drawn into the advertisements and model homes that pronounce how to live, the ideal role for a woman, how to be happy. I admit that sometimes it looks tempting, a husband, a large home in the countryside, two cheerful children, a dog. But then when I really think about it and imagine myself in that life, a life without the theatre and Olivia and the freedom of living right in the centre of London, I feel a sense of dread. What I really want, I suppose, is change. Constant, exciting, exhilarating change that makes me feel alive. The last few years at Sadler's Wells have given me that, the joy of growing with this new company, seeing our audience numbers build, reading the reviews in the newspapers. I worry, though, that this feeling isn't going to last, that soon I am going to be looking for something else.

Nathan is waiting for me in the foyer. It takes him a beat to work out who I am, his eyes instead following Olivia in my green coat as we walk through the entrance together. Perhaps I could persuade her to swap for the day, like we used to when we were little, tricking Aunt Alice into muddling us up. But I couldn't do that to her; Nathan is my burden to manage.

I tell myself to be cheerful and pleasant, but I don't take his arm. I keep hold of Olivia's and call out to him to hurry up or we'll miss the bus. He follows us, our growing group of young women, a few of the men joining too. In the bus we are noisy,

Bobby Helpmann entertaining us all with his comic stories of astonishment at our British ways. He is Australian, only arriving in London this year, and he finds us very strange. We find him strange too, but in a lovable, curious way. Just last week he had us in fits of giggles as he argued with Lilian Baylis over how much brilliantine he uses in his hair. He argued none at all, that he had his own concoction of Vaseline and paraffin. You wouldn't want to light a match too close to him. Now, he is up at the front of the bus, getting Hermione to point out London landmarks, which he deconstructs, scandalously. Even the grandeur of Buckingham Palace is a joke to him.

Turning, I look back at Olivia. She is sitting with Beatrice, the two of them talking intently, their heads close together. I long to know what they are talking about, but I don't think I would be welcome. I am with Nathan, and everyone expects me to enjoy his attentions. But I can't, not when all I can think about is how much I used to love taking the bus with Olivia and how far away from her I feel right now. When we were younger, we'd run onto the bus after ballet class, our slim shoulders easing effortlessly through the press of men with their briefcases and the women clasping their shopping bags. We'd make up stories about the people passing by, our faces pressed against the window, curiously watching as cyclists plaited in and out of the taxis and pedestrians marched onwards, everyone finding the tempo of their day.

Today London feels on edge. I notice policemen stationed outside Green Park and on the fringes of Hyde Park Corner, their faces alert and wary. I watch them as the bus stops and starts on our way to Olympia, a restless light bouncing off the silver star on their helmets. Along the side of the road is the debris of a march that took place yesterday, an anti-fascist protest that wound its way from Commercial Road to Hyde Park with determined energy. A cloth sign has been discarded on the pavement, the large bold letters that call for a boycott of German goods still showing through the dirt smeared across the fabric. The Vic-Wells dancers dominate the bus with their talk of it as we pass by Hyde Park, several of the boys giving their accounts of the crowds that had packed the streets yesterday. I wish I had been there, joining in as the protesters swept through the city. Olivia and I had read in the papers back at the start of February about Hitler's power. It had unsettled everybody, the dressing rooms noisy as we repeated the phrases we'd lifted from the stacks of newspapers we walk past every day on the way to the theatre. But we'd all moved on with our day quickly, forgetting as soon as the first bars of the piano heralded the start of ballet class.

As the rest of us chat loudly, Nathan is quiet. I have noticed that he prefers it when it is just the two of us. That is when he is at his most confident, talking endlessly, giving his opinions on everything. But now, when Bobby makes a comment about the czardas in *Coppélia* being played so slowly yesterday he thought his legs were going to fall off, Nathan says nothing. If it had been just me, he would have started a long lecture about why the piece had been played at exactly the right tempo. I try to ignore Nathan and his silence, instead taking part in the loud energy of the others. But when we arrive at the Olympia exhibition centre, I have to stick with him. He has our tickets.

The exhibition is vast, growing every year. This year's main attraction is a 'Rainbow City', and it is just as brilliant as advertised. In all the colours of the rainbow, the giant domed roof is lit up by a gigantic scheme of neon lighting. I look up, dazzled by the lights reflecting from the glass of the Grand Hall. I imagine our lighting designers at Sadler's Wells will be stealing some ideas from here. There are still the same categories as last year, the show homes, working-class housing, child welfare, 'homes fit for heroes', the results of the reader 'ideal homes' competitions. But there is also a series of 'Rooms of the Scientists', which apparently will show us the history of inventions from Newton, Faraday, Marconi and more. There is a section on the home cinema, one on the telephones of the General Post Office, another on modern sanitation and heating. I long for better heating, but Olivia and I will never be able to afford the luxuries on display here. Saturdays are the busiest days, of course, and we are immediately thrown into the crowd. I watch as Olivia disappears with the other girls, and I am left with Nathan. Reluctantly, I put my arm through his and decide I will have a good time, whatever the situation. I lead us towards the fashion area, past the 'ideal dinner party' displays, through the common-sense kitchens, along the village of ideal homes. It would be a shame to miss the fashion pageant.

There are displays set up either side of the central walkway, and I stop at a few of them, taking a mental note of the new styles and shapes of the clothing. Nathan follows dutifully, stopping when I stop, moving again when I do. I am fascinated by a set of removable dress shields that apparently can be sewn into clothing to prevent the dress or blouse staining from underarm sweat. This is absurdly exciting to me, and I wish Olivia was with me so I could share this. We have to throw away so many clothes far too soon because of stained underarms. I turn to Nathan.

'Now this would be useful,' I say, smiling.

'What exactly is it? It's hardly pretty.'

'It's not supposed to be pretty, Nathan. It's to stop sweat stains ruining clothes.'

He looks horrified. His eyes widen, and then he turns away. 'Don't be ridiculous. You don't need that.'

I refuse to let this go. It both amuses and alarms me that he thinks I might not be susceptible to the same bodily functions as himself. He's seen me sweat in ballet class; perhaps he thinks it is some sort of magical ballerina glow.

'Nathan, women get exactly the same sweat stains as men. It's foolish to pretend otherwise.' I see a cosmetics stand across the aisle and I drag him over. 'Look at this powder,' I say to him firmly. 'Do you think my nose and cheeks stay this smooth matte colour without it, especially in ballet class when I'm hot and sweaty?' I hold him by the arms, turning him to look at my face. Today I spent longer than usual on my make-up after class and I know my face looks flawless. 'This isn't my natural skin,' I repeat, laughing now at how uncomfortable he is looking. I remember a hilarious article in *Miss Modern* last year where a man was complaining about the Bank of England banning its female employees from wearing make-up. Little did they know that they might be surprised when the women did not look quite as perfect and polished as the men were used to. Yet I remember not being entirely enamoured by the male writer objecting because of his desire for women to introduce glamour and romance into 'our humdrum routine'. I had felt very sorry for those poor female office workers with the men ogling them in some fantasy world of romance.

'Come on, let's find the pageant.'

The fashion pageant is extremely popular. Already the hall is full, women vying for the best positions. I see Olivia has found a spot near the front, so we push our way through and join her. It is Penelope Spencer we have all come to see. She is famous in our ballet world, a great comic dancer, her choreography modern and daring. Olivia and I danced in some of the pieces she chore-ographed for operas several years ago, the most memorable being *Cupid and Death* at the New Scala Theatre on Tottenham Court Road, for which she made us go to the zoo to get inspira-tion for some of the characters. She is very bold and gets exactly what she wants. The theatre manager for the opera claimed he had no money to pay us, so she threatened to pull us from the night's performance. And lo and behold, we were suddenly paid in advance, the dance going ahead.

This sketch is called 'Ladies, Sigh No More!' and it features thirteen women as mannequins and one dancer. It is advertising five brands of stockings by I. and R. Morley, a comic display of the woes of finding the right stockings that won't tear, stretch or fade. The music starts and the 'mannequins' find their positions. It is wonderfully funny. I glance at Nathan and see that he too is lost in the comedy. He looks entirely transfixed by the mannequins, their long legs clad in the smoothest, sheerest of stockings. When it ends, I have to drag him away. I think he enjoyed it even more than I did; I am surprised by how warm it makes me feel towards him, the great Nathan Howell finally showing a sense of humour about something frivolous and play-ful. I had expected him to be stuffy and boring about it, making some comments about how lowbrow it all was. But he did noth-ing of the sort.

Olivia walks with us to the next hall and then heads off to meet the other girls. But before she goes, she turns to Nathan and says the funniest thing.

'Have a lovely afternoon with my sister. I hope you don't muddle us up this time.'

Nathan doesn't reply, just splutters some sort of mumble half-way between a laugh and a cough. I raise my eyebrow at him, but he just shrugs. 'I would never muddle you two up,' he says to me once she has gone. I am not sure that I believe him.

Olivia looks lovely today, but a little different to normal. It takes me a moment to realise what it is, but then I see it. She has styled her hair exactly like mine, loose around her shoulders, with just the front sections tied back in a low twist. With the green fur of the coat around her collar, the coat Nathan bought specifically to dress me and show me off to his friends, anyone would think she was me. Or I was her. It is confusing sometimes, and not altogether pleasant, trying to work out whether people think I am her double or she is mine. I suppose it depends on who you ask.

'Don't you want to know the surprise?' Nathan says, interrupting my thoughts. I had forgotten about this. Part of me is curious now that we are here, ready to be spoilt and treated to afternoon tea or champagne or a show. It is easy to get swept up in the exhibition. Everyone here is looking to escape into an imaginary world of idealness, visualise themselves in a new home, a new dress, owning a fancy refrigerator, illuminating their bedrooms with the glass light shades that hang resplendently around the Grand Hall.

I let Nathan lead us out of the main hall and into the Pillar Hall, a smaller space with rows of ornate marble Corinthian pillars and an elaborate ceiling emblazoned with rich decorative plasterwork. Little tables are laid out with crisp white covers, arranged with crockery and champagne coupes. A waiter comes to us, takes Nathan's name, and then leads us to a table at the edge of the room. It is a relief to be out of the noise of the Grand Hall and I enjoy looking around me at the other couples, the sprays of flowers at each table, the cakes and tea and wine that waiters in black tie are spreading through the room. It looks choreographed, a dance of nodding and smiling and order.

'My mother would have liked this place,' Nathan says, dragging me back to attention. I would be perfectly happy to sit without talking, to watch the varieties of life around me. But I agree; I can also imagine his mother here, the beautiful dead woman with the bright blonde hair, always perfect, her make-up never smudged. She has no need for powder and undergarments that protect her clothes from sweat stains. I find myself wanting to be cruel again, to say something harsh and unnecessary to Nathan, but I stop myself. He has organised all this and he wants it to be special.

'She loved everything to be dainty and elegant,' he continues. 'Anything loud and vulgar upset her. Afternoon tea was her speciality, the tea just right, the cake light and airy. We always had to have cotton napkins, bright white and pressed.'

'She sounds like a perfect mother,' I say. 'My mother would have taken to the bottle if she'd seen me or Olivia eating cake.' He frowns. I know he doesn't like it when I talk about my mother. She is too real and upsetting, a wild, mad woman that doesn't fit into his ideal.

'I found another photograph of Mother the other day,' he says, reaching into his jacket pocket. 'I was clearing out papers in the boat and I found this one hidden amongst some programmes from my concerts, the ones I played at when she was still alive.' He blows gently on the photograph, cleaning off the lint from his jacket. It looks like he is sending her a kiss. He passes it to me.

There she is, standing next to a grand piano. A very small and wide-eyed little boy is seated on the piano stool. Nathan. It is hard to imagine that he is about to give a concert to a packed audience. He looks perfectly calm. But it is his mother who I can't stop looking at. She has very white hair, soft like a cloud, and her eyes are large with long, even eyelashes. It is her youth that really strikes me. She looks barely twenty, but of course she must be older. And just a few years after that photograph was taken, she would be dead.

'I still can't believe she's gone,' he says. 'I remember the day it happened, when my father broke it to me, so gently, I simply couldn't understand what either of us had done to make her leave us.'

'You were a child, Nathan. You were too young to understand death, how no one can control those things.' I give back the photograph and take his hand. 'There was nothing you or your father could have done to keep her alive.'

I have tried asking him how his mother died. He doesn't like to talk about that, though. Instead, he likes to keep her memory alive with stories of how wonderful she was, how caring, how she made him feel like the most loved little boy in England. I envy him this. When I think of my mother, it is with guilt and anger. Guilt for hating every second of those monthly visits to Colney Hatch; anger at having to go in the first place. But then another feeling creeps in, slyly, cruelly. I am glad she is there, locked up, drugged too heavily to complain. It keeps her away from us; it gives me and Olivia the freedom to live our lives as we want.

When I look up from my plate, my mouth full of cake, I freeze. Nathan is holding out a ring. Silver, a dark red ruby encased in diamonds.

'This was my mother's engagement ring. She left it with us, a memory of how happy we were together. I want you to have it.' He is looking at me with very earnest eyes. 'I want you to be my wife.'

The noise of the room seems to vanish and all I can hear is a loud whooshing inside my head. At the edges of my vision, the waiters appear to have slowed down, performing a long and fluid *adage* as they dance across the room. I look down at my plate, transfixed by a gem of pale pink icing. I need to say something, but the words are stuck in my throat. Finally, I raise my eyes.

'Nathan,' I say. 'I can't marry you.'

All at once, I am afraid. His hands have clenched into tight fists and the skin on his neck is throbbing a mottled red. I know he is used to getting his way. But he gathers himself, readying for the next attack.

'It's too soon? You want to dance, I get that. I wouldn't get in the way of your career.' He is trying to keep his voice calm, but I can hear the strain in the words.

'No, Nathan. It's not just that. I can't marry you.' I push my chair away from the table. 'Please don't ask me again.'

He reaches across towards me, his hand finding mine. I pull away, standing abruptly. He looks shocked, and for a moment I feel a terrible guilt. I know I am supposed to say yes to him; this is what the girls in the dressing room gossip about, dream about. We have all imagined the scene a thousand times: the setting is perfect; he has surrounded me in idealness, an ideal home, an ideal life. But the feeling passes as soon as it arrives, and I know I need to get out of here.

I start moving, pressing my bag into my chest, weaving in and out of the waiters and the guests, avoiding a tower of cakes, a tray of champagne coupes. The crowds in the Grand Hall seem to bear down on me, the model homes and ideal kitchens looming large in a grotesque nightmare. A row of mannequins in silk evening dresses point their wooden arms at me as I run, the cloying floral smell of perfume thickening the air. It is only when I get outside, when I've run through the street and made it onto the bus, that I can breathe again.

ACT THREE

14

OLIVIA

I never sleep the night before a first performance. I don't think Clara did either last night, judging by all her tossing and turning. She came in very late, out with the musicians, no doubt. At one point, I opened my eyes to see her at the window, the curtains drawn, looking out into the night. I mumbled something and she returned to bed.

Coppélia has finally arrived and Sadler's Wells feels alive, delivery men going in and out, posters pasted onto the walls, the press sending their runners to collect first night tickets from the box office. This is the biggest production our Vic-Wells company has attempted, and Miss de Valois knows the pressure is immense. It is not only the cost of the production, which is significant and has required the support of the Camargo Society, but the knowledge that the critics will be out in force, waiting to pass judgement on Miss de Valois's success or failure in bringing one of the great Russian classics to London.

The whole cast take ballet class together this morning, packed like sardines along the barre. Miss Moreton leads the class, calling out the exercises with fast precision. There is no time to get left behind. Thankfully she keeps the barre simple today. There are too many of us to risk the *battements frappés* and *grands batte-ments en cloche* flying off in the wrong direction, legs clashing and crashing. We work through our *pliés* and *tendus*, our *relevés* and *ronds de jambe*. It calms us all to follow this daily routine, establishing order through our legs, reassuring each muscle and tendon that tonight will go as planned, that our bodies will know exactly what they need to do.

Clara has a furious, focused expression on her face all class. She looks hardly present, as though she is fixed in some labyrin-thine internal battle. But when we get into the centre, she doesn't dance with her usual brightness, and it worries me. Her *adage* and *port de bras* droop a little and I notice that she hides herself at the back. Miss Moreton sees everything, though, and calls out sharply to her to lift her elbows. Clara seems to wake up and the next exercise is better, her pirouettes showing her usual sharp head and strong lifting out of the hips.

Nathan is playing the piano this morning. I have noticed a tension between Clara and him this past week, ever since our trip to the exhibition. She doesn't wait for him after class or rehearsal any more, and she avoids his eye completely. He still stares at her though. It frustrates me, all this attention he wants from her, when she is clearly not interested. He should have known he couldn't catch her, couldn't keep her. My sister has always been restless. She used to sigh loudly and naughtily whenever she was bored in ballet class when we were younger, despite knowing Mother would tell her off on the bus journey home. She resented having to repeat an exercise over and over until the ballet mistress was happy. Clara was always ready to move on and try the next step.

At the end of class, Miss de Valois wants to rehearse the Act One mazurka one last time. We change into our character shoes, the heels feeling strange after a class in soft blocks followed by pointe shoes, our toes moving more freely when released from the tight pink satin. We line up, finding our partners, and the music begins. I love the mazurka, the strong rhythm reflected in the stamp of our feet and the swoop of our arms into *épaulement*. Clara is always the best, though, her musicality finding the exact notes to rise and fall. We are a chorus, a corps de ballet, but still she stands out.

After a few counts of eight, Miss de Valois bangs her stick. Nathan stops playing and we all fall out of our movements.

'Clara, come up here,' she calls. I turn to watch my sister hurry to the front of the room. Even Clara would never dawdle when our ballet mistress summons. But she doesn't look concerned; instead, there is a sharp look of defiance behind her gaze, as though she is daring us to challenge her.

'Watch how she does it,' Miss de Valois tells us. 'Listen to the music, watch how she finds the beat, becomes part of each note. The rest of you are not listening.'

Nathan plays the introduction again and Clara starts dancing, on her own this time. Miss de Valois is right. None of the rest of us can become the music the way my sister can.

'Now everyone,' she summons, and we join in, breathing into the steps, listening to the accent of the music. We watch Clara at the front the room as we dance, matching the stamp of our feet to hers.

'Better,' Miss de Valois tells us at the end, when we are all sweating from the effort. 'Costume call at five o'clock,' she announces as we leave. It is no change from usual that the costumes are only just ready. We've had productions before where we were pinning ourselves into our tutus with minutes to go before the curtain rose. There are nearly always missing items, a headdress, perhaps, or a lace armband. I have two costumes in *Coppélia*, first the villager dress with a white frilly blouse underneath and the soft leather boots with a little heel. Later I change into a romantic-style tutu, white with a red sash, for one of Swanilda's friends.

I love the choreography at the end of Act One where we all hold hands in a line and sneak into Dr Coppélius's house. He drops the key in the square and we have no qualms about breaking into his home. Lydia Lopokova is a very bold and lovable Swanilda, bossing us all around and enjoying the fun of her naughtiness. I am surprised Swanilda goes for someone like Franz. Stanley Judson is brilliant as Franz, all doe-eyed and pathetic, looking up at the doll Coppélia who sits in the balcony reading all day. I don't understand how Franz thinks she is real. Perhaps a more entertaining – albeit darker – version would be if Dr Coppélius really did steal Franz's life and transfer it into his doll. It would serve him right.

The afternoon is rehearsal-free for most of us. Everyone seems to disappear, so I go for a walk through Clerkenwell, dropping down to the canal at Duncan Terrace Gardens. I walk as far as Sturt's Lock, turning around after watching a barge and tugboat slowly rising and falling through the barriers of the lock. I enjoy looking at the boats, some of them packed with crates, deliveries to be dropped off at London pubs and markets. As I walk, I like to imagine the journey they have made along the canal networks of the country, like veins and arteries, ending up here in the heart of our city. A few of the boats clearly haven't moved in a while, flowerpots resting on the roofs, laundry hanging out to dry. I remember Clara telling me that Nathan lived on one of these boats, renting it far more cheaply than he could find a flat. He made a deal with a retired old boatman whose wife wouldn't agree to live on the boat any more; the old man had spent his life travelling the country along the canal, from warehouse to warehouse, and couldn't quite bring himself to sell this physical, nostalgic memory of his life. He installed a new engine, prepared it for sale, but at the last moment couldn't go through with it. Renting it out, keeping it close by, was a compromise. I hope I will feel like that about a home one day, somewhere special that I can build memories with Clara.

It is good to get out of the theatre, to calm my nerves. Sturt's Lock is eerily quiet, just the low clangs of metal and the hisses of steam whispering from the chimneys. It is hard to imagine the factory workers hidden inside the brick walls of the blackened buildings that line the water. The only evidence of their existence is a barge loaded up with stacks of wrought-iron bars ready to be carried along the web of waterways. But as I turn and start to walk back, the broken sound of boys fighting, their voices loud and rough, breaks into my path. I look towards the noise, strangely unsettled by the intrusion. Two young boys are in the water, their chests naked as they wrestle, their thin arms grabbing at each other in the slime of the cold and dirty water. I slow down, watching the way the water washes over their skin, hair sticking to their foreheads in greasy clumps. A green finger of mare's tail root clings to one of them, wrapping its tendrils around his arm. The two boys look feral, dangerous water nymphs emerging out of the muddy water. They seem entirely oblivious to the cold, their bodies alive and unafraid. It only takes me a second longer to realise this is just a game to them, their cries morphing into laughter. This is their affection, bold and physical; they grab at each other without shame, a primeval display of unapologetic power.

A whistle blows from above me, followed by the angry shout of a policeman. People drown in the canal all the time, foolish swimmers who think they are invincible to the dark swells and depths of the locks. Even walkers like myself are discouraged from the paths, seen as nuisances getting in the way of the trade and transport of the waterway. I watch as the boys swim fast to the edge of the canal, hauling themselves out and running, laughing, to where their clothes lie in the dust. They run with identical strides, throwing their shirts over their shoulders. They look like brothers, even their slim calves springing in exactly the same taut way as they move.

The policeman has walked away, and I hurry back towards the Islington Tunnel. It is the image of the two boys that stays with me as I get back to Sadler's Wells. There is something about the ripples of energy that danced from them, the green weeds of the canal that clung to their skin, the tangle of their limbs in the water, that makes me long for something unknown, something visceral and animal, something I can't quite define.

When I return just after four o'clock, I don't take long to get into costume, but when I try to dance a few steps in the corridor outside the dressing room, the heeled boots for the villager dances feel stiff. They need dancing in a little more, breaking in until the leather is supple enough to move. I walk up to the Wells Room, but it is already being transformed into a reception room, high round tables with white cloths laid out across the space. I try the board room on the top floor. That is all the space I need to dance a little, to knead the shoes up and down in *relevés* and *retirés* until they soften.

I hear piano music coming from the room. I suddenly remember the last time I came across Nathan in there, how tempted I had been. Now that I have seen my sister's dismissal of him, I don't feel so guilty. Perhaps I too can have a moment of love; I deserve some affection, some admiration. I've worked for it, danced for it, starved myself as my mother told me I would need to do if I wanted to be beautiful. I need some recognition of all the sacrifices I have made.

Standing outside the door, I look down at myself. I am wearing a costume already; I've taken on a role. I haven't done my hair and make-up yet, but that is no matter. Pulling out my bun, I redo it, piling my hair on top of my head as Clara does. I close my eyes and try to imagine myself as my sister. What would she do? How would she talk to him? Would she wait for him to acknowledge her, or would she just walk straight in, go to him, kiss him?

I step into the room.

It is gloomy, the only light coming from above the piano. Nathan is staring down at his hands as he plays, shadows dancing across his face. He looks up as I reach the piano, and I see a look of surprise and then fear move through his eyes.

'We worked well together earlier,' I say. I cannot falter. This is just a performance, I tell myself. I know how to do it. 'It must be all that practising we've done. You've taught me how to find the music in my movement.'

I continue walking to him and then crouch at his side, leaning my arms across his legs.

'Clara,' he falters, his voice uncertain.

My eyes widen nervously as I wait to see if he has realised who I am.

'Does this mean you've changed your mind?' he says, reaching for my hand.

I don't know what he means, but he sounds like he wants me to say yes. Looking up at him, I smile. He stands then and lifts me up with him, wrapping his arms around me. My lips have never been this close to anyone's before, not even in the ballets where we fold and bend from the waists, our partners holding on to our hips, drawing us close as we rise up from *arabesques*.

Nathan's hands feel so different to the hands of the men in class, their grip firm and safe around our waists and thighs. His hands feel hot and alive, moving down my back, gripping my buttocks. He pulls me in tighter and I feel him moving, hard against my pelvis. I lift my chin and he kisses me, his lips rough, his tongue finding its way into my mouth. He tastes stale, like old coffee, and his teeth clash against mine. But I try to transform every moment into the fairy tale I was expecting, closing my eyes and imagining that this is me, and not my sister, who is being kissed and adored.

His breathing is faster now. I have an urge to pull away from him, to get his tongue out of my mouth. But I don't. I have dreamt of this and even though it is not exactly as I imagined, I will not waste it. His hands move between my legs, lifting up the weight of my skirt. There are layers of net, topped with a red apron, and he struggles to find my skin beneath all the material. I am not wearing tights, but as I feel his hands brush my thighs, his thumb reaching up to the edge of my knickers, I wish I had put on the full costume, with the tights and the leotard to protect me. I flinch, but then tell myself not to be stupid. This is what I have asked for; I am in control.

But then he moves my knickers aside and pushes his fingers inside me. I gasp and jerk away from him. My mouth is wet and there is a line of saliva running down my chin. I don't think it is mine.

'Clara,' he says, reaching for me. 'I thought that's what you wanted.'

I don't know what to say. I push his hands off me. 'I did. I do. Just not right now. I…'

'Yes?' he says, his hands returning again to my hips.

'I need to get ready for the performance.' Extracting myself, I walk to the door, trying to stay calm. I want to run, but it would look strange, over the top. Right now I feel so foolish, my cheeks burning hot.

I open the door, the faint noises of the theatre downstairs returning. It is reassuring to hear the sounds of the stagehands and the musicians, even from a distance, muffled as though at half speed. A window out onto the street must be open nearby. I can hear a bus go by along Rosebery Avenue, the hard groan of the wheels. But then it disappears and the claustrophobic murmurs of the narrow corridor return, as though a door has been slammed shut and locked me in.

Nathan has caught me by the hand. I turn back to him, trying to pull away, but his grip is strong. He pushes me into the door frame, the lock digging into my back. Even with his breath steaming against my neck, all I can think in that second is that I hope my dress doesn't rip.

'You haven't answered my question, Clara,' he says, his body pressing against mine.

'What question?' I say, turning my head to the side.

'You know what question. What is this? A test to see if you really wanted me?'

'I don't know what you mean.' My voice is rising.

We both freeze. There is a sound of footsteps coming towards us. Nathan takes a step away from me and I run.

I go straight to the well, even without thinking: my feet guide me. I can't go back to the dressing room immediately. Clara will know something is wrong.

The heels of my boots echo against the steps down to the well. Thankfully no one else is there. I get down onto my stomach and dip my hands into the water. It swells then stills against my skin, giving away nothing. I haven't turned on the light, so just a faint glow spreads down from the top of the steps, fading until the corners of the room are plunged into darkness. It is a relief to see that none of my pointe shoes are floating across the water. I have found them here twice before, each time putting my nerves on edge, as if I am being followed. That same feeling lingers now and I keep rubbing my hands together in the water, washing away what I have done.

Then, with the cold travelling through me, I find stillness. I spread my fingers into the black, claiming this darkness, a hidden secret world where I can cleanse myself, wipe away the pretence, become Olivia once again. As the water cools me, I imagine green weedy fingers climbing up my arms, wrapping tendrils and twists and coils up and up until they find my throat. It should be terrifying, the darkness hiding the smooth porcelain of my skin. But I am not afraid. As I feel my body returning to me again, I know that I am different, stained inside with a new pattern, as though if you opened me up I'd be a painting of my desires. Unique. Spreading away from the identical design of my sister.

When I finally stand, my hands cold and sore, I realise that my costume is creased, the netting crumpled. I smooth it down as best I can and make my way back up the stairs, trying to find the composure and the focus that everyone expects of me.

Clara's gaze catches me in the mirror when I return to the dressing room. She raises her eyebrows, momentarily distracted from putting on the make-up that is scattered around her. 'Got into a fight with your costume?' she asks.

I mumble something about my shoes being too stiff; I got carried away breaking them in. The cold suddenly hits my body, but I need to stay in costume until Miss de Valois has been to do her checks. Clara's green coat is further down the row of dressing tables, draped over a chair. I reach for it and wrap it around my shoulders. But as I curl up on my chair in the corner, making a start on my hair and make-up, I feel the heaviness of the coat pressing down on my shoulders. Clara may have said I can wear the coat as much as I like, but it isn't mine. Nathan gave her this coat, bought it for her, chose it specifically for her to wear. The guilt of what I just did chills me and I shiver, even in the warmth of the fabric.

When I am finished on my make-up, I tentatively put my hands into the pockets, trying to warm my fingers, which are still cold and stiff. The coat is indulgently soft, but I can't get warm; it is as though the fabric refuses to accept my skin. Slowly, as I dig my hands deeper, I touch the sharpness of two pieces of paper, a small scrap and a card. They are right at the bottom, almost hidden in the folds. One of them feels like a business card. Clara is at the other side of the room, talking loudly to Hermione and the others. Something tells me these are not for me, so I alter my position, leaning forwards over the dressing table as I pull them out. The scrap of paper is just a line of poetry: *A lovely apparition, sent to be a moment's ornament.* The words make me shiver. *Lovely, apparition, moment, ornament.* These words are haunting, a little terrifying. They remind me of my mother when she was at her thinnest, less than six stone. She thought she was beautiful, admiring the bones and sinews on her back in the mirror, the cords of her neck twisted so she could see herself.

I turn over the other piece of paper, a card, feeling the sharpness of the edges against my fingers. It is addressed to Clara. The handwriting is bold and round, the pen pressed deeply.

Call me at my hotel when you have made up your mind. I can make you a star.
  Jacob Manton, the Atrium Suite at the Hotel Great Central
  P.S. America will love you.

I slip the poetry and the card back into the pocket, my heart thumping. When Clara returns to our dressing table, I look up at her, scrutinising her face. But there is nothing, no sign that she is hiding anything from me. Not even the giant revelation that she might be leaving me. I think of everything we have done together, right from the instant we were born, when we were children constructing elaborate games around the fallen trees in Hampstead Heath, when Father died, when Mother turned from us and forgot how to treat us like the children we were, when she was admitted to Colney Hatch. I can't imagine going forwards without my sister. There is no part of my life that exists separate to Clara.

As I watch her finish her make-up, I feel another more complex uncertainty. Part of me wants her to leave, to let me be more than one of those identical twin ballerinas, the pretty Marionetta girls. But another, deeper, part of me is scared. What if she leaves and people realise that I am nothing without her? I don't know if I can be talented enough, strong enough, beautiful enough, without my sister to reflect back at me. Without her I might just go back to being ordinary Olivia Smith.

15

SAMUEL

The orders are coming in even faster than before and there has been no time for Mr Frederick to consider Samuel's sketches. Samuel, too, has hardly been able to think of them, rushing as he does between home, the workshop and the theatres and ballet schools where he delivers shoes. A new ballet company is forming, Les Ballets 1933, and they, too, are in need of shoes. They will not be in London until June, Samuel has been told, but the Russian-born George Balanchine has heard about Freed and has given them advance warning of his needs. And dancers for the Ballet Club have been asking for more shoes, so Samuel has been busy creating shoes, labelling the soles with the names of more and more ballerinas, travelling across London to deliver them. They have a new shop assistant, Milly Bell, who works with Mrs Dora upstairs, sorting the shoes, cutting the ribbons, learning how to fit the dancers who come in. She has had to learn quickly to keep up with the growing numbers of dancers who seek out their shop. He has heard Mr Frederick say to his wife that they also need to hire a delivery boy; Samuel is needed in the workshop. Samuel isn't sure how he feels about that. The deliveries are exhausting, but how else would he get to see

Olivia, to watch her dance in class and rehearsal when he arrives at a lucky moment?

Tonight is the first night of *Coppélia*, and he longs to be there. He has seen enough snippets of rehearsals to excite him, and he loves the comedy, the joyful peasant dances, the angry Dr Coppélius who wants nothing more than for his creation to come alive. Samuel has some sympathy. But he is unlikely to get a ticket for tonight's performance. It is the talk of the town, and all the seats will have been taken. He will wait, he tells himself as he sits as his workbench, his hands moving securely over the shoes. One of the later performances will have some tickets still available. He might be able to afford one of the cheaper tickets, just over a shilling for a seat in the amphitheatre.

Halfway through the afternoon, Mrs Dora calls him up to the shop floor. He stands there, blinking in the light that reflects from the mirrors and the sparkling pink of the shoes.

'Do you like ballet?' she asks him as she rolls the pink ribbons into a tight spool. It seems like an absurd question. Of course he likes ballet. How could he not like watching his shoes come alive, the costumes that he would like to design one day, Olivia floating across the stage? He nods.

'Yes, I always like to watch when I have a chance.' He hopes he hasn't said the wrong thing, that this isn't some sort of test to see how much time he wastes when he delivers shoes at the theatres. But Mrs Dora isn't like that. She doesn't speak in riddles. If she had a problem, she would just ask, directly and clearly.

'Good,' she replies, looking up at him. 'Frederick and I have tickets for tonight's *Coppélia,* a gift from Ninette for all the shoes we've delivered for the production. But we don't really like going to the ballet, not after a long day here. Frederick is too tired; he'll just fall asleep.'

Samuel feels suddenly very awake. He doesn't speak, just in case he says something to make her change her mind.

'So, here is a ticket if you want it.' She hands it over to him. It is just a little piece of paper, but it has immeasurably changed his day. It should be edged with gold, not this flimsy white and red card. 'Milly is taking the second one, so perhaps you two can go together.'

He looks over to where Milly is sorting shoes into size order on the shelves. She turns to him, a shy smile on her face. Samuel is confused by her wary expression. He doesn't know whether she is nervous he'll say yes, that she'll be duty-bound to stay stuck to him all night. Or maybe she's afraid he'll dismiss her and go on his own, or not go at all. Samuel has no experience with these things.

'Well, that's settled then,' cuts in Mrs Dora. She makes the decision for them. 'Samuel, you'll meet Milly outside the theatre at 7 p.m. You both need to go home first, to get changed, so you can leave early today.'

'Thank you, Mrs Dora,' Milly says, her cheeks blushing prettily. Samuel has never really looked at her before. The clean and shining world of the shop floor is not for him. She is very small but soft and round, her face a smooth circle. Her blonde hair is neatly curled, short and pinned up around her face like a frame. The collar of her white shirt is high, a navy ribbon tied loosely underneath, and her skirt sits neatly over curved hips. Even her hands are small, Samuel notices as she turns back to stocking the shelves: small but soft and smooth, the skin plump.

Mrs Dora closes the shop early, sending him out at three o'clock with a final delivery of shoes to Sadler's Wells which he must drop off before he goes home to get changed. He notices that

Milly has already gone. Perhaps she lives further away than him, or needs longer to get ready. Samuel doesn't know what he is supposed to wear, as he can't possibly match the smart suits and evening dress of the audiences he has seen going in and out of the theatres. He considers asking Mrs Dora for her advice, but he doesn't want to seem inexperienced, uncultured.

She seems to read his mind.

'Do you have a jacket you can wear?' she asks as he walks through the shop to say thank you once again. 'It doesn't have to be an evening jacket. Times have changed, you know. Many people turn up at the theatre in exactly the same clothes they've been wearing all day at work. It's a good thing, in my opinion. We can't be expected to spend all that money on both a ticket and a dress. So, don't be embarrassed if the person you end up seated next to is looking all fancy in evening dress. A day jacket will be fine.'

Samuel nods. He has a jacket. He wore it to his interview with the Freeds. And he has a clean shirt, a waistcoat and a tie that he made himself from scraps of silk that were being sold for pennies on Exmouth Market one day last year. He thinks he can make himself look respectable if he asks the landlady to let him borrow her trouser press. He'll need to give his one pair of smart shoes a good polish too.

He arrives at Sadler's Wells just after four o'clock, weighed down by the bag of pointe shoes. Hopefully they don't need the shoes for tonight's performance, he thinks. It will be tight timing for the dancers to sew on the ribbons, darn them, wear them in until they are soft enough to be quiet on the stage. The main door on Rosebery Avenue is busy with deliveries of wine for the reception. Samuel has a ticket for the stalls, the best seats, but he knows he won't find the confidence to go into the Wells Room for the reception. They will all be far too finely dressed in there. And what if someone recognises him, the pointe shoe maker's apprentice lingering where he is not invited.

Samuel walks around to Arlington Street, avoiding a pile of bricks abandoned by one of the builders who occasionally show a reluctant commitment to continuing with the renovation. The theatre may have been rebuilt two years ago but the rest of the street remains tired. Samuel finds a door open. Discarded cigarettes are scattered about the pavement where stagehands have escaped to find a moment's peace before the chaos of first night. Inside, the corridors feel alive, the preparations for the show building and building to the inevitable climax when the curtain opens at half past seven this evening. For any passer-by walking past the worn and sagging buildings on Arlington Street, it would be impossible to imagine the scenes of creation and preparation going on inside the theatre walls.

He goes straight to Wardrobe and delivers the shoes. It is busy in there, a seamstress stitching on last-minute additions to the costumes and dancers searching through the cupboards for hairpins and make-up brushes they can spirit away to their dressing rooms. When he has finished, he lingers outside the dressing rooms, imagining Olivia is in one of them, preparing for the night's performance. He doesn't hear anything, so he moves quietly through the theatre, unnoticed, peering into the Wells Room, which has transformed for the refreshments. Samuel keeps on moving up the stairs to the top floor, drawn by a desire to find her, to glimpse her just once before she appears before him onstage. He is oblivious to the closeness of the air, the smell of damp and musk, as he moves steadily forward through the narrow upstairs corridor that houses offices and small rehearsal rooms.

There are voices at the far end of the corridor. He stops and listens. One of the voices is familiar: Olivia Marionetta. But the man, the other voice, speaks to her. He calls her Clara.

'You haven't answered my question, Clara,' he hears the man say. But it is not Clara who replies; it is Olivia. Her voice is rising. She sounds afraid. Samuel takes a step closer towards them. There she is, his Olivia, pressed against the door frame, her face turned to the side. He thinks he recognises the man: it is the pianist, the one who plays for their ballet classes. Samuel has seen him often with Clara, the two of them leaving the theatre together, sometimes hand in hand when they think no one is looking. He doesn't understand what is happening. Surely the man doesn't think it is Clara in front of him now, that it is Clara he is pressing into the door like that, breathing into her neck?

He takes another step towards them, the tread of his feet louder now. They seem to freeze, the pianist pulling away. Olivia runs past him, not looking up, the lace of her skirt flying behind her as she moves. The pianist turns and sees Samuel. He narrows his eyes and sighs in frustration, running his hands through his hair. For a moment, neither of them moves, but then he walks towards Samuel, his shoulder knocking into him as he pushes past.

Samuel wants to grab the man and shake him. He wants to shout at him how stupid he is. How can he think Olivia is Clara? Does he really, properly, see either of them? How can he love when he is blind to who they both are? But of course Samuel doesn't do any of these things. He watches the pianist walk away before he heads back down the stairs and leaves.

Milly is waiting for him outside the theatre when he arrives just before seven o'clock. Samuel is distracted, upset about what he saw, but he smiles nervously when he sees her and tries to be friendly. He doesn't know how to behave. This isn't a date: Mrs Dora wouldn't have thought of it like that, and would never put Milly in that situation. He still feels an expectation, though, a nervous tension hovering between them. It would have helped if they knew each other a little better, but they've hardly spoken, just a few nods as they pass each other in the shop, Samuel holding the door for her, Milly bringing him a cup of tea a few times when she is making one for Mr and Mrs Freed. She has dressed up for the occasion, wearing a plum-coloured crimped chiffon dress with frills around the hem and the collar. Her white fur stole sits high around her neck, her bright blonde hair resting above in tidy curls. Although she is too small and round to look fashionable, not at all like those glamorous photographs of Hollywood stars, when she smiles at him he relaxes a little. He has never been on a night out with a woman before, but this arrived so suddenly and unexpectedly that he hasn't had the time to get anxious.

Although Milly loves ballet and theatre, she has never been to Sadler's Wells before. She tells him about the theatres she has been to with her mother: the new Mercury Theatre, Drury Lane, the Old Vic. As the two of them walk in, get their tickets checked at the door, she talks with a natural cheerfulness, filling Samuel's silences and nervous replies. She went to ballet classes when she was younger, but stopped when she was fourteen, accepting that her body wasn't suited to the movements. Samuel finds it hard to tell how old she is, her round rosy cheeks giving her a youthful doll-like look. But she must be at least eighteen for Mrs Dora to have given her a theatre ticket and sent her out with just him, unchaperoned. Samuel feels a weight of responsibility towards her, and offers her his arm as they walk in to the crowded foyer.

'My ballet teacher said I would be more suited to cabaret or musical halls. I guess she meant I wasn't really elegant enough to be a ballerina. It's okay, though. Fitting the dancers for their pointe shoes is exciting enough for me now.' She says this with a bright smile, not a hint of regret.

They walk straight to their seats in the stalls. The foyer is too busy and there is nowhere to stand without feeling awkward or getting in the way of the attendants who sell little packets of Hunter's fruits and nuts, their harnessed wicker trays packed with sweets, chocolates and cigarettes. Already the auditorium is filling, a noisy medley of voices, instruments, the rustle of dresses as women shuffle their way down the rows of seats. Men and women light up their cigarettes as they wait for the perform-ance, ushers politely reminding them that there must be no striking of matches once the performance starts.

Samuel buys them a programme from an usher who walks along the rows, and the two of them read it together, Samuel pointing out names of dancers he makes shoes for, Milly asking him questions about the ballet, the rehearsals, the costumes. He tells her everything he knows and she is fascinated by the story of Swanilda and Franz, how they plan to be married at the Harvest Festival, how she shakes an ear of wheat to her head to see if he loves her. If it rattles, then he truly is in love with her. However, she hears nothing. And perhaps the wheat tells the truth, for Franz is enraptured by the doll Coppélia, who he thinks is a real woman. So much so that he creeps into Dr Coppélius's house to try to woo her. The old man drugs him and tries to steal his life-energy in order to magically bring his precious doll to life. Poor Dr Coppélius is tricked by Swanilda, who has dressed up as the doll and pretends to be Coppélia coming to life. It all ends happily, with Swanilda revealing the trick and forgiving her fiancé. It has taken a lively, naughty young woman to teach the men that there is more to women than dull, passive beauty.

Milly laughs at that. 'That should be a word of warning for all those young men who stare at photographs of movie stars all day. Greta Garbo, Joan Crawford. My brother has a whole stack of them that he buys from Woolworths: Mae West, Katharine Hepburn, Bette Davis. I don't know how any woman is ever going to live up to his standard now. Even those actresses don't look like that when they've taken off their make-up each evening.'

Samuel is thrilled to hear her talk this way, dissecting the beauty of these women just like the construction of a pointe shoe. For him, the shoe is just as beautiful before he turns it the right way out, the folds and stitches and glue hidden underneath the perfection of the satin. When he says this to Milly, she laughs again, a jolly, light sound that he enjoys. He is glad to have her here with him. They are surrounded by very smart-looking men and women, many of them in silk dresses and black tie despite what Mrs Dora had said. Without Milly he would have felt out of place, too large and too common for these seats. But her bright smile, her brilliant blonde hair, her fascination for everything around her, makes him start to relax.

Finally the conductor, Constant Lambert, walks to the pit and bows to the audience. As he dips his head the energy in the theatre changes, as though the air is charged with electricity, pulsing dangerously as it waits for the curtains to open. The clapping is loud and hard around Samuel, and he can imagine the dancers bending and stretching in the wings, pounding their feet into the ground, using the volume of the applause to disguise the final sounds of their warm-up.

The rest of the evening passes in a dream, a story brought to life. And of course it is Olivia whom he watches most of all, waiting for each moment that she returns to the stage. He is impatient during the opening dances from Swanilda and Franz and he is overjoyed when the friends of Swanilda enter. Olivia is amongst them, smiling so brightly as she dances. There is so much jumping, he notices, her feet moving fast in his shoes. He doesn't know how she manages to do it all without her face showing any effort. It is as though her legs are moving by magic, conjured to life by a spell.

At the end, as he walks Milly back to her home in Islington where she lives with her parents and brother, he finds it hard to concentrate on her chatter. He is still back there, in the stalls, watching his Olivia.

16

CLARA

I linger in the dressing room at the end of the performance, waiting until there is no one left but me. There is a party in the Wells Room, and I know I should attend. All the dancers will be there, as well as the usual critics and photographers. We know we are more likely to get a mention in the next day's papers if we make an appearance at the party afterwards, dressed in our evening best. The trick is to find Arnold Haskell, one of the Camargo Society founders, and let him manoeuvre us through the heaving room of moustached men. But I need to make a decision. I have a choice to make, the biggest choice of my life. I could continue as I am, dancing with the Vic-Wells, enjoying the opportunity to be part of this fast growth of British ballet. Or I could take this gift that Jacob Manton has offered me, and leave. Now, more than ever, it feels right. It frightened me how Nathan's proposal made me imagine my life. How easy it would be to slip into mundanity, Nathan controlling every decision.

Mr Manton approached me last night after the second dress rehearsal for *Coppélia*, and I have to say that I was impressed he had worked out which of the Marionetta twins he was looking for. This season he has been a regular presence, watching us in *Pomona* and *The Birthday of Oberon*, even coming into class one day. Miss de Valois did not look so delighted about that, but she couldn't exactly say no when he is a friend of the Camargo Society and promising to donate some large sums. He has been clever, gradually making himself familiar around Sadler's Wells. So when he came up to me, I wasn't affronted. Quite the opposite, in fact. All I could think about was this is my chance. This is how I escape Nathan. This is how I stop hating myself every time I join him in the theatre foyer, smiling absurdly as he leads me to the evening he has planned.

Jacob Manton is an agent from America. He represents movie stars and dancers, actors and comedians. He finds models amongst the masses, draws them out and makes them shine. He can spin gold from straw, he told me last night, which made me slightly worried that I am the straw. But apparently gold is just around the corner if I want it. And he knows the ballet world: he is currently working on George Balanchine, persuading him to set up a dance school and company in San Francisco.

He was waiting for me in the foyer, his coat folded tidily over his arm. I was struck by the neatness of his trousers, the way they fell in sharp lines down to spotless black shoes. We took a taxi to the Hotel Great Central in Marylebone and a waiter found us the best table in the courtyard, an indoor extravaganza of shining glass, exotic plants, a grand piano, opulent golden seating. I had never been there before last night, this vast atrium with warm lighting reflecting off the marble, and wished I had dressed more smartly rather than just throwing on my green coat over my dress in an unthinking rush. Olivia had worn it earlier in the day on the way to the theatre, but I doubted she would object to me taking it back just for the evening.

Manton ordered us champagne with a pretty selection of cakes and sandwiches as well as jams in the brightest of colours. The waiter looked a little surprised by the order, but Mr Manton laughed.

'I'm American. I need to try all these funny British delicacies before you kick me out for breaking all the rules.' He was quick to put me at ease, with his wide smile and comic mannerisms. Everything entertained him.

He gushed about the ballet, the Vic-Wells, everything Ninette de Valois is doing to put British ballet on the map. And he gushed about me. My artistry, my musicality, my eyes, my legs, my stage presence, my *allegro*, my pirouettes. It was exhausting listening to him. I kept trying to interrupt, to at least thank him for his compliments, but he wouldn't let me. He had to get to his climax.

'And so I want you to come with me to America. I have watched you perform, and I think you need more. You need to dance, yes, but you also need to act, to model, to shine on Broadway, to be delivered into the hands of the best Hollywood directors. You can make your career your own in America, and you can be central to the development of American ballet. We need more dancers like you, dancers America will adore.'

He was sitting forward in his seat, his dark eyes boring into mine, his hands pressed firmly into the table. I held his gaze; there was nothing in it to intimidate me, just the promise of change and excitement.

Slowly, he sat back, crossed his legs, his eyes finally leaving me. 'And you'll be paid twenty times what you're paid now.'

'You don't know that,' I said, laughing a little at the extravagance of it.

He looked at me again, totally serious. 'Yes, I do. It would be my agency paying you. We'd represent you, and for the first year your contract would be fixed. Sixty pounds a week.'

I almost choked on my sandwich. That was more than twenty times what I was paid here. It seemed absurd that I could arrive unknown in America and make that sort of money.

He continued, graciously pretending to ignore my reaction. I tried to regain my composure, taking small sips from the champagne coupe. American women were probably far more sophisticated around discussions of money. 'After the first year, we'd renegotiate payment. It may be you're doing so well by then that you prefer the agency to take a percentage of each engagement's pay. We'd put you up in a lovely apartment in New York, though you're likely to be on the road a lot for tours, so I can write in a guarantee of first-class hotel suites wherever you travel. Something like this, eh?' he said, gesturing around him at the brilliance of the courtyard bar.

I hesitated, unsure how to frame my first question. I wasn't sure what I wanted the answer to be.

'And it would be just me you wanted? I would be going alone?'

Manton tilted his head to one side, studying my face. He was definitely observant. He knew this wasn't a straightforward question.

'Look, obviously I've thought about it,' he said. 'I've imagined bringing the two of you, introducing America to the two identical twin ballerinas. It would be exciting. We would make headlines. There would be a real media thrill, the type you just don't get here in England. But it wouldn't last. Not if that was how we sold you, advertised you. One of you would get sick of it and want to go home. And then we'd have blown it. No,' he said, leaning forward again, 'we need to do this differently. We need to start with just you, make you a star in your own right. Then maybe, if your sister is interested, she could join you for a few seasons.'

I nodded slowly, liking this idea. For the first time in my life I felt as though something was being decided that was for me, just me. I had another question, though, one I was longing to understand.

'And why me? Why did you choose me and not Olivia?'

'Clara, your sister's gorgeous, obviously. She dances like a dream. But I've watched her too, and I don't think she'd last a week in America. She wants ballet and only ballet. She wants to do her morning class, rehearse, perform, repeat it all again. She's a purist, living for the ballet. But you, I think you're different. I think you want to try everything and be everywhere. I think you want fame. Your sister, well, she wants fame too, but in a different way. She wants a mysterious, aloof kind of fame. She wants to be a prima ballerina.'

He was right; we both knew it. But what I didn't know was whether I could leave her. Could I get on that boat and know, for the first time, that I would be drawing my own path, one that didn't involve Olivia? I did want to say yes, I really did. But it was too big a question to decide at eleven o'clock in the evening after a glass of champagne.

Mr Manton could tell what I was thinking. He took out his card and scribbled a note, handing it to me across the table. 'Think on it. I don't need an answer until the middle of April. If you said yes, you'd join me in the summer.'

'That's just a few weeks,' I said, biting my lip anxiously. It felt ridiculous that I was to make this decision so quickly. All I could think about was how I was going to tell Olivia. And there was Mother. I didn't know if I could leave Olivia to brave those monthly visits alone. It would be irresponsible, dangerous even. Mother had always had a stronger hold over Olivia, her words eating away at her, worrying her. Without me there to balance out those stinging criticisms, I didn't know if she would cope.

'You'll be surprised how quickly you make up your mind,' he replied. 'Take a day and imagine yourself in a year's time. For half the day, imagine you have stayed in London, with your sister, with the Vic-Wells. For the other half of the day, imagine you have decided to come to America. That you have a schedule set out for the next month: performances on Broadway, modelling for a fashion brand, perhaps a screen test for a movie role, an appointment with a group of dancers to help set up an American ballet school. Try to work out how you feel about each future. Which one makes you anxious, nervous, depressed? Which one makes you excited?' He stood up and offered me his hand. 'Call me here when you've made up your mind.'

I wanted to stuff those remaining cakes into a handkerchief to take home to Olivia, but I didn't. Making a good impression mattered so much to me, and I longed to emulate the sophisticated mystery of the dancers he must have assumed I could be.

He walked with me to the lobby and asked the concierge to call me a taxi on his account. There was just something about him that reminded me of my father, a steady certainty that had surrounded him until the last weeks in the hospital when he could barely recognise us. But Mr Manton was different in every other way: loud, confident, his hair shining from brilliantine, a big smile that showed his large white teeth. He was a neat man, his suit perfectly pressed and tailored, his shoes so clean that they shone. I enjoyed watching him flirt with the concierge, as he had with the waiter, a kind, warm flirtation. He made you want to be part of his circle, as though his hands lit up everything he touched.

Wiping away the bright stage lipstick and then reapplying a softer shade, I decide that I can't sit here all night, waiting for some revelation to fall upon me. I get changed into my evening dress, the last one left on the rail now that all the other girls are already at the party. My reflection gazes back at me. There I am, looking like a bolder, more beautiful version of myself, my dress a bright blue silk, falling in a bias cut over my hips. With my dark make-up still bold around my eyes, I look like one of those post-card pictures of movie stars, otherworldly, untouchable. Right now, I can imagine myself in New York, Hollywood, on the screen, in a magazine. This dressing room, with its chaotic piles of old pointe shoes, feels too small.

There is music and the busy hum of voices coming from the Wells Room, and I join them. The room is transformed from the sweaty studio of our morning ballet class into this party of beautifully dressed dancers, musicians, patrons, rich old women with jewels hanging from their wrists and fingers, pearls encircling their necks like collars. It is still sweaty, but now with the heavy musk of scent and powder. I join Olivia and the other girls who are standing in a cluster, not yet finding the courage to start weaving their way between the guests, smiling for the critics and photographers. None of our dresses are expensive, except Hermione's perhaps, but we know how to wear them to make them work. That is our reward for all those hours of exercises at the barre.

I glance around the room, trying not to fidget with the hair that I have re-pinned in a more fashionable shape after the tight bun required onstage. I see that Nathan is here, talking to a group of men by the drinks' table. He is nodding, listening to an older man go on about something, but I can tell his attention isn't quite there. Instead he keeps glancing into the room, as though he is looking for someone. It is probably me he is trying to find; I have been avoiding him since his proposal, terrified of a repeat. I know I should have ended it with him weeks ago, but I couldn't find the courage to shake him off; it was easier to accept his gifts and attentions. And now he wants to trap me, to bind me to him with a ruby ring. I cannot give up everything I dream of to settle down to a life of marriage. He said that I wouldn't need to give up my career, but I've seen it before, dancers determined that nothing will change when they marry but who are pregnant within months and picking out linens for their nursery. Thinking back to Jacob Manton, his advice of living half a day imagining each alternative to my future, I know I don't need to live half a day imagining a marriage to Nathan. I know it would be impossible. When I remember all those nights spent rehearsing together, his desire to make me perfect, his control over every weekend's plan and night out, how much he kept me for himself, I feel sick.

I know I should at least speak to him. I don't want to be cruel; he has done nothing wrong except want me to love him. But his just isn't the type of love I can let into my life.

Excusing myself from the girls, I squeeze my way through the room. 'Nathan, how did tonight go for you?' I ask, coming up to his group and nodding to the men around him. They seem to understand that he is to be released from their conversation, that the company of one of the Vic-Wells ballerinas trumps theirs. He walks with me to the edge of the room. I repeat my question, something easy and neutral to start us off.

'It was fine. Constant kept us all together and that rehearsal after class today really helped you dancers keep to the rhythm.' Already I am finding him irritating, his commentary on the dancing unnecessary. I don't think he means to annoy me; that is the problem. Increasingly, though, I am finding that everything he says jars, as if we are shouting at each other from different rooms. It is sad, really, considering how many hours we used to fill with our endless chatter. Maybe this is what happens when you fall out of love.

'And you,' he says. 'Did you enjoy yourself?' His tone surprises me. It isn't a kind question; it has bite, as though he is trying to make a point. I ignore it as best I can.

'Yes, it was wonderful. And Lydia was hilarious, even more so than in rehearsal. You must have heard the audience. They were in stitches when she pretended to be the doll, rolling her eyes at Dr Coppélius.'

He doesn't smile. 'What do you want, Clara?'

I sigh. This is more difficult than I imagined.

'Nathan, you know I am fond of you. I am sorry I can't marry you. I can't marry anyone right now. But I had hoped we could move on and be friends.'

'Really? You want to be friends. And what was that this afternoon then?'

'This afternoon?'

But he isn't looking at me any more. He is staring at the door and his face has gone an awful white. I start to turn, to look where he is looking, but he grabs me above the elbows and stops me.

'Just make up your mind, okay.' And then he leaves, pushing his way through the crowd and disappearing into the gentlemen's bathrooms. I turn to look towards the door, to see who it is that made him go that ghastly shade. But the space has already filled again with new guests, the room shifting and changing as each group divides and reunites, and I walk back to find the girls, grabbing a glass of wine on the way. I move too fast through the crowds, wine spilling over onto my hand and splashing dark shadows onto the silk of my dress.

Nathan asked me to make up my mind. But I am already entirely decided on that question. I will not be marrying Nathan Howell, or anyone for that matter. I don't know how he could possibly have interpreted me any other way. Something keeps stopping me from telling Olivia about his proposal. Maybe because I don't like to think about it. If I don't mention it, perhaps it will all go away. I will tell her tonight, I think, once we are both home and in bed.

'Where's Olivia?' I ask Hermione when I join them again. Hermione, I notice, is looking radiant in a long silver dress, the back scandalously low. She always has admirers, but there are more than the usual number of stares tonight, a musician from a film company lingering close by.

'Oh, she left a moment ago. Probably gone home. You know how she is.'

I do know how likely this is. But tonight I am disappointed. I want to walk home with her, like we always used to do before Nathan started to monopolise me; I want to open up to her about all these strange changes in my life. I know I have been distant recently, and I need to remedy that before I decide on America. She cannot think it is because of her. It would horrify me if she misinterpreted my journey towards America and all its promises as a desire to leave her. I know how sensitive she can be.

Somehow, I arrive home before Olivia. It is late, almost one in the morning, and I have been thinking up ways of explaining everything to her the whole way home. But she gets in just after me.

'Where have you been?' I ask her, surprised.

'Just out, walking. I couldn't sleep.' She looks exhausted.

We get ready for bed quickly, splashing water on our faces. Although we both still have dark eye make-up staining our skin, it is too late for us to care. I try to start a conversation, but she is so silent, her eyes glazing over. Now is not the time.

I am almost asleep when I hear her get out of her bed. In an instant, she has climbed into mine, tucking herself in, pressing herself against my back. She is warm, and I nestle closer to her. We fall asleep like that, wrapped up together as we used to do every night when we were younger, before Mother went to Colney Hatch, before we found that we could breathe easier when it was just us. Two sisters, together. I don't know how I will be able to break that apart.

17

NATHAN

Nothing goes right for Nathan Howell today. Miss Moreton snaps at him twice during ballet class. He is playing the wrong type of polonaise for the *petit allegro*; his tarantella is too fast for the pirouettes. And then there is Clara. She dances the mazurka demonstration perfectly, every tiny movement an extension of the music. How can she dance like that, finding the heart of his music with such ease, and for them not to be made for each other? When she comes into the board room later that afternoon where he is practising, he is overwhelmed. Finally, after this week of silence, she is responding. He has the ring still; he carries it everywhere he goes. As he kisses her, he thinks of it there in his jacket pocket. But he doesn't have the chance to offer it to her again, for almost as soon as she arrives, she is gone again. She leaves him frustrated, cold, angry.

He dresses for the performance with a full mind that darts from place to place. Slowing his fingers as he buttons up his shirt, he focuses on every little movement: he needs to force himself to calm down if he is to be ready to play. Nathan loves the music, the choreography fitting better than so many of these modern ballets where the score and the dance have to be forced to work together with no care for the nuance of the rhythm. He is angry that he is going into the first performance feeling so unsettled. It is not as he planned it. He has imagined a very different scenario, him confident and assured, kissing Clara in the wings, reminding her to take off her engagement ring before going onstage. She was to have looked down in delight at her hand, hardly bringing herself to slip off the ring. But, reluctantly, lovingly, she would have done it, holding it briefly to her lips before giving it to him for safekeeping while she danced.

But now she has made him feel lost, disorientated. Nothing is going as he had so carefully and indulgently imagined.

Settling at the piano in the orchestra pit, he finds the pace of his breathing. He looks over the score, not that he needs it; he knows the entire ballet off by heart. The piano sits behind the harps and from his position he can see out into the auditorium. It is filling quickly and he is calmed by watching the seats changing from uniform red to a portrait of richly dressed benefactors, coloured in furs, silks, pearls.

Suddenly, as though a memory is surfacing hard and fast from the depths, he is hit by another wave of panic, the day's onslaught of confusions and stress never-ending. He feels his heart racing, a shock of sweat breaking out under his armpits.

He catches sight of a woman ushering her two children, a girl and a boy, along the rows of the dress circle. A man follows. Then they are out of his sight, too far stage right for him to see. But her face is still clear in his mind, imprinted there like a flash from a camera. Tall and slim, bright white hair, a long sloping neck, dressed in the sort of simple elegance she always favoured. And she has the same quiet beauty, her hand on her children's shoulders with a light touch, a reassurance that she is just behind them.

But of course it can't be his mother. That is impossible. He remembers the funeral, although its details are a blur. Sometimes it takes place on a bright summer's day, the coffin showered with huge white lilies. At other times it is inside a dark and gloomy church, mourners following the coffin, black veils covering their faces. But that can't be right, as he also remembers looking up and seeing his mother by his side, her hair bright underneath her veil.

He has kept all her cards and notes, the little words of encouragement she would write to him before each performance. They are packed neatly into a box that he keeps safely in his boat on the canal. He had to fight to get them out of his father's hands after she died. His father tried to burn everything, every last memory of his wife. Any object that could remind him of her was too painful; he could not bear to keep those remembrances alive. But Nathan reacted differently, grabbing everything he could and storing it safely in a large trunk under his bed. That was one of the reasons why he moved out of his father's house in Richmond when he was twenty years old and he knew he would go mad if he had to stay there a day longer. He needed the space to remember his mother as he wished, and, to make matters worse, he could tell his father was drawing away from him. Once Nathan's piano career started to lose the star quality it had attracted when he was a child, his father found it hard to conjure up the same enthusiasm. He died two years ago, alone, miserable, too bitter to let memories of love sustain him.

When Nathan went back there to organise the sale, there was nothing left that even hinted that his mother had once lived there. Every dress had gone from the wardrobe, every bottle of scent, every flower she had ever pressed. He searched frantically through the bookshelves, trying to find a book that might hold one of her dried flowers. That was her one eccentricity, bringing in flowers from their little garden and pressing them between the pages of books. His father had not found it so endearing and would fuss noisily whenever a dried daffodil petal or snowdrop fell out from the pages of his book.

Nathan took that trunk from under his bed with him when he left home. He has it still, the items carefully placed around his boat. They are his memories, beautifully wrapped in the pale pink tissue paper his mother saved from department store packages. Her white silk gloves, her feather headpiece she used to wear to parties, her bottle of scent that he occasionally sprays over his pillow, sparingly. It needs to last forever. Her silk stockings, her little book of Shakespeare sonnets that, now he's read them, he finds surprisingly erotic. There is an evening dress, midnight blue with feathers edging the hem. A pair of shoes, silver with little buckles. A white fox fur piece that he stores with blocks of cedar wood to stop the moths getting to it. And everything she ever wrote to him, all her gifts, the miniature dolls she bought him for the playroom. He has quite a collection: soldiers, princesses, musicians, priests, ballerinas.

And so it cannot be his mother up there in the dress circle, seated with a man and two children. A trick of the mind, he tells himself as Constant raises his baton and the performance begins.

He is distracted in the Wells Room at the party. Usually this would be his opportunity to meet composers and musical directors from the top theatres in London, his chance to remind them of the Nathan Howell who impressed them all these years ago as a little boy. His heart isn't in it, though. In a backless blue dress, her slim white arms beautiful like smooth porcelain, Clara looks like a model. She acts as if nothing has happened when she comes to speak to him, as though she thinks he can forget it all and move on, establish some sort of friendship. But it is too late for that. She needs to be his, exactly as he imagined it. He is already regretting what happened in the board room; it wasn't supposed to be like that, her body coming too close and then pulling away, perfection tarnished. When she talks to him, he looks down at her hand. He would like to take the ring that even now is nestled in his pocket and slide it over her finger, catching it in silver and diamonds.

It is then that he sees her again. The woman with the bright white hair. Her children are at her side, a girl and a boy, both around ten years old. They look like her too, blonde, with big green eyes. A man is just behind her; he has a hand around her waist. Nathan watches as she turns to the man and smiles, moving her hips just a little.

Nathan cannot bear it. He runs to the bathroom, locking himself in the cubicle, but even here he cannot find the quiet he needs. Men walk in and out of the bathroom with noisy laughter, and he wants to scream. But he doesn't; he has enough control. He leaves the theatre, going out the back way onto Arlington Street. One of the stagehands catches him as he leaves.

'There was someone looking for you,' the boy says, handing him a note. 'She said she was sorry she couldn't wait any longer as she needs to get her children home to bed.'

Nathan looks down at the note, his hands shaking.

'She said she's your mother,' the boy adds. 'Nice of your folk to come to this, give you some support. Usually it's just the ballerinas I'm delivering cards and flowers to.'

Nathan doesn't hear him. He is reading the note.

Darling, please don't be angry. I've been trying to find the courage to visit you for years, but I didn't know if you wanted me to. I wrote to you so many times in Richmond but heard nothing back. I would love to be part of your life again. You can meet my family. I know you'll get on so well with Lily and Charlie. Please write to me. We live at no. 5 Hadley Gardens, Chiswick. Yours, your loving mother.

The words swim in front of his eyes. His mother is dead. She died the day she left them, the day she decided that he and his father were not good enough. He gave her a glorious funeral in his mind, dressed her body in a white gown, buried her. The letters that arrived regularly at their home in Richmond were not real. He had ripped them up, burnt them, expunged them from his mind every time they appeared on the doormat. Until finally they stopped. And he was left in peace. His memory of his mother was preserved, a perfect woman, a goddess, an adoring mother. He has built his shrine to her, a woman who would never leave them for another man, replace them with a new family. Better dead than to have rejected him like that.

He starts walking home to the canal. By the time he reaches his boat, he has ripped the paper up into little pieces. He throws them into the water and they disintegrate; there is no proof that they ever existed.

18

OLIVIA

I decide to leave the party early. My mind is too full of my sister, Nathan, the first night of the ballet. It's too much of too many things at once. I don't know how I feel about any of it, other than that I feel like an imposter. Maybe Sergeyev should have cast me as the doll in Act One, the immortally passive Coppélia sitting immovably at her balcony. If Clara goes to America, if she says yes to that note in the pocket of her coat, will I finally find out if I am enough, if I can make it by myself? I might have found the note in a coat that Clara is insistent we share, but the words from Jacob Manton are very clearly for Clara only. A thought keeps creeping, insidiously, into my mind. Why did he choose her over me? Is she better than me, a more talented ballerina, performer? Even today it was Clara who was pulled forward in class to demonstrate to us her perfect timing in the mazurka. She shines, while I fade into the background. But even as I think it I know it isn't true. I am a better ballerina; my technique is more precise; I take direction, adapt my movements to the demands of the choreographer. Clara isn't designed for the corps de ballet. She should be in America, on Broadway, in films. Jacob Manton was right to choose her.

As I leave, hugging my goodbyes and congratulations to the other girls, I notice Nathan over in the corner with Clara. It scares me to watch this conversation from a distance, hearing nothing but seeing the tension spread across Clara's back. I hadn't even considered whether Nathan might mention what happened in the board room. I don't know what Clara would do if she knew I had pretended to be her. She would never suspect me of something like that, which makes me even more terrified about how she will react if she finds out.

Nathan isn't even looking at her. He is staring right past her at the doorway. I turn to look, following his gaze. There is a woman framed by the entrance to the Wells Room, her two children at her side, a man behind her with his hand on her waist. Her hair is very white but it doesn't make her look old; quite the opposite, it lights up her face like a crown. She looks around her, then turns back to the man and shakes her head.

I follow her and her family out of the Wells Room. Without really intending to, I end up standing behind them in the queue to the cloakroom. I had taken my coat and bag with me to the Wells Room on my way to the party earlier, thinking there would be somewhere to put them, but it had been so busy that I'd asked the cloakroom attendant to look after them for me.

'Do you know how I can find one of the orchestra?' I hear the lady ask. She has a light, sing-song voice.

'They are probably all at the party in the Wells Room, ma'am,' the attendant replies, handing over a stack of coats. I watch as the woman passes them to her husband. He helps the children into their coats, tickling them under their arms and making them giggle as they wriggle out of his way. The boy is tired, his eyes glazed as he stares about the foyer. They look contented, like sleepy little cherubs.

'I tried in there, but I couldn't find the man I was looking for.'

'Who is it you are after? I might be able to tell you if he's left already.'

'Nathan. Nathan Howell, the pianist.'

I stiffen, listening more intently now.

'I haven't seen him leave,' the attendant says. I see her notice me. She is fairly new here, and we've only spoken a few times, but she knows I am one of the dancers. 'She might know,' she says, nodding to me. She probably knows I am either Olivia or Clara Marionetta but hasn't got a clue which one. Safer to stick to 'she', it seems. The lady turns to me and smiles.

'Do you know Nathan?' She pauses and smiles even more, drawing her hands to her chest. 'Oh, you're one of the dancers, one of Swanilda's friends. You were just wonderful tonight. We loved every moment.' She turns to her daughter, who is staring up at me with wide eyes. 'Lily, this is one of the ballerinas. Isn't it exciting?'

Lily does not seem able to speak, despite her mother's coaxing. Her eyes are fixed on me with intense curiosity. I remember looking the same way at ballerinas when I was even younger than her, when Mother would take us to the theatre and fight her way backstage, bullying the poor stagehands into letting us through.

I lean down slightly, smiling at the little girl. 'Do you like ballet?' I ask her. 'Have you started lessons?'

She is shy, shuffling a step closer to her mother. But she nods, blushing.

'Oh, she adores ballet,' the woman replies for her. 'We haven't been to many shows yet, but now the twins are a little older we're going to be more adventurous.'

I reach into my bag. It is stuffed with shoes, tights, hairpins, my wool leg warmers. The pointe shoes I wore for Act Two are already a little worn out. They might get one more ballet class out of them, but that will be it.

Taking out the shoes, I kneel in front of the girl. 'Have you ever held a pair of pointe shoes?' I ask her. She shakes her head, looking at the shoes with nervous excitement. 'Well, you can have these, if you would like,' I say, holding out the shoes. 'They're too big for you now, but one day maybe they'll fit and by then your feet will be ready. If you start ballet classes soon,' I add. 'These are the shoes I wore tonight; so you will always remember your first performance of *Coppélia*.'

'How generous!' exclaims the woman, kneeling down by her daughter. Lily looks up at her mother, seeking permission to take the shoes. She nods, and so the girl reaches out and takes them. The girl turns them over in her hands, so gently as if she were holding a bird. It is lovely to watch, a shy little girl dreaming of wearing such shoes herself one day. She has a pink bow in her hair and her dress is covered in frills and froth. I was the same at her age, transporting myself forward to the life I wanted to live.

The woman whispers something in her ear. Lily turns to me, more confident now.

'Thank you very much.' She blushes again. 'I love them.'

'You are so kind,' her mother adds. 'She won't stop talking about this for months, I can tell already.' I think she is right; Lily is swaying from side to side, lost in her own imaginary performance. 'Please will you sign our programme?' The woman holds it out to me and I take the pen that the cloakroom attendant offers. I lean against the counter and sign my name next to the cast list. *Olivia Marionetta*. I might not be at the top of the list, but it is only my name that is drawn in pen across the page. And it is my name that Lily will remember.

As I return the programme, the woman looks anxiously at me. 'Sorry, one more thing. You have been so kind, so I hate to keep asking questions, but do you know the pianist Nathan

Howell?' I nod and her face lights up. 'Oh, wonderful. I don't suppose you know if he is still here?'

I think back to that moment in the Wells Room when I saw him across the crowded room with Clara, that strange, shocked look on his face. He had bolted out of the room through the side door.

'He left the party, but maybe he's still backstage. I can try to find him for you?'

I really don't want to; I can't face the thought of speaking to him now, of trying to behave as though nothing has happened between us. The woman is looking uncertain and her son is nearly asleep, leaning heavily into his father's waist. 'Or I can ask a stagehand to deliver him a message, if that would be easier?'

'Could you? That would be a great help. We need to get these two home to bed.'

'One moment,' I say, moving quickly towards the auditorium. A young stagehand is sweeping, and I call to him. He follows and joins us in the foyer.

'This lady would like to get a message to Nathan Howell. Can you take it?' He nods and we wait while she scribbles a note on a piece of paper that the cloakroom attendant hands her. She gives it to the stagehand, lingering a little as she passes it over.

'Tell him it's his mother.'

I look at her in surprise. She seems too young to be his mother. And surely these can't be his brother and sister. I have a vague memory of Clara telling me his mother was dead. But I must have been mistaken.

Her husband takes her arm. It is a gentle movement, kind and patient. She looks up at him and nods.

'Time to go before we all turn into pumpkins.'

I wait until they have left, the children bundled out through the doors and into a cab that lingers on the street. Although I leave too, I am not tired. I can't go home just yet; I know I wouldn't be able to sleep.

It is too early in the year still for the nights to be mild and I shiver as I stand on the corner of Rosebery Avenue and Arlington Street, deciding where to walk. A bus goes by and I feel myself tempted to get on, see where it takes me. But even that is too daring for me, even tonight when I am feeling strangely wild, as though I have transformed into a different person. Perhaps it was the girl, Lily, her obvious admiration and excitement at seeing a ballerina so close-up. Giving her those shoes had been just as thrilling for me as it was for her. Or maybe it was meeting Nathan's mother. I had been afraid of him after that kiss, when he had pressed his hand between my legs. But there is something about meeting someone's mother that brings them back to the realm of the human; it normalises, takes away mystery. It makes a person seem just like the rest of us. And besides, I don't even know if I want Nathan any more. I thought I did, but in that moment with him in the board room, I had not felt the joy and exhilaration I had been expecting. Instead there had been guilt, disappointment, disgust.

Turning north, I start walking away from my usual homeward direction. Arlington Street is dark and quiet, the walls of the theatre windowless on this side. They loom high over me, a face-less stare of shadowy brick that seems to swallow the sounds of the street. There is an old pub further up, but it is shut and boarded, the chipped harlequin sign fading. I walk quickly past a narrow alleyway on my left that disappears into the gloom, piles of discarded bricks, crates and wooden pallets cluttering the entrance. Building work on the street started last year, catching up with the renovated theatre that has emerged, gloriously, from its ruins, but it is painfully slow, the debris of bricks more common than the sight of a workman. When I reach the end of

the street, I continue without thinking into the narrow passageway that leads onto Owen Street. Usually I would be afraid to
walk this way at night, avoiding the warbling calls of the drunks
who spill out from the public houses. But tonight I am not afraid.
When a man turns at the end of the passageway, I instinctively
press myself into the wall, hiding myself in the shadows of the
building. I see his face, partly lit up by a street lantern, one of the
old gas lights dimly fighting their yellow rays into the night.
Even with half his face in shadow, I can tell it is Nathan.

I feel an urge to follow him, as though tracing his journey home
will purge the fear I felt when he touched me, will give me the
power to move unnoticed and unafraid. Landing each step lightly
on my toes, I keep my distance. It is not difficult to keep up this
dance; I am used to balancing my weight forward, always ready to
jump and leap and turn across the stage. But now I must be silent.

He continues north, crossing Goswell Road and then the city
road. These roads are wide and open and I feel anxious for a
moment that he will turn and see me, but he seems intent on his
direction now, surging forwards with a certain step. He cuts
through the gardens alongside Duncan Terrace and Colebrooke
Row, and I follow. In the darkness it is hard to tell where I am
going, the trees reaching up and out of the ground either side of
me. A few squares of light from the windows above the two
roads taper in through the tree cover, but they are not enough to
provide a guiding path. At the end of the gardens, I look about
me, trying to spot him again. And just as I think I have lost him,
there he is, disappearing down a slope to the right.

I wait, unsure. I can see down to the canal, Nathan marching
along the towpath. The water is a yawning black, impossible to
tell how deep it is. It both frightens and rouses me, this water
that sits so still like spilt ink. It reminds me of my well at the
theatre, but without the luck that comes from dipping my toes

into its mysterious waters. This water, here, looks cruel and heavy, as if it might stick to me if I dared to lower myself into its blackness. I walk down to the canal, touching my fingers against the brick wall on my left for support. The brick feels cold and wet, and I draw my fingers away hastily as I feel something moving beneath my touch. Just moss, I tell myself sternly.

Standing at the bottom of the slope, I look out along the canal. To my right is a tunnel, its mouth gaping wide with darkness. I turn back to the open canal, the rows of boats set neatly against the path. And then, suddenly, the dim glaucoma of the clouds clears and for a moment there is a brightness from the sky. The moon is large and whole. It looks like a searchlight, scanning the area for intruders.

I can see him. He is standing on the front decking of a narrowboat, holding his hand out above the water. As he opens his fingers, white fragments flutter down into the water, twirling as they do so. At first I think they are pieces of satin, like the scraps we cut from the end of our pointe shoe ribbons. But as the last wisp of cloud disappears from the face of the moon, I see they are paper, torn and shredded in his hand.

There in my mind is his mother, the beautiful woman with the bright white hair, anxiously scribbling her note onto the scrap of paper. Nathan watches the water, the pieces of paper disintegrating on the surface of the canal. Once the last one has vanished, he crouches down, lowering himself inside his boat.

I get home late and I am too tired to talk to Clara. I don't tell her where I have been. There is nothing I can say. But still I can't sleep. It is only once I have crawled into her bed and wrapped my arms around her back that I feel my mind relaxing, and sleep finally draws me down into a quiet rest.

ACT FOUR

19

CLARA

Miss de Valois calls me and Olivia into her office after class. There is a telephone call for us. She leaves us alone, and I see her look back at us strangely as she closes the door. It isn't quite sympathy, nor is it concern. Instead, it is almost a nod of reassurance. She knows we can handle whatever the telephone call will reveal.

We both know it will be about Mother. We've been expecting a call like this ever since she was admitted into the hospital three years ago, both dreading and wishing it in equal measure. It is the senior doctor waiting for us on the telephone, Dr Morris, a man we have only met twice before. First, when he came to our house, coaxing Mother out of her bedroom, leading her by her skeletal arm towards his car. Then, in his office at Colney Hatch, about a month after Mother was admitted. I remember that a bar of light had been shining across his face and he kept blinking, as if he could make it go away. All I could think about was why he hadn't just closed the blinds.

And now we hear his voice again. I am holding the receiver, but Olivia has her cheek pressed to mine, listening in to the call.

'Miss Smith?' the voice asks. It is a while since anyone has used that name. The nurses know we are Marionetta now, instructed as they are by Mother, who talks about us endlessly, boasting to the other patients about her ballerina daughters. Not that any of them care, I expect.

'Yes, speaking,' I reply.

'It's Dr Morris, from Colney Hatch. I am calling with some bad news about your mother.' There is a fraction of a pause on the line, but then he continues, his voice steady. Dr Morris is too busy to do this slowly, though I imagine many of the patients have no relatives to call, none who would be interested anyway. 'I am sorry to have to tell you that she passed away this morning.'

Olivia and I reach for each other, our hands clasped together. I feel her press her cheek into mine more firmly, her skin hot and damp.

'Was she ill?' I say. It is a stupid question: of course she was ill. But it seems strange that she would die so suddenly, without any word of warning. Even as I think it, I know it is an unreasonable thought. Death, especially for someone like Mother, would not be a slow easing away from life. Nor would it be a long painful suffering, like our father's. Mother's death was always going to be dramatic, a sudden burst, a grand finale.

'Not as such,' he replies. 'She was doing well, in fact. I know you visited a few weeks ago, and she has been very positive and cheerful since then. The nurses thought she had turned a corner, fewer outbursts, more polite to the other patients. They were so confident in her behaviour that she was included on the morning walk today, to the park across the road from the hospital.' He pauses now, and I can hear a faint buzzing from the telephone line. It seems he is uncertain about how to continue. 'Would it be better if you came in to the hospital? It might be easier to explain in person.'

'Yes, okay. We'll come in this afternoon,' I reply. This is not how we should be finding out about our mother's final moments, with our faces stuck together, sweating as we both struggle to hear Dr Morris clearly.

'You can collect her belongings then, too, if you would like. There is no obligation to do so – we can dispose of them here. But you might not want to return too many times. And there is the funeral to arrange, if you feel able.'

It is too much to think about. 'Yes, fine. We'll do that this afternoon when we are there. It makes sense to do it all in one go.' I realise I sound harsh and unfeeling. And maybe I am, just wanting to process it quickly and move on. But I am sure the emotions will come later. There is only so much one can think in half a minute.

When I put the phone down, I forget where I am. The walls decorated with photographs of ballerinas, a pile of pointe shoes in the corner, a set of glasses with decanted sherry in an ornate bottle on a side table: for a moment I could be back in our family home in Highgate, in Mother's bedroom. But this room, Miss de Valois's office, is too tidy, too ordered, a professional office, not Mother's chaotic world of make-believe.

Miss de Valois gives us the afternoon off rehearsals, and we take the train to Colney Hatch. Olivia is quiet, her hands anxiously turning and turning on her lap. I reach across to her and she stills.

'It's going to be all right,' I whisper. And I truly believe it. As the train brings us closer, I feel more and more certain that we can survive this. More than survive this; perhaps it is what we need to move on with our lives.

A nurse is waiting for us at reception and she takes us straight to Dr Morris's office. I peer down the long corridor to the right. It is quiet, ghostly even. It always surprises me how empty the hospital feels, even though I know it is packed with more than two thousand patients. The corridor goes on and on, the end just a tiny dark speck in the distance. It must be nearly five hundred feet long, an endless tunnel of rooms and wards and offices, all hiding madness and pain.

Dr Morris stands when we enter, and gestures to two chairs across from his desk. He is a short man, stocky, with a wide neck that seems too large for his shirt. I remember this from the first time, how solid and sturdy he looked compared to our frail, birdlike mother.

'I thought we could take a walk,' he says, after repeating the condolences he expressed on the telephone. 'I can show you where your mother died. It may be easier for you to understand that way. First a few papers to sign. This for next of kin and this one to confirm that your mother died while living here.' He nudges some papers across his desk towards us.

'Shall I sign, or would you like to?' I ask Olivia.

She shakes her head. 'You do it.'

He waits for me to look over the papers, then stands. 'Shall we?' We follow him out of his office and back outside into the driveway. Another nurse is waiting for us by the gate. I notice how nervous she looks, her eyes flitting up and down as we approach her.

'This is Nurse Sarah,' Dr Morris tells us. 'She was there when your mother died.' The nurse nods at us, a sympathetic smile spreading anxiously across the width of her face. She is all large angles and lines, thick, straight ankles rising out of her brown shoes. Her white cap sits firmly on the back of her head, strangely at odds with her restless eyes.

We leave the premises and cross the road into a park.

'The nurses take the patients here for a change of scenery, if we feel they are sufficiently stable. It is good for them to get out and feel a little less cooped up. They always go early in the morning, before too many locals are out and about. And the patients are often more receptive in the mornings, before they have worked themselves up into tiredness and hysterics. Everything seems a little clearer in the mornings, don't you think?' he says, a friendly smile on his face. He is trying to engage us in conversation, but neither of us are in the mood.

'As I said on the telephone, your mother was doing very well. We thought she might start getting agitated if we didn't give her a little outing. But we misjudged her condition. She was clever, your mother. She knew what she was doing, I think.'

I turn to him sharply. 'What do you mean?' I don't like his suggestion that she somehow manipulated the nurses into thinking she was getting better. But of course that is exactly what she would have done. I don't know why I am surprised.

'Just that she knew she could control her behaviour in order to get what she wanted.' He stretches his hands out in front of him, his thick wrists too wide for his cuffs. 'That is not unique to a mental hospital, Miss Smith.'

I nod and he continues, leading us towards a large pond, almost a lake, that appears as if by magic out of the ground. It is lined with reeds, the grass merging into the water. A bank of swans swim across the surface, their long necks still and serene. Another group is resting by the edge of the water, looking around them with territorial suspicion. Nurse Sarah walks a few steps behind us. When I turn to look back at her, I catch her letting out a sharp sigh. This is hard for her, I realise.

'There were two nurses and four patients, which should have been fine. But one of the patients, a young woman with a nervous disorder, was upset. Something your mother said, apparently. The patient wasn't clear on what happened, but it was something about her feet. Your mother kept calling them lumps of clay. It wasn't really anything serious.'

I can't help smile a little and I turn to Olivia to see her, too, struggling to suppress a laugh. That was exactly what Mother used to say about the other girls in ballet class, especially those who had been given more attention than us by the ballet teacher. 'I don't know what she was looking so smug about,' Mother would snarl on the way home. 'Lumps of clay, her feet were. Absolute lumps of clay.'

Dr Morris continues. 'While the two nurses were calming down the other patient, your mother slipped away and ran off into those trees.' He points to a little copse of woodland just behind the pond. With the afternoon sun lighting up the leaves, it is hard to imagine them hiding Mother.

'When they finally located her, she had stripped off all her clothes and was walking, naked, towards the water.'

He shows no embarrassment at telling us this story. No doubt patients taking off all their clothes is not an uncommon occurrence at Colney Hatch. But now he turns to Nurse Sarah and gestures for her to join us.

'Perhaps you could explain to the Miss Smiths what happened next?' he asks, but it isn't really a question. He shows no sign of noticing the nurse's discomfort at being brought here to relive our mother's death. She must only be in her mid-twenties but her solid, sturdy frame makes her seem older, masking her nervousness from anyone unwilling to look too closely.

Nurse Sarah shakes her head as she speaks, as if she can negate the story she is telling us. 'Your mother kept heading towards the water and suddenly started speeding up. We were on the other side of the lake so couldn't get to her. She was taking quick, dainty steps and her arms were flapping all over the place. It looked as though she thought she had wings. She just kept going, bending her body up and down, her arms above her head, sometimes wrapped around her, sometimes flapping frantically. She went right through the middle of a group of swans and they weren't very happy about it. They kept hissing at her, beating their wings and winding their necks towards her, but she didn't seem to care. In fact, she started to move a bit like them, writhing her neck and shoulders in this very swanlike way. It gave us all rather a shock to see her like that.'

Olivia has moved closer to me and we both stare across the lake. I can picture Mother, her tiny naked body, her fading bones jutting out, her fragile skin draped with creases and folds. It was always her frustration, her flesh dissolving but leaving loose folds of skin that she could pinch between her fingers. I imagine her dancing towards the water.

I know what she was doing. This was her dying swan, her final performance. She always had a fascination for Fokine's *Dying Swan*, Saint-Saëns's music, Anna Pavlova's famous solo. She sought out opportunities to see it performed and when she returned home we would find her dancing around her bedroom, her arms twisting and turning, her feet trying to mimic the little *pas de bourrée*.

Nurse Sarah cuts through our thoughts. 'I ran around the lake towards her, but my colleague, Nurse Lizzy, had to stay with the three patients who were by now beside themselves, crying and screaming. Your mother walked right into the water and kept going and going until she was beyond her depth. I called out to her, but she sank down into the water and was not able to find the strength to rise out of it again. Perhaps she could not swim, or perhaps she was too weak from anorexia. By the time I had waded my way in and gone down under the water to find her, she had drowned. I dragged her out and pulled her onto the bank, but it was too late.'

I turn to Olivia and hug her. Neither of us are crying, though somehow I feel I should. Maybe the doctor expects it. Or maybe not. Perhaps no one cries when someone dies in Colney Hatch. It is a terrifying, haunting death, but it is also exactly as Mother intended. Of that I am sure. Finally, our mother found a way to become not only the ballerina but the muse itself. A dying swan, dancing to her death.

Dr Morris leaves us with a different nurse once we are back at the hospital. Nurse Sarah disappears immediately, before we have a chance to thank her. It must have been awful, running into the water after Mother, searching for her body amongst the reeds.

The nurse takes us to Mother's room. It is both disappointing and a relief to see it already packed up, her belongings neatly placed into two boxes.

'Sorry that we couldn't leave everything as it was. But this room is needed for another patient, and we couldn't wait.'

'Not even a few hours for us to visit?' Olivia says. She is upset, I can tell. This is all moving too quickly for her.

The nurse looks apologetic. She is young and pretty, just the sort of woman Mother would have courted. 'I fully appreciate that would have been better. But we had no choice. It was that or making a vulnerable patient in a busy ward wait until tomorrow to get a room of their own.'

Olivia looks down. 'Of course,' she says. 'The living take preference over the dead.'

There is an uncomfortable silence before the nurse gestures to the two boxes. 'There's no need for you to take any of this if you don't want to. We can dispose of it here if you prefer. But I'll give you some time to go through them and decide.'

'Thank you,' I say. 'We won't be long.'

I take the first box and open the lid. Mother's scarves and jewellery, her colourful headbands and trinkets that she must have convinced the doctors it was safe for her to keep. I close it quickly. 'I don't think there's any need to look through this one.' Olivia nods. She isn't touching anything, just standing there with her hands behind her back, hardly even looking at the box.

Then I open the other one. In it are the letters we have written to her over the past three years, stacks of photographs, programmes from theatre productions, memories of the days before Father died. I take them out and start to leaf through them. There are signed photographs of Pavlova, Lopokova, Nijinska, Massine. There are old reports from the many different ballet teachers Mother persuaded to train us over the years. There are a few photographs of me and Olivia, one from our first ballet class, one of us before performing in an operatic play at the Old-Vic, dressed in little sailor costumes. There are a few more recent ones that we have sent her since joining the Vic-Wells. It is interesting that in every photograph she has of us, we are in ballet clothes or costumes. Any image of us as ordinary little girls does not exist.

Olivia has joined me now, looking through another pile of papers that she lifts out of the box. She holds a photograph out to me. It is Father. He looks so young in the photograph, dressed in army uniform with his hair swept across in a side parting. An inscription on the back of the photograph says it was taken in 1915. Just one year after we were born.

He was in France then, fighting in the war. Mother would tell us the story regularly in those earlier, happier days before Father died. Apparently, as the two of us were fighting our way into the world, Father was escaping death by a matter of inches. He would take over the storytelling then: he was in the trenches that night, the night before a big offensive at the Marne. He was instructed to join a group of men to creep out into no man's land and cut through German barbed wire. Out in the field, mud creeping up around his boots, he heard the man beside him drop his wire cutters. Father reached down into the mud to pick them up, and reached out to hand them back. As he did so, there was a blast of gunfire. The cutters were blown clean out of his hand, sending shards of metal into his arm and fingers. In agony, he was rushed back to the trench by the men around him, finding help in one of the dugouts. The metal shards had missed a major artery in his arm by millimetres. He spent six months recovering at home, during which time he got to meet his beautiful twin daughters. Then he went back to the front. He avoided death throughout the war with his three lucky charms, his wife and two daughters, protecting him. But it was cancer that got him six years after the end of the war. His luck had run out.

In the end, we take just a few photographs. The memories of everything else belong to another time, when we were a different family to what we became. We find the nurse and let her know.

'And the funeral?' she asks. 'What would you like to arrange?' I feel lost by the question. How is anyone supposed to know how to arrange a funeral?

She must notice my look of confusion. 'Come and sit in reception and I'll talk you through the options.'

We decide on a small ceremony in the hospital chapel next week, followed by a burial in Highgate. Mother will be buried next to Father. The extended family in Brighton will be invited, but it seems unlikely they will attend. That will be easier, really, avoiding their stares and undisguised disapproval. Aunt Alice will overcompensate for her guilt at neglecting us so entirely and it will be unbearable.

'What happens to those who have no family to arrange their funerals?' Olivia asks.

'We organise it all for them,' the nurse replies. But she says it quickly, a little dismissively. It sounds as though she doesn't want further questions.

'Where are they buried?' I push her. I've heard rumours of large unmarked graves in the grounds at Colney Hatch, forgotten and unloved people left here to die by their indifferent relatives.

'There is a graveyard by the chapel,' she says, smiling and standing. The conversation is over. I feel glad that Mother has us, that we never neglected our monthly visit. I am glad too that we got to visit the place she died, to pay tribute to those final moments. She died as a swan, a dancing swan, and she will be buried with Father, her great love, the only person who could relieve her terrible anxieties. There, under the ivy and stone of their grave, they will be together again.

20

SAMUEL

If Milly Bell hopes Samuel will ask her out again, properly this time, without Mrs Freed to orchestrate it all, she is to be disappointed. While she longs for Samuel to take the next, obvious step, it doesn't even occur to him that she might like him. Perhaps if he wasn't so wrapped up in replaying Olivia's dancing in his head all night and all morning as he walks to work, he might notice the smiles and friendly attentions Milly gives him every time she finds an excuse to come down to the workshop. For days now it has been the same painful routine, Samuel oblivious while Milly tries her hardest to get his attention. Mr Freed, of course, notices nothing. Mrs Freed is more observant and feels for Milly every time she comes back up from the workshop, her face uncertain, disappointed.

The morning after the two of them had such a wonderful time at Sadler's Wells, Milly is filled with excitement. Getting ready in her little bedroom feels like preparing for a night out; even the morning light spilling in between her pink curtains takes on a different hue. Everything has a thrill to it: choosing her skirt and blouse, which shoes she is to wear, the pearl necklace she knows looks good against her skin. She takes longer with her make-up than usual, a light blusher on her cheeks, a new lipstick. Milly graduated last year from a tiny women's college next to Regent's Park. She was taught the importance of dressing beautifully and neatly every day for work, but sometimes she rushes her face in order to get to the shop on time. Madame Clement would be proud of her today, she thinks. The other girls at the college had been envious when Milly got the job with the Freeds. Several of them had applied, attracted to the glamour of ballerinas and pink satin shoes. It was preferable to a dull job typing up letters and making diary appointments for boring men in grey suits.

Downstairs in the kitchen, she hurries with her breakfast. Milly wants to get to Freed early, to be already behind the till when Samuel arrives. She thinks forward to when she can make him a cup of tea and take it down to him mid-morning. What she will say to him, how he will respond, how easy and friendly it will all be; she imagines it all. She refuses the egg sandwich her mother offers to make her, instead putting together her own plain roll and some thin slices of beef. Everything is deliberate this morning: she imagines Samuel watching her, eating with her perhaps out on the little bench in the square close to the shop. An egg sandwich would be too messy, too smelly.

Her brother Jonathan comes in, yawning, his hair a mess. He seems to drag himself awake as he notices his sister, searching lazily for something to tease her about.

'You came in rather late last night, Milly,' he begins, leaning forward on the kitchen table and picking pieces of beef from the plate. His mother pushes his hand away from the meat, passing a cup of steaming hot tea into the other. He is spoilt and he knows it. They all know it, but they are too fond of him to do anything about it.

'Not so late,' Milly replies, packing her roll into her bag. 'I was at the ballet, if you must know.'

'Who with? Go on. Tell us. I saw you coming back dressed up all fancy in that ghastly fox piece.'

'Hey,' she cries, hitting him on the arm. 'I like that fox piece.'

'I'm not sure the fox agrees with you,' he smirks.

'I went with a friend, a colleague actually.'

'That giant I saw at the end of the path? He's a colleague?'

'He's not a giant. He's a pointe shoe maker. They need to have very strong … arms.' She can feel herself blushing and turns away.

'Strong arms, eh,' he laughs. 'I bet he does.'

'Oh, be quiet, Jonathan,' his mother scolds. 'He was a gentleman and walked Milly all the way home.'

'I'd hope so too. It's not like he could just leave her stranded in the middle of London.'

Milly cuts in, her face gradually returning to its normal colour. 'So you've walked every girl home you've ever been out with, have you?'

'No, of course not. But not every girl is worth walking home,' he laughs, pinching her waist.

'Well, clearly Samuel thought I was worth walking home.'

'Oh, Samuel,' he teases her.

Milly leaves her mother and brother arguing over what sandwich he is going to take to his office for lunch. All the way to work she thinks about the route Samuel might take, whether they will bump into each other before they arrive. She'd like that. It would be almost as though they'd walked the whole way together, which of course they haven't, and she knows that would be an outrageous and shocking suggestion. But it is only inside her head, so it doesn't really matter.

She is disappointed when she arrives at the shop to find that Samuel is already there, stationed at his workbench downstairs.

It will be several hours until she can find an excuse to go down-stairs. Mrs Freed asks her about the ballet and she replies at length, going through every little detail she can remember. Talking always calms her nerves. She knows it is ridiculous to be nervous; she has seen Samuel every day for weeks and not thought anything of it. And yet one evening with him at the ballet has set her on edge, as though an entirely new person is downstairs crafting those shoes. She likes him, and she is long-ing to know if he likes her too.

After several days of awkward and polite exchanges, Mrs Freed decides something must be done. She cannot bear to watch Milly making a fool of herself day after day while Samuel is oblivious to it all. Samuel comes up to the shop floor just before lunch, carrying piles of pointe shoes in his arms. Immediately Milly blushes.

'Hello, Samuel,' she says, smiling at him from where she counts out a delivery of spools of pink thread. 'How was your morning?'

'Very good, thank you, Milly,' he replies, nodding in her direc-tion as he continues unloading the shoes into the shelves.

Mrs Freed cuts in. 'How about you show Milly your ideas for the character and ballroom shoes?' she says. At least they will have something to talk about, rather than skirting around each other. What Samuel needs, she thinks, is a chance to really notice Milly. And men, in her opinion, notice women most when that woman is praising them, complimenting them over something brilliant that they have achieved. Milly surely won't be able to look at those stunning designs without giving him lots and lots of praise.

'Only if you're interested?' he says uncertainly to Milly. But he looks happy, his chin lifted.

'Bring them up here and you can have lunch with Milly behind the desk while you look.'

He returns in a few minutes, some of his drawings wrapped up in string while others, the ones Mr Freed is thinking they might be able to use soon, are held flat between two pieces of leather. It was Mr Freed who bought him the leather case, dark brown with a strap inside to hold the designs. Samuel lays it open across the desk, unrolling the other sketches alongside it. He arranges them neatly while Milly leans over his shoulder. She gazes down at them, making little cooing sounds, pointing out her favourites: the green boots with the fur trim, the fur collar for a coat that clasps at the side with a beautifully cut felt button, the high-heeled dancing shoes with petal shapes cut into the toe. Milly can't believe that this man, this giant man, as her brother would say, is capable of creating such delicate and beautiful drawings. She imagines herself in the shoes and the fur collar, heading out on his arm to a restaurant. These are shoes to wear while drinking champagne.

'So, are you going to make these?' she says to him. 'You should set up your own dressmaking shop.' She blushes again when she says this, seeing the eyes of Mrs Freed on her. It wouldn't do to suggest Samuel should leave the Freeds, set up on his own, not when they have given him all his training. But why should he stay here making the same pointe shoes day after day? Not when his head is filled with the most glorious and varied designs.

He shakes his head firmly. 'Maybe Mr Freed will make some of the dancing shoes, the character ones, soon, when we think we'll get enough of a customer base to make it worthwhile. The others are just a bit of fun, something I enjoy doing as a hobby.'

'One day maybe,' Milly says, almost a whisper. Mrs Freed is the other side of the room and Milly is feeling bolder now, their hands close as they look through the drawings. 'Perhaps I could join you and run the shop. We'd have every woman in London coming to us wanting these,' she says, nodding to the designs. 'You're very talented.'

Samuel looks down at his designs, Milly's soft, plump hands grazing them. She has placed a seed in his mind, something he had never dared think before. Starting his own shop is a wilder idea than he has ever imagined. But of course it is what he wants. One day.

'Like Mr and Mrs Freed, you mean?' he says, stopping as abruptly as he began. He didn't mean it like that, not the Mr and Mrs part. But it's out now, and there is nothing he can do to take it back. As he looks down nervously at Milly's bright blonde hair bopping prettily at her shoulders, the little smile on her lips, he thinks perhaps she isn't offended. She turns her face up, her eyes directly on him.

'A little like that, perhaps.'

Mrs Freed watches them from the other side of the room, where she sits with her tea and her sandwich. She doesn't want to lose these two; they would be very hard to replace. But she doesn't think there is any risk of that just yet. They remind her of herself and Frederick when they first started working together, Frederick's shyness, her leading him subtly to every step forward in their courtship. While he might have been the one to propose, she had got him there. She wonders if he has any idea how much she had to do to make it happen.

Milly is full of chatter all afternoon. When she is ready to leave, the shop packed away neatly and the blinds down, she calls down to Samuel.

'Are you finished yet? I'm going home via a new fabric shop on Percy Street. Do you want to come too? I hear they have lovely new colours you could build into some of your designs.'

Samuel is just walking up the steps, his coat over his arm. He had been planning on working on his tutu design, the one for Olivia that he knows he will never be able to afford to make her. But he decides that can wait.

Mrs Freed watches them leave the shop, Milly a few steps ahead. She smiles before turning away to finish checking the till.

21

OLIVIA

The second performance of *Coppélia* is a whole week after the first, which gives Miss de Valois plenty of time to respond to the reviews and work us hard in rehearsal. Critics were, however, very positive. They enjoyed the chance to comment on our revival of a Russian classic, this story ballet so different to the choreographic experiments of Ashton and Miss de Valois. Clara and I collected all the newspapers after the first performance, laying them across my bed and poring over them indulgently. We read that it was a 'sparkling performance', that Swanilda danced with 'superb grace, ease and vitality'. We quickly glossed over the news report immediately next to the review: a man murdering his girlfriend on the towpath at Barnes hardly seemed in keeping with our joyful ballet. Of course we were both disappointed that our names weren't mentioned, but we hadn't really been expecting it. And then the next day Mother died. We forgot to look out for reviews after that. It didn't seem to matter.

I have been avoiding Nathan. He pays no attention to me, so it isn't difficult. It is my sister he desires. She still hasn't mentioned America to me. Sometimes I catch her looking thoughtful and I try to imagine what is going through her mind. Can she leave me here alone right after Mother has died? Does she want to give up her place in the Vic-Wells, just when it is getting started? Is America and all its promises worth it for all she would lose? If she would just speak to me about it, I could help her. Ever since I read that note in the coat pocket, I've been thinking about it more and more. And now I know, or at least I think I do: I want her to go. I want to make a name for myself here in London on my own, to prove that I am good enough just as me. And now that Mother is dead, well, I am even more certain. I don't need Clara to hold my hand any more, not now we don't need to suffer those monthly trips to Colney Hatch, Mother making me feel like a child again, her searching eyes checking that I still look like the ballerina she expects of me.

With the second performance finally here, the energy in the dressing room is high. It is different to the nerves of the first performance, instead a more certain, entertaining mood, with the girls making jokes about the ballet, mimicking the mime sequences with exaggerated movements. By now we are all experts at playing at being dolls, copying the stiff arm *port de bras* that Swanilda performs while pretending to be Coppélia, bending forward from the hips, turning our heads abruptly from side to side. We open our eyes very wide and blink in time to the beat, two slow and three fast, our dark eye make-up framing the movement. Some of the men have decamped to our room to share make-up tips, William Chappell drawing an extra line of pencil under our eyes: 'A miniature Clapham Junction,' he says, leaning back to admire his artwork.

When there is just an hour to go, we traipse to the well, the steps down to the storage room becoming congested with dancers who search for their luck. We need to dip our fingers into the water, our lucky charm to send us on to the stage with certainty. It is our moment of transition, resetting the muscles and the mind from an afternoon of rehearsing other ballets to the performance of the evening. Clara is already down there. I am surprised to see her there before me. She doesn't always bother with the ritual of the well; she has never been as superstitious as me. I am even more surprised to see her dressed in the costume for the doll Coppélia, the red tutu with the frills. That part is usually played by one of the students from Miss de Valois's school; there is nothing more to it than sitting in a chair on a balcony, reading a book. It requires utter stillness, but that is all.

'Oh, hello,' she says, looking up at us all as we fill in the cold gloom around the well, the men leaning against the steel beams, their dressing gowns, dirty with make-up grease, draped over their costumes. 'Miss de Valois asked me to put this on for some press photographs. It's all done now.' She stands and starts to move towards the stairs. 'I had better hurry if the girl performing Coppélia tonight is going to be ready in time. Is it Molly Brown tonight?'

I ignore her question. 'What photographs?' I ask. None of the rest of us were asked, and I feel let down that she has been chosen for this over me. Or, at least she could have told me about it and I could have gone along to watch. It would have been fun seeing her onstage, posing for the camera.

'They were mostly of Lydia, but they wanted the doll in the background, to set the scene. I just had to sit completely still, trying not to wiggle my nose when I had an itch.' She is trying to trivialise it, I can tell, reducing it all to a joke, a nuisance. And in that pretty costume it is hard to be cross with her. She really does look like a doll, her costume all frills and dark pink scalloped ribbons. In her hair she wears a crown of flowers, and there are more red ribbons around her wrists.

'See you onstage soon for a warm-up.' And then she is gone, running up the stairs and pulling the flower crown from her head as she does so. She is late as usual.

*

We drag the portable barres on to the stage behind the thick red curtain and warm up to the rhythmical clapping of Miss Moreton as she instructs us in a quick routine of *pliés, tendus, ronds de jambe* and *grands battements*. Raising our legs onto the barres, we fold forward to stretch out our hamstrings; we listen to the tones of the orchestra as they tune their instruments, their own warm-up that does not need to be hidden from the audience like ours does. We have a magic to preserve, one that relies on mystery and illusion. The stagehands hurry us off the stage as we get closer to the beginners' call and we continue our preparations in the wings, spilling further into the scenery docks. I notice a door is open out onto the street, a faint smell of cigarette smoke drifting towards me: someone's last minute attempt to calm their nerves, I expect.

As soon as the music starts and the audience settles into silence, I forget about everything else and just focus on the performance. The familiar smells in the wings centre me: the musk of the curtains, the heat of the lights warming the stage, the sweet sweat of the dancers, our bodies supple and warm. I love this ballet, the drama, the story, spinning a whole tale through dance. But in the interval there is chaos. Mr Healey is furious, storming in and out of the dressing rooms in a rage. The headpiece for the doll, Coppélia, is missing. So the girl from the school who was performing the doll had to wear the second one, the one that Swanilda needs in Act Two when she pretends to be Coppélia. I look over to Clara, who is redoing her lipstick in the mirror. She doesn't look at all concerned, shrugging as Mr Healey shouts at us all.

'This room is an absolute disgrace,' he cries, his arms flying about him as he gestures to our chaotic piles of coats, warm-up clothes, practice skirts, pointe shoes. 'And what is that ribbon doing on your dressing table, young lady?' he shouts at poor Gwyneth Matthews, who has left her face cream open right next to part of her costume. She goes bright red and gathers up the ribbon into her hand.

He sees Clara. 'You,' he says. 'You wore the Coppélia costume earlier for the photographs. Where did you put the flower crown?'

Clara turns to him, coolly, without the panic of the rest of us. She doesn't stand, just crosses her legs and leans back into her chair. 'I returned the costume to Wardrobe for whichever one of Miss de Valois's students is performing the role tonight. I can't be responsible for whatever happened to the costume after that. I put the flower crown back on the mannequin head on the shelf above the rail. Have you checked there?'

'Of course I checked there.' Mr Healey stares back at her. He looks as though he might explode. We all sit very still, trying to avoid his eye as he starts rummaging through the dressing room, lifting up our piles of coats and bags. But he doesn't find the crown.

He leaves and the tension slowly dissolves, but we have to force ourselves to find the same ebullient mood for Act Two. Lydia looks sternly at us when the movements turn her away from the audience, which wakes us up and reminds us that we need to be performing with much greater energy. When Swanilda mimes to her friends to wind up the clockwork dolls positioned around Dr Coppélius's workshop, I think she is really telling us all to brighten up our performance. By the time we take the curtain call, I feel better again, but I go down to the well at the end anyway. I need a moment to settle myself.

The light bulb, shaded in its enamel frame, is just strong enough for me to see after the darkness of backstage. I am still in costume, a shawl around my shoulders for warmth. It is quiet and relaxing down here, strange after the raucous applause from the audience, and I stretch my arms up to the ceiling, shifting my weight from side to side as I reach up and up out of my hips. I let my head lower and I roll forwards, stretching out my hamstrings. It feels glorious to hang my head upside down like this, letting the weight of my body pull me down. I wrap my hands around my ankles and touch my lips to my knees.

As I draw my body slowly upwards, I catch sight of something in the water behind me. I pull myself upright immediately, so fast that my head spins and my vision blurs. Kneeling to centre myself, I creep slowly, nervously, towards the edge of the well. My legs feel heavy, dragging behind me, and I can hardly bear to look down into the water. But I do look, my hands gripping the stone.

I throw myself backwards, drawing away from the water in horror. I think I must have screamed, because I hear concerned voices coming down the stairs. It is Clara and Hermione.

'What's wrong?' Clara cries, running down and kneeling next to me. I must look a sight, thrown back against a beam, breathing hard.

'In the water,' I whisper.

'What, this?' Hermione says. She is reaching down in the water. I watch, transfixed, as she pulls out the head of a mannequin, one of the light, hollow ones that we use for storing wigs and headdresses. In her other hand she is holding the flower crown. 'How on earth did that get in there?'

'I thought…' I begin, but then I stop. It sounds too ridiculous. When I looked into that water, I was sure I had seen the head of a woman, floating there in her floral crown. But I was mistaken. Just the costume Mr Healey has been searching for, thrown into the well by someone mischievous.

I look up at Clara and Hermione. They are staring anxiously at each other. It might only be a costume, but it's enough to scare us.

Another image comes to me: a pointe shoe drifting amongst ribbons, rose petals wilting in the dark water. A suspicion lingers, just enough to make me shudder. That large man with his bag of shoes, his ungainly tread as he moves through the corridors of Sadler's Wells. I remember him watching us at the shoe shop, his heavy body blocking the shine of the pale pink shoes. Ever since he gave me the rose before the first night of *Coppélia*, I have been wary of him. A disturbing, reluctant feeling has been lingering at the edge of my mind recently, a feeling that it might have been him that wrote that note. I have tried to push the thought away, preferring to think that the rose and the note are from a worthier admirer. Now, I feel disappointment, but worse than that, dread, as my suspicions of the pointe shoe maker's apprentice grow into something solid, menacing, real.

22

NATHAN

When Nathan goes into the orchestra pit a few hours before the performance to check his music is in place, he is surprised to see Clara on the stage, dressed in the Coppélia doll costume. She is entirely still, up on the balcony of Dr Coppélius's home, book in hand, staring down at the pages with large eyelashes that rise up slowly. For a moment he thinks she really is a doll. Someone has created a doll of Clara Marionetta, he hears himself think, absurdly. Nathan is envious of whoever had such an idea. He would like to lift her out of that chair and take her home to his boat. Then he could have her forever, in doll-like perfection.

But then she moves, just a little flicker of her eyes. Of course she isn't a doll. There is a photographer on the stage, kneeling as he holds up the camera. Lydia Lopokova is moving in and out of a low *arabesque* and the photographer is straining to capture the image. Clara is part of the backdrop, setting the scene for the ballet. Nathan watches from the pit, leaning against the piano. He doesn't care if Clara can see him; why shouldn't he stare at her? She never minded before. They were so close, Clara grateful for his love and admiration until he proposed. Since then she has been drawing away and then pulling in close, confusing him with her rejection and advances. It has unsettled him. But not only that: seeing his mother surrounded by her new family, her pretty children, has turned everything upside down that he thought was straightforward and simple. It is harder to make himself believe in her death now that he has seen her. But that isn't her, not the mother he remembers. That mother is dead, preserved forever: she would never leave him for someone else.

Clara is utterly still again. It amazes him how long she can go without blinking. Perhaps she is testing herself, some sort of personal challenge. That would be just like Clara: to turn this into a game. Some of the other musicians have joined him in the pit. They are checking the angle of their seats, the height of their music stands. One of the flautists starts playing snatches of the music, breaking the silence of the auditorium. Clara shifts, just a little note of surprise. She has awoken from her doll-like sleep, Nathan thinks. The photographer stands, pressing his free hand into his thigh. This is the cue for the world to begin again. Clara rolls her shoulders, opening her lips a little. It is as though she has started breathing again, a doll come to life.

As Nathan stares down at the flawless ivory and ebony of the piano keys, he has an idea, or less an idea than a vision. It reminds him of when his mother first left and he knew that he wouldn't accept it. He remembers sitting on his bed after his father told him what had happened, remembers reimagining the entire conversation, changing the words, changing it all. After that he couldn't go back. And now, with Clara, he thinks he knows how he will get her back. He will make her his again.

The auditorium starts to build in noise and movement, ushers checking there are no old programmes lying around, the stage-hands sweeping the stage before the dancers emerge to start their warm-up. Nathan can predict every movement in that hour before a performance, the ushers, the stagehands, the dancers, the musicians: he knows exactly where everyone will be, the routines and rhythms of the theatre ingrained into him like clockwork. He follows Clara at a distance, watching her tutu bob up and down as she walks. She goes down to the well; the dancers' daily ritual. Although he is fascinated by their superstitions, he understands. Nathan has his own routine before performances: he whispers the mantra to himself, even though the words have become hollow and meaningless. He is special, he is talented, the world is lucky to have him. When his mother said these words, he believed them. But now they do nothing except trick his brain into preparing for the ballet. As he whispers them, he touches every black key on the piano lightly with the tip of his finger. Then he visualises himself in the prelude of performance, the conductor raising the baton.

Dancers are coming the opposite way along the corridor to the well, their voices loud and fast. The second night is always easier on the nerves than the first, everyone a little more relaxed. Nathan pulls back and waits for them to disappear down the steps. He doesn't want them to wonder why he is hovering in the corridor.

Clara runs up a few moments later, pulling off the headdress. She dashes along the corridor away from him, the crown of flowers hanging down from her hand. He smiles bitterly. It is just like her to rush through life treating everything with careless disregard. He is angry with her. Why can't she slow down? Why can't she be more like that doll Coppélia, content to sit, passive, with a book in her hands?

As he follows her along the corridor around to the dressing rooms and Wardrobe on the other side of the auditorium, he feels his anger growing. He wants to get hold of her and keep her still. But she moves so fast, she always has. He doesn't know why he ever thought he would be able to have her.

She is in Wardrobe for a few minutes. Nathan waits in the shadows behind a properties storage container; if anyone sees him he knows it will be hard to explain why he is hiding there, but he feels compelled to stay and wait for her. When she comes out again, he finds himself gripping the edge of the storage box.

She is naked. Not quite, he realises, the blood pulsing hard in his neck. She has taken off the costume and is wearing only her pale pink tights and pointe shoes. Although she has pulled her tights as high they will go, they do not cover her breasts. She looks around her guardedly before dashing down the corridor to the dressing rooms. Her room is only a few doors down, and he hears peals of loud laughter coming from inside as soon she enters. The musicians love to joke about what goes on in those dressing rooms, some of the men making dirty jokes about the ballerinas' flexible legs and hips. It seems that perhaps they weren't so wrong after all. Naked dancers daring each other to run through the corridors: he can imagine the leering laughter if he tells this story to the other men. But he won't. This is just for him.

It is quiet inside Wardrobe. There is no one else there. He sees the Coppélia doll costume back on the rail, hanging on its side with the netting sticking out. He goes to touch it, feeling the softness of the bodice, sticking his hand inside the net knickers. He rubs the tulle between his fingers, where it has been resting against Clara's thighs. He wants to take it, but he knows that would create uproar. Someone will be coming in to put this on soon. He looks up. The flower crown is resting on a mannequin head. Before he thinks about what he is doing, he has reached up and grabbed it.

The well is quiet now, all the dancers warming up onstage. He holds the mannequin head in front of him. There are no eyes, no features, just the shape of a head moulded out of hollow plaster. He tilts it to one side and bows a little in response.

'Clara Marionetta,' he whispers, 'may I have this dance?'

The mannequin head nods in return, the flower crown dipping down over where the eyes would be. Nathan starts swaying from side to side, the head held level with his eyes. He hums a tune. It is the waltz that his mother used to put on at home before she left: 'The Blue Danube'. His father didn't like it though. He'd always turn off the gramophone whenever his mother wanted to dance; he had no time for such frivolity. And now Nathan thinks of those notes drifting across mourners. It is easier to conjure a picture of her coffin down here, in the quiet gloom of the well room, dancing with plaster and paint.

He presses the head to his shoulder. They are dancing closer now. He dips his forehead against her, the flower crown tickling his cheek. Nathan closes his eyes and sees her again, as she was when she appeared out of Wardrobe. The pale pink of her tights and pointe shoes merge into her naked torso. She could be entirely naked. He sees her breasts, small and high, her nipples like raspberries. She doesn't even try to cover them with her arms. He pulls the head into him, even tighter now. There is a heat within him and his breath is faster, the tune of the waltz distorted. They dance together, around and around.

'Nathan, is that you?' A voice is calling down the steps.

In shock, Nathan wakes from his dance, his tune cut short. He hears footsteps coming down the stairs.

'I thought I saw you coming this way. We want to rehearse the bolero, the Spanish dance, before the House opens.'

He panics. Constant Lambert is coming down the stairs, every step bringing him closer to finding Nathan there holding the mannequin head. Nathan has seconds to spare. He throws the head into the well. There is a small splash and he watches as the head dips and then bobs up again, floating on the water's surface. Flowers spread themselves across the darkness of the well.

'What are you doing down here?' Constant asks suspiciously. 'You've not fallen for those same good luck charms as the dancers, have you? What are you going to do, anoint yourself with holy water?' He is laughing and Nathan laughs too, joining him on the steps.

'I just needed some quiet. I've had a headache all day,' Nathan lies. It comes easily to him.

'Try smoking. A cigarette before a show usually sets one up all right.'

'Yes, maybe I'll do that.' Nathan nods and follows Constant up the stairs.

It is one of the girls from the school as the Coppélia doll tonight. Nathan, at the piano, keeps finding himself turning towards the stage, studying the contrast between the fast, dancing feet and the calm stillness of the doll up in the balcony. When Swanilda and her friends creep into Dr Coppélius's workshop, he glances around and up at the stage. Clara is in the middle of the line of girls, her white skirt moving smoothly as she places each foot firmly onto the stage. Nathan is almost late with his cue and he turns back to the piano swiftly, sensing Constant's stare on him from the conductor's stand.

He knows what he must do. He just needs to find the perfect opportunity.

23

OLIVIA

Mother's funeral is a small, quiet service. It is a bright April day and we squint in the clean light of the chapel at Colney Hatch, the glare exposing the smallness of our group. There is just me and Clara and some doctors and nurses who come to pay their respects. It seems Mother was rather a celebrity around here, which doesn't surprise me.

Aunt Alice and her family do not come. She sent us a note yesterday, written in a neat, careful hand. She is too shocked, too upset. Her presence would be a hindrance and we will, she tells us, be able to mourn for our mother more appropriately without her there. It is just an excuse, of course. Aunt Alice never could cope with Mother's madness. She blamed ballet more than she blamed the stress of war and of loss. We were a reminder of everything she could not endure. She preferred to keep a stiff lock on emotion, pain, memory: life must go on.

After the service, the chaplain offers us a lift in his car. We follow the undertakers as they drive Mother to Highgate Cemetery. The chaplain is young and fresh-faced, new to Colney Hatch. When we ask him questions to fill the silence of the drive, he tells us that it is different to his previous post at Edgware hospital. There he had administered to the sick in body, the elderly, the frail, easing them gently towards an acceptance of death. He had comforted families and helped them prepare funeral services. At Colney Hatch, death comes suddenly and when you least expect it. No one thought our mother was going to die, not for many years. It was a shock to them all. I nod, make soft noises of sympathy. But then I stop and stare out of the window at the passing cars, buses, an old man bent double at a bus stop. It is my mother who has died. The chaplain does not need my sympathy.

We get out at the gates of the cemetery while the chaplain finds parking down the street. The porter lets us through, nodding politely. Clara and I have visited the cemetery every year since Father died. For the first few years it was always with Mother, the three of us standing very close at the foot of his grave, laying a small posy of flowers by the headstone and then leaving after a few silent, strained minutes. In recent years it has just been me and Clara. Each year we stay a little longer, kneeling in the grass, reading the stories Father used to tell us, the ones he had been so drawn to after the war. Tales of Rat and Mole, the Wild Wood. They were glorious escapism for us all, a brief respite from his memories of those awful years in France. Now, each year on the anniversary of his death, we spread out a picnic blanket on the patch of grass by the grave, on the top of a little slope less populated than other areas of the cemetery. A large canopy of trees shades us, ivy and ferns creeping up around the tombstones. The Western Cemetery, where Father is buried and Mother is about to join him, is dark and wooded, trees packed tightly together around the graves. Every year it is a little wilder, more and more moss and ivy taking over the graves. Even the imposing Egyptian Avenue is fading under the growing green of the wood, the old cedar tree looming darkly over the graves. Father's grave is at risk of being swallowed by the neglect, but we make sure to clear the tendrils of the ivy, wiping the headstone free of moss.

As we reach the grave, the undertakers are already there, waiting silently by the open hole in the ground. It is a shock to see the grave disturbed like this, and we stand a little further off, waiting for the chaplain. When he arrives, he smiles at us and nods. We follow him towards the grave. Mother, Father, the two of us: it is strange how close we all are right now. There is so much I want to say to them both, my anger at Father for leaving us when we needed him, my disappointment at Mother for failing us. But I will never be able to say these things. And perhaps it is better that I don't. I have blamed them too long for every anxiety, every self-doubt, every fear. It is time I start taking responsibility. Time to move on.

The ceremony is short, and I don't think I am really listening. It is only when they lower Mother's coffin into the grave that I reach towards Clara and take her hand. She squeezes mine in response. I turn to her, looking straight at her profile. She is gazing up at the tree in front of us, her eyes still. Neither of us can cry.

The walk home is well over an hour, but it is preferable to taking the bus. We don't want to go inside just yet, don't want to face the stillness of our flat and the quietness of loss. Out here in the streets, with London hurrying by, it is easier. We talk of tomorrow's performance: the third night of *Coppélia*. There is significant cast change and we have been rehearsing for the past few days to prepare. At the end of the last performance, Lydia Lopokova gave a curtain speech, curtsying low to the audience and then holding out her arms to quieten their applause. She teased them, laughed and bowed, saying that while this was her final performance in this run of *Coppélia*, she would not promise never to appear again. I expect she cannot bear to give up; to retire is to be old, acknowledging the frailties of the body. We have all seen her struggling with her knee in rehearsals, hobbling back to the dressing rooms between Acts. But onstage she is wonderful, full of the wit and joy that makes her so perfect for the role.

Ninette de Valois is to dance Swanilda for the final few performances. When this was announced, Miss de Valois called me back at the end of class. I am to take on her old role of leading peasant girl. It is wonderful news, and I have been working hard outside of rehearsals to prepare, going over and over the steps, the music, the rhythms. I was surprised it was me she asked, to be honest. After Clara had demonstrated the mazurka in class, I was convinced that she would be the one to be promoted. I worried that Miss de Valois had made a mistake in asking me to take on the role, that really she had meant Clara the whole time. I couldn't bear it if it was taken away from me now. But she had definitely asked for me, Olivia. She had used my name several times. No matter how strong my self-doubts, I could not deny that it was me she wanted.

Clara stops suddenly. It takes me a moment to realise that she is no longer walking by my side, and I have to turn and walk back to her. The pavement is narrow and getting busier as people start leaving work, the early April sun still bright. Clara is blocking the path, her shadow merging with the commuters who are walking fast and determined in each direction. They are yet to adapt to the warming weather, a block of browns and greys and blacks, coat collars rising high around their faces.

'What is it?' I say, avoiding the sweep of a satchel from a man charging past me. My voice is carried away by the grinding wheels of a delivery truck that rocks unsteadily past us.

'Let's keep walking,' she says eventually. She looks unsettled, nervous. 'I need to talk to you about something, but it's too noisy here.'

'When we get home, then?' I think I know what this will be about. Or at least the different options start playing anxiously through my mind as we continue the walk home. I too feel nervous all of a sudden. It could be about the peasant girl role, though that seems unlikely. Clara has shown no signs of caring about that. Or maybe she has found out about what I did with Nathan, how I pretended to be her for that brief moment. I feel sick when I think about that. Or perhaps she is finally going to tell me about America, the note I found from Jacob Manton, whoever he is.

When we are nearly home, she suggests we stop in Gordon Square. The gate to the garden is open, and we find a bench under a tree. We love this garden, how quiet it is, the residents of the square the only ones to use it, and us when we can find a gate that has been left unlocked. Sometimes Lydia is here, dozing under a blanket, reading a book, even practising her conditioning exercises, her white feet stretching and flexing in the sun. She likes to escape from the intellectualism and pretensions of her husband's Bloomsbury Group friends who haunt Gordon Square. They don't understand her, she tells us; they complain about the noise of her *allegro* on the wooden floors of the flat but really believe her an unsuitable wife for a man like John Maynard Keynes.

She always leaves the gate open for us if we ask her.

'Olivia,' Clara says, turning to me but not quite looking at me.

This is hard for her, I think. It has always been this way; the longer we wait to tell each other something new, the harder it becomes. When we were children it was so much easier, our whispered confessions binding us together against the paranoid stares of our mother.

'I have been trying to find a way of talking to you about this. I haven't made up my mind yet, as in I don't know if this is what I want, but I've been offered a really exciting contract.'

I nod once but say nothing. She continues, a little more certain now that she has begun.

'It's in America. I'd be working for an agent and performing on Broadway, modelling, maybe even doing some film work. And he wants me to help set up an American ballet school. It's a really exciting opportunity for me.'

'Who is he?'

'Jacob Manton. An agent. He's been watching performances at Sadler's Wells this season and noticed me.'

This hurts a little. If he noticed Clara then he noticed me too. There is no avoiding the two identical twins. I just didn't stand out for him. He didn't want me too.

'How long would you be gone for?' I ask, holding back the lump settling in my throat.

'A year to start with. But maybe longer if it goes well and we want to renew the contract.'

'And what's holding you back from saying yes? You seem really excited about it.' I try to keep the bitterness out of my voice, but I can hear myself failing.

She sighs. 'You know what's holding me back. I don't want to leave you, to be without you. Would you be okay without me here?'

I don't like this. I don't like her assumption that I can't cope on my own, that I need her by my side to survive. Perhaps there was a time when that was the case, when Mother had first been admitted into Colney Hatch, when our monthly visits took their toll. But not now. Now I am a different person from that anxious, afraid little girl.

'Clara, I'll be fine. If you want to go, you should go. I can manage by myself.' I struggle to keep the harshness out of my voice. I want to say something cruel, to shake her confidence, her certainty that she has a brilliant career mapped out for her in America while I languish in the corps de ballet in London. But there is nothing I can say.

'Will you stay living in the flat on your own?' she asks.

'I have no idea. You only told me you were leaving about a minute ago, so there have been other things to process first.'

'Sorry. Of course.'

'Have you told Miss de Valois?'

'She already knows. Jacob Manton went to her first. She gave him her blessing, as long as he promised to give me access to daily ballet classes.'

'And Nathan?'

'What about Nathan?' I notice an impatience in her voice.

'Have you told him? Surely he deserves to know. You are so close.'

'We're not that close. Not any more, not really.'

'What happened?' I am wary of asking too much. It seems like dangerous territory. But I need to know if it was my fault, if what I did pushed them apart.

'He proposed to me,' she replies. Then she laughs, rolling her eyes. 'Can you believe it? As if I would marry anyone right now. I'd go from independence, a career, doing what I love, to folding his pocket handkerchiefs and making him dinner. It's laughable really.'

I nod. It is making more sense now, why he behaved the way he did in the board room that afternoon.

'I thought you liked him?'

'I did. I do, I think. But he's changed. He wants me to be this perfect woman and I'm just not prepared to fit into his ideal.

We've never even done anything more than kiss, you know. I used to be so frustrated by it. It was as though he would only love me if I was held at a distance, chaste and innocent. I can't take any more of that.'

An image comes to mind of how he pushed himself against me, his hands hot against my thighs, his tongue hard. What was it about me, how I behaved, that made him do that to me? I had assumed that he and Clara had slept together, or at least got close to it. Finding out now that they haven't, that there was something about me that pushed him to do that, even if he did think I was Clara, makes me feel ashamed.

Clara is staring at me, looking concerned. 'What's the matter? Why does it matter what happened between me and Nathan?'

I shake my head. But there are tears threatening.

'Do you like him?' she asks, her voice shaking a little with laughter. 'I've seen you looking at him. If you want him, don't let me stop you.'

'How can you say that?' I cry out, standing abruptly and stepping away from her. She spreads out her hands, tilting her head.

'Don't get upset, Olivia. I don't know what you want. It was just a suggestion. Perhaps you'd be suited. You're exactly the kind of perfection he wants.'

'I am not perfection. Don't say that as if it is some sort of compliment. We both know you think I am dull. I don't break the rules like you do, I just get on with what I'm asked to do. Of course your Jacob Manton didn't ask me to come to America too. I don't have the personality and the charisma for such a privilege. I should stay in London, dancing in the back row, waiting for someone like Nathan Howell to propose. Is that it?'

'Olivia, no. Why are you being like this?'

But I don't wait to reply. I press my bag to me and run to the gate, nearly colliding with a couple coming into the square. They exclaim indignantly as I barge past them. When I get home, I rip off my clothes and get straight into bed. Clara gets home soon after and I pretend to be asleep. I hear her padding around the flat, hanging up my clothes, making dinner. Eventually she comes into our bedroom and sits on the end of my bed. I can feel the weight of her as the mattress sinks, but I don't move. My eyes are tightly shut. I hear her voice, barely a whisper.

'Olivia. I don't know why I said that about Nathan. I guess I've been feeling bad about turning him down. And I'm feeling bad about going to America and not telling you about it straight away. I don't know why I kept it from you. I suppose I wanted to have a clearer idea of my answer before I told you.'

She pauses. I can feel the heat under her hand as she rests it against my shoulder.

'Maybe I thought that if you wanted Nathan and Nathan wanted you, I wouldn't have to feel so guilty. I could even make you both feel guilty about it, about taking him from me, and then I could go to America without feeling so wretched about myself. But I know that's unfair, more than unfair. I should have been honest with you. I'm so sorry, Olivia.'

I shift a little under her hand. She knows I can hear her. I turn and open my eyes. She doesn't know how close she is to reaching some sort of truth. But any longing I have ever had for Nathan has vanished. It started fading away in the board room when he reached up between my legs. It vanished entirely this evening when Clara revealed the truth about their relationship. I don't want to become her replacement, a second-choice Marionetta.

Reaching up to her, I pull her in towards me, kissing her on the cheek. I hear her sigh. It is a sigh of relief, I think, that she can go to America without the guilt she was waiting for me to absolve.

ACT FIVE

24

CLARA

Final nights are bittersweet. And this final night more than most. *Coppélia* is my last performance at the Vic-Wells, at least for the next year. I sent a note to Jacob Manton last week accepting his offer and within hours a giant bouquet of pink flowers had arrived at our lodgings. Olivia put on a delighted front, laughing as we tried to find a vase big enough. In the end we had to separate them into several vases and jars, decorating our flat with pastel pinks and hot shocks of red. She struggled for the first few days after I told her, but she gradually eased back to me, accepting it, seeing it differently from that first angry reaction. I imagine she is coming around to the idea, realising that we could both do with some time apart. Now that Mother is dead, we have the space to be who we want to be, to be different, to be ourselves. And we need to find a way to let that difference flourish.

Olivia left before me this morning. She has a rehearsal to get to: *Les Sylphides* at the Ballet Club, a Fokine revival, and she will take ballet class at the Mercury Theatre. I did feel a little sadness that I couldn't be involved, but preparations for my departure are building, Jacob sending me schedules and performances and bookings he's sorted for me almost daily. It will be so busy when I get there that taking it a little quieter now is probably good.

I leave the flat mid-morning, stepping out of the downstairs front door into a warm block of bright light; the April weather promises to behave today. I lock the door, first letting the little tabby cat who belongs to our neighbour upstairs run out into the street. When I turn back to the road, the light has changed. I give an involuntary cry of shock as I realise it is Nathan standing there, his shadow stretching up the steps.

'What do you want?' I ask him. But I realise my voice is hard, suspicious, and so I smile, trying to be polite. And yet this is difficult when he is the last person I want to see right now. I know I need to talk to him, to tell him about America before he finds out from someone else. It isn't fair on him. I may have fallen out of love, but I still owe him an explanation.

'I thought I could walk with you to the theatre,' he replies. 'Like we always used to do.'

'All right.' I am irritated. I had planned to walk slowly, taking in the spring air, the flowers springing up around the grass verges, dotting my way through the little gardens and parks there for anyone who bothers to look for them. It won't be the same now that Nathan is with me, looking at me in that wounded, expectant way.

I set off at a fast pace, taking the most direct route. The morning has been ruined, so I might as well get to Sadler's Wells as fast as possible. Nathan keeps up with me, taking large strides.

'No Olivia this morning?' he asks.

'No, she's already left for Notting Hill Gate.'

'Is she rehearsing at the Mercury today?'

'Yes, she's dancing for Marie Rambert at the Ballet Club in May. She's joining them for class this morning.'

'And not you?'

'No, not me.'

We fall silent, the sound of the road and the breeze too loud in my ears. Nathan's footsteps echo on the pavement. I am tense, waiting for the moment I can find the courage to tell him. When we reach the New River Head garden, I know my time is almost out.

'I don't think I've mentioned to you about America, have I?' I begin. It is a coward's approach to trivialise it, to pretend I don't realise this will be upsetting for him. But it's all I can bring myself to do right now.

'What about America?'

'I have a contract to go over for a year, maybe more, to perform. I leave next month.'

'Next month.' He stops now, turning to me. A bus lumbers by and we have to wait until it has passed for the road to be quiet enough to speak. I stare up at him, determined to hold his gaze. I cannot read his expression. It is not as I expected, instead a strange mix of confusion, hostility, defiance.

Finally I can speak again, the noise of the road fading as the bus continues its journey to Angel. 'Yes, it's come around so quickly.'

'And you've only just told me now?'

'I don't understand. Why should I have told you earlier? Surely you see that I wanted to wait until it was all confirmed?' Of course, I know exactly why I should have told him earlier, but I'm not going to admit that right now. I turn away from him and catch the eye of a small boy who is crouching down in the grass on the other side of the road, waiting for his mother. A worm is struggling to escape from his determined grip.

'Clara,' Nathan says, reaching across to me and taking my wrist, 'I proposed to you. I thought you might say yes, that you'd think about it and decide you wanted me too. The least you could do is tell me. I think I deserve a straight answer.'

I pull my arm away from him and take a step back. 'I'm sorry. But I thought I'd made it very clear I didn't want to marry you, or anyone. I don't know how you could think I would change my mind.'

'That's not how it seemed to me.'

We stand there on the pavement, neither of us knowing what to say, neither of us moving. I watch his face as it starts to shift and change. At first I think he is about to cry. But he doesn't. His lips twist into a smile and he laughs. One loud, hard laugh. I look back at him, confused.

'You really think you'll make it to America?' He drawls his last word, contorting his voice into a parodic attempt at an American accent. 'Well, good luck to you.' He turns and resumes his loud, long strides until he reaches the stage door.

'What do you mean?' I call to him. But my voice is drowned out by another bus. I follow him towards the stage door, gazing up at the large poster advertising *Coppélia* on the side of the theatre. Lydia Lopokova, smiling in a low *arabesque*. And there, in the shadows behind her, is me, dressed as the Coppélia doll, gazing down at a book with complete stillness. I give an involuntary shudder and enter the theatre.

25

NATHAN

The first thing Nathan does when he enters the theatre is steal the Coppélia doll tutu. It is even easier than he thought it would be, with the dancers all in their daily ballet class and Wardrobe empty and quiet. Constant is playing for class today, his weekly duty that gives Nathan time to practise for performances. There is just the gentle hum of the stagehands cleaning, the carpenters preparing for the next production, the deliveries of drinks for the interval. If he closes his eyes he can picture the entire theatre like a dolls' house, each occupant precisely where they should be. They will shift and change and shuffle between rooms exactly as he predicts, like the clockwork dolls' houses his mother took him to visit when he was performing in Nuremberg as a child. All Nathan has to do is walk into Wardrobe, lift the tutu from its rail, and walk out again. He lingers a little, feeling confident no one will find him, and identifies the headdress, the ribbons for the wrists, the heart necklace. These he takes too, pressing them tight to his chest as he walks quickly down the corridor towards the well. If anyone sees him, layers of tulle pressing against his chin, he will have a lot of explaining to do. But the corridors are clear.

Down in the well room, he makes his preparations. He is relieved to find that the cupboard at the back of the room is not locked. The door opens easily, and he carefully lays out the tutu and the accessories amongst the pipes and brooms and mops. Bundles of rope that look as though they were once used by the stagehands for securing scenery are coiled in piles on the ground, gathering dust. Stacked against the wall, looking strangely out of place, is an assortment of sport equipment: a set of tennis balls, a racket, golf clubs, a cricket bat. Perhaps props from a production that never found a permanent home. He takes out the cricket bat, blowing dust away from the edge. It is covered in little flecks of paint. Nathan has always marvelled at the strangeness of theatres, the medley of items that pile up in dressing rooms and scenery docks. He thinks of his boat, his home, his own museum of the past, a carefully curated selection of items that centre him, write the story of the life he wants to remember. Soon there will be a major addition to his collection. He places the cricket bat in the corner of the room, hidden in a patch of shadow.

There will be chaos when they find out that the costume is missing. But they have spares for the second cast performers; and perhaps Swanilda and Coppélia can find a way to double up, the woman and the doll sharing the same tutu. He finds it quite comical that he is concerned about this: the show must go on, even amongst his plotting and planning. It has always been this way, this irrational desire for the production to succeed despite his deep-seated resentment at being consigned to secondary importance, the piano player accompanying the dancers as they rehearse. When they arrive for company class each morning, it is as though he is invisible, Miss Moreton only speaking to him to give instructions for the *allegro*, whether she wants a tarantella or a mazurka for the pirouettes, the type of waltz she requires for the *grand allegro*. It never used to be this way, not when he was a star and his dressing rooms became confectionery shops of treats and toys, offered indulgently by the wives of the other musicians who fawned over him backstage. From the moment he arrived at each theatre, concert hall, grand mansion of a wealthy patron, he was treated like a prince. He didn't have to think of anything but placing his hands on those keys and performing.

Once all is set, he walks back up the stairs and goes to find Constant. Ballet class will have ended but he knows where he will be, and he is right. He bumps into Constant as he is coming out of Miss de Valois's office, a cigarette balanced between his lips.

'Constant, I've been looking for you. I need to talk to you about tonight's performance.'

'Yes, what is it?' Constant replies, preoccupied as he digs through his jacket for a lighter.

Nathan coughs heavily before taking out a handkerchief and wiping his brow. 'I'm not well. A horrible cold, and I don't want to risk ruining the performance with this cough all night. I'm really sorry. Could you ask someone else? Charles Lynch maybe? He'll know what he's doing.'

Constant lets out a long exhalation of smoke and then grimaces. 'Fine. But you've got to make sure Charles is up to speed.'

Nathan coughs again, a great racking cough that vibrates through the corridor. 'Actually, don't worry about it. I'll sort it out,' says Constant with a sigh. 'If you stay here a minute longer you'll infect us all. Go home and get better.'

'Thank you. I really am feeling very rough. I'm sure a day in bed will sort me out.'

'Perhaps if you lived in a real house with real walls, this wouldn't happen. It can't be good for you to live amongst all that damp.'

Constant takes a long drag on his cigarette and walks off, shaking his head.

Nathan has one more job to do before leaving the theatre. He waits until he knows the backstage crew will be on their lunch break and then makes his move. It throws him a little to see that a new stagehand has stayed behind. The young man is sitting alone in the scenery dock with a sandwich and a newspaper, easing his nerves on his first day at Sadler's Wells, but he doesn't notice Nathan.

Once he has completed his task, Nathan enters the building again via Arlington Street and makes his way through the theatre to the main Rosebery Avenue entrance, nodding at the dancers who have spilled out onto the street for fresh air between class and rehearsal. A few loud coughs announce his departure to anyone who cares.

Walking quickly towards Duncan Terrace and down the slope to the canal, he imagines the next time he will do this walk home. On his way he checks the pavements, the roads, the height of each drop between the two. He will need to plot his route carefully. When he gets home, he sits for a long time at the front of the boat. People walk by, making the most of the warm spring weather, but he ignores them all, even the dog that barks up at him, trying to jump on his boat. There is a new narrowboat moored just above him, its hold stacked with crates, an awning protecting them from bad weather. It is rare for anyone to stay long, so he doesn't worry about it. Most boats are working boats, gliding through the country's canal network collecting and delivering goods. Using it as a home, as he does, amuses the boatmen, who like to salute him on their way out of the tunnel's mouth under Duncan Terrace. They are entertained by him, why he would choose a boat when he has no connection to the water, no history of travelling through the waterways, of striking deals at the locks, of searching for the best pubs, of haggling with suppliers. He is a pretender, they think, but a harmless one, especially when he offers them a whisky as they come to peer at him in the evenings: the strange pianist with this narrowboat that hasn't left its mooring spot for nearly two years. Nathan always explains to them about the man who owns the boat, his refusal to sell up, his delight when Nathan met him in a pub and offered to live there for rent. One day the old man will find the courage to say goodbye to his boat, but for now he is happy for Nathan to live there, occasionally visiting him and waving from the canal's edge. He never comes in, just pats the boat lovingly, as one might pat a dog.

Nathan doesn't react as the man from the new narrowboat waves at him. He needs to plan and prepare. Closing his eyes, he thinks about the inside of the boat. There is his bedroom at the back with a door leading out to the tiller, the bed not so narrow that it couldn't fit two people. The blanket is navy and white, the same nautical colours in which his mother had fitted out his room back in Richmond. A small bathroom, a stove fitted tightly, a wooden table that cuts out into the room, narrow seats with red cushions. There is a space where he could fit another chair, right next to the gramophone. And opposite is his trunk, surrounded by a wall of photographs, programmes, memorabilia of his life, exactly as he wants it. He smiles to think of it all, his shrine, so perfect, now to be added to in such a significant way. The little ballerina figurine is centre stage on top of the trunk, her skirt fixed and stiff. He touches her every day when he gets home, a little gesture of luck.

At six o'clock he eases himself up from the front deck and goes down into the boat to do one final check. All is ready.

He starts the walk back to the theatre with a spring in his step.

26

SAMUEL

Samuel goes home immediately after work. This is no ordinary Tuesday evening, and he needs time to think. The final performance of *Coppélia* is tonight, and he wishes he could be there. He would like to sit in the stalls; the back row would be just fine. Perhaps he would even send flowers to the dressing rooms for Olivia, maybe write her a note. Of course, any flowers he could buy would be pitiful compared to the huge bouquets he has seen delivered backstage by couriers and chauffeurs. The dancers are not short of admirers. But he has no ticket for tonight's performance. *Coppélia* will have to go on without him; and it will. No one will care that he wasn't there to watch.

In fact, he has other plans, something which surprises even himself. He often has plans these days, a walk after work to a little café Milly wants to try, the cinema with Milly, a Sunday walk through the park, Milly bringing a picnic. He doesn't remember ever actually coming up with any of these ideas himself, but he has a good time anyway, Milly's tireless energy not giving him a chance to be distracted by the eternal doubts that plague him. Milly always has a plan: exactly how far they will walk, when they will stop for lunch, what drinks they will order, what film they will see. He likes her certainty, how easy everything is. She never doubts her decisions.

Tonight, he has been invited to her house for dinner. Her parents will both be there, as well as her brother, Jonathan. He doesn't know who he is most nervous about. Probably the father, Mr Bell. Milly has tried to reassure him. Her father is an academic at University College London, in the English Literature department. He is close to retirement, Milly tells him, as if his old age will somehow reassure Samuel. Milly's father is writing a book on the absent mother in Shakespeare's plays, and all his conversations will come back to this particular theme, she warns him. Her mother finds it particularly tiresome, but they all humour him. Once the book is published, he will be much easier. Samuel is also nervous of the brother. As an only child, he doesn't know what to expect. Milly talks about Jonathan as though he is a child, naughty but harmless; she is clearly very fond of him and so he wants to make a good impression.

Samuel changes into a clean shirt and tie, peering uncertainly at himself in the small mirror above his sink. Milly has told him what to wear: a jacket and tie, nothing too smart. Her father will be wearing a jumper with holes in the elbows and her brother will strip down to his shirtsleeves as soon as he gets in from work. If Samuel dresses too smartly, they will think him very odd. He is to bring a small bunch of flowers for her mother, a box of chocolates for her father. She helped him pick them on their way out of Covent Garden that evening, telling him exactly which colours her mother would most like, which flavours her father would be pleased by. Not too expensive, of course. Milly knew it wouldn't do to embarrass him with instructions to buy something far beyond his means.

He leaves his flat on Exmouth Market just as the sun is starting to dip towards the highest buildings, a warm glow lighting up the road behind him. The market traders are packing away, just a few stalls left with sad piles of sagging vegetables and stale-looking loaves of bread. He often picks up a simple dinner from here at night: some bread and a few slices of ham from the butcher, who spreads his produce out into the street on long tables, flies congregating as soon as he lifts the cloths from the meat. Sometimes he adds an apple from the greengrocers. They are used to him now, his daily routine. Samuel hasn't brought Milly up this street yet. He is nervous about it. She likes everything, is enthusiastic about even the smallest spot of life in the most mundane corner of London. If she doesn't like his street, his home where he's learnt how much more he can be away from the cruel laughter of his father, he doesn't think he will cope. It is silly, he knows, this self-preservation. But still he avoids Exmouth Market when he walks her home, instead continuing along Rosebery Avenue and up to Islington Green.

Sadler's Wells looks alive, the lights glowing in the Wells Room, the front doors to the foyer buzzing with life. He cannot resist going past the stage door, imagining the excitement in the dressing rooms as they prepare for the final night. Cars and taxis pull up outside the entrance and he watches for a few moments as men and women dressed in their finest furs and jewels step out onto the pavement. He feels a warmth running through him as he remembers meeting Milly here those few weeks ago, how lovely she looked in the plum chiffon dress. She had made him feel as though he belonged, even though it was him explaining the story of the ballet, pointing out the shoes he had made, telling her about the dancers. He had been glad to have her by his side.

He needs to hurry up or he will be late. And Milly told him very pointedly that he was not to be late or her brother would be insufferable, teasing her that she'd been stood up. The road is quiet behind the theatre, just the distant whisper of the orchestra's warm-up that spills out from an open door somewhere along Arlington Street.

As he walks past the end of the theatre, he hears a strange noise coming from behind him. He turns for a moment. A man is throwing his arms around in a narrow alleyway to his left. He seems determined to unearth something, but a layer of broken wooden crates is weighing down whatever it is, bricks wedging it into place. Samuel is about to go and help him when the man stands up tall and pulls something clear from the mess of bricks and crates piled up at the edge of the passage. It is a chair, a wheelchair perhaps. The shadows of the alleyway make it impossible to tell.

There is no need to help, so Samuel continues on his way. It is only when he reaches the end of Duncan Terrace and gets into Colebrooke Row that Samuel realises he recognised the man. It was Nathan Howell, the pianist. The one he caught pressing his body into Olivia before the first night. The one who could not tell the two sisters apart.

Samuel is suddenly anxious. It has been several days since he's seen Olivia. That pull, that desire to be near her, has started to fade recently. And he hasn't objected. It is easier that way. But remembering that moment with Nathan has brought it back again. He has a sudden urge to turn around and go back for her, to run backstage and check she is all right. Right now she should be waiting in the wings for her moment to appear, pressing her feet up and down in his shoes as she warms up. But the flowers and chocolates in his hand remind him that he has no right to do this. Olivia has never really acknowledged him, not since that day in the corridors of the theatre; she doesn't even know his name. It is Milly who is waiting for him, her whole family there to meet him. He keeps walking onwards, not looking back.

*

Milly is right about the flowers. Mrs Bell looks delighted, giving her daughter a sly smile as she takes them from him. Mr Bell receives the box of chocolates with genuine pleasure, leading Samuel straight through to the living room, where he offers him a drink.

'Best not to linger in the kitchen too long,' he says to Samuel with a conspiratorial raise of the eyebrow. 'You never know what you'll get roped into doing.'

A young man with wild, floppy hair steps into the room. Just as Milly predicted, his sleeves are rolled up and his tie is loose around his neck.

'This is my son, Jonathan,' Milly's father says by way of introduction before turning with mock severity to his son. 'How you get away with looking like that at your office, I'll never know.' He addresses Samuel again. 'Jonathan is training at one of the best law firms in London, but you wouldn't think it to look at him.'

Samuel holds out his hand to Jonathan. The boy, for he looks far too young to be a man, offers his own in return. Jonathan is suddenly shy, all the teasing and joking to which he has subjected his sister for the last few nights disappearing. He is, if he is honest with himself, intimidated by this large man whose shoulders look as though they might burst through his jacket. Jonathan is tall but as skinny as a child, his fragile wrists looking even smaller against Samuel's broad arms. He is so different to his sister, who is small and plump, with soft round cheeks; he looks as though he would blow away in the wind.

The two women join them in the living room, the warmth and smells from the kitchen following and spreading indulgently between them. Samuel says little to begin with, just answering the polite and interested questions of the family, Milly standing by his side with a happy smile on her face. But at dinner he starts to relax, the easy familiarity of them all moving through him. It is so different to his own memories of family dinners, his mother nervously offering his father more potatoes, the silence as they ate, just the sound of his father's loud chewing and his mother's nervous gulps as they finished their meal. Here the family tease Mr Bell, mocking him as soon as he starts talking about the effect of the absent mother on Cordelia, Goneril, Regan, Hero and Beatrice. Samuel is lost by this list of names; it is a world he does not understand.

'No one is interested, Father,' Milly says, smiling.

'How sharper than a serpent's tooth it is to have a thankless child!' Mr Bell replies. The family groan in mock despair.

'So, Samuel,' Mrs Bell says when their laughter has calmed, 'Milly tells us you are designing shoes for the Freeds. She says you are very talented.'

Swallowing his mouthful, he looks up. He assumes they will be bored by his answer, just asking out of politeness, but he is surprised to see them all looking at him with genuine interest, even Jonathan waiting expectantly for his reply. Samuel imagines his own mother asking him about his work. His father would grunt and say dinner is not the time for such nonsense.

'Hopefully, yes,' he manages to reply. 'I have some designs, and Mr Freed is considering whether they will be a popular addition to the pointe shoes we already make.'

'They are gorgeous,' Milly adds. 'One day we'll all be wearing his shoes. And his clothes! You should see Samuel's design for a winter hat. It's got the prettiest trim of navy lace embroidery.'

'It sounds lovely,' replies Mrs Bell. 'Do you take commissions? You could start your business from home perhaps, just with the occasional item when you have time on the weekends and after work. And then one day perhaps you can open your own shop.'

Milly has been suggesting this to him recently, dropping it into conversations as though it is the simplest thing in the world. But he doesn't have a sewing machine, not even close to enough money to buy one, and the costs of starting up would be too immense. It feels like a dream too far off to grasp.

'Not yet,' he replies. 'But if I can save up enough for a sewing machine, then I can start practising and maybe be good enough to take commissions one day.'

'Why doesn't Samuel borrow our sewing machine?' Mr Bell says as he pours a thick layer of custard over his pudding. 'I don't think I've seen either of you use it for months.'

Milly looks up excitedly. 'What a brilliant idea. Jonathan and I can bring it over this weekend.'

It is all moving too quickly. Samuel feels unsteady, as though the walls are expanding and swelling around him. He doesn't know what to say, but the excited chatter of the others means that he doesn't really need to say anything at all. When there is finally a lull in their noise, he speaks.

'Thank you.' And he adds in his head that this is the kindest thing anyone has ever offered him, but he doesn't have the courage to say it out loud. He turns to Mrs Bell. 'Perhaps you could request the first commission?'

The rest of the meal moves between planning Samuel's first design projects and Mr Bell trying to squeeze in anecdotes from his book. The laughter and the noise do not die down, even when Jonathan and Mr Bell take to the sink, continuing their conversation as they do the washing-up. Samuel offers to help, but Milly and her mother put their hands on his arm, keeping him at the table. He has never, in all his life, seen his own father do the washing-up after a meal.

When he leaves just after ten thirty, the family press into the hallway to wave goodbye. 'See you in the morning,' Milly shouts at him as he walks away. Samuel turns back to wave, feeling an immense relief that it is fewer than twelve hours until he sees her again. He will time it so that he arrives just as she does, the two of them appearing at the turning down to Cecil Court at exactly the same moment; he knows her schedule now, as precisely as if it were his own. It will be like they never left each other's side.

At first, he thinks he is hallucinating. But then the figure comes closer, materialising out of the darkness. He knows her run, the shape of her shoulders as she moves, the rise of her breath now hard and panicked. Olivia Marionetta is running towards him. Duncan Terrace Gardens transform, and all his thoughts of Milly, the sewing machine, the laughter around the table in the little home off Islington Green, dissolve and vanish. He is only here, in this moment, waiting for Olivia Marionetta to reach him.

27

CLARA

Tonight, I am the last to go down to the well. I need to do this alone. My final performance, my final routine of getting ready for a show in this theatre I have grown to love so much. The energy in the dressing rooms is high, not even dampened by Mr Healey's noisy hysterics about the missing Coppélia costume. It is a mystery but probably easily explained. Maybe it was taken to the cleaners a day too soon; maybe someone has stolen it – it could be anyone. The theatre is hardly the most secure place, suppliers in and out all day, audience members who might be tempted to sneak backstage. You could make a lot of money from a costume like that. But we nod sympathetically as he charges around our dressing rooms, and then we get back to our conversations. I have told them about America now. Everyone reacts in different ways. Some of the girls seem envious, while others think I am crazy for giving up all we have created here at the Vic-Wells. I can see them turn subtly to Olivia, trying to gauge her reaction. But she just smiles and gives them nothing.

I haven't finished my warm-up, but the quiet of the well room is what I need tonight. So I linger after all the others have left. I lay my shawl across the ground and lower myself down slowly, stretching out my hamstrings. Then I rub my feet, flexing them, rolling my ankles. I have my pointe shoes with me, hanging over my shoulder with the ribbons loosely knotted. Tying my pointe shoes has become a part of my body, a muscle memory I could do with my eyes closed. But tonight I think about each movement, each turn of the ribbon, how the shoe feels against my foot, exactly how tight the ribbon needs to be around my ankle. Once they are tied, I stand and pad out my feet, walking through the pointe, pushing my arches forwards. I know I will need to keep up this discipline, taking class every day, keeping my body in the condition it requires to be able to dance as I expect of myself. It will be hard in America to be strict with myself without Miss de Valois and Miss Moreton pushing us through our barre work every morning. But I am excited about the chance to do more. I long to travel, to meet people, to explore a new theatre every season, to meet actors and dancers and musicians on tour. I long to get away from the still waters of this well. I want an ocean, not a dark puddle that drags me back here every day, reflecting back a face that is not sure whether it has chosen this path. Now that Mother is no longer judging and shaping us, I can re-evaluate every decision I have ever made.

There is a noise from the other side of the room, a rustle and then a bang, as if something has fallen over. I look up with a jump, startled by the intrusion on my preparations. But there is no one there. I start to gather up my belongings, wrapping the shawl around my shoulders. The moment of calm has come to a sudden end and I need to return to the dressing room to do my last few preparations before the performance.

I start to walk towards the steps. But there is a louder noise behind me now, footsteps gaining on me quickly, heavy breathing. I start to turn but then there is pain, darkness.

28

NATHAN

Nathan holds the cricket bat in his hand, suddenly afraid. What if he has killed her? Throwing the bat aside, he kneels beside her, pulling her head into his lap. When he feels the back of her head where he hit her, a bump is already forming. He leans forwards, his ear to her mouth. She is breathing, a mist of air hovering above her lips. He lifts her wrist, feeling for her pulse; he can just feel it, faint through the delicate white of her skin.

Lying her on her side, he gets up and goes to the broom cupboard. He has been hiding in there for nearly an hour and his limbs are stiff from the effort of staying so still. Nathan had hoped he would find her alone, but he hadn't really thought it would work out like this. His alternative plan was more complex, more risky, but he'd practised it enough times in his head that he was convinced it would work. He was going to find that new stagehand, the one who hadn't been here long enough to know what Nathan Howell looked like. Nathan would send him to find Clara Marionetta, to tell her there was an American gentleman waiting for her with some news. The gentleman wanted somewhere quiet before the start of the show and had found out from the dancers that the well was the best place in the theatre for a private conversation. Nathan knew that she would come running, afraid her precious contract was about to be taken from her. But in the end he didn't even need to do that. She'd lingered. He'd been there to catch her.

Nathan can sense the movements of the theatre around him, even from the secluded darkness of the well room. There are a few minutes until the beginners' stage call and then the corridors will fall empty and quiet just long enough for him to move her. He brings the Coppélia costume from the cupboard and lays it on the ground next to Clara. She looks so peaceful like that, sleeping on her side, her legs stretched out elegantly, one foot crossed over the other. Kneeling, he feels for the clasps on the back of her peasant girl costume. They are tight and firm, but he manages to loosen them. Nathan rubs her collarbone with his thumb as he draws the straps down her arms, pulling the skirt and bodice from her body. He stands and looks at her, casting her costume to the side. The skirt ends up on the stone wall of the well, slipping too close to the water; the netting soaks from the bottom up within seconds. Slowly the costume sinks into the well, floating there in a mess of satin, net, lace.

Now he turns his attention back to Clara. He has seen her like this before, when she ran half-naked out of Wardrobe. But she was moving then, a flash of fast flesh and motion. He can really look at her now, the curve of her breasts, her small, firm waist flat beneath the band of her tights. Her spine is protruding, each vertebra poking through the skin, and he draws down them with his finger, stopping in the middle of her back where one of them is red, the skin abraded. He has seen the dancers doing their exercises, lifting themselves up and down on their backs to harden their stomachs, caring nothing for the pain of their bones against the studio floor.

It is not easy getting the doll tutu over her legs and pulled up to cover her body. For a moment he wishes he had waited until later, instead keeping her in the peasant girl costume, but he knows that wouldn't do. He needs her as Coppélia from the moment he possesses her.

Nathan adjusts the tutu around her thighs, running his fingers around the net gusset, settling the knickers into place. Clara murmurs as he tightens the bodice around her. He freezes, his hands still, but she doesn't wake. The ribbons are easy to tie around her wrists, and the necklace fits perfectly around her neck. He is less skilled with the headpiece, his hands slipping as he tries to pin the floral crown into her hair. The final result is not perfect, a little skewed, making her look wonky, a faulty doll. Not happy with it, he tries again, his heart beating faster now. He needs to hurry.

Finally, she is ready. He lifts her to her feet, groaning with the weight of her lifeless body. She falls forward over his shoulder but he catches her, holding her under her arms. He takes a step to the side and her legs drag with him. It is a dance of sorts, a sleepy, heavy dance of acceptance. She has accepted him at last, he thinks.

The drink is prepared. His Sleeping Beauty. He takes the bottle out of his jacket pocket: water mixed with sleeping pills, crushed into powder. They will take effect quickly, especially after the blow to her head. Her shoulders drop forwards, her head lolling over to the side, but he catches her, holding her upright again. He lowers her to an awkward seated position, holding her head back as he tips the bottle towards her lips. Clara is almost awake, but lost in a haze. She resists, murmuring a protest, but she has no strength and eventually he manages to get the contents of the bottle down her throat. A trickle of water has dripped down her chin, and he wipes it away. The skin beneath is paler now, her stage make-up fading. Nathan dabs at it with his finger, trying to even up the colour of her foundation. It unsettles him, this flaw. He needs her to be perfect.

From the quiet of the well, he can hear the orchestra starting to tune up, the hum of the audience filling the auditorium. Someone must have left a door open onto the pit, he thinks; the noises of the stage are louder than usual. There are footsteps above him, at the top of the steps, dancers running to the wings to complete their warm-up. He will need to wait until the performance has started and the corridors are quiet again. Nathan thinks of Charles, the pianist taking his place for the night, and he hopes he doesn't mess up. He thinks, too, of the dancers, the missing costume, the missing doll's wheelchair, their missing peasant girl. They won't think of him though, the pianist who sits silently in the corner, who has learnt every beat of the rhythm of the theatre.

Suddenly, a voice at the top of the stairs. He freezes, gripping Clara with shaking hands. It is Olivia, looking for her sister. Her voice carries down to him with unnerving strength, as though the sleeping woman in his arms has sprung into life in the bright light at the top of the steps.

'Clara, if you're down there, hurry up. We're on in minutes.' He stays still, not daring to make a sound. If he is silent, maybe she won't bother coming down. And he is right. He hears her sigh, muttering something about where Clara could be, and the tap-tap of her pointe shoes disappearing down the corridor.

Nathan needs to move. The performance is starting and he knows he has just a short window of time in which the stage-hands, dancers, musicians will be occupied with those opening moments of the performance, all attention on Constant Lambert making his way to the podium. Already the discordant notes of the orchestra warming up are starting to metamorphose into harmony. Clara is heavier than he expected, her body giving him no help, limbs falling uncontrollably. How do the male dancers make it look so easy? he thinks, envious of their effortless strength at lifting and throwing the ballerinas up in the air. But of course they have help, the women taking half the effort, their muscles taut and strong. Clara is giving him nothing; she collapses like a puppet.

He is sweating with the effort by the time he gets to the top of the stairs, but fear and anticipation keep him moving with a power he did not know he had. The door to the street is not far, and it is easier once he is not climbing the narrow stairs from the well. He kicks the door open and looks around him before stepping out in the street. It is still light, too light, and for a moment it feels as though a spotlight is directed right at him, his body lit up as it used to be when he was performing at concerts, the child star. These longer evenings have arrived so quickly, he's missed it, somehow expecting it to be pitch black by the time he leaves the theatre with Clara. The street is empty so he surges forward, his back aching with every step. Sweat drips down his forehead and he can smell the cloying dampness on his top lip.

Nathan reaches the alleyway opposite the theatre, a narrow lane off Arlington Street used as a dump by workmen. Finding a hiding place for the Coppélia doll wheelchair while the stage crew were on their lunch break had not been easy, but he'd been relieved to find the chair still in place when he'd returned this evening, covered by the broken crates and pallets he'd pulled across it. He lowers Clara down behind a pile of bricks, covering her gently with his coat.

As he shuffles about in the alleyway trying to release the wheelchair from its hiding place, a man walks past carrying a box of chocolates and a bunch of flowers. It seems so out of place, this ordinary man continuing along the road for his ordinary evening. Nathan waits for him to get to the end of the road before he hauls the chair out and steadies the wheels. He is grateful for how silently it moves, greased regularly by the stage-hands who are instructed to keep it quiet onstage. When he turns back to Clara he is dismayed by the sight: she looks like a discarded china doll, a smear of dirt across her cheek. He wipes it off tenderly before lifting her into the wheelchair.

It is with reluctance that he places his coat over her, hiding the tutu from view. She looks so small all of a sudden, her body disappearing under his long heavy coat. He wraps a shawl around her hair, very gently so as not to disturb the angle of her floral crown. And finally she is ready. As he wheels her out into the road, he feels calm, in control. Now that he is wheeling her steadily, no longer sweating under the weight of carrying her over his shoulder, he feels better. At the end of Arlington Street, he looks about him, watching as a steady stream of cars, three women on bicycles, a bus, continue past him. A taxi pulls up further along the road, its navy body rocking as four men rush out, the bottles of beer in their hands splashing over onto the pavement. They ignore him. He is just a man wheeling a sleeping invalid back home after an ordinary day. They do not notice the tiny flash of pink satin peeking out under the bottom of the coat. Two young women stop right next to him, waiting to cross the road. He turns his head just an inch to look at them, to see if they are staring curiously at his sleeping doll. But they don't even register the wheelchair. Their heads are close, both of them in matching grey hats, and he sees that they are holding hands. One of them notices Nathan looking and pulls her hand away. They take a step apart from one another, their faces taut. Nathan feels relief. Everyone has their own personal adventure to worry about tonight.

A break in the traffic emerges and he crosses the road, quickly slipping between the warehouses on Owen Street and then into the shadows of Colebrooke Row. A mother and daughter walk towards him and he feels his chest tighten as the little girl stares at Clara with wide-eyed curiosity. But her mother yanks on her arm to hurry her up, and they move on.

It would be safer to stay hidden, to wait in the darkened alleyways until the streets clear, but there is a part of him that wants to be seen: he deserves her. He has waited long enough, worked hard enough. She belongs to him, dressed forever in the same red skirt with the same pink shoes tied around her ankles. Lace and net graze her motionless thighs. Her skin is smooth porcelain and her lips are pink. Never has there been a lovelier figure, unchanging, unbroken by the pace of time. Soon she will be home with him and he can start to preserve this memory, this moment of perfection. Her sightless eyes will not fade. She will be a beautiful statue, preserved forever. He has watched her for so long, holding her in his gaze, locking her into position like a photograph. Now she can join his mother, but it will be so much more real this time. No more pretending. No more fantasy.

He imagines dancing with her, the two of them arm in arm under the stars. Silent, of course, but that is no matter. It is better that way. She is a dancing doll, his Coppélia, created at last. He can finally believe it, now that he has her in the wheelchair.

Pausing at the top of the slope down to the canal, he reaches down to her wrist, which has broken free from the coat. He lifts her arm above her, as if she is waving to a crowd. Ice-cold. He drops her arm in fright. Life lingers, like a promise; but he is afraid of what will happen when she wakes.

He needs to move quickly.

29

OLIVIA

I am convinced that Clara will turn up. Just before we are about to run onstage, she will appear, a little apologetic, making up some excuse. And so we delay rearranging the order, the patterning of our corps de ballet, until the last possible moment. When we finally realise she isn't coming, I take charge and give everyone their new places, a little shuffling of the positioning so that the audience won't notice the missing peasant girl. One of the men runs around to the other side of the stage to pass on the message to those entering stage right. Everyone seems to feel it is my responsibility to sort this out. She is my sister after all.

We are all nervous, me more than anyone. It doesn't feel right. Clara has never missed a performance; and besides, I saw her ready in costume just half an hour ago. My stomach is in knots and I can't keep still, repeatedly rising and lowering in *relevé* and *échappé* until my legs feel warm and awake. It is easy to tell when we are feeling unsettled before a performance. The rosin box at the back of the wings is always crowded with our feet, all of us returning too many times to dip our toes into the powder. There will be no slipping onstage for anyone tonight.

It is not only Clara's absence that is strange. One of the Coppélia costumes is still missing. And even stranger is the missing wheelchair. The backstage crew realised it had gone as they were preparing the stage this afternoon. They have had to make do with an ordinary wooden chair instead, which doesn't quite have the same effect, and we are all hoping Sergeyev doesn't notice the small change to the choreography.

I hear the applause of the audience as our conductor walks into position, the moment of silence as he lifts the baton, the first slow notes, like an awakening. Taking a deep breath in, I find the pace of the music, let it wash over me. It is so familiar; I can hear each note, each bar, even before it arrives. The melody, high and strong, comes in after half a minute. Usually this is when I start to picture myself onstage, visualising each step. But tonight I feel nothing. The music sounds strange, distorted, as though I am listening to it underwater. I watch Miss de Valois onstage, the Swanilda variation that she performs with such lightness, the mime usually so clear it is as though she is speaking the words. Tonight I cannot read the language of her gestures; it seems to me that she is dancing another story altogether. It is just a chaotic mix of waving arms and legs.

All I can think about as I run onstage and start dancing is where Clara could be. The audience are even more of a faceless sea of shapes and shadows than usual, and the swaying movement of the orchestra unnerves me, like a leviathan rising from the depths. In the interval I search every dressing room. I even consider running home, to see if she is there, but I know I won't make it back in time.

Just before Act Two is about to begin, I realise that I haven't checked with Nathan. He might have spoken with her; perhaps they had an argument. I hurry to the dressing room where the orchestra spend the interval. It is packed in there, a crush of white shirts and black jackets. Most of them ignore me as I ease my way into the room, asking them if Nathan is around. But finally one of the percussionists takes pity on me and asks me again who I am looking for.

'Is Nathan Howell in here? Or do you know where he is?'

'Nathan isn't on tonight. He's unwell. A cough or something. Constant told him to go home.'

I leave, disappointed. Act Two should be a moment of celebration, our final night. But I can't find the energy and I know my dancing as the mischievous friend of Swanilda is flat. After the curtain call I get changed as quickly as possible, ready to hurry home. The other girls are preparing to go out with feverish excitement, refreshing their make-up, loosening their hair and re-pinning it into glamorous styles, smoothing out their party dresses. A bar in Covent Garden has been booked for the evening, but I can't join them. Not without knowing what has happened to Clara.

'You're not going to know where Clara is all the time when she moves to America,' Hermione scolds me playfully, as I fret with the buckle on my shoe. 'I'm sure she's fine. When has she ever not been fine?'

'This isn't like her. She's never missed a show before.' I have no patience for the persuasions of the girls. I know they are just trying to help, but I can't focus on anything they say.

As I walk along the corridor to the stage door, I try to remember how she was when I last saw her, what she was doing. It was down by the well, all of us dipping our fingers into the water and trailing the drops over our toes. There was quite a crowd of us, laughing and joking as we mocked ourselves for our ridiculous superstitions; Clara was the last to arrive. I can't remember seeing her after that.

Reaching the door that opens onto the staircase down to the well, I am nervous again, as though I might find something horrible down there. A memory of the night I found the flower crown in the well comes back to me sharply. It spooked me, seeing those flowers floating in the water, the mannequin's head bopping up and down. And now the missing tutu, the wheel-chair. I don't know if anyone thought to look down here in the dark corners or the cupboard at the back. Perhaps no one wanted to try.

I turn on the light as quickly as I can, but it offers little clarity, the shadows and shapes of the room lurking. When I reach the bottom of the steps, I move quickly towards the water. At first I think it is her, drowned, the net of her dress consuming her body. I hear my cry, a loud, sharp scream. But the silence of the room swallows it just as I realise there is no body. Just a mess of costume half in, half out of the water, her shawl in a heap on the ground.

I call out for her, but there is nowhere she could be. The room is empty. My sister has vanished.

30

CLARA

I struggle to find myself. Sound comes back first, a strange discordance of familiar music, ripples splashing against a surface, low slapping footsteps, water under a bridge. My head aches, a dull pounding through my temples, a sharp pain near my neck. I try to open my eyes but they feel glued shut, my eyelids heavy. There is music coming from very close by, soft at first but gradually getting louder and clearer. I recognise those notes. Long, slow, a little haunting. The melody comes in with a brightness that hurts my head. The opening of *Coppélia*. That is when I panic. It feels like hours since I was getting into my costume, warming up, putting on my make-up for the start of the performance. I try to think. Has the performance happened? Did I fall asleep? Am I in the wings, waiting to enter the stage? Or am I at home, having some horrible dream? It would make sense, I reason with myself, to be plagued with nightmares about missing the show, a manifestation of my decision to go to America. I try to feel my body, bring it into my consciousness, find its location. No, I am sure the performance hasn't happened yet. Either I am dreaming or I have missed it altogether. My thoughts dance and drift over each other, not grasping anything real.

I try to move, but I can't. My legs feel like lead, and it is as though something heavy is sitting on my chest. My mind jumps painfully to a copy of a painting Olivia and I were obsessed with as teenagers: Fuseli's *The Nightmare*, with its terrifying creature pressing itself down into a woman's body. Right now, with my eyes refusing to open, I feel its claws working their way into my ribs, my lungs struggling to find enough air. The image was in a book Mother kept in her bedroom, an illustrated history of Romantic art and literature. We would sneak in and look at it when Mother was out. I can't get that awful image out of my head now; it is imprinted in the dark pink and black behind my eyelids.

My body is slowly coming back to life. I move my fingers, stretching out my palms, though my grip fails me when I try to fold them into a fist. Extending my consciousness down my body, I think about my feet. But they feel trapped, restricted. I register that familiar feeling of tightness around the balls of my feet and realise I am wearing pointe shoes.

I feel a soft brushing on my arm. It moves up and down, gently, rhythmically, out of time with the music that continues to build around me. I try to let it soothe me, like the way Olivia and I would tickle the inside of each other's arms with the lightest of touches when we were tired and scared. But the more I try to open my eyes, the more I think about that stroke on my arm. I don't know what it is and it unsettles me. I want to push it away, brush it off. Eventually it stops. I think I can hear footsteps moving away from me.

It takes great mental effort but I manage to pry open one eye, just a little, before it closes again. I feel myself drifting in and out of sleep. But what I see when I open that eye stays with me, turning itself over and over until I can decipher some of what is around me. Red, brown, dim golden light, wooden surfaces with red curtains and cushions. Directly opposite me, a trunk. Papers, maybe photographs, chiffons, dresses, a fox fur piece, a pile of hairpins, silk stockings, a little music-box doll. It reminds me of a dressing room. Perhaps I have fallen asleep in the dressing room. Why would no one wake me? I can hear the music, but it doesn't sound quite right; a low crackle stains the clarity of the sound. My entrance is just minutes away. I need to be warming up, preparing my body for the first steps across the stage. I try and try, willing my body to get up. But it does nothing.

I must have fallen asleep again, because I jerk awake this time, my eyes opening and flicking wildly around me. I am in a narrow room lined with wooden seats, a small table that juts out from the wall, a stove in the corner. The light is dim, just a few candles dotted on the surfaces, a paraffin lamp lit low against the wall. I try to stand, pressing my hands down against the sides of the chair to lift myself up. The ceiling is low and I feel breathless, as if the walls are closing in around me. With my feet firmly on the ground, I take a step forward. The ground doesn't feel right, as if it is shifting and rocking ever so slightly. My head pounds and I suddenly think I am going to be sick.

'You'll feel better if you sit down,' a voice says from an inner door to my right. I turn my head too sharply and reel. Although I recognise the voice, the pounding in my head is muffling everything and I can't think straight.

He comes into the room, the light from the lamp just reaching the edge of his face. I lean against the chair but don't sit down; my legs quiver with the effort. He takes another step forward, and that is when I realise who it is.

'Nathan,' I say, alarmed when my voice refuses to work properly. It is barely a whisper, but it hurts my head, the word reverberating through my skull.

He comes to me and puts his hands around my waist, gently lowering me back into the chair. I murmur a protest, but I need to sit. If I don't, I think I might collapse. The seat is uncomfortable, a hard wood, but it feels faintly familiar. I look down and to the side and notice wheels attached to the chair. I am in a wheelchair; there is a block of wood wedged under one of the wheels. This is the Coppélia doll chair, I am sure of it. I can't make sense of it, this strange mix of Delibes's music, the chair, my feet in pointe shoes, this long, thin room. Now that my neck is moving more easily, I can see my body. Red ribbons are tied around my wrists and I am wearing a tutu. It is uncomfortable sitting in the skirt, the netting at the back sticking into my thighs. I will be crushing it. We've been taught never to sit like this in a tutu, but right now it doesn't seem to matter.

'It suits you,' Nathan says. He is leaning against the door, watching me with an odd expression. He seems so different somehow, as though the Nathan I know has morphed into someone new. 'I saw you wear that for the photographs, for the poster. I'd never seen you sit so still as when you were posing for the photographer.'

'But I'm not Coppélia tonight,' I insist, moving awkwardly in the chair. I try to pull the back of the tutu out from under me and it fans out behind me, the netting reaching high against the chair. 'It's one of the students. Mr Healey will be needing this tutu. Why am I wearing it?' I don't really think Nathan will have the answer, but I ask it all the same. He should be in the orchestra pit right now.

'You're wearing it because it suits you,' he replies. I don't understand him. 'I chose it for you. The perfect costume for my doll.'

'Your doll.' As I speak the words, I start to panic again. There is something about his tone, the way he is looking at me, that I don't like. It reminds me of when he proposed. I think that was the first time I truly felt afraid of him. Before then there had been no reason to, not even when he was at his most controlling, leading me from restaurant to café, dictating the rhythm of my evenings, what I must wear, when I should dance, when I could go home. He had never done anything to suggest he'd hurt me, or anyone for that matter. I had always felt balanced on the edge of control and submission, as though a word from me and he'd give in, let me choose my path. But I realise now that I have never really tested that hypothesis. I always gave in to him, right up until his final demand, the marriage proposal that I finally found the courage to refuse. Looking at him now, he is different. Dangerous, even. I shift uneasily, the bodice cutting into my waist. Someone has done it up too tightly.

He steps forward and kneels in front of me, placing his hands around my ankles. I try to move my legs away from him, but his grip tightens.

'Would you like to see my collection?' he says, smiling up at me with a new hardness I have not seen in him before. 'I've got to share it with you, now you're finally here.'

'But where am I?' I look around me again, trying to piece together some order to the dull shapes that dance in the candle-light. I hear voices and footsteps close by. We must be near a street, I think, but there are other sounds too that confuse me. The music continues to rise and fall around me, but I see now that it is coming from a gramophone to my left.

'You've always said you wanted to visit my home,' he replies. 'Well, here we are. My boat. What do you think?' He gestures around him. 'Is it how you imagined?'

'But how did I get here, Nathan? The last thing I remember is getting ready for the performance, warming up. I was by the well.' And then I remember those footsteps behind me, the pain in my head. Nathan is still holding on to my ankles. I flinch away from him, trying to kick his hands off me. But my feet can barely move.

'Steady, Clara. You're okay now. I brought you here. You needed help.'

'Why did I need help? Did you hit me?'

'Yes. Of course I did. As I said, you needed help.'

'How was hitting me over the head and dragging me all the way to your boat helping me?'

'Let's not get ahead of ourselves. You're tired. You've had a shock. Just rest a moment, and then we can talk further.'

'What is it you want from me? I need to be onstage right now.'

'It's a bit late for that, I'm afraid.'

'Olivia will be wondering where I am. She'll come looking for me.'

'I'm sure she will. But by the time she's worked out where you are, it won't matter any more.'

'What do you mean by that?'

'Hush. It's okay.' He pauses and looks up at me, his hands relaxing their grip on my ankles. 'Let me give you a guided tour of my boat. That will make you feel better.'

I stand up in one strong effort, pushing him as hard as I can from where he is crouched on the floor. He falls backwards, letting go of my ankles. I try to step forward, my body propelling itself towards the door at the other end of the boat. But there is something stopping me, a rope perhaps, tying me to the frame of the chair. I fall onto my knees. The chair bucks behind me, knocking into my back painfully.

Nathan stands quickly, lifting me back into the chair. I struggle against him, but he is too strong, his weight pressing into me. He has a piece of rope in one hand and I fight him as he winds it around my chest and arms, pinning me to the chair. My head still aches and my throat is dry. When I cry out, I don't know if I am even making any sound. It feels like I am in a nightmare. I must be making some noise, for he drives himself at me, holding his hand against my mouth.

'Clara, it's okay. I don't want to hurt you.'

I shake my head at him. I want to believe him, but I can't. Not now that I am tied to this chair, my head swimming in pain.

'I'm going to tie this around your mouth if you can't be quiet,' he says, looking at me with eyes I don't recognise. He has a thin silk scarf in his hand. It looks delicate, a silvery blue with half-moon patterns printed across the silk, but I don't want it near me. It transforms into something terrifying, held like that in his hand. 'Can I trust you?' he says, his face close to mine. His hair is burnt gold, fading just a little above his temples. I have never looked at him this closely before, not even when we were out in London, at cafés, restaurants, exhibitions. It is as though I am seeing him for the first time.

I nod, desperate for him to remove his hand. I can feel the wetness of my breath pooling in his hand; the rise and fall of my chest is strained and heavy.

He pulls back, watching me carefully. I move my jaw from side to side, easing out the ache across my face. He's looking at me strangely, critically, as though there is something about me that is not quite right. He reaches behind him towards the trunk and picks up a powder compact. It is an old style, the type my mother had when we were very young. There is a pretty floral design interwoven across the case.

There must be lipstick on his hand, perhaps even some smeared across my face. Nathan wipes his hand on his trousers as he comes towards me, opening the compact. He leans over me, dabbing the sponge against my skin. I twist my head away, but he turns me back again, holding my chin with a tight grip.

'I need you to look just right,' he says as he straightens up, staring down at me as though I am a painting. 'There.' He turns the compact around and holds up the mirror. 'Don't you look lovely. Like a doll.'

I stare at my reflection. I do look like a doll. My make-up is heavier than usual, rosy cheeks rising up into my hairline.

'I added a bit of make-up once you'd got here,' he says, as if reading my thoughts. 'The journey didn't do you any favours. But it's okay now. You're here.'

'What is this?' I say, my voice rising uncomfortably. 'Why have you brought me here?'

He ignores me, instead going to the trunk opposite and starting to tidy up. He puts the make-up back into a box, rolls the stockings into a ball. The hairpins are scattered amongst the photographs. He draws them all together and tucks them inside a velvet purse. There is a little box on the trunk. I know what is inside: the engagement ring I refused to accept.

'These all belonged to my mother.' He picks up each item tenderly before setting it down again more neatly. 'This was her favourite fur piece,' he says, stroking a white fox fur shawl that is fraying a little around the edges. 'And she loved an occasion to wear these shoes.'

His hand lingers over the ring box but then he moves on, placing the shoes back on a shelf above the trunk; they are silver with delicate buckles. Hanging from a hook on the wall next to the trunk is an evening dress: it is blue, trimmed with feathers, the sort of dress I remember my mother wearing too. It makes me sad to think of how much he has saved. He has all these memories of his mother, while Olivia and I threw it all away. We took nothing but a few photographs from Colney Hatch. All of Mother's clothes, her jewellery, her make-up, they would be discarded by now, thrown out amongst the belongings of those patients who have no family to preserve their memories.

'Do you want to try on her gloves?' he says, holding out a pair of white silk gloves. I shake my head.

'Probably for the best. I don't want to muddle up the artefacts.' I don't like the way he calls them that, artefacts, as though this is a museum. But looking at the way he handles her belongings, his memories of his precious mother that he has told me so much about, it really could be a museum.

'Do you want to see my toy room?' he asks me, his voice rising in excitement. 'Don't you dare say no,' he warns. He is smiling, though, like a little child showing his new toys to a friend. I do nothing, just stare blankly back at him. He is a stranger to me, this talented pianist I thought I knew so well, reverting back to some childlike state. 'Don't you move,' he says, laughing. 'I'll bring them to you.'

He disappears into the room from which he first emerged. I have never been on a narrowboat before, but there is no bed in this main room and nothing that looks as though it could be converted into one. The other room must be the bedroom, I think, shuddering as I remember all those times I had longed for him to bring me back here, how much I wanted him to run his hands over me, to press his mouth against my skin as we lay on his bed. Now, the thought makes me sick. As soon as he leaves, I strain at the bindings, pushing my arms against them. But all that happens is the wheelchair comes loose from the wooden wedge holding it in place and I roll forwards, crashing into the trunk.

'What's going on?' he says, appearing quickly out of the bedroom. 'Clara, you have to stay still. This is only going to take longer if you struggle.' Nathan wheels me back to the same position against the side of the boat, placing the wedge back under the wheel. He disappears again but this time comes back immediately. In his hands is a tin box.

He collects a few candles from around the boat and places them on the table diagonally across from me. I have a clear view of the space, and I watch with reluctant fascination as he opens the box and starts to empty its contents onto the table.

Nathan starts with the soldiers. With a steady hand, he lines them up in two rows at the edges of the table. They are all standing to attention, painted in bright red and gold.

'These were my first. Mother bought them for me after each concert as a reward. They were unpainted and I would sit the day after each performance and paint them in the finest detail. I still have the workbox, all the tiny brushes and the bright tubes of colour. It became a routine, a reassurance, I suppose, that I was still a child and could do childish things. Mother found all the best toyshops in London, Paris, Venice, Geneva. It was the first thing she would do when we got to a new city for a concert – find me my next doll.'

Gradually, I watch as he fills the centre of the table with more miniature dolls and figurines. There is a priest, painted in long robes with a purple chasuble. There are many musicians, some medieval minstrels with lutes and recorders, some in modern dress attached to miniature musical instruments. A little boy plays at a piano, his hair painted golden. There is a woman in a long blue dress playing the violin. A choirboy stands with a hymn book open in his hands.

'I had a princess stage, which amused my mother and horrified my father. Here's Sleeping Beauty.' He lays her out on the table, a little doll resting on a bed lined with roses. 'I remember painting her, how careful I had to be with her lipstick. I have a very steady hand. Mother said it was because I was so good at the piano. All those scales.'

'Why are you showing me all these?' I say. I have been here too long without understanding what he wants from me. These dolls are scaring me, the way they are lined up in perfect rows with the candlelight flickering gloomily over their faces.

He ignores my question. 'And finally we have the ballerinas.' He places three dolls along the front of the desk, one of which he picks up from the trunk. There is one kneeling, with her arms crossed over her legs. She is wearing the dying swan tutu, the feathers painted with careful precision. Another is in chiffon trousers drawn in at the ankle, a bright red cropped top that is studded with jewels. The attention to detail is remarkable. It is the Firebird costume, recreated in miniature. The final doll is familiar. It is the music box figurine, the one I saw him steal from the dressing room all those weeks ago. I don't know why, but it is this one that scares me most, its stiff skirts and hard skinny arms sending a shiver down my spine.

'And you, Clara, you have just joined them. You are my greatest creation, my Coppélia doll brought to life.'

'What do you mean, I have joined them?' I say, trying to control the fear in my voice. I want to ridicule him, show him what a child he is being. 'Who do you think you are? Dr Coppélius?'

'Now perhaps that wouldn't be such a bad idea,' he laughs. 'For years I've kept Mother dead, convinced myself, convinced you, that she died when I was twelve. I created a story that worked for me. I needed that story, that version of my life. I couldn't let Mother leave me, to choose to leave me. And what is that, I suppose, but being a doll-maker, a Dr Coppélius, creating someone who would never be able to fight me, hurt me, leave me. And then you came along. We were supposed to get married. You were supposed to love me. You did love me, I thought. But no, you decided you didn't want me, that I wasn't good enough for you. You refused me, you walked out on me. And now you are moving to America. You're leaving me too, just like she did. Well, this time I am not making any mistakes.'

He is standing very close to me now, the music box ballerina gripped in his hand.

'I did love you, Nathan,' I whisper, afraid of him and the way he is staring at me. 'But people fall out of love. It happens all the time. It's nothing to do with you or me or your mother. It's just what happens to people. We love and we stop loving. There is no other explanation. You can't let your happiness ride so entirely on the decisions of others.'

'As I said, Clara, I'm not making the same mistake again.' His voice has taken on a new grimness, a hard determination.

'What mistake?'

'My mother came back to life. She turned up one day, with her new husband, the children who replaced me. Her very presence reminded me that I was not enough for her.'

'So your mother isn't dead?' I whisper, uncertain. 'I thought she died years ago?'

'Don't you understand anything I've just told you? It would have been better if she *had* died.'

He walks to the end of the boat and opens a cupboard. I strain my neck to see what he is doing. In the gloom it is hard to see what he has picked up. He comes back towards me, holding up a box. At least it looks like a box. But as he gets closer, I realise it is a camera.

'Clara, I need you to stay very still for me. I'm going to take some photographs.'

31

OLIVIA

I kneel by the well, as I have done so many times before. I don't know what I expect it to give me. Hundreds of times I have reached down into its mouth, straining to reach the magic waters that spring up from the borehole that plunges more than six hundred feet down to the chalk below London. I think of all those people who travelled to visit the spas of London over two hundred years ago. It would have been a countryside retreat, an escape from the censorship controls of the city centre. Perhaps not much has changed. Perhaps this theatre is a fantasy world where we get lost in the seduction of dance, music, creation. We search for something outside ourselves to find hope, certainty. But now, with Clara missing, not even the most holy of waters would comfort me. I feel a wrench deep within my body, like there is part of me gone too. I am afraid that if I stand I will fall, a vertiginous descent into the well.

I pull out Clara's costume, a stream of water soaking me as it escapes the netting. As the water runs down and pools around my feet, those other discoveries in the well flood my memory. My pointe shoes, the white rose petals, the flower crown, the mannequin head. And now this. An entire costume drowned. I try to piece it all together, but it doesn't fit; I can't match the shoes floating there amongst a bath of petals with this sodden dress. Desperately, I try to think where she could be. I know I need to go home, to check she hasn't gone straight there. Maybe something has happened, some news. I can't think what it would be apart from about her contract to America. Now Mother is dead, we have stopped waiting for the phone to ring, a doctor's voice telling us the news. That chapter of our life is closed. We are both ready to move on.

There is one room I have not tried. The board room. I don't really want to go back there, not after last time. Every time I go to the top floor of the theatre, I think of Nathan. It makes my cheeks hot to remember what I did. I don't understand why I wanted him; it feels like madness, an irrationality that I can't connect with myself. But if the ballets and operas in which I have performed have taught me anything, reason is an irrelevance when desire is involved. Yes, I admit it. I desired him. But now when I think of him, it is with horror and shame. I wonder if I really did want him, or whether it was what he had with Clara that dug its way, insidiously, into my heart. It scares me a little to know that I am capable of changing so quickly, from obsession to disgust in minutes. The catalyst for that change: the sudden arrival of reality. The hard, cold, unpleasant reality of his tongue pressing between my teeth, his fingers inside me. Or maybe the reality of how it felt to betray my sister.

The board room door is closed but unlocked. Nervously, I fumble for the light switch. I don't know what I expect to find. Nathan and Clara locked in an embrace? Clara alone, hiding from us all? There is no one there, just a piano, an empty stool, a few boxes of music stacked at the side of the room. I walk to the piano, looking around me for any clues that Clara has been in here. There is nothing.

It is colder than usual in here; the window has been left open. I pull the coat around me tighter, pressing the green fur high around my neck. Part of me is glad to be wearing her coat today, a little piece of Clara wrapped around me. But it also makes me think of Nathan, the heat of his hands that have lingered around the collar when he kisses my sister. I shudder. There are some music scores on the piano stand, several of them stacked open on top of each other. I flick through them as if they will miraculously reveal a map to Clara. The end of Act Two of *Coppélia*. Berners' *Foyer de danse*. Rachmaninoff's 'Prelude in D Major'.

There is something else tucked between the scores. It is a photograph, fallen in amongst the pages of music. Taking it out, I hold it in front of me to catch some light. I recognise the woman immediately. Younger, dressed in the fashions of a decade ago, but it is definitely her. Nathan Howell's mother, the beautiful woman with the two sleepy children who came to the first night of *Coppélia*. The woman he seemed so determined to avoid. I remember watching him walk home to his boat, ripping a note into shreds.

I turn over the photograph. There is an inscription on the back, written in a hand that looks vaguely familiar.

Mother, died 1924.

I squint at the words. But she isn't dead. I saw her just a few weeks ago, right here in Sadler's Wells. And who writes the date of their mother's death on the back of a photograph? It makes me uneasy, these bold, certain words. There is another note written below the date.

Her beauty shall in these black lines be seen,
And they shall live, and she in them still green.

These lines jog a memory. Clara and I used to love searching through Father's bookshelf, the slim volumes of poetry with his light pencil markings in the margins. His little book of Shakespeare's sonnets, green leather and small enough to slip into a coat pocket, had delighted us. We had pored over those poems, unpicking them like a riddle. We had taken childish joy in laughing at the poet's arrogance, his belief that his lines would remain when the youth's beauty had long faded. It is, I realise now, a chilling thought that he believed his art could triumph over life: and perhaps he was right in some way. But our dance, our ballet, denies art this change; it lives only in the moment, that split second where the dancer flies through the air, spins round and round.

Taking the photograph, I put it in my pocket. I want to show Clara. She should know that Nathan has been lying to her, pretending his mother is dead when I have seen her in this very theatre, alive and well.

There is another note in my pocket, the one I found next to the card from Jacob Manton. I remember how it had confused me, the line of verse strange when taken out of context, alone on the scrap of paper. I take it out now and read those lines again. The hand is identical to the writing on the back of the photograph.

A lovely apparition, sent to be a moment's ornament.

As I stare down at the words, trying to make sense of them, I can feel my chest tightening. *A moment's ornament.* I think of Clara's complaint about Nathan after Mother's funeral. How she didn't want to fit into his unrealistic ideal. How controlling he had become. Now, reading these lines of verse, something feels terribly wrong.

I start to run. Out of the board room. Along the corridor. Down the stairs. Out of the stage door, ignoring the waves of the others who are congregating in the entrance, their long dresses and bright red lips signalling their readiness for a night's celebration. I cannot be part of them, not now. Not with my sister missing. And I think I know where she might be.

Turning north, I run up through the back streets, across the two roads, narrowly avoiding a cyclist who shouts back at me angrily. The air is cool on my skin, but I am sweating inside my coat. Clara's coat. Now I am starting to understand why she wanted me to have it, why she was drawing away from anything that bound her to him. I run fast, the heels of my shoes loud against the pavement. The houses either side of the terrace loom down, lights from the windows dotting on and off; I imagine my footsteps waking up their occupants, a running woman charging through the London streets. I fly between the pools of light that paint the ground underneath each street lamp, running faster than I have ever run before.

A man has stopped in the street just ahead of me, his large bulk blocking my path. I am aware of him watching me, waiting even. His chest and shoulders seem huge in the shadows from the street lamps, his face dark.

'Olivia,' he calls to me. At least I think that is what he says, but my own breath is too loud in my head for me to be sure.

I need to turn off the terrace and go down to the canal, and he is blocking my way. As I try to push past him, he says my name again, holding out his arms and taking me by the shoulders.

'Olivia, is everything okay?'

I shrug him off me and stand back, finally stopping. He releases me immediately, his arms falling heavily down to his sides. I must look a mess, my hair flying loose around my face, sweat pooling above my lip.

'What do you want?' I manage to gasp.

'I'm just walking home,' he says, looking down at me strangely. 'Why are you running? Is everything okay?' he repeats.

As I look back at him, I realise that I see this man everywhere. The pointe shoe maker's apprentice. I do not know his name. He is always there, watching our ballet class from the doorway, lingering in the corridors, in and out of Wardrobe. He was there that afternoon when I pretended to be Clara; he saw Nathan kissing me. He knows everything about us, when we take class, when we start warming up for the shows, when we go home, when we come in again in the morning. He creates the shoes we wear on our feet; he understands our strengths and weaknesses. I have ignored him for so long but he has been there all the same, watching me, watching Clara.

I look at him again, really look at him this time. And I am afraid.

32

NATHAN

The first few photographs he takes will not turn out right, Nathan thinks. She looks frightened and angry. In black and white she will appear sinister, demonic. He needs her to be flawless. This is not what he wants, and he places the camera down for a moment, working out how he should proceed. He wishes he could process the photographs immediately, transform his bedroom into a darkroom. Sadly, that is not possible, and he will need to wait until he can access the darkroom off Dean Street, tucked away in the corner of Soho, where no one asks any questions. He has been there before to develop his photographs, the ones he's taken of his toy soldiers and princess dolls, all of them arranged in complex stories and scenarios. They were a little blurred and it was disappointing to lose the vibrancy of their colours, but it was a good test of the lighting in the boat at night. He knows what he is doing now, his hands comfortable with the camera and its functions.

Nathan was fascinated by the darkroom, the men moving in and out of the corridors, their photographs hidden away for their eyes only. And the assistants who took bundled cash payments for silence. Not so secure, though, once one was inside that shabby door at the end of Diadem Court: Nathan walked into the wrong room while he was waiting for his photographs to develop, only to be quickly ushered along by one of the assistants. But he saw a glimpse of those photographs hanging from the line, naked limbs contorted and bound, open mouths like dark tunnels, men and women stripped down to their wildest, barely human. He hadn't liked it; all this rawness, it terrified him. Nathan wants order, precision, perfect lines of the corps de ballet, not a hair out of place. There will be none of that grotesque display of desire in his photographs tonight, he assures himself.

He goes to the little sink and takes out a bottle of champagne. It has been chilling all afternoon on a bed of ice that he bought from the local fishmongers on Exmouth Market. The woman asked him if he was having a party. He supposes he is; this is the closest he is going to get to a party with Clara. But that is her fault, not his. The ice is melted now, the label of the bottle wet and fragile. The cork makes a loud popping noise, the bubbles fizzing over onto his hand. He pours two glasses.

'Just imagine it exactly like it was before,' he says to Clara. 'When we would go out dancing together after shows, trying every new cocktail we could find. You wanted me then, didn't you? You were desperate for me to bring you back here.' He drops more of the crushed sleeping pills into her glass, careful not to let her see. The music is loud, the end of Act One of *Coppélia* singing out from the gramophone, and Clara will not be able to hear him mixing the powder into her drink with a spoon. The bubbles dance against the metal. As the previous dose is still in her system, he estimates it will not be long before it takes effect. He knows all about barbiturates; the little pot of pills by his father's bed became a frequent sight after his mother left them. Nathan knows how quickly they start to work, how long they last, which ones are fast-acting, which ones will keep her asleep. He will need to act fast, persuading her into the poses he wants.

Nathan picks up a knife from the drawer next to the stove and tucks it into his trousers. He turns around to her with a smile. 'Champagne?'

'No. Of course not.' She glares at him. 'What do you want from me? You have to let me go now.'

In one tidy sip, Nathan drinks from his own glass of champagne, neatly dabbing his mouth with a handkerchief. Then, he walks to Clara. He leans over her, the other glass held in his hand. Swiftly, she turns her head away, her lips tight. He grabs her face and twists it back to him, tilting her chin back. She struggles to move away from him, but he has tied the ropes too tight.

'Don't fight or you're going to get champagne all down your tutu. Come on, you'll feel better after a drink. You always say that, don't you, when we're finding a table in one of those cafés you like so much. You love this champagne. Pol Roger. I got it especially for you.'

She closes her eyes as he forces the glass to her lips, squeezing her jaw and cheeks to press her mouth open. Much of it streams down her chin and neck, but finally he gets her to drink. She coughs loudly. He strides over to the stove and returns quickly with his handkerchief, wiping the spilt champagne from her skin. It has pooled down between her breasts and he gently reaches the handkerchief under the tutu. He hopes the stain will not show in the photographs.

'I'm going to untie you now. But you're not going to fight me, or scream, or try to run away. It won't be a good idea, I can promise you that. I just want a few more photographs, and then I'll stop.'

'And then you'll let me go?'

'We can talk about that afterwards. It really depends on how you behave with these photographs.'

'You could have just asked me if you wanted a photograph, Nathan. It didn't need to be like this.'

'I've already explained to you,' he says with a sigh. When he takes the knife from his trousers, Clara shifts in the chair, knocking the wedge from under the wheel again. 'You've got nothing to fear if you stay still and do as I ask,' he says sternly, placing the wedge back. 'I will only use this knife if you give me reason to do so.'

The drugs are taking effect, Clara's head falling to the side. She immediately jerks herself to attention, but Nathan can tell it is a struggle for her. He kneels in front of her and places his hands in her lap.

'As I said, I'm going to untie you now. You don't need to get up. I just want you to take this book. Imagine you are the Coppélia doll, reading in the window of Dr Coppélius's workshop. Okay?'

Clara nods, her eyes following the knife. Nathan reaches around her and finds the knot, releasing her arms first and then her feet. He watches her carefully, the knife gripped in his hand. She shifts uneasily as he leans over her, the blade grazing her skin. Even though her feet and arms are now free, she cannot find the energy to move. He hands her the book, a hardback of *Tess of the D'Urbervilles*, which he opens to a random page. Clara holds it in front of her, the words swimming. She tries to stay awake and alert, forcing her eyes to travel across the page. But she cannot take in the words, just a sea of Angel and Tess and the fire in the grate and horrible laughter. She blinks and the words do nothing to reassemble themselves. Once Nathan has prepared her feet, manoeuvring them up to a tight parallel resting en pointe, he moves away and picks up his camera.

'Just read the words. No blinking now. That's it. Soften your lips a little. No scowling.'

He takes two photographs, one from directly in front of her and one from the end of the boat, filling the lens with her body.

'You can stand up now. Put the book down.'

'I don't think I can. What did you put in the champagne?' Clara can barely whisper the words; it takes tremendous effort.

'Yes you can. Just a few more minutes, then you can sleep.'

Clara pushes herself to her feet, trying to thrust sleep to the edges of her mind.

'One of those low *arabesques*, please,' Nathan instructs her. 'One hand to the side of your face, the other stretched out behind you.' She slowly eases her body into position, *arabesque allongée*, her shoulders in *épaulement*. Nathan holds out the camera, takes several photographs, murmuring softly to Clara as he does so. Lift your chin, dip it again, open your eyes wider, part your lips. All the time the knife is at his side, back in the belt of his trousers. Clara is just conscious of it, the glint of its edge floating in and out of her consciousness.

Nathan turns to put down the camera. As he does so, Clara forces sleep away for just a moment longer. With great effort, she breaks out of the *arabesque*, one great *glissé* followed by a determined jump, landing her right by the door that leads out to the front deck. She pushes it open, the music from the gramophone dancing in her ears. It is the gigue from Act Two, the tempo fast and strong. It propels her towards her escape, the cheerful notes so strange against the frightening shadows of the boat.

Nathan grabs her and slams the door shut. She feels the edge of the knife against her jaw, the metal cold and hard. But then even that sensation fades as the drugs take over.

This time, he doesn't bother putting her back on the chair. He drops her to the floor, her legs and arms falling to the side like a rag doll. Looking down at her, he feels a strange, unexpected sensation. He thought he would only want perfectly curated photographs, his Clara preserved forever like a china doll. But there is something about the way she lies now, her tutu rising awkwardly, that reminds him of those secret, sensual photographs in the darkroom on Diadem Court. He leans over, his camera ready to capture the images he wants. Her thighs, her lips slightly parted, the thin slope of her neck, her collarbone. He places the champagne bottle to catch the light, the glass reflecting the flame from the candle. He photographs her feet, their high arches pressed between the pink of her shoes. He travels upwards, his camera searching between the folds of her net tutu. A collage of body parts. This is not what he expected, but he feels himself enjoying it, testing the boundaries of his desire.

Eventually the camera clicks empty, signalling the end of his cataloguing.

Leaving Clara sleeping on the floor, Nathan goes onto the deck and starts to prepare the boat for departure.

33

SAMUEL

'Your sister?' Samuel stammers out in confusion. 'Is she here?'

'I'm asking *you* that,' Olivia cries, looking wildly around her into the dark of the street and down the slope towards the canal. They are standing above the Islington tunnel, where the waterway disappears under the surface of the streets for half a mile. 'She's missing. I thought maybe she was here with Nathan. But you're here instead.' Her voice is accusing, afraid. 'I see you everywhere, watching us, hanging around. What have you done?'

'I don't know what you're talking about. Please, Olivia, tell me what's happening. Maybe I can help you find your sister.'

'You can't deny it. Why are you always there? Why do I see you all the time, in and out of the theatre, always lingering?'

Samuel has been afraid of this moment. His father drilled into him the importance of staying in the shadows, hiding from attention, from ridicule. Why risk being laughed at, mocked for his desires and ambitions. But Olivia has got it all wrong. He never meant to scare her. He didn't even know she had noticed him. And he doesn't know where her sister is; how could he? There is only one thing he can do now, but it terrifies him. He needs to tell her the truth.

'Olivia. I don't know where your sister is. I haven't been following her; I don't know anything about her.' He takes a deep breath; the next words will be the hardest. 'It is you. I love to watch you dance. And when you started wearing my pointe shoes, well, I think I started to love even more about you. I was drawn to you.'

Olivia has taken a step back from him. 'What do you mean, your pointe shoes? Doesn't Mr Freed make them?'

'I make shoes too. I make yours, and your sister's, and ones for several of the other dancers in the company.' Samuel pauses. He needs to be honest with her. She is staring at him apprehensively, doubt still creeping across her face. 'Your shoes are different to the others. I wanted to do something to make them special. Have you ever noticed the rose engraved into the sole?'

She nods. 'Surely they are on everyone's shoe?' But as she says it, she looks uncertain, trying to picture the soles of her sister's shoes.

'No, just yours.'

She looks horrified, but worse than that, disappointed. 'The note. With the rose sketch. It was you?'

'Yes, I wrote you that note. I wanted to sign my name, but I was afraid you would laugh at me. You have so many admirers, always getting gifts and flowers sent backstage. I am no one, just a pointe shoe maker's apprentice. You don't even know my name.'

'And the shoe in the well, the rose, the flower crown, the mannequin head?' She gestures manically around her. 'And what is your name?' she adds, her voice accusing.

'Samuel. My name is Samuel Steward. But I don't know anything about a head and a crown. That wasn't me. But I admit that I took one of your shoes and scattered the rose around it in the well. It was supposed to be a good luck charm. I thought you'd like it, part of your routine of visiting the well before each performance.'

'Maybe I'd have liked it if I knew who'd done it,' she replies, her voice a little softer now though still suspicious and wary. 'But I had no idea. You scared me. Why couldn't you just say something to me?'

'I couldn't say anything to you. There is a world between the two of us.'

Olivia says nothing, shifting from foot to foot as she thinks. She wants to believe him; but she can't help but feel disappointment now she knows who was leaving roses in her pigeonhole, who wrote the note all those weeks ago. And to think she had believed for a moment that it was Nathan. She feels stupid, so blind to what was going on around her. Samuel is standing before her now, telling her all this, admitting to loving her. As she looks up at him, trying to work out how she feels, all she knows is that her sister is still missing. She still doesn't understand why Samuel is here, so close to where she thought she would find Clara. There is no time to take this all in.

'What are you doing here then?' she snaps at him, her chin lifted in anger. Samuel shakes his head, scared of her and this strange ferocity that he has never seen in her before.

She continues, her words faster now. 'You need to explain why you're here. Where is my sister? You need to help me find her.'

'I'm not here specifically. I'm just walking home. I was invited to dinner at a friend's house a few streets away and I'm heading home, to Exmouth Market, where I live. I only stopped because I saw you and I wanted to check you were okay.'

Olivia nods, not really hearing him. Her eyes are turned to the canal, down to where she was headed so determinedly before Samuel appeared and all she had been so certain about dissolved into doubt. She isn't interested in his dinner, where he lives, what he is doing. She only wants to know about Clara. But still, perhaps he can help her.

'I'm sorry I never noticed you, Samuel.' But her words are hollow, spoken only as a way of using him to find her sister.

He realises he has been holding his breath. Now, hearing her say his name, he lets it go, a long slow exhalation. He is sorry she never noticed him too, but it doesn't hit him as hard as it would have done a few weeks ago. There is Milly. And she has noticed him. He doesn't have to creep around in the shadows, watching her from a distance.

Samuel shivers in the cold. There is the faint ripple of water below them, a boat pressing its bow through the canal. He thinks he can hear music, its notes distorting as the sound moves beneath them, but it is too quiet to be sure. It must be dark down on the water, he thinks, the canal giving up no secrets in the gloom of the night.

'You said that you thought your sister might be with Nathan?' he offers tentatively. 'The pianist?'

'Yes, I thought so. He lives down here, on a boat on the canal. That's why I was so confused when I saw you here instead.'

'I saw him earlier this evening outside the theatre. I didn't think anything of it at the time, but he was acting strangely. He was dragging a wheelchair out of an alleyway.'

'A wheelchair? Like the one for the doll in *Coppélia*?'

'Yes, I suppose so. Now that I think about it, it might have been the same one.'

'Why did he take it? The stage crew were losing their minds trying to find it before the show.'

'I didn't stay to watch, I'm afraid. I was late for dinner. With Miss Bell, my friend,' he adds after a pause. If he says her name, keeps reminding himself of his happy evening with her family, perhaps he can prevent himself from falling for Olivia again. He doesn't know if he can cope with the anxiety, the disappointment, the pain of loving someone who barely acknowledges his existence.

'Will you come down to his boat with me?' she asks, moving towards the canal entrance. 'Just in case there are problems.'

'Of course.'

The two of them start walking down the steep slope to the water, Olivia in front, Samuel pressing his fingers against the mossy wall to secure his footing.

'It's not far,' she calls back to him. 'I've seen it before. His is one of the only boats that never moves.'

They walk in the dark, the dim lights from the moored boats barely spilling their glow onto the path. The warehouses on the other side of the water are closed up like sleeping giants, their shadows pressing down on the water. Olivia pushes aside the branches of a willow tree, continuing up the path to where she remembers seeing Nathan's boat before. She stops before she gets to the bend in the canal, looking around her. The boat was here last time; she is sure of it.

'It's gone,' she says, turning to Samuel. 'He's taken her.' She doesn't know what to do, standing there at the edge of the canal staring into a blank space where the boat should have been.

'It can't have gone far,' Samuel reassures her. But he is not so sure. They don't even know which direction it has gone. 'Why don't we ask on some of the other boats? They might have seen something.'

Olivia nods and they start walking back up towards the tunnel. The next boat along has a long cargo hold with a short living area, boxes and crates packed tightly underneath a tarpaulin. A light burns on the front deck and Samuel can just make out low voices inside. He knocks lightly on the side of the boat and then steps back, waiting.

The voices stop.

'What do you want?' calls out a man's voice. It is not a London accent. Birmingham perhaps, Samuel thinks.

'We just want to ask if you've seen a boat leave here recently? We're looking for someone.'

The door opens onto the deck and a man comes out, pressing his cap back down onto his head as he leans against his boat.

'You mean the one who's here all the time?' he says, lighting up a cigarette and exhaling the smoke that lingers around him. 'He was here earlier, but I heard him leaving not long ago. You've just missed him.' He pauses, scratching his chin. The strong stale smell of cigarettes and old yeast escapes from his mouth. 'You know, I've been on these parts of the canal maybe ten times these past few years. Never once seen that boat move. And now you come along just as he does, wanting to know what's going on. Seems odd to me.'

Olivia has stepped up to Samuel's side. 'Did you see him bring anyone on to the boat? A woman?'

'A woman, eh? What's this about? He your sweetheart?' The man laughs, the smoke from his cigarette drifting further away from him. Olivia says nothing, waiting for him to reply properly. 'No, miss. I've been inside for the past few hours. I ain't seen anything.'

'How about a wheelchair?' she presses.

'Nope. But as I said, I've not been out on deck. Some people have walked past, I guess, but I didn't look out. Look, he didn't leave long ago. He went into the tunnel. You'll have to go back up to the streets, but if you're quick you might catch him somewhere on his way to King's Cross. It's slow going there, and he'll have to pause at St Pancras Lock.'

'Thank you. We'd better get going then,' said Samuel, nodding to the boatman. They start walking briskly away, Olivia breaking into a run as soon as the street lamps from above the tunnel's entrance start to breach the darkness. The man calls out to them.

'You might be able to hear him. He's been playing this damned music all evening. That's how I knew he was leaving. His music faded away into the tunnel.'

Samuel waves his thanks and they run towards the edge of the tunnel.

'How far do you think he's got?' Olivia says, just as much to herself as to Samuel. 'I wish we could get in there. I don't like to think of him in that tunnel with her. What if something happens in there?'

'There's no towpath. We can't follow. As the man said, it's not far to the other end of the tunnel. If we're quick, we'll catch him coming out the other end.'

Olivia presses herself against the mouth of the tunnel, leaning out as far she can over the water. 'Perhaps we'll be able to see them?'

'Be careful, Olivia.' Samuel comes up to her. 'At least hold on to me so you don't fall in.'

'Okay. You hold my hand and I'll lean around.' Samuel wraps his hand around her wrist, widening his stance to secure his footing. She leans further now, peering down into the tunnel. It is pitch-black, the curved walls and the dark waters merging like paint.

'Can you see anything?'

'Not a thing.'

But then there is a moment of complete stillness, as though all of London has held its breath. From not far away she hears the notes of Delibes's *Coppélia*. She can't quite place the piece, perhaps from Act Three, the part they didn't perform. She leans out even further, pressing her arms away from the tunnel's mouth. There it is, the smallest flicker of a light. A candle perhaps, or an oil lamp, its flame reflected against the water and the wet walls of the tunnel.

She pulls back and turns to Samuel. 'They're in there. I think the boat has stopped not far into the tunnel. I can hear the music. How are we going to get to her?'

Before he can reply, another noise joins those quiet notes. It echoes and vibrates around the walls of the tunnel. Heavy shunting, a scraping noise, dull banging. And then a splash. One, and then another.

Olivia doesn't stop to take off her coat. She jumps down into the canal and starts wading through the murky waters into the darkness. Her legs move too slowly, so she throws herself forward into a swim. She hears Samuel call after her, but she doesn't stop. Not even when her clothes are heavy, their weight pulling her down, each stroke making her muscles scream. Samuel has no choice but to follow her. The gaping mouth of the tunnel swallows him whole.

34

CLARA

I am trapped in a nightmare where I want to scream but I can't; my throat is stuck, my limbs are too heavy to move. I drift in and out of waking but it is so dark that I cannot be sure when I am asleep and when I am awake. Time is impossible to grasp, the sound of Delibes's *Coppélia* weaving its way into my mind and then vanishing again. For a while I sense that I am moving, a slow steady floating. But then the movement stops and I feel as though I am suspended between two walls gradually filling with water.

Now the sounds around me have changed; they are echoing, cavernous. I am certain I am awake this time. It feels different, as though my body is coming back to life, a sharpness edging around my mind like a mirror gradually clearing of steam. I look up. The darkness is vast, like black paint smeared across my vision. But gradually my eyes adjust, the faint light from the boat casting slow shapes into the air. A curved brick ceiling flickers into view, the walls domed and falling to unseen depths below the waterline. We are in a tunnel, the smell of damp and algae and cold wet brick hovering thickly. Nathan has placed the oil lamp on the floor of the decking and I can see that I am lying on the floor next to it. Lifting my head off the ground, I peer as far around me as I can; I cannot see Nathan. I try to roll onto my side, to push myself up off the floor. That is when I realise my hands and feet are bound. I strain against the bindings. They are not too tight and I can shuffle my feet against each other, the knots of my shoe ribbons rubbing against my ankle bone. But I cannot get out of them, not with my hands tied behind me.

The engine of the boat shudders and then stops, leaving an eerie stillness. In this stillness, I realise that I am shivering, my arms exposed to the dampness of the air. My tights feel wet, and the netting of the tutu sticks into me uncomfortably.

Although I am afraid, my anger overwhelms my fear. I am furious that I am held like this, prevented from dancing, walking, making my own decisions about what I want to do next. Even the simplest task has been taken away from me.

When I hear Nathan's footsteps coming back out onto the deck, I struggle more determinedly. I can't be trapped here. Not now. Not with my life laid out for me with such promise: travel, fame in a new country, the freshness of change. Nathan has always tried to stifle me, making me adapt to his version of what he wants me to be, a prize possession to make him feel as though he is still a star, beloved by all. And now I fear he is taking this vanity to its extreme. With a slow, nauseating tightening deep within my stomach, I realise what he meant when he said he wasn't going to make the same mistake again. He created a fantasy for his mother, one that suited his inflated ego. It makes sense now, the way he has always talked about his mother as though she was a goddess, the perfect woman. And she was, in a way: he created her; she was a religion for him. Then she ruined it when she revealed her living, breathing self to him, refused to play his game. He isn't going to let that happen with me. Those photographs he was taking – I had hoped, prayed, that they were the extent of tonight's madness, his strange obsession needing an even stranger outlet. But of course the photographs weren't enough. Here, in this tunnel, he is going to kill me.

'Stay still, Clara,' he whispers, kneeling next to me. 'It's almost over now.'

'Nathan.' My voice comes out high and pleading. I try to calm down, but I can feel the panic washing through my body. 'You can't do this. It's insane. Do you really think you'll get away with this?'

'No one knows you're here. And if, as you say, your sister does turn up, she isn't going to find you. She won't even know where the boat has gone. We're halfway along the tunnel, hidden under London.'

'She'll look for me. She'll find me.'

'Unlikely. And I'll be back in my usual spot by morning, nobody the wiser.'

'You don't need to do this. What do you want from me?'

I don't know how to reason with him, not when he has convinced himself of such a wild, irrational plan. And this just makes me more terrified. It is as though the Nathan I thought I knew has transformed into a madman. Part of me, the part that knows I need to fight to stay alive, tells me I should beg him. I should offer him an alternative; I should promise myself to him, a future where I stay in London, marry him, become his ideal wife. But even as I think it I know I can't do it. And it's too late. I can see that he doesn't trust me any more.

'I have what I want from you now; I have no more expectations. Not from you, not this Clara on the ground in front of me. I'll build a new Clara now, one that lives just in my head, exactly as I want her. I have learnt the hard way. People make promises, they let you expect the world. And then, nothing. They take it all away again. I was loved, famous, the best child pianist across Europe. And now look at me. Even a dancer in the corps de ballet thinks she is too good for me.'

'I didn't think I was too good for you. You know that wasn't it.'

'No, you were too good for all of us. Even your sister. And your mother, who you left to die in a mental asylum. The Vic-Wells. London. It always has to be the biggest and the best for you, off to America to fulfil some crazy dream.' He leans over me. The light of the oil lamp illuminates the gold of his hair, casting shadows across his forehead. 'Maybe I should have gone for Olivia from the very beginning. Maybe I still can. When you're gone, she'll need someone to turn to.'

'Don't you dare go near her. She won't love you. No one will love you.' I spit out the words.

He stands up, dragging me with him. My legs buckle, but he lifts me by the waist. It is a strange, painful dance, my weight falling awkwardly, a *pas de deux* with no harmony, no connection, no sharing of body weight, the momentum carrying each step. This is ugly, angry, my toes scraping against the wooden decking. I fight him, tossing and turning in his grip. But he drives us forwards to the edge of the boat. I see the black of the water, an endless tunnel with no light marking out its end.

And then I am in the air, just for a second, before landing with a hard splash in the water. The cold immediately rushes over me, my bottom sinking first, then my torso, legs, feet, head. Dirty water presses me down, goes over my hair, into my mouth, drenching my skirt. Pushing myself up to the surface, I gasp for air. I try to move my arms and legs to keep me afloat, but it is hard with them tied together, and I have no idea how deep the water is, whether if I attempt to find the canal floor I will sink too far to rise again.

It is the tutu that protects me: a life jacket of tulle and satin. I find myself floating, the smallest of leg movements enough to keep me above the waterline. Turning away from the boat, I start to kick out, propelling myself forwards down the tunnel, into the darkness. I need to get away from him. If I can find the end of the tunnel and crawl onto land, I will be safe.

There is another splash behind me. I don't dare turn. Eyes forward, determined not to lose my sense of direction, I swim with as much force as I can, my back and legs aching, my hamstrings on fire. I push the water away with my feet, my neck straining to keep my head above water.

I don't know how far I get: it could be yards or it could just be a few, futile inches. A hand grabs my foot. He pulls me back to him. I try to scream, but the water rises around me, rushing into my mouth.

And this time I do not float back to the surface.

35

OLIVIA

I shrug off my coat as I swim. It is so heavy, weighing down every movement I make. Swimming away from it, the cold hits me once again, but I don't stop, even though my arms are in agony. I know Clara is on the other side of the boat; I know that splash was her. I need to reach her.

As I swim further into the tunnel, darkness folds over me. It is terrifying, impossible to tell where the surface of the water breaks into air. I force myself onwards, my arms stretching and disappearing with each stroke in the black night.

Eventually, I can make out the outline of the boat that creates an even block of darkness in the tunnel, framed by a flickering glow that creeps out onto the walls. But I don't seem to get any closer; the darkness distorts my sense of distance. By the time I am at the boat, I am cold and exhausted. I reach up, my feet pressed against the hull. One foot finds the rudder and I rest my knee on a rope fender that hangs wet and heavy over the edge of the boat. In one movement, I propel myself up onto the back of the boat. It surprises me, this strength. I did not know I could lift myself out of the water with such power. But my arms ache painfully, a sharp throb running down my sides and across my shoulders.

Peering into the shapes and shadows, I try and decide on a route. There is space to edge my way between the wall of the tunnel and the side of the boat, but finding a footing will be a challenge; there is only a thin edge jutting out above the hull. Instead I lift myself onto the roof, grabbing a small chimney pipe and dragging myself upwards. There isn't much space between the roof of the boat and the ceiling of the tunnel, just enough for me to crawl forwards. I know I need to be as silent as possible, but I can do that. I'm used to moving swiftly and silently across a stage, merging effortlessly into the corps. I remove my shoes and leave them on the decking at the back of the boat. My stockings are slipping so I remove them too, throwing them overboard into the water.

I creep forwards, my toes gripping the boat. The roof is flat and stable but I rock in panic as a shape flies towards me, its wings stretched wide. I just manage to stop myself from screaming. Bats, congregating in the dark dampness of the tunnel. When I reach the front, the light improves, and I can see around me a little more clearly. There is no one on deck, just an oil lamp sending shadows up the sides of the tunnel walls.

'Olivia.' A voice reaches me, a shaking whisper.

I turn abruptly. It is Samuel; he has followed me over the top of the boat and is lying down flat behind me, his head almost disappearing in the pitch darkness between the boat and the tunnel ceiling. I am relieved to hear him.

'Can you see them?' he whispers. We both jump down onto the front decking and lean over the edge of the boat. I wince at the noise of our feet landing against the wood. He holds out the lamp, the light pooling down across the water.

'There!' I exclaim, pointing at a dark shape not far away from us. It is hard to make them out but it looks like they are struggling, two bodies expanding and contracting in the darkness.

'Wait,' Samuel says, holding my arm. 'We need a plan.'

'There's no time for a plan. Don't you see he's drowning her? You pull him off and I'll get her out.'

'Okay.' He sounds unsure. I turn back to him, placing my hand on his.

'Samuel, thank you.'

I don't wait for a reply. I jump into the water and start to swim towards them. The water seems to fall away from me this time. There is no tiredness, no effort. I have only one focus, and that is getting to my sister.

Samuel is right beside me. We surge forwards until we are upon them. He grabs Nathan and wrenches him backwards. Nathan cries out, releasing Clara as he falls back into the water.

Clara disappears down below the waterline. She is unconscious. I reach for her, but she slips below me. Taking a deep breath, I duck under the surface until I am right above her; the water is deeper here in the tunnel, just above my head when my feet find the slime of the canal floor. I kick underneath myself and lift her out, keeping her head high.

I start to swim, supporting Clara with one arm, desperately trying to stop her head from sinking. It is exhausting and slow-going, but I press on, finding my way back to the boat. I can vaguely sense Samuel to my right. He too is moving towards the boat, dragging Nathan with him, who is coughing and choking as he is heaved through the water. I reach the edge of the boat, but I don't have the strength to lift Clara over the side onto the deck. I need to do something, though; I don't even know if she is breathing.

Holding on to her with one arm, I wade to the edge of the water, wedging myself between the boat and the tunnel wall. Grasping a rope fender, I try to calm my shaking arms. I lift one leg up and over the boat, contorting my body into a position even the most flexible ballet dancer finds a challenge. My hand is wet and cold but I keep it tightly wrapped around Clara's arm as I lift my other leg over, my stomach tensing. It is a relief to find dry, stable ground once again, but it is not over yet. I lean back over the side of the boat and take Clara under her shoulders. Digging my feet into the decking, I heave, pulling her over the side and into the boat. Pain shoots through my back and legs and I collapse heavily from the momentum. She lands on top of me, her soaked tutu covering my face.

I roll Clara off me and kneel by her side, leaning down towards her mouth. As I do so she jerks up towards me, vomiting out water and coughing painfully. The light of the oil lamp reveals her face, pale and stained with streaks of black eye make-up.

'Clara,' I cry. 'I'm here. Are you okay?'

'Where's Nathan?' she chokes, sitting up and looking down at her hands. I can just make out red marks around her wrists, where she must have been tied with a rope. 'You untied me?'

'No, the rope came loose in the water.' I look down at her legs. Her ankles are still bound together. I reach down and start to unpick the knot, but it is tight from the water, the fibres stuck together.

'Where is he?' she repeats, more urgently this time. 'We need to get away from here before he finds us.'

'Samuel has him,' I reply, concentrating on the rope. My fingers are so cold, every effort sending angry shocks through my hands.

'Samuel? What Samuel?'

'Our pointe shoe maker. There's no time to explain now. You're freezing. We need to get you out of here.'

Samuel nearly has Nathan back at the boat.

'Watch out,' he calls to us. 'I'm bringing him up.'

Samuel has no trouble lifting Nathan out of the water and heaving him onto the deck. Quickly, I position myself between Nathan and Clara, still fumbling with the rope, which is finally starting to loosen. Samuel is back in the boat before Nathan has a chance to move. He presses him to the ground, holding him still.

'What do we do now?' he says, his body pressing against Nathan, who is struggling to sit up.

I turn to Clara. 'What do you want us to do?'

She doesn't speak, just stares over at him, her face stony even as she shivers.

'Clara,' I insist. 'What does he deserve?'

36

CLARA

I want to kill him. I want Samuel to throw him back in the water, to hold him down until he drowns. I want him to be afraid, like I was afraid. I look at Olivia. I can tell she wants it too. Together, we can do this. We can overcome him, just like we have overcome all our fears. I think back to that awful night when Father died. Mother hadn't even been able to look at us; our pain was too much for her. She sent us out of the hospital room, waving us away with a dismissive flap of her hand. We had to deal with it alone, sitting for hours in the gloomy hospital waiting room in Finchley, wondering whether our father was still alive. It was a nurse who finally told us, bringing us sweet tea while we sat there shivering with grief. Mother walked straight out of the hospital without even collecting us. We walked home in the dark, two eleven-year-old girls, holding hands as we avoided the drunken stares and shouts of the men coming out of the public houses. We found her at home, hours later, lying in bed in the dark with a bottle of brandy on the side table. Olivia and I knew we only had ourselves to rely on from that moment onwards.

Samuel has his hand over Nathan's mouth, his legs pinning him down. He looks up at Olivia and me and shakes his head.

'I'm not killing him, if that's what you're thinking.' He looks terrified, this poor boy dragged into the canal by my sister, involved in a mess that hasn't anything to do with him.

'Of course not,' I hear Olivia say, but she doesn't sound convinced. I want to scream at him. Just do it, I want to shout, just press your hand around his mouth, his nose, squeeze his throat. But he won't do it, I can tell. He doesn't hate this man enough; he hasn't seen what he is capable of.

My legs are free now. Slowly, I push myself up onto my feet, Olivia getting up with me and helping as I find strength in my freezing muscles. The flower crown has fallen over my eyes and I wrench it off, pins flying out of my hair and into the water.

'I'll do it,' I say, taking a step towards Nathan. Olivia follows me and we kneel either side of Samuel. Nathan looks up at the three of us, his eyes wide.

'You can get off him now, Samuel,' Olivia says, starting to position herself at Nathan's legs. 'We won't ask you to be involved in this.'

Samuel shakes his head. 'Don't you see? I'm already involved. I can't let you do this. How can I live with myself if I just sit here watching the two of you kill him, whether you think he deserves it or not? It isn't for you to decide.'

I feel frustration building inside me; I could be a doll, a wind-up doll ready to explode into life. That was how Nathan saw me, only he didn't want me to spring awake. He wanted a passive, lifeless marionette. He wanted to pull all the strings.

Samuel turns to me; he looks scared, but not of Nathan. Of me. 'Please, Clara,' he says, almost a whisper. 'Don't do this. It isn't just his life you'd be ending. None of us would ever be the same again. I don't want to be a murderer. I just want to go back to my flat, my work.' He pauses, turning away from me. 'And

Milly.' He says this woman's name, Milly, as though it is the saddest thing in the world.

'Milly?' I repeat. 'Who is she?'

He shakes his head again. 'I can't talk about her, not here, not right now. She is better than all this. She's just like me, I see that now. Ordinary, hard-working, wanting something but not everything. She understands me better than I've ever understood myself. I thought that this mad life you all live, always on the edge of pain and exhaustion, was somehow worth it. It was glamorous, beautiful, justified by art. But she's taught me that happiness doesn't come from producing something beautiful, something that everyone will admire and celebrate. I don't want to be celebrated. I just want to love and be loved.'

Olivia has gone very still. I turn to her and see her staring across at the water, her face unmoving. In the darkness she feels far from me, as if her features have blurred and deepened into something unreadable and unknown. She turns back to me.

'Clara,' she says. 'Maybe he's right. It isn't up to us what happens to Nathan. We can't live with that sort of responsibility.'

I sit back against the edge of the boat and put my head in my hands. There is something about what he said that hurts me; it lingers too close to the truth. And I think it hurts Olivia too. What is left when there is no love, Father dead, Mother gone before she could acknowledge what she did to us? Instead, we search for beauty and art and fame. It is the only way to hide from ourselves.

Olivia crawls over to me. 'You're shivering,' she says, placing her arm around me. She holds me close and I can feel the faint heat of her body, even through the chill of her wet clothes. 'You know he's only partially right, don't you?' She pulls me even closer. 'We may live a mad, painful life. But we do have love. We have each other.' I put my head on her chest and sob, my shivering changing into deep shudders that vibrate through my ribs. 'You'll go to America,' she continues, 'because it's exciting and new and I'd never keep you from that adventure. But you'll go knowing that you're loved and that I am loved. You'll come home one day and we will always have each other.'

She stands and holds out her hand. 'Let's get you inside the boat. We need to find some warm clothes.' I follow her inside, and she searches in Nathan's bedroom, bringing me a towel and a blanket. It is strange to be back inside here again, the trunk still loaded with Nathan's strange memorabilia, the box of figurines lying open on the table. The music has stopped and there is just the low sound of the needle crackling against the record. The bottle of champagne is half full on the sideboard, a pot of pills lying open in a puddle of ice. I pick up the pot and read the label. The words are faded, smudged from the ice. These are what he drugged me with, I realise. They are fast-acting sedatives, sleeping pills. I can just about make out the instructions: *Take one pill ten minutes before sleep.*

'He gave these to me,' I say to Olivia. 'I know Samuel's right, but I wish I could crush the whole pot into this champagne and send Nathan to sleep forever.'

'There's part of me that wants that too,' she replies, coming over to me and putting her arm around my shoulders. Her arms are thin but taut with energy and power. 'But we can't. Let's just leave him and go to the police station. They can come back to deal with him.'

'And we'd tell them what? It will be his word against ours. He has no criminal convictions. He used to be a famous piano player, a golden boy. They'll take one look at us, at our mother's mental illness, me dressed in a stolen costume from the theatre, two ballet girls. No one will believe us.'

'Perhaps the police don't need to believe us. He's not going to come back to Sadler's Wells now. Not after this. He won't want the embarrassment of us spreading this story. He cares about his public image more than anything.'

I nod, reluctantly. But I know she is right. Nathan isn't going to be playing for ballet class now. More than anything he wants to be remembered forever as the piano-playing prodigy, remarkably talented, on a level with Constant Lambert. Already this image of him has faded; if we tell this story he will be condemned forever as a freak, a criminal, and that is what people will remember.

We go back out on the front deck. The oil lamp is still flickering and I can see that Samuel looks exhausted. Nathan has stopped struggling. He stares up at me, unable to speak with Samuel's hand still pressing down on his mouth. I gesture to Samuel, and he slowly eases his hand away. Nathan takes in a big, stuttering breath of air.

'Leave London and never come back,' I tell him, trying my hardest to keep my voice firm and level. It is difficult, especially when my teeth still shake from the cold. 'I will tell this story to everyone at the Vic-Wells, to Constant and the rest of the orchestra, to everyone in the Camargo Society. We have your camera with those photographs of me, and we know about the fantasy world you created about your very much alive mother. But more than that, the three of us will be looking out for you. And if we see you again, we're not going to let you go free again.'

'I'll go now,' he says, his voice high and strained. 'You don't need to tell anyone. Just let me go now and I'll leave. I'll go straight to King's Cross. I'll get the first train in the morning out of London. You'll never see me again.'

I think he is telling the truth. The loss of his reputation would be far worse for him than a nomadic life away from his home.

What I don't know yet is whether this is enough for me, whether I will be able to resist this desire for more, for something unspeakable and horrifying, for something that reveals a power that has always been there within me, waiting, afraid.

Olivia and Samuel keep glancing into the dark of the tunnel, anxious that another narrowboat will appear, but it's not likely, not at this time of night. We take Nathan inside and seat him in the wheelchair, Samuel still keeping a firm grip on his shoulders. He slumps forward as soon as Samuel releases him. But then he looks up and says my name, an uncertain whisper. I go over to him, taking care to keep my distance. We found the knife in his trousers when we carried him inside; Olivia threw it into the canal. I nod to Samuel, who moves slowly and cautiously back through the boat to find the engine.

'It doesn't have to be this way,' Nathan says, his voice low. 'Perhaps I can stay, just playing for class quietly in the corner. I'll keep out of your way.' He can barely look at me, so different to the man who proudly paraded his toy soldiers across the table not long before. 'I can try harder. I can start afresh. I won't ask for anything. I can be different.'

'No, Nathan. You can't be different. All you want is to be special. You want to be treated like a spoilt child. That isn't just going to go away overnight. Perhaps you brought that out in me too, made me doubt myself. You made me feel as though I wasn't good enough. I had to be this perfect doll you could parade around on your arm, shining brighter than anyone else's girl-friend. I am better off without you.'

I am not sure if he hears me; his eyes have glazed over and he stares listlessly out at the macabre museum to his desires. I lean down towards him.

'If I ever see you again, I'll tell your mother what you've done. I'll tell her how leaving you was the best decision she ever made.'

He shifts in the chair, his gaze fixed on a tiny toy soldier that has fallen into a puddle at his feet.

'I've found the engine controls and tiller,' Samuel says, coming back in through Nathan's bedroom from the back deck of the boat. 'It looks complicated, but I think I know how to get this boat to move.' Samuel looks enormous in the cramped corridor of the boat, but with his neck craned to one side he seems anxious. I see him staring uneasily at Nathan.

'Are you sure he'll be all right?' he asks, though no one answers. I don't have to be responsible for Nathan any longer, not now, not after tonight.

Olivia and I watch Nathan as the engine starts running and the boat inches slowly back along the canal. He doesn't even flinch when the loud bang of the engine going into reverse announces itself, the sound vibrating and dancing between the canal walls. The tunnel is entirely straight, no side currents to take us off course, but we are all nervous as Samuel steers the boat, emerging out of the mouth of the Islington Tunnel. If anyone looked down now from the wall above Duncan Terrace, they would just be able to make out a reversing boat, creeping slowly towards a mooring spot on the towpath. But the courage of Samuel and Olivia's actions remains hidden in the waters of the tunnel, a secret I'll never forget.

When we feel the boat gently nudging the side of the canal, Olivia and I run out onto the deck. I glance back at Nathan, but he is still staring ahead, his hands gripping the arms of the wheelchair. My legs feel suddenly light, liberated, as I make that step off the boat and onto the towpath. Olivia is clutching the bag of Nathan's belongings: his camera and the photographs of his mother that he's labelled with the date of her fantastical death. I've picked up the flower crown too, though I don't think it's in any condition to return to Mr Healey.

I look around me, feeling the firm ground of the path. The night sky is so dark that for a moment I am not even certain we have made it out. There are no stars, not a single ray of moonlight. And perhaps that it is for the best, I think, no one to watch as we climb out of the boat, our clothes still drenched, the tutu flopping heavily over my thighs.

Olivia is looking down into the water by the entrance to the tunnel. A large mass is floating across the surface like a swamp of algae. She kneels and tries to grab at it, but I pull her away. I can see now that it is the coat, that green coat with the fur collar that I thought I could escape if I just parcelled it off to my sister, silently, stubbornly, without explaining why wearing it made my body feel heavy, trapped.

'Leave it,' I say to her. 'Neither of us will ever wear it again.' The two of us press the coat down under the water, forcing it into a bundle that sinks to join the London debris of waste and dirt and discarded memories. She stands up and takes my hand, squeezing it gently. There is no need to say anything more.

'I live ten minutes away,' Samuel says to us. 'Let's get there as fast as we can and get warm.'

I want to leave this canal; I want to run from the suffocating walls of the boat that held me captive. But first there is something I need to do. I take two determined steps back onto the boat and push open the door. Nathan is still in the chair, his shoulders hunched forward and his hands heavy on his thighs. I go to the trunk opposite him, ripping the programmes and photographs and notes from his mother down from the wall above it. They scatter, ruined, at his feet, instantly drenched in the puddles of canal water that soak the wooden floor. I watch as he reaches down to pick up the wet fragment of a photograph, his chest heaving with sobs.

But it is the dolls I am after, those rows of tiny painted soldiers and musicians and princesses. The Firebird ballerina has fallen into a line of soldiers, knocking them in chaotic disorder. I scoop them all up and throw them into the tin box that sits beside them.

I hesitate, my hand hovering over the final doll.

This one he can keep, a reminder of all that he has lost. I place the ballerina figurine alone on the trunk, one thin arm pointing in *arabesque* at Nathan.

When I get back outside, I empty the box into the canal. The miniature dolls float lifelessly on the quiet surface of the water.

I turn and look down at my body, plastered in a wet tutu with a towel wrapped around my shoulders. Samuel offers me his coat, collected from where he left it, dry, at the edge of the path. I take it gratefully. I am still in my pointe shoes, but they are soft and malleable now from the water.

'Are your feet okay?' Samuel asks me as we are dragging our exhausted legs up the slope back to the road. I look up at him and smile.

'Never been better. Whoever made these knew what they were doing.' I wink at him and he smiles back.

It is late, long past pub closing hours, and the streets are still and quiet. No one would notice us anyway, three ordinary people rushing home, finding our way back to safety. It is only when Olivia finds my hand, wraps her cold fingers firmly around mine, that I know we are going to have to return before the night is over.

37

OLIVIA

Samuel's flat is on Exmouth Market, a tiny one-room home. But right now it feels luxurious, safe, warm. Perhaps this can be how the night ends, I tell myself, like collecting the needles stuck in a ball of darning thread and tidying them neatly away. I know that isn't possible, though. We strip off our clothes while he lights the tiny fire, the room still too dark to make out its features. The coal slowly starts to glow and we huddle around it, wrapped in his small selection of towels and jumpers. He gives me his dressing gown. It is a thick wool, hugely long, and I immediately start to warm up. I have never really looked at him before, this huge man with shoulders that must be twice as wide as mine.

He boils the kettle on his stove in the corner. And I thought our kitchen was tiny. He doesn't even have a space that could be called a kitchen, just a collection of pots and plates and tankards stacked on a shelf in the corner. But the tea he makes us is delicious, just as good as any made in the finest London hotel, and for a moment I let myself relax.

As the fire builds, a warmth starts to spread through the flat. Samuel lights a few candles and I look around as the room gradually comes to life. What I see surprises me. There is a desk by the window that is covered in sketches, a leather case, rolls of paper. Pencils, chalks, a pot of scissors and rulers, a measuring tape. I look at the wall to the right of his desk. It is crowded with designs, the most detailed and intricate sketches of shoes, hats, dresses, a coat. Clara is looking now too, both of us gazing around the room, astonished at what he has created.

We have all gone silent; Samuel seems to be holding his breath.

'You designed all these?' I ask. But of course he did. He made my pointe shoes, didn't he? The best shoes I have ever danced in, as if he understands how we move, what we need to be able to dance with power and grace.

He nods. 'Yes, I'm going to start my own shop one day. These are my designs.' He says it shyly, quietly, as if it is an effort to say these words. Perhaps he has never said them to anyone before.

I get up and walk across to another collection of sketches on the other side of the room. A few scraps of tulle and satin are pinned up next to them. I reach up to the drawings, not quite touching them.

There, in a series of sketches of different angles and scales, is a design for the most perfect tutu. It is white, a matt satin bodice, layers and layers sketched out for the skirt. Measurements are written out in pencil, but with a space next to waist and hips.

'Are you going to make this?' I say, turning to him in excitement.

'That's the plan,' he replies, tentatively coming to stand next to me. 'But I can't afford the materials without being paid to do it. And no one is going to commission me for a tutu. Not yet, while I am no one, just a pointe shoe maker's apprentice.'

'But you think you could make this? If you had the materials?'

'Yes. I am sure of it. I know how I will make every cut of fabric, every stitch. Milly is lending me her sewing machine this weekend. I'm going to start with a turban hat for her mother.' He points at another drawing pinned on the wall: a navy silk hat with a net butterfly pinned to the side.

'What about if I asked you to make this tutu for me?' I say to him. Of course it must be Samuel, my pointe shoe maker, the man who saved my sister: he must be the one to make the tutu I've wanted for so long. An act of creation rising out of the pain of this night. 'I've been saving up. I can give you £3. Will that be enough?'

He looks at me with an expression that I can only describe as shock.

'Samuel?' I urge. I turn back to the sketches, admiring the cut of the skirt on the hips, the delicate layers of tulle.

'Yes,' he says. 'I will make it for you. But I think £3 will be too much. The material won't cost quite as much as that.' He sounds uncertain. Even without looking at him, I can tell he doubts me. He doesn't trust me. After tonight, I have transformed from a ballerina into something too real, too human. I am a woman who would jump into a canal and swim in darkness to her sister; a woman who wanted to put her hands around the throat of a man; a woman who is no longer afraid of her own body.

'You'll keep the rest, though. I need to pay you for your time as well as materials. And perhaps you can start saving up for a sewing machine of your own.' I turn to him and smile. In that look he knows I refuse to be in anyone's debt.

When we are dry and warm, Clara no longer shivering, we say goodbye. We look ridiculous, in clothes far too big for us and thick socks instead of shoes, but it is better than my dripping dress, Clara's tutu. Samuel tries to insist on walking with us, but we don't let him. He has done enough, fulfilled all that we need from him.

As soon as we are out on the street, we forget Samuel, our minds focused on what we know we must do.

When we get home, we change our clothes again, this time into dark dresses and our solid boots with the low heels. There is no need to speak, to plan. We both move as one in the cold light of our bedroom. The rest of the building is so silent, not a single squeak of a floorboard or slam of a door; it feels as though we are the only ones awake, two sleepless sisters claiming the night as their own. Standing in front of the mirror at the sink, we brush out our wet hair so that it shines in long straight strands around our identical faces.

Clara lowers her eyes, her brows knotting together with uncertainty. But when she raises them again, the doubt has gone. We wrap dark headscarves around our wet hair and go out once more into the night.

38

SISTERS

Nathan is not in his boat. We hadn't expected him to be; there are too many signs of his failures staining the fabric of the walls. The ballerina figurine lies stiffly in a puddle on the wooden floor and the champagne bottle is smashed in the tiny sink. A dark spray of blood patterns the panel behind the worktop, fine drops of red feathering out along the wood. Nathan must have cut himself as the bottle broke into pieces, an angry explosion of glass.

We keep moving, our steps light against the dirt of the canal. Our shadows fall darkly in duets every time the moon breaks through the clouds and the lights of the dim street lamps creep down onto the canal path. We walk steadily, our shoulders grazing, our hands finding the light cold brush of each other's fingers. Our breath mingles and floats upwards in the frigid air but then disappears, mute to the indifferent night. The boatmen in their barges and narrowboats sleep on, oblivious to our journey. It is we who hunt now, Artemis and Atalanta, searching along the dark water for the man we cannot allow to go free. I can feel the muscles in my legs springing with power, my arms bristling with an electric energy. My sister, too, her neck long as her eyes dart about in the darkness, her chest pushed out as though wings rise from the blades of her shoulders.

A flash of light from a car on the road above breaks onto the water and for a moment the surface glows, like a river of fire. We are almost at Sturt's Lock, the wooden arms of the gate jutting out into our path. A tall chimney from one of the canal-side factories looms above us, a black and solid shadow that seems to lurch into the water, but then we move on, our pace quickening.

Our gaze is set firmly on the man standing by the water.

He turns when we are just a few feet away from him. Nathan Howell. He has no power now to try to charm us or control us, to wrap us up in fur or tulle. He cannot reach up to kiss us or press his hands against our skin.

'Clara. Olivia.' His voice stumbles over our names. That is all he can say. Still, he does not know how to tell us apart.

I watch my sister spring and grab him by the throat, her full weight against him. She is flying, soaring fast, a silhouette of fury. My body strains to join her, the air making a tunnel just for me, a cord drawing us together. But I don't move, not yet.

Then he falls, his head hitting the beam of the lock gate. Suddenly, I am on him too, stamping the music out of his hands.

He struggles, his eyes flitting fast between us. But it is too dark, and we are too strong, four long arms smothering his body.

And then it is as though he has forgotten to fight; his arms go limp and his body slackens.

We roll him into the water and his limbs bounce listlessly against the lock gate. The canal is high on this side, a dark swamp that will rush down to fill the chamber the next time a boat tries to navigate along this passage.

There is silence, something uneasy that hangs above us now that his grunts and moans have been muffled by the waves lapping against the lock.

We, too, seem to be holding our breath.

I stand and turn away, my hand light on my sister's shoulder.

I don't see the final thresh of the body, the bubbles springing from his mouth, the heave of his back as he tries to draw himself out into the air. When Nathan reaches up, I barely notice.

With the swiftest of kicks I knock his hand away from my sister. He falls backwards, stumbling further into the water. I kick him again, a hard blow to his chest. The energy ripples through my leg, powerful like the staccato strike of *battements frappés* in ballet class. He topples back beyond my reach into the middle of the canal. All is shadows and dancing swells of water, his face a ghastly grey.

When the moving light of a truck on the bridge ahead catches him across the cheek, I know he is going to die.

The water flashes with Phlegethontic fury and then dims, returning to a bleak and murky dirt.

My sister turns back around and glances at him, her face motionless. She is already walking away as he sinks beneath the surface, this time with no chance of rising again.

I wait for her under the Wharf Road bridge. She is running, her heels barely touching the ground. When she reaches me, she smiles grimly, gives a little shake of her head. There is no need to speak: what would be the point of trying to reframe our actions into something softer, death setting us free?

The canal path comes alive as we walk towards home, the wind starting to murmur with whispers of excitement. A long branch of a weeping willow strokes my face and I let my fingers lightly graze the bed of wet moss that has grown into the wall. I turn to my sister as we walk, glancing at the straight lines of her profile. Her headscarf has fallen down and a strand of hair is sticking to her cheek.

She has changed. Or perhaps not.

Perhaps it is what I see when I look at her that has changed. There is no comparison, no terrified weighing of myself against her. Instead, it is my own power, my own beauty, my own ruthless determination, that I see reflected back in the fierce tilt of her head as she finds her way forward in the dark.

39

SAMUEL

Any exhaustion Samuel expected to feel the next morning vanishes as soon as he steps outside onto Exmouth Market. The street is already busy with sellers setting up their stalls. There are piles of rosy red apples tumbling over each other; carrots, tomatoes, courgettes all seem to glow like jewels. Great chunks of meat, collected that morning from Smithfield Market, are displayed on the butcher's tray, and the baker has laid out steaming rolls and buns on a bright yellow cloth. There is a chill in the air, but Samuel doesn't feel it. Not today.

The cars and buses and bicycles spread through the roads, filling every artery of the city. Watching them rush past him reminds him of a game he used to play when he was little, on the rare days his mother would take him to the beach in Norfolk when they went to visit her parents. He would dig intricate passageways through the sand and then wait to watch the high tide surging in and filling his tunnels. Today he feels part of the city, in step with the other pedestrians, all marching in time to the rhythms of London, its melody and its bass.

As he rounds the corner onto Long Acre, the energy lifts its tempo, cars jostling for space as they drive in and out of the car dealers' halls, the big double doors all wide open to the street. There are people everywhere. Mechanics in their overalls, car salesmen in suits and ties, shop girls in slouch hats, coats tied tightly around their waists. He used to think everyone looked the same, their tired eyes shadowed in the black and grey and brown of their hats and coats. But this morning they are different, or perhaps he is different. A girl with bright red shoes walks past him; a mechanic, he notices, has a floral handkerchief poking cheerfully out of his pocket; a woman on the other side of the street has pinned a silver dove brooch onto the slant of her hat, its shining tail reflected in the sunlight. He smiles and keeps on walking, imagining them all in his designs, his shoes, his colours that will bring light to the city.

Just as he turns onto St Martin's Lane, he sees Milly hurrying down from Seven Dials. He waves to her and she joins him on the pavement; they both slow their step, walking side by side towards Freed.

'Did you get home okay last night?' she asks, smiling up at him.

He wants to laugh. It feels like a strange dream now, as though he had watched the events unfold at a distance. 'Yes, eventually. A few hold-ups along the way. I'll tell you about it when we have more time.'

'Sounds exciting.'

'Yes, I suppose it was. But not as exciting as the dinner with you and your family. Please thank everyone for me. It was a wonderful evening.'

'You made a very good impression,' she laughs, nudging him lightly in the ribs with her elbow. 'Even my brother said nice things about you, which really is saying something.'

They are almost at the Freeds' shop. Samuel doesn't want to go inside, not just yet. He knows he needs to say more, be bolder.

He needs to tell Milly how he feels. Last night woke him up to what really mattered, exposed those old obsessions as danger-ous, false, based on a fairy-tale fiction.

He takes Milly's hand and gently ushers her into the entrance of Cecil Court, away from the busy flow of pedestrians.

'Milly, I want to ask you something.' He is nervous and he can feel his hand starting to sweat. But Milly doesn't let go. Instead she squeezes it and smiles at him encouragingly. So different to Olivia and her remote, suspicious eyes. He takes a deep breath. 'Meeting you has been the best thing that has happened to me.' She shakes her head, but she is still smiling. 'No, I'm serious, Milly. You've made me realise so much about myself that no one has ever let me believe before. But it's not just that. I think about you all the time. Last night, for instance, when I got held up on my way home. I just kept thinking about you and how I wished I was with you.'

She takes a step closer to him. 'And all I think about is you, Samuel.'

'I feel as though I know you and you know me.' He looks nervously about him, his voice lowering as a bookseller on Cecil Court throws open his door and looks out into the narrow street. 'I'm not asking you to commit to me forever, not right now. But I just want to know if we could be together, more than colleagues, more than friends, I mean.' He is flustered, not sure how to say what he wants to say. But it is no matter, for she rises up on her toes and kisses him.

Mrs Freed looks up at them as they enter the shop together. She recognises that look, the first stages of love, the moment after the connection has been made, the words spoken. She smiles at Milly, who blushes crimson as she takes off her coat and hangs up her bag.

At ten o'clock Mrs Freed asks Samuel to deliver a new order of shoes to Sadler's Wells. The order is so big that he packs the store cart full of shoes, covering them with a waterproof cotton gaberdine. The half-hour walk to the theatre feels different now he is wheeling a cart, avoiding the potholes and the sharp edges of the pavement. It makes him think of Nathan's journey to his boat the night before, how he must have struggled to hide Clara from view as he manoeuvred the chair over the kerbs and the stones that would have threatened to jam the wheels. Nathan should be on the train out of London by now, Samuel thinks. But he isn't certain he will have kept that promise. Samuel remembers the desolate look on Nathan's face when they left him there in the boat. His eyes had been fixed on that strange museum of fabricated memories, his desires stripped away and exposed.

A group of stagehands are gathered outside the Rosebery Avenue entrance when he gets there, the smoke from their cigarettes clouding his path. He hears fragments of their conversation as he wheels in his cart.

'They pulled a body out the lock. The police sent me a different way. Made me late in, it did.'

'It was a barge that found it first thing this morning, drowned in Sturt's Lock. That's the third drowning this year on that part of the canal,' one of the men pronounces with the air of someone delighted to be in the know.

'Suicide?' one asks.

'Probably. Or a drunken walk home gone wrong.'

'Never seen so many policemen on my way to work,' another adds, shaking his head. Samuel feels the cart lurching unsteadily in front of him, the shoes rolling to the side. He keeps his eyes forward and continues into the foyer.

*

Wardrobe is empty as usual, so he takes his time placing the shoes into the dancers' pigeonholes. He remembers that time those few months ago when he placed the white rose in Olivia Marionetta's pigeonhole, how he hoped she would somehow understand his love, anonymous, in the shadows. This time he has no rose. But he finds a scrap of paper from the wardrobe master's desk and a crayon. He leans over the desk and writes.

Dear Olivia,
If you are still interested in the tutu, please send your measurements
to me at Freed at a time convenient to you.
                                              Yours, Samuel Steward.

He takes the note over and places it above her new shoes. For a moment he considers ripping it up, distancing himself as much as he can from this woman for whom he feels no love, not any more. She has transformed in his mind since last night, as if the woman he obsessed over has vanished, rebirthed into something new and strange. When he closes his eyes, he can see the two sisters crawling over to where he held down Nathan on the wet decking of the boat, the look of murder in the hard lines of their jaws. It is impossible now to imagine her in the white tutu that he has sketched with such care on the walls of his home. That obsession that dug its way into him like a worm on a sick rose, that turned the theatre into a beautiful monster: it has gone.

As he leaves Wardrobe, he sees a heap of red in the corner. He can't help but smile to think how angry Mr Healey will be when he finds the precious Coppélia tutu wet and ragged, smelling of dirty canal water. He's a little surprised that Clara and Olivia have brought it back here; it might have been easier to destroy it. But he doesn't blame them. He too would find it difficult to throw away that quantity of tulle and satin.

*

On his way out he goes via the Wells Room. Perhaps if he sees her dancing once again, those feelings of horror when he thinks of her will dissipate. The familiar sound of piano music meets him from the end of the corridor, and for a moment he is afraid. But there is no way Nathan would have turned up today as if nothing had happened. He quickens his step anyway and goes to the open doorway. Ballet class is in full swing, the dancers performing a *grand allegro* across the room, their legs high as they jump and turn. The room is full of the sounds of the piano, the tap of pointe shoes on the floor, the gentle thud of the men landing from their *grands jetés*, the exhalations of the dancers as they throw themselves across the room. They make it appear effortless, but Samuel knows it isn't. Even ballerinas are subject to gravity. At the piano is Constant Lambert, thumping out the notes with vigorous energy. He looks hungover, not at all delighted to have been called in to play piano for class the morning after a final night of a show, his loud playing compensation, no doubt, for his exhaustion. He will not be impressed that his protégé has failed to turn up this morning.

Miss Moreton bangs her stick and the music stops. The dancers transform from performance mode into exhaustion now that there is no music to cover the pace of their breath. They wipe their brows and lean against the barre. Samuel glances anxiously into the crowd of sweating men and women, trying to find Olivia. A deep shudder of panic travels through him. Two twin sisters, both in identical black practice leotards and skirts, the pink of their shoes scuffed grey in the dirt of the studio floor. But then he looks again. Of course he knows which is Clara, which is Olivia. Clara is on the floor by the mirror, her legs stretched out in front of her. Samuel watches as she leans forward over her legs, her back flat. He can't even touch his toes, he thinks without envy, as he watches her rock from side to side, pressing her body further in towards her legs. Olivia walks over to Clara and reaches out her hand. Clara looks up and takes it, getting to her feet with a groan.

'We start rehearsal in five minutes,' calls out Miss de Valois. Even she looks a little tired, but she hides it well, the indomitable ballet mistress who never has a hair out of place. He wouldn't want to get on the wrong side of her.

Olivia sees Samuel standing in the doorway and she waves at him. His first instinct is to think she is waving at someone else, someone just behind him. But she starts coming towards him, saying his name. She speaks in fast sentences, walking up and down en pointe, pushing her arches out over her shoes.

'Samuel, you're here.' She is smiling, but there is no warmth behind her eyes. She is all efficiency and business. 'We've got all the clothes you lent us. They're in our dressing room. Can you stay and watch the rehearsal? Then we'll get them for you?'

'Yes, of course,' he replies, a little thrown at the invitation into this sacred room. 'I just need to be back at the shop by lunchtime.' It is Milly he is thinking about. They have planned to eat lunch together in Trafalgar Square, by the fountain.

'Perfect. It's just a short rehearsal. We're learning the "Rose Adagio". The Sleeping Princess repertoire. Miss de Valois wants to get everything she can out of Nicholas Sergeyev and his notation books before he decides he's had enough of us.'

Clara has joined her, and the two sisters lead Samuel into the studio.

'Let me talk to Miss de Valois,' Olivia says, offering Samuel a seat at the front of the room. He feels a little awkward, but no one seems to object.

'This is Samuel Steward,' he hears Olivia say to the ballet mistress. 'He is going to watch the rehearsal, if that's okay with you. He makes our pointe shoes with Frederick Freed.'

Miss de Valois looks over to him. 'Yes, I know all about Samuel. Our guardian angel.' Samuel looks confused, Olivia too. How could Miss de Valois know what happened last night? But then they realise Miss de Valois is talking about his pointe shoes, the way he creates perfection with satin and paste and a welting machine. 'Enjoy the rehearsal,' the ballet mistress says to him, a smile just about breaking beneath her arched brows, those piercing eyes that see everything, every tiny detail.

Samuel watches with a new sensation. He feels admiration, certainly, but it is different to before, when he thought ballerinas were beyond human, their dancing effortless and weightless. The 'Rose Adagio' requires balance, poise, shoes that keep the feet firm and strong. Four princes, four white roses, one Princess Aurora. Miss de Valois divides them into groups, Clara, Olivia and one other woman going first, each with a set of four men. When Olivia and Clara stand tall in an attitude en pointe, he sees the muscles in their legs tense. They lift their hand up into fifth position, holding a moment of balance before the next prince arrives to provide the support of his hand. Neither twin sister wobbles. Samuel is certain that if those four men vanished, Olivia and Clara would still be there, balancing en pointe, strong, powerful, complete.

HISTORICAL NOTE

While Clara, Olivia, Samuel and Nathan are entirely fictional creations, the corridors of Sadler's Wells Theatre in *Clara & Olivia* are filled with dancers who would have been taking morning class, rehearsing, performing, right there in 1933. I wanted *Clara & Olivia* to be a story of new beginnings, twin sisters learning their strength. And so I decided to set the novel at a time of great significance for British ballet, its own new beginning.

It is interesting how many of us assume ballet has always been part of Britain's heritage, an old, established art form. However, before the work of the remarkable Ninette de Valois, British ballet was little more than divertissements in variety shows. De Valois transformed it into an art form that rivalled the contemporary cultural developments of art, music and literature. By 1933 it was firmly on its journey to becoming the successful, world-leading institution that we perhaps take for granted today.

Dame Ninette de Valois, known in the ballet world as 'Madame', met Lilian Baylis in the late 1920s and the two of them worked together to transform the ruins of Sadler's Wells into a successful theatre. Lilian Baylis ('The Lady') was manager of the Old Vic Theatre; she campaigned tirelessly to find funding for the project, with sponsorship coming from many directions, including famous names such as Stanley Baldwin, Winston Churchill, John Galsworthy, G.K. Chesterton and others. When the theatre opened in 1931, de Valois set up the Vic-Wells Ballet company and moved her school into the theatre's studio. Sadler's Wells Ballet School and the Vic-Wells Ballet have evolved into today's Royal Ballet School, Royal Ballet and Birmingham Royal Ballet.

The 1930s was a momentous decade for British ballet, and I have brought many of these influential people into *Clara & Olivia*. In addition to Ninette de Valois, Constant Lambert was integral to the success of the Vic-Wells. He was the musical director, bringing with him his experiences of working with Diaghilev, both as a composer and conductor. Richard Shead's 1973 biography of Constant Lambert describes those years, and Antony Powell's memoir at the start of the book gives a taste of the vibrant life Constant Lambert lived.

Dennis Arundell gives a fascinating account of the early productions in his 1965 book *The Story of Sadler's Wells*. He also writes about the Camargo Society, a group which helped to fund many of the early productions. They were led by the economist John Maynard Keynes, Lydia Lopokova, the music critic Edwin Evans (for whom I have given a fictional role in his cruel review of Nathan Howell), Constant Lambert and the ballet critic Arnold Haskell. Interestingly, it was a different production of *Coppélia* (two June 1933 gala performances at the Royal Opera House) that marked the end of the Camargo Society's work; with the increased popularity of ballet, it no longer needed the funding of the Society.

Another key personality, both in *Clara & Olivia* and in the early days of the Vic-Wells company, was Alicia Markova. She brought the necessary celebrity excitement to the fledgling company and can be partially credited with ensuring the success of the Vic-Wells. Her beautiful book *Markova Remembers* (1986) provides photographic details of many of the performances at Sadler's Wells in the early 1930s, as well as productions at the Mercury Theatre, staged by the Ballet Club run by Marie Rambert. Ninette de Valois, in her 1957 autobiography *Come Dance with Me*, talks of those early years with great fondness. She also describes just how challenging it was to establish British ballet's reputation when both the public and press seemed determined to associate great ballet only with the celebrated Ballets Russes. She suggests that it was the death of Diaghilev in 1929 and Pavlova in 1931 that gave British ballet the space to grow.

All the productions mentioned in *Clara & Olivia* really did take place, including Penelope Spencer's sketch 'Ladies, Sigh No More!' at the 1933 Ideal Homes Exhibition. The protest to which Clara alludes on the bus took place in July 1933, so I have moved that forward by a few months to fit into the novel's time frame. Similarly, I have taken liberties with the date of the unveiling of Boris Anrep's mosaic *The Awakening of the Muses*, bringing it forward from the actual date of July 1933. I have tried to include many of the real dancers who danced with the Vic-Wells in 1933. Robert Helpmann had just joined the company. Frederick Ashton was already creating his ballets; also appearing in the book are Beatrice Appleyard, Ursula Moreton, Hermione Darnborough, Nadina Newhouse, Gwyneth Matthews, Antony Tudor, Stanley Judson and William Chappell (whose 1951 book *Fonteyn: Impressions of a Ballerina* captures the essence of life behind the scenes at Sadler's Wells; it was my ballet teacher Valerie Hitchen who gave this book to me just before I started at the Royal Ballet School back in September 2000. She wrote that she hoped I would keep the book nearby as an inspiration. I have certainly done that, if not quite in the way she and I expected).

I danced scenes from *Coppélia* many times during the years I was training at the Royal Ballet School. It is a ballet of which I have very fond memories, and so it was an easy decision to set the novel during the rehearsals and performances of a historical performance of the ballet. The Vic-Wells Ballet put on a production of *Coppélia* in March 1933, and many of the named cast were indeed dancing in those performances. Lydia Lopokova is one of the great ballerinas of the first half of the twentieth century, and her role in *Clara & Olivia* comes at the end of her ballet career. She danced Swanilda for the first two performances of *Coppélia* in March 1933, after which Ninette de Valois took over the role for the remaining performances. She had a fascinating life, and the wonderful biography *Bloomsbury Ballerina* by Judith Mackrell (2008) follows Lydia from her childhood at the Imperial Theatre School in Russia to her life in London, her marriage to Maynard Keynes, and how she coped with the intellectual snobbery of the Bloomsbury Group, who felt she did not match up to their standards: how wrong they were! While Olivia and Clara Marionetta are fictional characters, I feel certain that they would have been inspired by the energy and fierce independence of Lydia Lopokova.

Clara & Olivia tells another story of new beginnings. Frederick and Dora Freed set up their shoe shop in 1929. From humble foundations in a workshop in the basement of his first shop in Cecil Court, Covent Garden, Frederick Freed started what is now Freed of London, the world's leading designer and manufacturer of professional dance shoes. While Frederick Freed was a quiet and ingenious creator, it was Dora Freed who helped to build the shop's reputation. She was a dynamic woman, confidently making connections and spreading the word about how different these shoes were to the previous offerings from other shoe companies. In 1933, there was just one apprentice working with Mr Freed. Samuel Steward is a fiction, but there really would have been a hard-working cobbler down in that basement to help produce these beautiful shoes. When I started writing *Clara & Olivia*, I got in touch with Sophie Simpson, the senior manager at Freed of London. She fitted me for my very first pair of pointe shoes when I was eleven years old and at White Lodge, the Royal Ballet School, and since then I have worn hundreds of pairs of Freed shoes. Speaking with her about the history of Freed and the process of making a pointe shoe was fascinating and led to the creation of my character Samuel Steward.

The Freeds famously said that they would make shoes to fit the dancer, not the dancer having to fit the shoe. Individual dancers, especially regular customers, would even have their own specific shoe last created for them, moulded to fit their needs. Indeed, Margot Fonteyn wore Freed shoes with a specific colour of satin just for her. The discerning reader may have noticed that Fonteyn has a tiny role in the novel. She was just fourteen years old in 1933. When her mother brought her to Sadler's Wells to audition for the ballet school, she forgot to bring her ballet clothes and shoes. Ursula Moreton told her to take off her shoes and stockings and audition barefoot in her petticoat. She was enrolled in the school and quickly became one of de Valois's favourites. Fonteyn's autobiography (published 1975) gives many detailed accounts of those early years of the company, with descriptions of Nicholas Sergeyev and his pianist Ippolit Motcholov. She also writes about Madame Manya, the dressmaker. An account of the young Fonteyn visiting Madame

Manya to persuade her to make a tutu inspired my fictional tale of Olivia making her own journey to Maida Vale. Fonteyn, however, was rather more successful than Olivia, coming away with a tutu that cost her £16.

The well in the basement of Sadler's Wells exists and is still used today by Sadler's Wells Theatre to source the water for the theatre. The stone cover, found by Richard Sadler's builders in 1683, is on display in the foyer of the theatre. However, the room which it inhabits in *Clara & Olivia* is a fiction, an embellishment of the existing well into a place for the dancers to play out their routines and superstitions. The description of the well itself is also fictional. In reality, it is a rather unglamorous hole in the ground, covered over so that it would not be possible to reach down into the water. I was inspired by memories from my years training at the Royal Ballet School: the bronze statue of Margot Fonteyn was the site of our superstitions. We would rub her finger every time we walked past, leaving that one finger highly polished and far brighter than the others. In the fictional creation of that dark storage room and its mysterious well, I hope to have recreated that same feeling of compulsion towards good luck charms and routine.

Coppélia is a joyful, comic ballet, the choreography packed with entertaining mime sequences and energetic national dances like the mazurka that Clara dances so well. The ballet is inspired by E.T.A. Hoffmann's 1816 short story 'Der Sandmann', a much darker, more sinister story of a man called Nathanael who falls in love with an automaton doll, Olympia. The first ballet *Coppélia* was choreographed by Arthur Saint-Léon in 1870, with Léo

Delibes composing the music. The version performed in 1933 was the Petipa version, first performed in 1884. Only the first two of the three acts were performed. In *Clara & Olivia* I have drawn on elements of both the comedy ballet and the gothic Hoffmann story. In fact, I took the names of Nathan and Clara directly from Hoffmann's work.

While the story of the Marionetta twins is fictional, there are many true stories to be found within this novel. Frederick and Dora Freed's revolutionary pointe shoes; Ninette de Valois's wisdom and perseverance; Nicholas Sergeyev's trunks, smuggled out of Russia and filled with notation books of the great classics; Lilian Baylis's renovation of Sadler's Wells. All these people came together at the perfect moment to spark the expansion of British ballet. It is into this world that Olivia and Clara Marionetta have danced, finding love and strength together.

ACKNOWLEDGEMENTS

Thank you to my agent Antony Topping who has always believed in this book. I will never forget the excitement of our first meeting. His wisdom helped to shape the story and sharpen its edges. Thank you to everyone at Greene & Heaton agency for making me feel so welcome.

Thank you to my brilliant editor Jenny Parrott. Working with Jenny is a joy; I know how lucky I am. Thank you to Molly Scull for her invaluable suggestions and to Sarah Terry for her rigorous attention to detail and infinite positivity. I am grateful to everyone at Oneworld for guiding me along this road to publication, for the exceptional work on the cover design, and the wonderful energy devoted to introducing *Clara & Olivia* to readers. Meeting the team at the Oneworld offices was a day I'll never forget – thank you.

Thank you to Sophie Simpson at Freed of London for sharing her knowledge of the history of these fascinating pointe shoes, as well as her enthusiasm in answering my research questions.

There can be no doubt that all the ballet teachers of my youth had a profound effect on the creation of this novel. Special thanks go to Valerie Hitchen for always believing in me; Nicola

Gaines for her beautiful passion for dance; to Tania Fairbairn, Anita Young, Patricia Linton, Nicola Katrak, Petal Miller-Ashmole, Hope Keelan, Irene Axon, and Brenda Last. You all taught me how to work hard and how to strive for perfection, even if it was impossible to achieve. Thank you, also, to Anna Meadmore for her kindness and support.

Thank you to Bryerly Long, my dear friend who worked tirelessly to find opportunities for us to dance together alongside our academic studies.

Thank you to the English teachers in my life. To Suzanne Gunton and all the English teachers at the Royal Ballet School, thank you for making certain that my love of reading stayed strong even amongst the busy ballet schedules. Thank you to my A-Level English teachers for making me believe I could read English at university; thank you to my tutors at St Hugh's College, especially Nick Perkins, for teaching me how to slow down and think deeply about what I was reading. And thank you to my fellow English teachers for sharing in my early excitement about this novel; our Byron Reading Room coffee breaks are a joy!

I am grateful to Joanna Bratten for encouraging me to write and submit my work to literary journals; reading her stunning poetry inspired me to seek out publication. Thank you to my glorious, enthusiastic, book club. Special thanks must go to Natasha Bassett who is always keen to find an excuse to celebrate: thank you for those walks along the canal – you made me fall for that little stretch of water and I couldn't resist writing it into my novel.

I am grateful to Jim Buckland: your support has been so important to me.

Thank you to my twin sister Suzie for her love and kindness. Thank you to my sister Jo: I don't know anyone who appreciates

ACKNOWLEDGEMENTS

the joy of escaping into a story like you do. To my parents, thank you for reading every word I have ever written, and always thinking of something lovely to say. Your endless belief in me has meant I have never given up on this dream.

And finally, to Erik. You knew I could write this book. Your love made it happen.

© Alex Fine

After training at the Royal Ballet School for eight years, Lucy Ashe decided to change career plans and go to university, where she read English Literature before becoming a teacher. Her poetry and short stories have been published in a number of literary journals and she was shortlisted for the 2020 Impr... Prize for New Writers.